Endorsements
for *Rock Bottom*

"Experience can be a valuable teacher. It is through the backdrop of influential years in a rural setting that Sandra Konechny has developed a delightful love story that merges romance, intrigue, generational blessings and curses throughout this storyline laced with truth. The realness of characterization resonates with our own experience… and leaves the reader hungering for more."

Connie Hundeby (pastor's wife)

"As the reader is drawn into the rural community of Minitonas, and the lives of Ellie and Hugh, these characters become our friends with whom we can relate in their hardships, joys and soul-searching questions. The sovereignty of God and His unconditional love shines through and encourages us to trust Him with our lives as well. An encouraging read!"

Sheila Wiebe, B. Ed (teacher)

"A compelling and inspirational story highlighting the value and life-giving nature of friendship and the redemptive power of the Gospel to heal broken people."

Pastor Gary & Joyce Sawatzky

"The transformation in the lives of these characters is inspiring and will challenge you to engage honestly with both God and those around you as He accomplishes His purposes in your life."

Leilani Bauman (test reader)

Enjoy!

ROCK
Bottom

THE MINITONAS DIARIES

——— BOOK ONE ———

SANDRA V. KONECHNY

Hebrews 13: 20, 21

Sandra V. Konechny

Printed in Canada

ISBN: 978-1-4866-2429-4
eBook ISBN: 978-1-4866-2430-0

Word Alive Press
119 De Baets Street Winnipeg, MB R2J 3R9
www.wordalivepress.ca

Cataloguing in Publication information can be obtained from Library and Archives Canada.

Dedicated to my daughters
and daughters-in-law

Whitney, Lark, Andrea, and Jacqueline

Foreword

AT SOME POINT in my preteen years, I watched a black-and-white movie of which I remember nothing except that a man had experienced something devastating and the only solution left to him was to return to his roots and pick up the pieces. His return home led him to confront lonely old buildings that were hardly habitable anymore. The scene of him sitting sadly at the table of his derelict house has never left my memory. Sometimes, during a wakeful night or a daydreaming spell, I would think up stories about how that man's fortunes might have transformed into a tale of restored happiness.

That scenario is the *seed* for this novel.

The story had to happen somewhere, and following a visit to the Swan River valley in midwestern Manitoba I determined that this would make for a good and appropriate setting. This was where my relatives had homesteaded and lived from the late 1920s until sometime in the 1960s, and it was where my nuclear family lived for three years when I was eight through ten years old.

I remember a lot about how the area was back then. While I've tried to remain true to the geography of the place, at least for the period between 1980 and 1981, I have also taken some poetic licence. For example, although the neighbouring farms I chose for the Bauman and Fischer families are real locations, the details of these properties are fictional. One of these sites truly borders the East Favel River, but the pond I frequently refer to is made up.

Please note that all of the characters are fictional. Not one of them is based on a real, living personality in the Swan Valley region—or anywhere, for that matter. Each one is a new creation, a composite based on the entire history of people I've known, read, or heard about in some way. If the characters remind you of a local personality, it's further proof that human nature is common amongst us—and that includes the many challenges with which we stumble along over the course of our personal journeys.

Acknowledgements

SPECIAL GRATITUDE IS extended to my beta readers, consisting of a few family members and friends. Their feedback always asked for more to the story, which is what inspired me to keep writing. The encouragement means a great deal to me.

I must also thank my good husband, Michael, who when asked if I should pursue publishing said, without batting an eyelash, "Go for it!"

My gratitude goes out to my parents, Edward and Ruth Tiede, who instilled in me a love for God and the Bible since I was born to them. (Dad lives with Jesus now, but it is still appropriate to give credit where it is due.)

I would like to express my deepest gratitude to the editor and staff at Word Alive Press for their commitment and expertise in refining the manuscript and for ensuring the message is clear to reach the heart of the reader.

My deepest gratitude, however, is reserved for Jesus. We wrote the story together. Every time I got stuck, I'd pray, *What happens next?* Soon insight would come. If the reader comes away with a blessing, a wise thought, or a word of help—thank Jesus, the Saviour. Such as it is, I cast this meagre "crown" at Jesus's feet. To Him be the glory forever and ever.

One

"**YOU NEED TO** figure yourself out." The tone in Hugh's boss's voice clearly indicated that he was out of patience. "Seriously, I would like to know what's with you. This is the third time in as many months that I've had to take the heat for your rudeness to our customers. Ever heard the expression, 'The customer is always right'?"

Hugh stood quietly, his blackened, greasy hands stuffed in the pockets of his coveralls. He met the man's gaze without defending himself. After all, he had no leg to stand on. He *had* been discourteous and testy with another patron. His temper seemed to simmer just beneath the surface of late and he couldn't altogether account for it. It was just that people were such idiots sometimes.

"Look," the man continued. "I'll write you a letter of recommendation. You're a good mechanic as far as that goes. But your manners could use some work. I think it's best we part ways. Clean out your locker. I'll have your separation papers ready in half an hour."

By the time Hugh had emptied his locker and got his walking papers, he had transitioned from fed-up resentment to hopefulness. On the drive back to his bachelor's apartment, he found himself reviewing an idea he had kicked around in his brain now and again for close to three years.

Why not? he asked himself. *It has to be better than sucking up to stupid people every day.*

The more he thought about it, the more sense it made. By the time he parked in his designated stall, he had gone from entertaining an attractive idea to forming a plan.

~

It was just about one-thirty in the afternoon of a sunny Monday, June 9 day in 1980 when Hugh Fischer approached the Highway 10 intersection where turning left on the 366 would take him into the small town of Minitonas, Manitoba; turning right onto Road 150W would take him to the precise farmyard for which he had left everything behind in Winnipeg.

It hadn't been a snap decision. He had often turned over the idea of going back to the place of his mostly miserable youth, especially since he'd begun having issues with abrupt anger at work. Had his parents still been alive, it would have been out of the question. But they weren't, as a result of a single vehicle accident three years earlier.

Returning home had promised solitude, something Hugh felt he needed—for the next few months, at least, if not the next few years.

From his standpoint, his entire life of thirty-one years had been marred by a disastrous chain of events that had left him disagreeable and unhappy. He could count the happy occasions on the fingers of one hand.

Well, perhaps that was an overstatement. It had been good luck to become friends with the Turners. That friendship had helped salvage his ill-fated existence and set the stage for him to finish school and improve his social skills. It was anyone's guess how things would have turned out for him if not for their serendipitous intervention fourteen years earlier.

Nevertheless, it was time to take stock, reflect on his priorities, and maybe engage in some self-analysis... if he was brave enough to be scrupulously honest with himself. He wanted the peace and quiet—not to mention the space—to engage in the kind of introspection that would take his life in a more positive direction.

In the meantime, he needed a break from people. All of them. Bosses. Customers. Landlords. So-called friends. And women. Perhaps women especially. As far as he was concerned, they represented nothing but mystery and heartache. The idea of living as a recluse, responsible only to himself, sounded perfect. And if it proved to be too lonely, a TV should suffice. And perhaps a dog for company.

As he turned north onto 150W and aimed his shiny red and silver pickup truck for the old Fischer place, Hugh was surprised at how little had changed in the fourteen years since he had sworn to never set foot on this land again. The radio began to belt out the first few lines of Kenny Rogers's "The Gambler," and Hugh spontaneously sang along. The words, this time, suddenly seemed prophetic. He had arrived.

The short driveway was nothing more than a pair of tire tracks with quack grass and weeds growing between them. The grass had recently been cut, but apart from that the place looked utterly desolate.

Hugh parked in front of the house and turned off the ignition. He took a minute to look around and reacquaint himself with the layout of the yard. Heaps of metal and scraps of wood held up the farm buildings. Junk and bits of old machine parts were strewn here and there with tall grass poking through them.

At last he opened the door of the truck, repositioned the blue cap over his shaggy brown hair, and swung his six-foot lanky frame out. He was home, whatever that meant.

~

That same evening, Ella Rose Bauman packed up all her personal belongings and stuffed them into her blue sedan. Having carried out the last of her boxes, full of novels and textbooks from her days of nurses training, she stepped back inside the elevator of the apartment block and hit the fourth-floor button. Her immediate objective was to take one final look around the apartment to see if she had forgotten anything.

It hadn't been an easy breakup with Paul, with whom she had shared the apartment for close to three years. After numerous heated discussions, he had agreed to end things and pay her fairly for her contributions to the furnishings and housewares. She had decided to keep little more than her clothes and a few collectibles she had been given over the years. Her plan was to return to her roots and start over, and that meant parting with everything that represented her past, specifically the past ten years of pointless, misguided, foolish living.

She had hoped to leave the city by 6:00 p.m., but sorting and packing had taken longer than she'd thought and now it was close to 8:00. It was too late to make the five-and-a-half-hour journey north, so Paul had offered her the couch to sleep on. After some serious deliberation, she had agreed. She hadn't wanted to stay with any of the so-called friends they had in common, and she'd already said goodbye to her co-workers at the hospital.

Paul had also suggested they go out for coffee one last time. The very idea made Ellie's stomach feel nauseous. The man she'd once loved had hurt her too profoundly to make amends. No bloody way.

To kill time, Ellie thought she might take in a movie. She got in the car and drove toward the theatre, but none of the titles stirred her interest. Instead she opted for a strawberry sundae, which she slowly ate by the window while watching the never-ending stream of cars and trucks pass by.

She returned to the apartment only after it was fully dark. Relieved that Paul had already gone to bed, she tiptoed to the sofa and lay down, pulling the well-worn throw over herself.

Sleep was long in coming—and it didn't stay long either. She awoke at 4:00 a.m. with the first streams of daylight coming through the window. Time to go.

Ellie removed the apartment key from her keychain, laid it on the table, and quietly slipped out. She never looked back.

The air felt fresh and cool on her cheeks as she drove out of the city. What was she feeling? A new sense of freedom, for one thing. The terrible ache of guilt and sadness that had been her constant companion for several weeks now was as present as it had ever been. Part of this was related to their bad breakup; the other had to do with her mother's recent passing, leaving a large, empty, extra-sorrowful space in her heart. But Ellie believed she had made all the right arrangements to deal with it. Going home, she believed, would help recentre her.

Thus, the further behind she left Winnipeg, and the closer she got to Minitonas, the more hopeful she felt. It was around 10:00 a.m. when she turned north off Highway 10 onto Road 150W. Almost there.

To get to the home of her youth, she had to drive past the Minitonas Cemetery, as well as the old Fischer place across the road to the west. Two hundred yards further would take her to the well-established Bauman farmyard.

Her gaze caught on the red and silver pickup in front of the Fischers' place—and the tall, lean man topped with a blue cap standing next to it. She briefly wondered who he might be and offered an automatic wave, as was the way of country folk. He lifted his hand in acknowledgment.

Twenty seconds later, Ellie turned east onto the well-worn lane and crept along it till she came to a stop in front of the garage. Turning off the engine, she sat still. Nothing much had changed. Home sweet home.

Two

STEPPING OUT OF the truck, Hugh stood in front of the house and stared at it for what seemed like a long time. His sister Margo had probably been right; it was too far gone to salvage with a few renovations. While the clapboard siding was weathered grey, the only "colour" Hugh had ever known it to be, it was coming apart in rotting pieces. The front porch was falling away and the structure listed northward like the leaning Tower of Pisa. He guessed the windows were cracked and broken despite being boarded up, on account of the tilt. He was glad he'd brought along a tent and all his camping accoutrements. He would need them if he stuck to his plan to live here.

His desire to check out the house fell to the side in favour of having a look at the remaining farm implements. Logic dictated that the equipment would be sheltered in the largest of the dilapidated buildings, the one they'd called the machine shed.

When he got there, he found the side door secured with a padlock. This struck Hugh as a little humorous; as if there was anything on this sorry, abandoned farmyard with enough value to make it worth stealing! Not to mention, it would only take a swift kick to break the door off its hinges.

Eventually he located the right key to unlock the door, although it still took a couple of shoulder pushes for it to swing inward. He stepped inside a pitch-black space and gave himself a few moments for his eyes to adjust to the dim interior, facilitated by tiny shafts of sunlight streaming through knot holes and other cracks in the siding.

He picked his way through the narrow space between the harvester combine and swather until he got to the chains which, when pulled, would raise the big door through which the large equipment came and went.

After much screeching and groaning, sunlight filled the shed and Hugh could clearly see that his father had made a few additions in his later years. There was an unfamiliar tractor with a cab. Not new, of course, but an update from what Hugh remembered. The combine was an update too. The swather and disc tillager also seemed newer than he remembered.

Perhaps his notion to begin farming for himself would be feasible after all. He hoped so. He wouldn't know for sure until he got around to seeing if any of this equipment still ran.

He closed all the doors and walked over to the barn. It was a small, hip-roofed structure as ancient and worn as all the other buildings. Although it stood straighter than the farmhouse, the roof sagged dangerously in the middle, reminding Hugh of a horse's saddle. The side door was also chained and padlocked. Nailed to one of the double sliding doors at the front of the barn he saw a faded black on yellow sign that warned *KEEP OUT* in large lettering. He wondered whether Margo or his pa had put it there.

When he finally opened the lock and got inside, all he saw was scrap and rubbish heaped into corners. Then he noticed the desiccated remains of animal dung that no one had ever taken the pains to shovel out. It stank faintly of barn, but it was easy to see that the place hadn't been used for several years. Fourteen years ago, he recalled his mother milking one cow and keeping about a dozen laying hens. In his estimation, the barn hadn't housed country critters for at least ten years.

An old grain truck from the 1940s was parked in the centre aisle of the barn. It had plenty of rust but looked like it could still be coaxed into service. The half-ton pickup he remembered his father driving was gone. It may have been replaced in the years he'd been away. Even so, whatever their last vehicle had been, Hugh figured it had been written off and towed to the wreckers after the fatal accident.

After checking out the barn, Hugh walked over to the row of granaries, a series of six wooden buildings that looked like miniature houses. Once upon a time, they'd been used to store grain until it was taken to the elevator and marketed. Each one was empty and rickety. The farmers in the area had mostly upgraded to round metal bins, but the Fischers, who by all appearances had always lived near the poverty line, had not. Between each granary were stashes of sundry items of wood or metal. To Hugh's eyes, it amounted to junk. He doubted he would find anything useful here with which to begin a new chapter of Fischer farming.

So far Hugh's initial tour had taken about an hour, although there were two sites he had so far purposely avoided. One was the house itself; the other was the hydro pole near the barn where he'd reached that great and terrible turning point with his father.

Sucking in his breath, Hugh approached that pole now, taking less than a minute to cross the yard. The pole still stood tall, straight, and strong, long grass and thistles surrounding its base.

He expected a flood of very strong emotions to sweep over him, but that didn't happen. He stood longer... waiting. Still nothing.

Hugh couldn't decide if he should be disappointed or relieved. Likely it was both.

He left the scene of the hydro pole and strolled back to his truck. He'd lost interest, for the time being, in opening the house and checking it over. Instead he wanted to set up camp, the temporary "home" he'd brought along. He wanted to be situated and organized before nightfall. After that, he would need to put together an orderly plan to resurrect this poor old excuse for a farm.

He erected the canvas tent, purchased at an army surplus store, near the outhouse. Hugh was glad he had chosen a larger model, for it had enough space to stow his duffle bag of clothing, a large insulated picnic hamper, his plastic bin of keepsakes, and useful miscellany. He also had room for his cot and sleeping bag. Other necessities like the camp stove and tiny charcoal grill, together with tin pots, pans, plates, and cups, got left behind in the back of the half-ton, along with his collection of tools. The tailgate on his truck would have to serve as his kitchen until he could figure out something better.

By the time Hugh had arranged his personal effects, it was nearly six o'clock. Supper time. His first meal was a tin of pork and beans, with some cut-up wieners and chopped onion thrown in, heated on the stove. A couple slices of bread, lightly toasted, completed the meal. He filled a thermos with drinking water from the five-gallon drum he had brought, thinking it would be enough to slake his thirst until morning.

Satisfied and rather pleased with himself, he rummaged through his plastic bin of miscellany until he came up with a pad of paper and a pen. The sun was low in the sky when he sat in his folding lawn chair and began to write out a couple of lists. One was a to-do list; the other was a to-buy list.

When dusk made it too dark to read his own writing, he turned into his tent, kicked off his boots, and lay on his cot. Sleep came quickly and he slept that first night untroubled.

At about eight the next morning, Hugh awoke immediately aware of the dry, stifling heat. Although early, the sun was already bright and Hugh felt hot and sweaty in the confines of the tent.

Outside, the air was cooler and pleasantly crisp. He set about making himself a traditional breakfast of eggs with toast and fried wieners. A pot of camp-style brewed coffee simmered on the second element of the stove and the cheerful aroma soon filled his senses. If there had been anyone around to ask, Hugh would have said that on this first morning at the old Fischer homestead he felt cautiously optimistic, even confident.

After that satisfying breakfast, Hugh set about tackling the first item on his to-do list: establish a good source of water for drinking and washing. There used to be an old-fashioned pitcher pump on a stand in the lean-to room off the farmhouse's kitchen. It was the closest thing the Fischers had been able to claim as running water. Hugh assumed it must still be there and recalled that it was connected to the cistern located partially beneath the house. He hoped the reservoir was still intact or he would be facing an expensive setback.

When he found the door to the house also padlocked, he turned to get the ring of keys he had tossed on the seat of the pickup. He leaned against his truck for a few moments to once again assess the stability of the lopsided house. As he did so, the sounds of an approaching vehicle got his attention. It turned out to be a navy-blue car. A woman he didn't recognize waved to him as she passed, then slowed down to make the turn into a farmyard a little further down the road.

That used to be the Bauman place, he recollected. Whoever this woman was, he hoped she wouldn't come by to investigate. He wasn't ready for prying questions, however well-meant. He was on a mission—perhaps mission: impossible—and didn't have any interest or time for distractions.

It took some doing to get into the kitchen, because the shifting of the house had warped and jammed the door, making it nearly immovable. Eventually Hugh prevailed, however, and entered with caution. The boarded-up windows made it almost too dark to see at first, but his eyes soon adjusted. Much of the kitchen was just as he remembered it, although the old woodstove had been replaced with a smaller-than-average harvest gold electric stove.

The kitchen was connected to the lean-to, a small back room that served as a storage space for a collection of old-fashioned household items such as a wringer washing machine, a pantry cupboard, and a washstand. The pitcher pump, complete with pail sitting on an old stool under the spout, remained in place.

In the main kitchen, he spotted another new addition: a small, fairly modern refrigerator with a freezer compartment on top. It was avocado green, as had been popular in the 60s. He marvelled that his mother had been able to swing these upgrades when he knew his father would have been unsympathetic to making life easier for her.

Hugh tried pumping the handle of the pitcher pump, doubting that any water would emerge. Yet he nursed some small amount of hope...

At last he felt a surge in pressure and water tumbled out of the spout. It was brownish in colour, like tea. No surprise there, since the system had been idle for at least three years. The operational pump, however, made Hugh feel hopeful that other parts of the old home-stead might still be in working order.

Before leaving the house to check on the cistern, he walked into the living room. The same old worn and frayed furniture stood as it had in the past, the wooden pieces a little worse for wear.

Then Hugh noticed the odour, strong of mice and something else... much like slough water. He opened the door off the kitchen and peered down the uneven steps into the dirt cellar. Sure enough, water had filled the space to within a foot of the main floor.

He let out a sigh. Well, that explained why the house was atilt. The timbers supporting the house must be completely rotten.

Back outside, Hugh went about examining the antiquated cistern through the manhole. It appeared to be about half full. He knew it would no longer be sanitary enough for drinking and cooking, but he hoped to still use it for washing.

Another memory returned regarding a well somewhere behind the barn. It was an old-fashioned thing they had used to bring up pails of water by rope for their farm critters.

After a bit of searching, he found it levelled, the shaft now covered with an old sheet of plywood. He peered into the well and saw, in the depths, his own reflection. Water then. A ray of hope.

Having replaced the plywood, he stood up and looked around. The darkness of depression gradually descended upon him all over again as he realized the immense amount of work it would take to make this place liveable, not to mention a viable operation. It would require a lot more money, and a lot more know-how, than he current-ly had.

Margo had warned him. He now saw that he had been overly opti-mistic.

"I'm a survivor," Hugh said to himself through gritted teeth. "I just need to figure this out. I *will* make this work somehow!"

He walked back toward his tent with determination, trying to stifle the rising fear that threatened to overtake him. By the time he reached it, he recognized that this fear and dread was the same he had lived with, with little relief, while living on this farm with his parents and sisters.

Suddenly his anger erupted.

"Get away from me, Fred Fischer," yelled Hugh furiously toward the mental image of his father, shaking his fist in the air. "You're dead and gone! Good riddance too! You can't hurt me anymore."

But the rage wouldn't remain boxed in.

A sudden urge arose to throw in the towel *before* he invested himself in the plan he had imagined would revitalize his life, but Hugh fought it. He knew he had to stand his ground, at least symbolically, if he hoped to overcome these dreadful memories and move forward.

"Somehow I'll do what you did not," he vowed, shouting again. "*I will* turn this place into something to be proud of. *I* will get rid of every-thing that is old and rotten, just like you. I *will* rebuild Fischer Farms. And I *will* have the respect of my neighbours and never have to be ashamed or embarrassed again. So help me, *I will!*"

After Ellie stepped out of her vehicle, she noticed that her brother Robert's truck was parked in front of the Quonset, which meant he must be around somewhere. But instead of searching, she turned to enter the house through the commonly used back door. It opened onto a small landing which led straight down to the basement, or up two treads into the kitchen.

Ellie inhaled deeply of the comforting smells of home: that wonderful combination of baking bread, canning vegetables, pickling cucumbers, rendering lard, roasting meats, and even the aroma of just-washed floors. She found everything neat as a pin, as she'd known it would be. It had been little more than a month since the family had buried their mother in the graveyard next to her father, who had died a year earlier by heart attack. Her mother had continued to live in the house up until the day she'd passed away in her bedroom of a massive stroke. Ellie believed she could still sense her mother's presence about the place.

She walked through the spacious bungalow where she and her three elder brothers had grown up, refamiliarizing herself with each room. Since she didn't have to share the house with anyone, she could choose any bedroom she wished. Naturally she chose her own former room. The furniture was the same, but all the little items proclaiming it as the domain of a teenaged girl had long ago been removed.

Ellie was glad that the reminders of past rebellion with her old-fashioned parents had disappeared. Now both parents were gone and, to her enormous regret, she hadn't renewed her relationship with them. That was because she had taken up a lifestyle she had known for certain would have caused them great anguish. John and Elizabeth Bauman's stringent religious beliefs would have had no toleration for a child who sampled the wicked ways of the world, which actively enticed young people into doing drugs, sexual promiscuity, living together without the commitment of marriage, defying authority, excessive drinking, and Lord only knew what else.

As a curious teenager, Ellie hadn't liked being so obviously different from her more carnal friends at school. So with a few white lies and the assistance of some fellow conspirators, she had largely been successful at living a secret double life in high school, and then in Winnipeg thereafter.

The thing was, the costly consequences her parents had warned about in their "preaching" had eventually turned out to be all too true. How many people had she witnessed fall prey to drug addiction? How

13

many young people had she known to contract venereal and other diseases through their "make love, not war" philosophies? They had chanted for peace whilst crying themselves to sleep at night because of all the turmoil they lived with.

Ellie had remained on the fringe as much as possible, with one foot in the hippie movement and the other entrenched in the world of her traditional upbringing. Not being all-in for either camp had meant she'd walked down the middle of the road—and as with real traffic, walking down the middle of the road was a good place to get hurt.

And that she had.

Ellie left the bedroom and returned to the living room. Acting on a sudden urge, she crossed the floor to open the stereo parked in front of the picture window. Just as expected, a few LP records were stowed beside the panel of dials. These would have been her mother's latest favourites. There were some gospel quartets, the Bill Gaither Trio, and then she saw an album entitled *The Top Ten Gospel Favourites of the 70s*. She set it up to play and turned up the volume. Some singer she didn't recognize belted out "O What a Saviour."

Suddenly, she saw Rob, her eldest and favourite brother, filling the entrance to the room with his six-foot frame. His sandy brown hair stuck out around his ears beneath a beige, sweat-stained baseball cap. His blue plaid shirt fit close, revealing a paunch that suggested a contented life of eating well.

"I would never have guessed you were into these old gospel tunes," he teased.

"You guess right," she said, turning down the volume. "They aren't my personal favourites, but they are *so* Mom and Dad! What a blast from the past. I can just see them, Dad especially, humming and singing along, tapping fingers and toes… When he did that, it always looked like he was directing a choir."

Ellie sat in what used to be her father's favourite armchair and mimed the actions.

Rob laughed. "You have that down pat." Then he changed the subject. "I was hoping to get here ahead of you. Sarah baked bread this morning and wanted a loaf left on the table for you as a welcome home present. She wanted the house to be as homey as possible when you arrived, which we didn't think would be until sometime this afternoon."

He handed Ellie the fresh bread.

She pressed her nose against the loaf. "That's so sweet of her. I'm going to enjoy this very much. Sarah makes good bread…"

"I noticed you haven't yet unpacked your car," he pointed out. "Would you like some help with that?"

"That would be great. I've got some heavier boxes in the trunk. I can handle bringing my clothes inside."

Between the two of them, it didn't take long to empty the car of all Ellie's things.

"Thanks, brother," she said when they'd finished. "I very much appreciate you letting me live here for a while. I believe it's the right place for me to do my soul work."

She wondered if Rob and Sarah would be as welcoming if they knew all there was to know about her. They'd kept the faith and shared the same values as their parents.

Rob nodded, murmuring that he was happy to help her out, and then returned to his own tasks in the machine shop.

Time passed quickly while Ellie hung her wardrobe in the closet and filled the drawers. The cosmetics and cleansers went in the bathroom and the few books she'd brought found spots on the shelf in her bedroom. Amongst them was a large coil-backed scribbler of lined paper that she intended to use as a journal. She also had a smaller one which could play the part of a daily assignment notebook. Then there were the three fine-point pens in different colours and her King James Bible, which had only rarely been cracked open since high school. She'd also been given a new Bible some time back.

She took both Bibles to the living room and set them on the coffee table. She reasoned that this would be the scene of her soul work journaling. But later, not now. She wasn't yet ready. Besides, she needed to eat something.

Curious whether anything had been left for her in the fridge, she opened it and felt immediately relieved to find assorted condiments and a jar of her mother's homemade crab-apple jelly. It was the perfect thing to slather onto bread. Hopefully there was some peanut butter in the cupboard.

There was. Was there anything better than fresh bread smeared with peanut butter and homemade jam of any kind? It was the main dish and dessert all in one.

Satisfactorily fed, Ellie next went on a walk around the yard. Quite a few of her mother's favourite perennials were now in bloom. She wanted to enjoy their beauty and think about her parents. A lot had changed in the ten years she had been away, having returned only for brief, occasional visits. Few of the old buildings remained. Her father, and later Rob, had regularly updated the farm to keep it on the cutting edge.

Although when it came to his personal life, her father had been as strictly religious and conservative as a man could possibly be.

Elizabeth, Ellie's mother, had followed the pattern of a traditional homemaker, a lifestyle that had served her well. She had sympathized with the feminist movement's calls for equality with men because nothing in her personal creed conflicted with that notion. In fact, she had seen herself as a full-fledged partner with her husband in their farming business, but her role in it had been distinct. She ran the house; he ran the business of seeding and harvest. She cooked, baked, and mended; he kept all things in good repair. They had gotten along by understanding their roles and sticking to them.

But to Ellie, her parents had been the most old-fashioned of the old-fashioned. Some of this could also be attributed to their age, since they'd been considerably older than the parents of her friends. In junior high, Ellie had felt embarrassed to be seen with them; to her, they'd appeared so dowdy. More like grandparents than parents.

Underneath all this, however, Ellie had known her mother as a wise woman with a wealth of knowledge on many topics—and she'd taught Ellie accordingly.

When Ellie had moved to Winnipeg, she had been amazed at how little her girlfriends understood about maintaining a home, basic kitchen skills, and keeping clothing in good repair. No one had known the right way to do laundry, how to prepare a balanced meal, or what to do when they were sick. Thus, wherever she went to live, she was soon elected to manage the kitchen and keep the apartment organized.

Ellie thought of all these things as she wandered the yard, recognizing her mother's touch in the floral borders and the neatness with which both her parents had maintained their homestead. She felt a palpable sadness at losing her mother and regret that she no longer had the opportunity to express appreciation for her training in the arts of homemaking. If her mother were still alive, Ellie knew she would eventually have summoned the courage to confess her many wrongdoings. Ellie was certain her dear old mom would have known how to heal her broken heart.

She had allowed pride and deceit, not to mention rebellion, to keep her away and cover up many secrets. And now it was too late. She would somehow have to figure things out for herself. After all, that was why she had come home...

Ellie wiped away a tear and rubbed her nose. Her walkabout complete, she re-entered the house and thought she had better take stock of what the kitchen had on hand and what she should buy in the way of groceries.

A half-hour later, she climbed into her car and got on her way to Minitonas. Passing the Fischer place, she noted the half-ton still parked out front. But she didn't see the young man in the blue cap.

She did, however, notice the tent pitched on the property. This detail struck her as a little odd, but then again it was none of her business what the neighbours did. It crossed her mind that perhaps the land had changed hands. She would try to remember to ask her brother about it.

Three

AFTER PURCHASING HER groceries of mostly fresh produce, Ellie decided she had better look in on Rob's family before going back to the farm. His wife Sarah and their three kids greeted her enthusiastically and urged her to stay for supper, a favourite meal of farmer sausage and perogies. She graciously accepted, and Rob arrived soon after.

Initially the conversation around the table revolved around what had happened at school that day—which was nothing much. Then talk turned to the garden, which was "up," and how the crops were looking, which was good so far. In less than three weeks, the church picnic would be held at the Bible camp by Wellman Lake and Ellie should plan to come along. It was normal conversation that reflected the kind of loving talk this average family had always engaged in.

Only Ellie was now realizing that the reality of it wasn't all that common out in the real world. Many of her friends had spoken of the troubles in their homes, such as parents frequently fighting, and sometimes divorcing. They hadn't gotten along with their siblings and people often seemed to walk on eggshells around each other.

But Ellie had grown up in a home much like this one. Sure, there had been spats between members of the family, yet underneath it all had been a strong current of respect, love, and loyalty.

It's true, what they say, Ellie thought. *You don't know what you've had until you don't have it anymore.*

She was thankful she could still choose to change course and get back on the track she had once known and had for too long rejected.

"Rob, what do you know about what's going on at the Fischers' farm?" Ellie asked out of the blue. "I saw a guy in a blue cap looking around there, and I didn't recognize him. He had a canvas tent set up."

"There's a truck there I haven't seen before, and yeah, I noticed the pitched tent," Rob replied. "I haven't seen the man himself, though, and I haven't heard anything about the property changing hands. If it had been for sale, I'd have been interested in it."

After supper and helping Sarah tidy the kitchen, Ellie hugged her nieces and nephew, said goodbye, and made her way home. Sleepiness was trying to overpower her, but she fought it, despite looking forward to a good night's sleep.

There was something she wanted to take care of first.

She prepared herself by having a shower and dressing in nightclothes. Then she sat on the accent chair opposite the sofa in the living room. She planned to speak to each of her parents, as well as Jesus, as if they were still alive in the flesh and sitting in the same room with her. She understood very well that this would be a symbolic act, but it seemed the best way to begin her soul work—to express her thoughts and confessions aloud to each of them.

Ellie envisioned her father sitting in his favourite armchair, relaxed and waiting for her to speak. She visualized her mother sitting on the end of the sofa nearest her father, her hands folded on her lap, while Jesus sat at the other end.

She crossed and then uncrossed her legs.

Finally, she spoke. "Okay, Jesus, You first. You know everything about me and I've spoken to You many times recently, confessing the wild things I've done since high school. You know I'm sorry for all of it. There is so much I wish I hadn't been part of. In all that time, I was never honest with my parents. It's important to me to admit to my sins to them too, not just to You, Jesus, even though they're no longer alive on the earth. I need to own up to them and let them know they were right all along. I understand that they're now with You, but if it's possible for them to listen in from the portals of heaven, I would like for them to hear what I have to say. I want to get back on track and live an upright life. Please help me talk this out. Somehow, it's still harder than I expected."

Ellie coughed and cleared her throat.

"Mom. Dad…" She looked toward the other end of the living room. "I guess it goes back to high school when I wanted to be like the other girls. You wanted me to dress in clothes that were out of fashion while my friends wore miniskirts and the latest styles. You wouldn't let me go to any of their parties, or to the school dances, or out with boys, or try smoking, or *anything*. I didn't want to be a bad girl. Honestly, I didn't. But I hated being so obviously different from the other young people. I felt so left out and uncool. So not-with-it. So I did something about it…"

Once she got going, it became easier to say what she wanted to say. She named the girls from their church, as well as others from her class at school who had felt they wanted to be seen as cool. Together they'd finagled opportunities to participate in parties where alcohol was present, and even a few drugs. She admitted that they'd paired off with boys to enjoy stolen moments of necking and petting.

At their high school grad, some of these girls had made a pact to share an apartment in Winnipeg and live modern lifestyles where they could do whatever they wanted without parents around to get on their case. Ellie had participated in this pact.

She confessed to her parents that while going through registered nurses training, she had gotten sexually involved with more than one boy. She'd had guilty feelings about that, but only when she thought of her family or church and how they would disapprove of her behaviour. But everyone was doing it, and so she was able to suppress her misgivings and go along with this "enlightened" and liberated way of life.

After nurses training, she had secured a position at St. Boniface Hospital. Soon after, she had met a very handsome and entertaining intern, Paul Richter. Their relationship had stayed at the friendship level until Ellie had dared him to kiss her at a party. He had, and neither had expected such passionate chemistry to explode within them. After that, they became nearly inseparable.

About three weeks later, Paul proposed they move in together. They chose a modest but attractive apartment not far from the hospital and set up house together. It had been a lot of fun choosing furniture and housewares. And they'd had a ball camping, canoeing, seeing movies, and biking together.

When Ellie had brought up the subject of marriage, Paul demurred, arguing that a relationship like theirs, where the love was real and deep, didn't need a piece of paper to prove or confirm it. Mutual love was its own commitment.

Ellie lost that argument, but seeds of doubt began to sprout in her heart. She wanted to nest, while Paul wanted things to stay as they were, at least until he became a full-fledged doctor.

Then an accident happened, and Paul blamed Ellie for it entirely.

At this point, she began to cry. "Sorry, Mom and Dad. I might not be able to tell you everything about this tonight. It's still too fresh and painful."

She wrapped her arms around herself and rocked back and forth in her chair, weeping quietly.

"I will say this, however," she continued after a few minutes of silence. "I remember you told me that there is pleasure in sin for a season, but afterward come the consequences, sometimes irreversible, and you were right. All those things I used to think were so much fun, I now find them empty, boring, and costly. For a while life seemed exciting and interesting. Not anymore. The highs always faded back to grim reality. We partied all the time, consuming one drink after another and philosophizing about what makes life worthwhile, but really, it was so much bull!"

Ellie sniffed, then pulled some tissues from the box on the coffee table to dab her eyes and blow her nose.

"I've given it a great deal of thought. I know now, and have probably known all along, even while I was trying to live totally different from what you taught me, that you were right. There's no joy in life, no meaning or purpose or contentment or freedom, or..." She trailed off, unable to think of any other things to add the list. "...apart from faith in Jesus, being in relationship with Him, and living the Bible way. I truly understand now that all your dos and don'ts were about preventing me from getting hurt." She paused. "I still wish, though, that you could have come up with some way of keeping me straight without me having to look and feel so different from the other girls at school. Cuz that's what started it. Whatever. We can't go back and do those days over again."

She wiped her nose again, trying to figure out what to say next.

"I just want to tell you that you don't have to worry about me anymore. Your prodigal daughter has come home, both physically and in spirit. I mean to live for Jesus again, the way you raised your children to live. I also want to tell you that you were good parents. I didn't show you nearly enough appreciation, and I'm sorry for that. Everything is going to be okay now. You can rest in peace..."

Ellie's voice cracked and she began to sob quietly.

After a couple of minutes, she turned her focus to the other end of the sofa where she imagined Jesus sat.

"Dear Jesus," she prayed. "I'm asking for Your help as I begin my soul work tomorrow. Guide me in my thoughts and feelings and get me back to mental and emotional health. Show me what to do, where to go, and all of that. I want You to be Lord of my life, this time permanently. And please help me to sleep well tonight. Amen."

On that note, Ellie left the room and went straight to bed. Sleep came mercifully quick and provided rest without the troubled dreams that often plagued her.

Four

ELLIE WOKE TO a light-flooded bedroom and the cheerful chirps of birds through the open window. It felt like it must be late in the day, but upon checking the clock on the dresser it was only 6:15 a.m. Still, she had slept well and was eager to begin the day.

After a couple of cat-like stretches, she got up, wrapped herself in her tatty chenille housecoat, and went down the hall to the kitchen to put on some coffee. While it brewed, she fixed herself a breakfast of buttered toast, cheese slices, and pieces of fruit. Moments later, she carried her breakfast plate and steaming mug of coffee into the living room and settled herself in the armchair. She could understand why it had been her father's favourite place to sit; it was one of those large, wide-armed bouffant pieces that seemed to hug its occupant from all sides.

Before settling in, however, Ellie picked up her two notebooks, Bible, and pens. Now she was ready.

She once again imagined Jesus sitting at the far end of the sofa. She pictured Him smiling and pleased that she was following through on her quest to re-establish a life of faith.

She opened the larger notebook to the first page and wrote with her blue pen:

Private Property
of
Ella Rose Bauman & the Lord Jesus Christ
June 11, 1980 - _____

Soul Work Journal

Then she wrote out her code, associated with the different-coloured pens.

> BLACK pen: Hard, revealing questions that I sense the Lord would put to me and have me answer from my heart to show the truth about me.
>
> BLUE pen: My most brutally honest replies to those questions.
>
> RED pen: Insight from a third voice, such as scripture, a quote from someone wise, something Mom or a friend might have said that is pertinent, etc.

After this, she turned over the page to begin her first entry. She paused for a moment, then picked up the black pen and wrote, *What specifically do you want?* It was a question from the Lord that deserved serious reflection, so Ellie closed the larger journal and picked up the smaller one.

On the first page she wrote in large letters:

Daily Assignments for Ella Rose Bauman.

On the next page, she wrote: *Name ten things you are thankful for.* She set it aside as well, planning to fill it in later.

She picked up the brand-new Bible, the gift she had received from her parents at the family Christmas gathering in 1977. It contained the text of the Good News Bible, a recent translation written in contemporary English. It hadn't been an unusual sort of gift for her family, but Ellie thought her parents had probably suspected that she'd not been keeping the faith as she once had and she imagined it was their attempt to entice her back to the fold.

Opening the pages, she reflected that she'd grown up with the traditional King James Version and was most familiar with its archaic language. However, now that she was on a mission to start over, the newer Bible seemed like the right place to begin.

But where to start, specifically? How about Matthew, the first book of the New Testament? Upon locating the opening page of Matthew, Ellie decided to read it through in one sitting, as if it were a novel. All she was after was a reminder of the stories in it. An in-depth study could come sometime later.

She did read it in one sitting, but it wasn't quick work. It took all of three hours to read a mere fifty pages. Quite often, a passage seemed to home in on her personal experiences, sometimes to convict her, other times to encourage and comfort her, and occasionally to wow her into learning some new or forgotten detail.

When she was done, the clock read 10:10 a.m.

Ellie already felt considerably better than she had for many weeks. The morning had been sweet and peaceful so far, but now she felt the need to move.

After dressing in her comfiest jeans and a faded blue T-shirt, she crossed the yard to the machine shed to look for her old bike. Hopefully it was still around somewhere. She had in mind to follow the road beyond the farm until it came to the bridge which crossed the Roaring River. She hadn't been there for many years, but she had once found it to be a pretty area. Maybe there would be a conducive spot to occasionally visit with her journal and do some soul work.

Only one way to find out.

It turned out to be a good afternoon, not just for rediscovering favourite places from her youth, but also for her visit to the cemetery to see her parents' graves.

After a light supper, she pulled out her journals in the living room and got ready to focus. She intended to write out her most heartfelt thoughts. She got out her blue pen:

What I want is:

- to be fully healed in body, soul, and mind
- to get back into a relationship with the Lord Jesus that is intimate and very real
- to establish habits of time spent daily with the Lord
- to know His voice when He should speak to my heart (apart from all other voices) and to be obedient to it
- to feel joyful again
- to know God's will for my life (what should I, a trained nurse, do with myself?)

That was all she could think of at present. She told herself she could always come back and add more items as she thought of them.

Next she opened her assignment book:

I am thankful for:

- good food
- a clean, safe place to live

- my brother Robert
- beautiful flowers
- Jesus
- the Bible
- good health
- my parents (especially Mom)
- my career training (nurse)
- my car (which gives me independence)

It was a simple, non-profound beginning, but it felt good to be still and listen to her heart. The home of her youth promised to be a safe place to be honest with herself, face hard questions, and take appropriate actions as they came to her.

~

That same morning, Hugh woke up grumpy and thoroughly annoyed. He'd had a restless night that included a bad dream, the details of which he no longer remembered or cared about. It was those stupid birds that tweeted so ridiculously early that triggered his irritation.

Getting up signalled an aching back. He missed sleeping in a real bed, and it was only the second night.

A fresh pot of coffee improved his mood some, but not a lot, since some of the food in his hamper already showed signs of spoiling. Clearly he would have to come up with some means of refrigeration. That meant having the meter on the hydro pole reinstated. Not a problem, but which of the farm's buildings would be sound enough to install the fridge and stove from the house?

The answer came easily: none.

ly after picking up copies of *The Star and Times* and *The Western Producer*. That's where he'd find the classifieds.

Hugh would have liked to leave for town immediately, but it was only six in the morning and he greatly doubted anything would be open before 8:00 a.m. What was he to do to kill a couple of hours? Unload the rest of his stuff from the back of the truck, for starters.

He didn't have many possessions. Aside from his tent and camping gear, he had a duffle bag full of clothing, a couple of jackets, including a winter parka, and some footwear. He also had a sizable collection of quality tools, mostly the kind that were used in the field of motor mechanics, but he also had all the basics for carpentry and electrical work. He was quite proud of his tool collection, which represented a sizable investment. Finally, he had a radio/cassette player. He'd brought no furniture, thinking he would buy what he needed when the needs presented themselves.

After his flight from Minitonas fourteen years earlier, he had been rescued and unofficially adopted by the Turners and lived with them in Winnipeg. He'd stayed as long as he could, but eventually he had taken room-and-board elsewhere. His focus had been on establishing himself in a trade where he could excel—and when he had started to make real money, he had saved every penny he could. Growing up in the Fischer household hadn't provided him with many opportunities to earn money for himself. On his own, he purchased only what was necessary and stored the rest with the bank. He enjoyed watching the figures on his account grow larger over time.

His first vehicle had been a subcompact car that served to get him to and from classes, and after that to and from his place of work. His heart was set, though, on one day owning his own fancy pickup. It was a proud day when he had been able to buy his dream truck and simply write a cheque to cover it.

It hadn't been long after that when he'd gotten the fateful call from Margo letting him know about the single car accident that had claimed their parents.

Here he was, three days into his new life, and already discouraged by the mammoth task ahead. Yet he wasn't willing to give up; he was determined to find the people who could help him with facts and prices. Rome hadn't been built in a day, he reminded himself.

Hugh figured the safest place to stow his tools would be in the barn. The second stall was the emptiest of paraphernalia, but he first tidied it up using a nearby shovel and the remains of an old corn broom. It didn't take long to get rid of the desiccated straw and dung and set his tools in place, as well as his radio, and cover them with a sheet of plastic tarp. That done, he hastily drew some water from inside the house to splash on his face and smooth down his sleep-messed hair.

Minitonas showed few signs of activity. He drove around the streets and avenues, reacquainting himself with the lay of the land. The town seemed smaller than he remembered. Following the fires of the 1960s, none of the affected businesses had rebuilt. The number of active businesses appeared to be few.

However, one new building at the intersection of Main Street and Second Avenue caught his attention: the Family Foods Community Store. It was a huge building. The posters and sale ads taped to the windows suggested it served as a general mercantile where hardware, paint, and housewares were sold alongside groceries.

But first up, breakfast. The café was still closed, so he parked in front of the building and waited, dozing off and on.

At last the waitress unlocked the front door. He took the first booth, a perch from which he could watch the townsfolk come to life. He ordered coffee and an omelette plate with hashbrowns and sausage as well as the latest copy of *The Star and Times*.

Soon the waitress, a plump, salt-and-pepper-haired woman, delivered his meal.

"Where're you from?" she asked. "It's not often we get out-of-town visitors stopping in for breakfast."

Hugh answered in generalities. "I drove up from the south to scope out the area. If I like what I see, and things work out, I may stay a while."

"That's different. The young people around here tend to look for greener pastures. Not many stick around after they graduate. But welcome here!"

"Thanks," said Hugh, feeling briefly encouraged.

He savoured his meal, paid his tab, and left with the newspaper under his arm. He then crossed the street to enter the only bank in town and made arrangements to have his money transferred from Winnipeg to a new local account. Afterward he aimed for the community store to buy a few non-perishables.

As Hugh drew near, he noticed a short elderly man wearing a soiled plaid shirt tucked into grease-stained green workpants. He appeared to be watching Hugh from the side of the store—not just watching, but studying him intently.

Hugh was just about to go inside the store when the old man squealed, "Weeell, if it ain't Freddie Fischer all over again."

Wary, Hugh stopped short and looked the old man straight in the eye. "You got it wrong, mister. I'm not Freddie Fischer." Then, after a slight pause, he added, "Whoever he is…"

The old man followed him inside. "Yer right, ya can't be the old man hisself, 'cuz he died a few years back. But otherwise, I'd say yer the spit of him. I'm thinkin' mebbe yer his kid that run off."

The stranger cocked his head to one side and smiled, revealing a few missing teeth.

Hugh didn't like the way this was going. "I don't know you. I'm pretty sure I've never seen you before in my life."

Hugh picked up a grocery basket and went looking for the tin cans.

The old man kept following him. "Folks 'round here call me Tipper. Yer old man did too. We was friends fer a long time."

Hugh ignored him, studying the labels on the tins.

"Yer not the friendly type, now are ya? Yer pa could be like that. Until he had something he wanted to sell, that is." Tipper chuckled to himself. "Then he'd talk the hindleg off a donkey."

Still ignoring him, Hugh pushed past the old man to where the cookies and crackers were kept.

"Let's see…" mused Tipper, still smiling toothlessly. "Yer prob'ly here 'bout the farm. Maybe ya want to make a go of it yerself. Or maybe yer gettin' ready to put it up for sale. Nah, I reckon yer gonna follow in yer pa's footsteps and become a farmer." His face brightened as if a new thought had suddenly occurred to him. He lowered his voice conspiratorially. "Are ya gonna get yer pa's moonshine business going again? Man, he could cook up some powerful spirits, I'll tell ya."

Hugh feigned no surprise, but inwardly it was a shocking revelation. "Nope! Never. I'm not much of a drinker."

He sighed audibly. Drat! He had given himself away, having as much as admitted to everything Tipper already suspected.

Tipper knew it too and looked at him with an even bigger smile, as if to say *"Gotcha."*

"I gotta go, Tipper. Got lots to do. Maybe we can chew the fat another day," said Hugh, but internally he thought, *When pigs fly*.

He hurriedly added a couple more items to his basket, as well as a copy of *The Western Producer*. He paid for them and left without saying another word.

His next stop would be the hydro office in the larger town of Swan River. As he drove up Highway 10, he realized that his encounter with Tipper had rattled him. He didn't like it observed that he looked like his pa. He had made a vow to himself years ago that he would *not* be like his old man in any way, shape, or form. Not if he could possibly help it.

It was the other revelation, though, that consumed his thoughts. His pa had run an illegal moonshine business? He wondered when that had started. It didn't explain everything, but it explained a lot.

Such as why he had been so adamant that they never have guests over, and that any visitor be sent away as soon as possible. It also explained why his pa had often smelled of liquor despite never actually going out and buying any.

So the farm had held a secret! And Hugh suspected that where there was one, there were probably more.

Numerous changes had taken shape in Swan River since he'd last walked its streets. Lots of new buildings.

It turned out that the cost to have the farm's hydro meter remounted wouldn't be as expensive as he'd feared. He could also get the well water tested, although he had neglected to bring a sample.

Since he couldn't think of anything else he needed, he decided to return to the farm.

He put away his groceries, then determined to go looking for the still his pa was supposed to have set up. He looked around, trying to surmise its likely location. There was a bit of bush along the north side of the yard that stretched long and wide out to the west, well past the farm buildings. He figured the still, if there really was one, was likely hidden somewhere out in that direction.

As he walked through the tall grass between scrubby trees, he saw what a graveyard the bush had become. Old pieces of rundown equipment were scattered and piled up everywhere. Included in the mix were rusted-out milk cans, barrels, tires, stones, rolls of barbed-wire fencing, and lots of broken glass.

It's a good place to get seriously injured, thought Hugh. Something else to add to his to-do list.

Eventually he came upon a pond, which triggered one of the few good memories he had of the place. It was a natural swimming hole, shaped roughly like an egg. At its widest it was about thirty feet, and seventy feet at its longest, or so he guesstimated. In the summers, he had sometimes come here for a dip to cool off. He'd forgotten all about that. He could come here again to bathe himself whenever he got sweaty or dirty from his labours.

Once again, things were looking up.

Then he saw the shack tucked in amongst some skinny trees. It was roughly made and hardly bigger than an outhouse. The once well-worn path that led to it was still discernible.

Bingo! Hugh was sure this was it.

Sure enough, opening the crude door revealed some copper tanks, now covered in green tarnish, and all the other accoutrements needed for the operation.

The sight gave Hugh pause. He didn't know what to do with this information.

Well, nothing for now. He refastened the door and headed back to his camp.

The return walk wasn't the same. He believed he felt a presence, as though he wasn't exactly alone. Sometimes he imagined he saw the furtive figure of his pa just ahead of him, dodging behind trees as he came up behind him. Hugh didn't believe in ghosts, but he was beginning to feel spooked.

When he got to the edge of the bushes, he could have sworn he heard his pa yell after him. *"You don't tell anyone what you just saw, you bastard, or I'll beat you within an inch of your life!"*

Even though it wasn't real, it felt real enough.

Hugh was thoroughly rattled by the time he reached his tent. Feelings of dread and fear washed over him for the second time in as many days.

"Stand, Hugh, stand," he instructed himself. "Don't let him get to you."

What to do now? He pulled out a soda and an apple and sat in his lawn chair. He would pass the time reading his newspapers—catch up with the goings-on of the world, scan the classifieds, see what Ann Landers had to say…

When darkness arrived, Hugh turned into his tent while reflecting on a grim reality: he had all the space and quiet he had ever longed for, but no tranquillity had come with it. He worried he had a monkey on his back, in the shape and spirit of his pa, and that it was going to hound him forever.

Five

ELLIE ROSE THE next morning in good spirits. Looking forward to the quiet time she would spend with the Lord reading, listening, and writing, she randomly chose the letter to the Ephesians. As before, she read through it in one sitting to get the overview. It didn't take as long to get through as Matthew had the day before, but she found herself pausing here and there when the instructions spoke directly to her heart and revealed areas of her life where she fell far short. An example was found in Ephesians 4:31–32: *"Get rid of all bitterness, passion, and anger. No more shouting or insults, no more hateful feelings of any sort. Instead, be kind and tender-hearted to one another, and forgive one another, as God has forgiven you through Christ."*[1]

These were supposed to be brutally honest sessions, so Ellie expressed her honest feelings to the image of Jesus she envisioned on the end of the sofa across from her.

"I get it, Jesus," she murmured. "This is where it all comes to a head. Forgive and be healed, or don't forgive and become bitter and ugly. The thing is, I'm not there yet. I find that I can't get over my hurts just like that. So I'm pleading for You to be patient with me. Bring me to a place where I can forgive and let go and move on in the freedom You have promised."

---

[1] GNT.

Ellie reached for her smaller notebook and wrote out the following assignment: *Name all the things that make you angry and why.*

Oh boy, she thought. *This could take quite a while.*

She set it aside to open the larger journal. She took out the black pen and wrote, *What exactly is your problem?* The question seemed straightforward enough, yet Ellie didn't find it easy to articulate a brutally honest response.

After several false starts, she set this journal aside too. She would try again later.

She started on the anger assignment and surprised herself with the lengthy list it produced. By 11:00 a.m., though, her legs were cramping. She needed to set aside the soul work and do something physical.

Ellie soon realized that she needed something to do with her hands. For the moment she settled on losing herself in baking. After rummaging through the cupboard, she decided to make bran muffins with some diced apple thrown in.

While the muffins baked, she played some gospel quartet music on the stereo. It lifted her spirits after so much introspection.

All fifteen muffins turned out perfectly! She then remembered one of her mother's habits. Whenever she had baked multiple loaves of bread, she gave one or two loaves away.

"Life is often hard for people," she would say in explanation. "If we can bring a blessing to others, it helps lighten the load a little bit."

For Elizabeth Bauman, tithing her baked goods had been one more way to be a blessing to others.

Ellie wondered with whom she could share these muffins—and immediately her new mystery neighbour came to mind. Perfect!

She found a suitable basket and came up with a cloth napkin to line it before filling it with nine muffins. She didn't need more than six for herself, she reasoned.

Rather excited about meeting the new neighbour, she left the house toting her wicker basket.

When Ellie pulled into the driveway, the mysterious stranger was outside working on a tractor just outside the farm's largest shed. He appeared both surprised and wary to see someone coming onto his property.

She pulled up close to where he stood and turned off the ignition. Stepping out of the car, she held the basket out in front of her.

"Hi there," she said with a smile on her face. "I'm Ella Bauman from just up the road. We've noticed someone set up camp and supposed it meant we were going to have neighbours again. So I thought I'd come and meet you, and welcome you to the neighbourhood with muffins."

She held out the basket.

Hugh looked at his hands, black from handling greasy tractor parts. "Ah, that's mighty nice of you, Ella Bauman. Maybe you could set it somewhere. My hands are too dirty…"

Ellie looked around but saw no convenient surface on which to set the basket.

"Perhaps inside your tent?" she asked tentatively.

"Sure, that would be great. That's real nice of you."

Ellie walked over to the tent and set the basket down just inside. Walking back, she noticed the man staring at her with a look she couldn't read.

"I wasn't expecting to see you, Ellie," he said. "Look at you. You're all grown up, and no more freckles. Still got blond hair, though."

Ellie's eyes widened in surprise. "Do we know each other?"

"We do, or at least we used to… a long time ago." Now it was Hugh's turn to smile. "You've brought those muffins to Hugh Fischer. It's been a while… like, fourteen years. I'd like to shake your hand, but my hands are filthy."

"Oh my gosh," exclaimed Ellie, "I… we… didn't know. We guessed that maybe the property had changed owners. What can I say? Welcome back. Are you here to stay, or are you just having a campout holiday?"

"Tell you what—let me clean up and then we can visit a while. I'm kind of hungry too, so those muffins are timely."

Before going into the house to wash, he pulled up his only lawn chair and invited Ellie to sit in it.

"I'll be back in a jiffy," he promised.

In the few minutes he was gone, Ellie assessed the property. It was rundown for sure, but abandoned homesteads often had cool, old-fashioned relics lying about. It was all she could do to stay put while waiting for Hugh to come back out.

When he returned, he brought with him one of the wooden chairs from inside the old house and plunked it down across from her.

"All right then, let's see about them muffins," he said. "And it's ladies first to tell what you're all about these days. I have to say, I would have thought you were the kind of girl who'd split from these parts and take up city life." Hugh took a muffin, peeled off the paper cup, and took a bite. "These are good…"

"As a matter of fact, that's exactly what I did," began Ellie. "After graduating from high school, I moved to Winnipeg and took up nurses training at the Winnipeg General Hospital. Then I got a position with the hospital in St. Boniface and have worked there ever since—that is, until I put in for a leave of absence at the end of May. You may not know this, but my dad passed away over a year ago, and my mom died of stroke in April."

"I'm sorry for your loss."

"Yeah, me too." She looked down at the ground. "Anyway, the house was empty after losing Mom, so I asked my brother Robert, who runs the farm now, if I could come home for a while. Let's just say I had some disappointing experiences in Winnipeg. I wanted some time and space to figure out what to do with myself going forward. So here I am. It's been less than a week, but I already feel better about a few things. My goal is to come up with a plan… to start over… and hopefully do right by myself this time. Your turn."

"That's actually very interesting." Hugh shifted his weight on the chair. "Because I came back to see if it's possible for me to start over too."

Ellie nodded to encourage him to keep talking.

"You probably know that I ran away from home when I was sixteen," he said. Ellie nodded again. "Well, I fell in with a family in Winnipeg who offered me a place to stay. They persuaded me to finish school and helped me get training as a mechanic so I'd have the skills to make a decent living. I did pretty well, generally speaking. It wasn't until my folks died—you knew about that, didn't you?"

"I'm sorry for your loss too, Hugh."

"Aww, well, I didn't take it hard, though I admit it was weirdly unexpected. After my folks were gone, I began to wonder if I could get interested in taking over the farm. I talked to Margo about it once in a while."

"Margo is your sister, if I remember right?"

"Yes. She handled all the stuff one has to deal with when somebody in the family dies, like funeral arrangements, signing off on taxes, and whatever else. Dying is a complicated business. Anyway, the more I thought about it, the more I thought the country life would suit me better than the hustle and bustle of the city. I worked long and hard to save up a bunch of money to come back and, like you said, start over. And here I am. I got back on Monday. How long have you been here?"

Hugh helped himself to another muffin.

"Since Tuesday morning," answered Ellie. "I wish you every success. What you have in mind is a good venture. I wish I had a good worthwhile project like that. I'm not ready to get back to nursing, but I need something to do with my hands." She changed the subject. "So what's your plan to get this place going under the Fischer banner again?"

Hugh sighed. "Before I got here, I had hoped the main buildings would at least be in good enough shape for me to use until I could afford to replace them. Margo warned me it wasn't likely. Now that I see it all for myself, it's even worse than she thought. It should all be knocked down and lit with a match. Trouble is, I don't have enough capital to replace the house and also get started in farming. So to answer your question, I'm still considering my options."

"Can I have a look inside the old house?" asked Ellie hopefully.

"What? Why? It's a total wreck, and probably home to all kinds of bugs and rodents."

He didn't say so, but she could tell he must be a little embarrassed to have her see the poor conditions in which he had grown up. Ellie tried to dismiss his concerns.

"Of course it is," she said. "It's a rickety old house, probably one of the first original homesteads to pop up in this area. I don't expect it to be neat and tidy. I just find it interesting to poke around old houses and imagine what life was like in the olden days. I do it every chance I get, and I've been at it since I was about ten years old. It's fun."

Hugh looked at her like she had a few screws missing. "Are you telling me you trespass on people's property to snoop around?"

It was an obvious attempt at teasing her and Ellie caught on to the joke. "I prefer the word *exploring* over *snooping*. Come on, give me the royal tour."

They rose together.

"Okay, Miss Ellie, but don't say I didn't warn you."

Upon entering, it took Ellie a moment to adjust to the dim light. When her vision was clear again, she gasped.

"Oh my gosh, it's still completely furnished! It's like a time capsule in here." Her voice sounded almost reverent.

"Well, it is what it is. Maybe the fridge and stove still work. They weren't here when I left. Everything else is broken down and should go down in a fire, along with the rest of the house."

Ellie caught the dark edge in his tone and instantly understood something about him. Hugh had grown up in a poor environment where they seldom, if ever, enjoyed the nicer things that most other families took for granted. It also seemed to her that Hugh had no idea about the value of antiques.

She got the hint, too, that more than the furnishings should be burned with this house, although now was *not* the time to pursue that avenue.

"I beg to differ." Ellie trailed her fingers along the Hoosier cabinet stationed between the fridge and the stove. "You have a house full of antiques and people would pay good money for them. If you don't want them, I'll take them. And I'll give you a fair price."

She stepped over to the wooden table, which showed a split along one of the glued seams. The mismatched wooden chairs had a few spindles missing. But out of the five chairs, each with missing parts, three or maybe four could be rebuilt.

"I think you're a bit loony, Ellie Bauman. These old things are just junk."

"Apparently I know something you don't. You're sitting on a few bucks here." She turned and walked into another part of the house. "What's in this room?"

Next, Ellie entered the little room behind the kitchen, noting another old cupboard. The room also featured a pitcher pump with a stool and pail. Beside it sat an old wringer washing machine, a metal bathtub, and a washstand still supporting a chipped enamelled basin.

She took the lead in moving on into the sitting room, with Hugh close behind.

"Oh!" she cooed. "Look at that cool old-fashioned sofa. It even has an armchair to match. The style makes me think they're from the 1930s. And what a dear looking secretary..." Ellie pulled down the lid that served as a writing desk and noted the empty cubby holes inside. "I'll take those too."

"Why would you want them?" asked Hugh in disbelief. "There's a spring popped. The material is worn and frayed. It's trash!"

"Nothing that an upholsterer can't fix. It's just a matter of pulling out the old stuffing and fabric and replacing it. Then you have a gorgeous sofa." She spied something else that caught her interest. "And I love this old steamer trunk. What's in it?"

"I have no idea. Most likely more useless stuff."

"Don't be so sure." Ellie made a beeline for the stairs. "What's up here?"

"Not sure," he said. "Haven't been up there yet."

40

"Let's explore! Come on."

"I think you mean *snoop*," he countered. "I sure hope we don't fall through the floor…"

The stairs creaked and groaned ominously, but they both made it to the upper level without mishap.

"Wow!" exclaimed Ellie as she peered into the first bedroom. "Look at that wrought iron bed. It still has all four brass knobs on the corners. And the linens are still on it! It's like a moment frozen in time. Oh, and the dresser! I love that oval mirror. The silver is starting to go, but it's still in pretty good shape. I'll take all these pieces."

Hugh snickered. "Okay, now you're just being greedy."

Ellie moved into the next room. "This must be the master bedroom."

It contained a double-sized bed, a model with a metal head and footboards made of tubes. A larger metal tube shaped the outside frame. The design included a flat panel about ten inches wide in the centre with two thinner tubes on each side.

The single dresser was a highboy with a short mirror in a tiltable frame across the top.

Before Ellie could add these items to her list, Hugh said, "I can see myself having a use for these items when I get a permanent place set up."

He didn't seem to mean it, though. It was more about having a little fun with Ellie.

"Uh-huh. Okay. Fine. What's in here?"

The next room was the smallest on the second floor and it held the treadle sewing machine, a few stacked boxes, and a narrow cot against the wall.

His voice got quiet. "That's where I slept as a kid."

"A lot too short for you now," Ellie quipped, wanting to keep the mood light.

Although long abandoned, Ellie could sense that the house still retained a lot of heartache and sorrow, misery and anguish. It was eerie. And if she could feel it, she wondered how much worse it was for Hugh. No wonder he just wanted to throw in a match and be done with it.

It was time to get back outside, away from this dark and depressing scene.

They took care descending the stairs. The boards squeaked so loudly that Ellie became concerned for their safety.

But once outside, the world looked cheerful again.

"Whew, that was fun." Ellie smiled brightly. "You have a virtual museum here, I think. What else can you show me?"

Hugh thought about it for a moment. "Are you into old vehicles?"

"Possibly."

"There's an old grain-hauling truck in the barn you might find interesting."

As they walked in the direction of the barn, Hugh told Ellie that he was looking into buying a used mobile home to live in since the house was uninhabitable.

Ellie stopped short, then turned to look at Hugh with a screwed-up nose. "May I please weigh in with my opinion on that?"

"I guess so."

"I think buying a mobile home is similar to buying a car. If you buy a new car from the lot, and try to return it the next day, will the dealer give you what you paid for it?"

"No," said Hugh. "He'll deduct a certain amount of depreciation."

"Exactly. It begins to depreciate as soon as it's driven away, and it keeps depreciating year after year until it dies and becomes worthless. Similarly, a mobile home won't keep its value very well. And I personally don't think they're very practical in the long run. Or attractive. You told me that you came back to start over, so I would very much like to encourage you to start over with as much quality as you can muster. Take it one structure at a time. That way, when the basics are in place, they'll truly fill their purpose and be sound structures that last a long while."

She turned in a circle, taking in the whole farmyard.

"I'm guessing that you're thinking of an old house trailer that somebody wants to get rid of for a couple thousand, maybe less," she said. "Then there's the cost of getting it here and hooking it up to all the utilities. Then, because it's past its prime, it will need constant repairs. That same amount of money would pay for a small, energy-efficient cottage that will last many years and look good too. I'd hate to see you throw good money after bad. If you have limited resources, it's especially important to invest wisely. Get my drift?"

Hugh nodded. "You make a good point," he said. "How did you get to be so smart?"

She let out a laugh. "If I'm smart, it's because I'm the daughter of John and Elizabeth Bauman, and the sister of three older brothers, every one of whom are efficiency experts and pros at just about everything they put their hands to. It's a blessing and a curse. And some of it might have rubbed off on me."

"The thing is, building takes time and I need a place that shelters me from the elements, especially winter, not to mention cooking facilities and the means to keep myself clean."

"That's fair. You make a good point, but you can spare a few days to work out a reasonable solution. You want to think of all possible options and then select the one which would dictate the best and wisest ways to spend a limited supply of dollars. In the meantime, you're welcome to refill your drum of drinking water and take showers as you need them from our place. Shoot, it's the neighbourly thing to do."

What she had thought would be a short visit turned out to last a couple of hours, and by now she was sensing that it was time to part company.

Ellie walked over to her car but didn't get in. She stood there, her forehead stitching up in concentration. Hugh was watching her from his stance near the tractor where earlier he had been in the process of taking the motor apart.

She turned back and walked toward him. "I gotta tell you, neighbour, I've been bitten by your bug."

Hugh looked confused.

"I mean, I've only been here a couple of hours and the ideas are rolling in nonstop. Can I be part of your think tank? You know what they say about two heads being better than one."

If anything, Hugh suddenly looked relieved. "As you were walking away, I was thinking how much it felt like we'd been friends for a long time. Seeing as I'm short on ideas, and since you're apparently overflowing with them, yes please. I'd like to know how you think a guy like me could rejuvenate this place."

Ellie beamed and extended her hand. "It's a deal!"

They shook on it.

"All right, I'm off to buy some graph paper," she said, walking backward to her car. "I'll need a couple of days, maybe more, to get my ideas on paper."

As she drove off, she yelled through the open car window, "Thanks for the tour!"

Six

IDEA AFTER IDEA surfaced in Ellie's brain as she drove down the highway. She was almost giddy with excitement at the thought of designing a plan that made sense for all the buildings that would someday be erected on the Fischer farm. She was most excited to design a cottage that would be practical and beautiful and economical with all the modern amenities for living independently, a true place for Hugh to call home.

God is real, and He listens to our prayers, she thought. *This morning I was clamouring for something to do with my hands. This afternoon I scored a great assignment. Thank You, Jesus!*

About forty-five minutes later, Ellie left the store with an armful of folders, paper, and pencils. She'd picked out a cheap sixteen-by-twenty picture frame at the last minute, as well as a magazine at the checkout that was devoted to house plans.

Ellie didn't go directly home but instead turned again into the Fischer driveway. Hugh was still working on the tractor when she pulled up just as before.

"I wasn't expecting to see you so soon," he said. "What's up?"

"I've got all the supplies I need, but before I go at it I need a bunch of measurements. Is it okay if I go around and measure a few things?"

"Sure. Do you want some help?" Hugh reached for the rag on the ground next to him and began to wipe the grease from his hands.

"I'll need to borrow a tape measure from you… if you don't mind."

"I don't mind. Just a sec while I fish one out of my toolbox." He returned shortly and handed her a tape measure that was good for fifty feet.

"Perfect! Thanks. Now, I can manage the small stuff, but we can work out the length and width of the yard together. Can I go into the house?"

He gave his permission.

Inside, she took measurements of the fridge and stove, then moved from room to room checking all the other items she thought she could use. All the while, she wrote their dimensions on a pad of paper.

By the time she came back outside, Hugh was ready to assist. Together they took down measurements of the yard as a whole, then each building and where they all stood in proximity to each other. Also noted was the location of the hydro pole and well.

Armed with facts, Ellie returned to her car.

"You're really taking this seriously," said Hugh, sounding amazed at Ellie's enthusiasm for a project that actually had nothing to do with her.

"I am. And if you're wondering why, it's like I told you before. I need a job, something to do with my hands. This sort of thing sparks my imagination! I love to draw. It's one of the few things that causes me to lose all sense of time. I'm very grateful to you for allowing me to have some input into your plan."

He hesitated for a moment. "Okay… but what if I don't care for your proposal? What if I think it doesn't suit me, or it's too expensive or something?"

"You're under no obligation to use my ideas."

"Alrighty then. I look forward to seeing what you come up with."

Once back home, Ellie set up her office on the kitchen table. She fixed herself a quick sandwich for supper, intending to begin work right away, but then remembered that she hadn't yet responded to the question she'd written that morning in her journal. She wasn't in the mood anymore for personal reflection...

Nonetheless, she went into the living room to talk to Jesus about it.

"Lord Jesus, I'm super excited about the assignment I've been given to design a new plan for the Fischer farm. Could I please be excused from our conversation this evening?"

The answer came immediately to her heart: *"But seek ye first the kingdom of God, and his righteousness; and all these things shall be added unto you."*[2] It was a verse out of Matthew she had read only yesterday, albeit in the translation she had memorized as a kid.

"Okay. I have to keep my promises to meet with You every day too. Could we at least change the topic of our conversation?"

The impression on her heart was that this was okay.

Ellie went into the kitchen and pulled out yet another notebook from the stack of paper products she'd bought. This one would be dedicated to the questions she put to God and the subsequent perceptions she received in reply whether through Scripture, quotes, or other sources.

After the title page, Ellie wrote out her first question to God with the blue pen: *What would You have me do for Hugh Fischer?*

Picking up the black pen, she listened for a few moments and then began to jot down the insight that came to her. It was close to seven o'clock in the evening when she felt she was done. The valuable exercise had slowed her eagerness to a rational and thoughtful pace.

She closed the journal and set it on the coffee table along with the other two.

Free to begin work on the Fischer project, Ellie decided that the assignment could be separated into three parts. The first phase would be a better interim shelter for Hugh than the tent, something he could move into straightaway. The second phase would be a small but well-built house to serve as his permanent residence. The third phase would be a plan for the entire farmyard, laying out all the structures and features to maximize their effectiveness.

---

[2] Matthew 6:33, KJV.

She turned her attention to phase one: a shelter for Hugh's immediate use. Ellie already had a brilliant idea that wouldn't—or at least, shouldn't—cost a dime beyond nails and screws. In fact, her guiding rule would be to only use salvage from around the property.

She consulted some of the measurements she'd taken earlier and began to work out the necessary dimensions. Even the draft sketches looked pretty good.

Confident that she had a winner, Ellie carefully drew up final copies. She also sketched a 3D version of what she nicknamed "The Ritz." It would merely be a summer cabin, for all intents and purposes, but giving it a fancy name added an element of humour. There wasn't too much of that anywhere around here! Using watercolour paints, she filled in the lines. The final product was practically a work of art.

"I dare you to reject this proposal," she said aloud.

This little project hadn't taken long at all, so Ellie moved on to writing out a few notes on how it should be accomplished in light of her stringent rule for only using existing components recycled from around the house and yard.

She went to bed that night well satisfied with her work and marvelled at how the day had unfolded, filled with so many unexpected but wonderful surprises.

In the morning, Ellie woke to grey weather and strong winds howling around the house. Her thoughts soon turned to Hugh and how he was managing, having only his canvas tent for shelter. She hoped he would feel free to come by if the weather got too miserable, but she doubted it. Their friendship was only budding, and men tended to deal with hardship more stoically than women.

So be it. He was a big boy. She needn't mother him.

For her soul work, Ellie read through the Gospel of John. She noticed that after reading scripture she felt calm, confident, and ready to face the day.

She picked up her daily assignment journal and assigned herself a task: *Name your fears, and explain why you fear them.* She left the other two journals sitting on the coffee table, since she had no sense of a question coming from the Lord, nor had she one to put to Him.

Identifying her fears, though, was sobering. Upon reflection, she realized that quite a lot of things troubled her.

Suddenly she felt utterly alone and lonely. Her eyes teared up. What she wouldn't give to be able to talk things over with her mom—in the flesh! Of course that wasn't possible, and never would be. She could talk to Jesus, but occasionally that was less than satisfactory too.

"It's nice that I can talk to You anytime and anywhere," she said aloud to Jesus-sitting-on-the-couch. "But sometimes I very much wish I could talk to You, or at least my mom, with skin on..."

At about ten o'clock, Ellie dressed in fresh jeans and a sweatshirt. A little of the excitement she'd felt the evening before returned and she looked forward to showing Hugh her first proposal. She brushed her hair, pinned it up with a clip, and grabbed her purse, along with the folder, on her way out the door.

When she got to the Fischer farm, his truck wasn't there—surefire proof that he wasn't around. Ellie debated whether to wait for him, which could take all day, or carry on to Minitonas. She decided that visiting her sister-in-law, Sarah, over a cup of coffee might expunge some of her loneliness.

As soon as she turned onto Second Avenue, she spotted Hugh's truck parked in front of the community store. She parked next to his vehicle, determined to wait until he appeared.

Her wait lasted a mere five minutes. She caught his attention with a wave, which he noticed right away.

"Hey, what are you doing here?" he asked, smiling as he walked over. "I thought you'd be busy at home designing houses and land-scapes for me."

"I need to come up for air occasionally, you know," she joked. "However, I had planned to stop by your farm. I have a proposal ready to show you."

Hugh looked puzzled. "Already? You said you would need a couple of days at least."

"True. But I decided there were at least three phases to this assignment. The first one, coming up with better accommodations for you over the summer, is the most urgent. That's what I want to talk to you about. Would you like to look it over at your place, my place, or somewhere else?"

"If you have it with you, then how about the café across the street?"

"Perfect."

There weren't many customers at the café, since it was too early for the lunch crowd. Hugh led her to a booth along the wall and then called for the waitress to bring two coffees.

Ellie slid onto the bench opposite Hugh and laid the folder at the centre of the table.

"Okay, let's see what you got," Hugh said once the waitress had brought the coffees.

There was a look about him that made Ellie nervous. She interpreted it to mean that he wasn't expecting much from the presentation she was about to make.

She took a deep breath, swallowed hard, and dove in. "Yesterday we talked about the need to make money stretch as far as possible. We also talked about your need to have better living conditions, including refrigeration, better all-weather shelter, and easy cooking. So my suggestion is to separate the salvageable from the unsalvageable and use whatever you can to erect a basic structure to last until the cold season arrives. Afterward it could still be useful as storage too. Perhaps as a garden shed."

Ellie opened the folder to the first page, which showed the drawing she'd made of the one-room cabin. It was plain, since the materials she hoped to use were modest, but the design had an attractive quality that showcased the recycled windows and door.

The second page laid out the overall dimensions of the cabin and how its interior could be arranged. She'd drawn the fridge along the back wall, alongside a stool topped by Hugh's blue water drum. Then there was the Hoosier cabinet, a garbage can, and the small electric stove. Along another wall, Ellie had designated a place for Hugh's bin of useful miscellaneous items—and his sleeping cot. Finally, she'd left space for table, a couple of chairs, and the antique dresser she'd noticed.

Hugh stared at the drawing for what seemed like a long time. At last he nodded, maintaining a poker face, and Ellie turned the page again.

On the third and fourth pages were notes about where the building materials would come from. The shell could be salvaged from boards on the old granaries and the floor could be pieced together from the plywood that currently protected the farmhouse's windows. The two windows, door, and electrical wiring could be salvaged from the house as well. Of course, the fridge, stove, cabinet, dresser, table, and chairs would all be reclaimed items.

At the end of these notes, Ellie had identified the pros should her proposal be accepted. Very little cash would need to be spent, and the tasks of salvaging and clean-up would kill two birds with one stone, as the saying went. And as she'd just explained, the cabin could serve other purposes in the future.

Before ending her spiel, Ellie admitted to two possible cons. The first was that what she was merely hoping that the wood from the granaries would be salvageable to construct the shell; the boards might prove to be too old and brittle. In that case, the whole proposal was doomed. The second con was that she couldn't think of how to solve the problem of sourcing readily available water. Her only idea was to hire an expert to rig up a standpipe indoors. She confessed that she knew very little about water systems.

Having concluded her proposition, Ellie sat back, sipped her coffee, and waited for Hugh to say something.

Hugh said not a word. He sat on his side of the booth quiet as death. As she waited, he picked up the papers and studied the drawings on the first two pages more closely.

At last, he closed the folder. "The brittle wood from the granaries can be prevented from splitting by drilling pilot holes first."

Ellie nodded. "That should work."

"You did this last night in just a couple of hours?" asked Hugh.

"It took me about three hours."

"How come you're not a draftsman or architect or something like that?"

"I just like doing it for fun. Remember, my career is in nursing."

To her surprise, he broke into a smile. "I hardly know what to say. This is amazing! It's great. It's also incredibly simple. I don't know why I didn't think of it myself."

"I think the answer is that I'm coming at the project with fresh eyes. You see buildings that are tired and decrepit and want to put them out of their misery, partly because you share a history with them. I don't have that. I can see new possibilities. That's why two heads are better than one."

In the ensuing silence, she leaned forward, feeling hopeful. "So… what do you think? Are you gonna go for it?"

"If the wind dies down, I'll start this afternoon." Then he changed the subject. "You might like to know that I found the problem with the tractor and fixed it."

"Wonderful!"

"And after that, I picked up the little piles of junk littering the yard."

"Did you leave nothing for me to trip over?" she teased. "That's rather thoughtless of you. I was planning to use that obstacle course as part of my exercise routine."

"Well, the obstacle course is no more. Actually, I was thinking of my truck. And if it's a choice between you and my truck, my truck wins! I got priorities, you know."

The smile on his face, even wider than before, told her that he was only kidding.

Seven

AFTER HIS UNPLANNED meeting with Ellie, Hugh left Minitonas in much better spirits. On the drive home, he thought about her drawings, which lay beside him on the passenger seat. They were inspiring, not to mention the perfect solution to his most immediate problems. Most important of all, this plan was simple and cheap. He was anxious to get started and couldn't help but start thinking about which tools he would need to dismantle those rickety granaries.

Back at the farm, Hugh walked toward the machine shed and located the farm tools strewn across the workbench. A ton of nails, screws, and washers were mixed up in a series of little tin cans. He looked through the disorganized collection, searching for crowbars, both large and small, and some kind of container in which to throw the rusty, bent nails.

As much as Hugh wanted to get started with taking apart buildings, he saw the value of reorganizing these tools and sorting through all the hardware. They would be useful to him; they were his tools now, and he would look after them in his own way.

It took the rest of the day to accomplish that task. This was all right, because the strong, cool winds which continued to blow would have presented a problem for dismantling the obsolete buildings. Upon completion, Hugh knew exactly what he had on hand, and where to find each tool, which contributed to his overall sense of ownership.

On Saturday, the sun rose without much wind. Hugh tackled two of the granaries.

Despite the tedium, it felt good to be doing real physical work. As he went along, he set up several piles, each representing different lengths and classifications of wood. At the end of the day, he was seriously tired and glad for his cot.

The "ghost" he'd felt a couple of days earlier—if that's what it was—didn't bother him at all.

~

After having coffee with Hugh, Ellie went to visit Sarah—and that's when she realized she wasn't feeling quite right. She tried to ignore it on her way and get to work on more drawings of the Fischer farm's current layout.

As the day waxed on, she felt increasingly worse. Finally she made herself a cup of tea and went to bed.

On Saturday morning, she awoke to cramping pain in her belly. This triggered the dark feelings of depression that had been her companion for more than two months now. She forced herself to get up, drink a cup of coffee, complete with painkiller, and eat one of the bran muffins she'd made.

She tried to get into her soul work but couldn't concentrate. After that she attempted to pick away at her drawings but couldn't focus on that either.

Giving up, she climbed back into bed.

On Sunday morning, Ellie felt quite a bit better. Although she didn't feel like going out, she dressed to go to church anyway. At nine-thirty, she got into her car and took off. Passing the Fischer farm, she noticed Hugh tearing down a granary. Of the six buildings, two were already gone.

As a new idea flashed across her mind, Ellie slammed on the brakes. She backed up and turned into the driveway.

"Wow, you work fast!" said Ellie, getting out of her vehicle.

Hugh stepped away from his work. "Actually, the work isn't that hard."

"Say, have you taken pictures of all the buildings? You should do that before they're all torn down."

"Nope. Not interested." His tone was firm.

"It's for posterity... for preserving Manitoba's prairie history... for putting together a before-and-after album as you renew this place. It's for showing your grandkids what it was like in the olden days..."

"Still not interested, Ellie. There's nothing here worth preserving in pictures." Then he sighed, feeling bad for having spoken so brusquely. "Look, it's not like anything historically important happened here, and I don't have any nostalgia for these buildings. It will be a happy day for me when they're all gone."

"Is it all right if I take pictures for my own collection?"

From the look on his face, Ellie suspected he wanted to say no.

Hugh sighed, wanting to discourage her from her growing interest in his property. But she had been good to him. What should he care about her personal photographs?

"Fine," he said begrudgingly.

Ellie fished her camera out of the glove compartment and made quick work of snapping photos of the remaining granaries, barn, house, chicken coop, machine shed, and even the outhouse. Then she waved goodbye and continued on her way to the First Baptist Church, FBC, in Minitonas.

The church was one of the newer buildings in town, having replaced the original structure in the 60s. Yet this morning she nostalgically remembered the quaint building where she had first learned Bible stories in Sunday school, memorized the words to the hymns and choruses, and came to appreciate what it meant to be a follower of Jesus. The newer building reminded her of her teenage years when she hadn't been so keen on living out the faith.

I'm back, Momma and Dad, she thought as she pulled into the parking lot.

The pastor, someone different than had stood behind the pulpit ten years ago, preached a stimulating message on the parable of the Sower and the seed in Luke 8. It was one of a series of messages that covered all the parables in the Gospels. Ellie's takeaway was that she should transform from being rocky soil, in which the seed of God's Word was received but prevented from taking root, to being fertile soil for the Word of God to bear mature fruit.

Also lovely were the warm greetings she exchanged with former friends. It was a relief when no one plied her with prying, personal questions. Everyone just seemed glad she was in their midst again.

Ellie's plan for the afternoon was to lay low and do some reading.

About mid-afternoon, the weather changed. Dark clouds rolled in and then rain pelted the earth. It poured steadily.

Within the hour, that familiar red and silver pickup made its way up the driveway. From the kitchen window, Ellie watched the sodden form of Hugh Fischer emerge from his truck toting his blue water drum and large duffle bag.

She met him at the door and hurried him inside.

"Look what the cat dragged in!"

"Sorry to bother you, Ellie. I just couldn't think of where else to go in all this rain. The tent sure isn't comfortable in this weather!"

"Come in," she said. "Let's get you dry."

"Uh, is your offer to have a shower still good?"

"Yes, of course."

"And can I pay you to use your laundry facilities? Minitonas doesn't have a laundromat."

"You can do that too."

Hugh showered, then sorted his clothing and towels into colour groups. Before long, he had gotten the laundry underway.

"I've got some soup simmering," said Ellie when they returned to the kitchen. "Would you like to have supper with me?"

"Thank you. I'd like that."

Hugh peered over Ellie's drawings, which were still laid out on the kitchen table. The topmost page showed the current layout of the farmyard.

"I'm looking forward to your next round of questions regarding my projects," he said without commenting on the drawing itself.

Ellie noted the omission but allowed it to slide. "I hope I can have something for you in a few days."

She restacked the papers on the table so they'd have space to eat their soup, including the biscuits she'd made earlier.

After the meal, Ellie poured mugs of fresh coffee and, carrying a plate of cookies, invited Hugh into the living room to have dessert. She took the favoured armchair and gestured for Hugh to seat himself on the sofa.

Once they were settled, they both spoke at once. They laughed awkwardly, but then Ellie invited Hugh to continue.

"I want to apologize for speaking so rudely to you this morning," he said. "You didn't deserve it, and I'm sorry."

"I forgive you," said Ellie sincerely. "However, I really do think it's time to tell me what's behind the comments you keep dropping. Like 'All this junk should be burned with the rest of the house' and 'There's nothing here worth keeping' and 'I'm not interested in keeping a record of the history of this place.' I'd really like to understand, Hugh."

Hugh's face flushed. He was uncomfortable hearing his own comments reflected back at him. He'd said those things to throw off, not peak, her interest.

Ellie saw that he was struggling and decided to encourage him. "Look, I'm not trying to pry, scout's honour, but I have the sense that there's a deeper story going on than merely old, decrepit buildings. Help me understand where you're coming from."

Hugh rubbed his forehead without answering; then brought his hand around to his chin and rubbed it too, deliberating over what to say.

His reluctance to launch into what should have been an ordinary explanation tipped Ellie off that she had hit a nerve. She adopted a softer, kinder tone, hoping to disarm the discomfort she had inadvertently uncovered.

"I see that I've made you uncomfortable," Ellie began carefully. "It takes one to know one. I'm seeing a guy in pain 'cuz I have my sore spots too. Can I say this? I know what happens to people when they don't talk about their suffering... when they keep it bottled up inside. The pain doesn't fade away and disappear altogether. Instead it festers and makes one sick with bitterness and resentment. After a while, their words come out of their mouths like knives and their faces take on hard edges. If they don't deal with their pain, eventually it comes out sideways. I think you're at the place where it's coming out sideways. I saw a bit of the hurt in you when you gave me that tour of the house, and I saw it in you again this morning when I asked about taking pictures. It needs to come out, Hugh, or it'll wreck you."

Hugh considered what to say. So far he'd only told the Turners about his family and home life. He hadn't wanted anyone else to know about the shame he felt regarding his past. In his mind, it should be buried and forgotten, never to be unearthed again.

He continued to rub his hand across his chin, deliberating over whether to open up this can of worms with his neighbour.

Hugh heard the truth in Ellie's words. He also recalled what Tipper had said about him, and they hadn't known each other one bit.

"Yer just like yer pa..."

Bottled-up pain, Hugh now realized, probably explained why he had so often been impatient with customers in the auto repair shop in Winnipeg. He had concluded that he should just stay away from people and live alone. Now here was Ellie, who seemed to be able to see through his skin. Could he trust her with his shameful and embarrassing story? Could he trust her? She seemed a good sort. He heard kindness and compassion in her words.

"When we were kids," he began hesitatingly, "and you were living here in this big, warm house eating great home-cooked meals, my ma, my sisters, and I were living in a hellhole..."

It hadn't always been terrible. In his earliest years, he'd been cared for without great trauma. But year by year, his father had become more unreasonable and controlling. As a child he'd been given only a few spankings; they became more frequent and unpredictable when he got older. Gradually, he and his sisters were living a fearful existence, never knowing when they might unleash the wrath of Freddie Fischer.

Hugh couldn't recall a time when he'd engaged in "normal" conversations with his old man; he'd always been threatening, calling him names like *idiot*, *stupid*, *insect*, or something else just as nasty. For Hugh, a favourite was *boy* or *bastard*. Whenever his pa spoke, every third word was a cuss word.

Over the years, his pa's power over the family grew to such an extent that eventually no one dared to challenge him. To be honest, they feared the consequences could be deadly.

"I once challenged my pa over something I believed was perfectly reasonable," Hugh said in bitter remembrance. "It didn't work. I paid a hefty price for 'crossing' him, as he put it."

Ellie listened in spellbound silence, not daring to ask a single question as he told his appalling story.

"The most controlling tool he had over us was money," Hugh went on. "He commanded every penny of it..."

No one in the family had been able to figure out where he kept it. The kids certainly never got any—ever. He had grudgingly doled out a few dollars to their mother, Alice, for groceries or clothes for the kids, or some other necessity after she'd begged long and hard for it. He seemed to take pleasure in making her beg. And it was never enough for anything beyond the basics. They didn't starve, but they were forced to eat a lot of oatmeal, pancakes, and sourdough bread.

Eventually the Fischer kids had figured out that their family was different from the other kids at school. Their clothes were a little shabbier and came mostly from the local thrift shop. Other kids would show off the latest in toys or gizmos, but the Fischer kids never boasted any of those. Other families drove late-model cars and trucks; the Fischers tended to ride around in old rust buckets. Other families lived in nice houses painted bright colours while the Fischers lived in an old house that looked like it had never worn a single coat of paint. And it was more of a shack than a proper house, adding embarrassment to their other difficulties.

Somewhere along the line, it had been noticed that their pa's drinking was heavy enough that he was frequently drunk. And when he got drunk, he was extra mean. Sometimes downright cruel. He often made their mother cry.

"Believe it or not, although going to school was hard, because we were so different from our classmates, it was also wonderful," Hugh said. "For six or seven hours a day, we could get out from under his watchful eye. We became avid readers too. Library books were like toys we could freely borrow without repercussions. Reading books made it a little bit more bearable. Mind you, if Pa called for you to do a chore or something, you dropped everything and did it. You didn't dare make him mad if you could help it. Does that paint enough of a picture for you, Ellie?"

"Oh my gosh," said Ellie in a rush. "I... we... had no idea this was going on so close to our place. I'm sure if we Baumans had known how awful your dad was to his family, we'd have staged an intervention and got you out of there. Nobody should have to live like that!"

"Actually, I think your parents might have suspected something. Every once in a while, your dad would drive into the yard and have a farmer-to-farmer chat with Pa. On those occasions, the transformation in my pa was incredible. His acting could be good enough to win him an Oscar! Mind you, I think we all learned to be actors when other people happened to come around."

Hugh sighed, trying in vain to stop the memories from coming back.

"Your mom would come by now and again to get neighbourly with my ma, and she'd always bring a fresh loaf of bread. She'd claim that she had baked a batch and one was to be given away as a *tithe*, whatever that meant. Pa didn't like it when your mom gave us food. He complained that he didn't want other people's charity. But then he'd practically eat the whole loaf himself."

"That would be just like my mom, for sure," Ellie remarked. "Hugh, I'm so sorry you had to grow up this way. I totally get why you'd want to get rid of everything connected with your past."

He hung his head, not knowing quite what to say to that.

Suddenly, she jumped up and fetched a couple of sheets of paper and pencils from the kitchen table. She settled in next to Hugh on the sofa.

"We did this little exercise at a party I once attended while I lived in Winnipeg," she said. "It's one of those a-picture-is-worth-a-thousand-words kind of things. Using simple shapes, you draw your family dynamics. I'll go first to show you what I mean."

Ellie flattened one of the sheets of paper on the coffee table, leaned forward, and drew a circle in the middle of it.

"This is my mom in the centre." She continued to add other, smaller circles around it. "And around her are my dad, Rob, Gus, Harold, and me. Mom was the glue that kept us all together. Our world revolved around her."

She sat back and passed him the pencil.

"Your turn. How would you draw your family dynamics?"

Hugh thought for a moment before taking the pencil from her. "This is my ma in the centre too," he started. "Then this is me and my sisters huddled close behind her."

Next, he drew bars in a frame. It looked like the stick family was in a cage. He then added a stick man outside the cage with a whip in his hand.

"That's what our family life was like," he said quietly. He dropped the pencil. "It's getting late. Thanks for supper and a good evening, but I think I'll go back to my tent now."

"No way," said Ellie. "It's still wet out there. Tonight you can sleep in my brothers' old bedroom. I don't want you to come down with a cold."

"For real? I think that's an offer I can't refuse." Hugh smiled. "Thanks loads."

He followed her down the hallway where she showed him her brothers' former bedroom. After she left, he stood by the door and listened as she returned to the kitchen and began cleaning up. When the house grew silent, he sat on the edge of the bed, his mind racing and his heart heavy. He didn't know if he would be able to sleep that night.

Eight

ON MONDAY MORNING, Ellie didn't open her eyes until the alarm clock showed 8:10. Then, remembering she had a guest, she threw off the covers and speedily pulled on some jeans and a T-shirt. Glancing down the hallway, she saw the door was open to the other bedroom; the bed was made up perfectly as if no one had slept in it.

When she reached the kitchen, she realized that Hugh's truck was gone too. She figured he must have left with his refilled water drum and freshly laundered clothing. She checked the laundry room and found it void of Hugh's things.

There was, however, a piece of paper lying on the kitchen table:

> Thanks for everything! This is to cover the laundromat services.

A five-dollar note lay nearby. Obviously he had been in a hurry to get back to work. She hoped he wasn't feeling regret over sharing his deeply personal history with her.

With no guest to serve, Ellie resumed her new routine. Soul work came first, and this time she read through Galatians. One verse in particular jumped out at her: *"Help carry one another's burdens, and in this way you will obey the law of Christ."*[3]

---

[3] Galatians 6:2, GNT.

She immediately thought of Hugh and wondered how much she ought to involve herself in his life. Was it possible for them to be friends without eventually wandering into the tricky labyrinth of sexual attraction and feelings of the heart? She was doubtful.

Later, she promised herself, she would discuss this with the Lord.

In her daily assignment notebook, she wrote out her task for the next three days: *What are your skills? Talents? Giftings?* Identifying her skills would be fairly easy.

In her bigger journal, she felt the Lord Jesus asking her to discuss a few sobering questions: *What do you trust Me for? What don't you trust Me for? Why?* She gave herself time to explore them.

Around eleven, she put her journals and Bible aside and went outside for some fresh air. The air smelled clean after the previous day's rain. The spring sun felt wonderfully warm on her skin.

She went poking around the garage, looking for enough space to stow the antiques she intended to bring home from Hugh's place. She found space in the Quonset, but it would require Rob's approval.

Back in the house, she scarfed down a peanut butter sandwich and went back to work on the plans for the Fischer farm. She was able to focus and narrowed down her suggestions to two arrangements that should work for Hugh. She put the finishing touches on the final drawings and then applied watercolours. They looked wonderful, if she did say so herself.

Leaving the papers to dry, Ellie decided it was time again for exercise. The clock showed three-thirty in the afternoon, and she determined to head over to the neighbouring farm. She wanted to see how far Hugh had come with his teardown project. There were also a few things she wanted to say to him, and hopefully he would allow her to lend a helping hand.

Before leaving, she borrowed a nail-puller from the farm shop and a pair of work gloves. She placed these in the basket of her bike and rode off.

As Ellie pulled up to Hugh's worksite, she found him beginning to take apart the last of the little granaries. He stopped and turned to grin at her.

"I figured you would be showing up today," he remarked.

"I see that I'm just about too late. You sure work fast. I brought along our nail-puller so I could give you a hand."

"The longer I've worked at this, the better I'm getting at removing the boards with efficiency. I'm darn near an expert now. Maybe I should go into the demolition business!"

"If you pull off the boards and nails, I'll stack them in the right piles," said Ellie.

They worked together in sync without saying anything more for several minutes. Then Ellie couldn't help herself.

"Can you walk and chew gum?" she piped up.

Hugh looked at her quizzically. "You mean at the same time? Sure! Who can't?"

"It's just another way of asking if you can hold a conversation while you work, silly."

"What's on your mind?"

"For starters, I'm ready show you the farmyard proposals I drew up."

"And you say I work fast."

"A rolling stone gathers no moss," she quipped. "Even after I've finished drawing up plans for the yard site, I'd like to keep working with you as your assistant. You're going to need someone to hold up boards, fetch tools… or whatever. I'd like to be that guy. It'll keep me busy. I'd also like to be involved in sorting out the junk around your place. After all, you don't seem to know the difference between true junk and what's valuable. I do."

Hugh stopped pulling off boards and straightened up.

"What I'm trying to say is that I would like for us to be friends," she continued, talking quickly. "Kind of along the lines of brother and sister. But I'm not open to letting things progress beyond that. It's not about you. I think you're an attractive guy and you seem very nice. It's just that when it comes to men, I'm seriously jaded."

Hugh shifted uneasily but didn't interrupt.

She kept going. "Look, you were honest with me yesterday, so I'll be honest with you today. One of the biggest reasons I left Winnipeg was a nasty breakup. Considering all the other disappointing relationships I've had with guys over the years, you're looking at a girl who's really put off men right now. I'm sure I'll get over it at some point, but that time is not now."

Ellie ended her speech and waited for Hugh to say something.

Hugh took off his cap and raked his hand through his hair. He took a deep breath.

"You're welcome to be my assistant," he finally said. "It should help with getting things done quicker. But I'm not offering wages. You can have those antiques, as you call them, in exchange for all the help you give me."

Ellie nodded. "Agreed."

"And you're also welcome to sort through the trash, separating out the good stuff. You're right. I have no knack for that. And quite frankly, my dear, I don't give a damn."

She smiled, recognizing the quote from *Gone with the Wind*. "Thank you."

"As for pretending to be my sister, we can give it a try. The truth is, my experiences with women haven't been so good either. My attitude right now is that they can't be trusted. It's not about you, Ellie. I think you're pretty, and you seem very nice. And smart to boot. But I'm off dating girls at this point. That's three for three."

"We understand each other then."

"I believe we do."

Hugh went back to prying boards off the granary studs.

Ellie didn't move, although she wore the expression of someone who wanted to say more.

"What?" asked Hugh with a bit of impatience.

"I... I just wanted you to know how much I appreciated you sharing your story with me last evening," she began tentatively. "Your words have been on my mind, and I've given a lot of thought to the things you said."

"Zip it, Ellie. My problems are not your problems. I didn't ask you to get involved. Anyway, the past can't be changed or fixed. I only told you so you wouldn't keep riding me about these old buildings and saving all the trash inside them."

Her voice firmed up. "I understand, but please hear me out. Remember what you said when we first met? You came back to start over. Well, there's more to that than destroying old buildings and replacing them. I hope you know that wherever you go, you take yourself with you."

Hugh exhaled a long, irritated breath, yet refrained from interrupting her.

"What I mean is that the way your story unfolded represents baggage that weighs heavily like a great burden. From where I stand, it seems poised to crush you. Can you see that?" Ellie's tone was both urgent and caring.

Hugh heard the genuine concern which caused him to relax a bit. "I guess, since you put it that way… It's true that I can't seem to shake off my past experiences very well. But I *am* trying my best to get over it."

What he didn't tell her was that sometimes he thought he heard voices in the breeze, voices that sounded like his pa cussing him. He also didn't mention that he occasionally almost, but not quite, saw furtive and insubstantial figures around the old buildings and in the bush.

Maybe that meant he was delusional, God help him.

"Your plan to *start over* has to include who you are inside your own skin," she continued. "You can't just get rid of old buildings and put up new ones. The way I see it, to get to a place of genuine peace and contentment, you'll need to learn what you can about your roots. If you could find out where the evils that plagued your dad came from, you can understand the nature of them and forgive your parents." She paused. "Unforgiveness keeps one in a cruel and heartless prison."

Hugh had kept listening to her with consideration—that is, until she inferred that he ought to forgive his pa. How could she say this after he'd dared to divulge how horrible it had been to live under his roof? Had she not heard a word he'd said?

He lost it.

"You want me to forgive that dirtbag?" thundered Hugh. "Never! I want that old man to roast in hell, if there is such a place. He doesn't deserve forgiveness. If I could, I would turn the tables and treat him the way he treated me to see how he liked it!"

Ellie backed up a step, a little frightened by Hugh's outburst. It revealed a core of undiluted hatred. For a couple of seconds, his countenance had changed, twisting into something almost violent.

It took a few more seconds for Hugh to calm himself.

"I also have someone in my life that wronged me," she carried on empathetically. "I came back to purposely work at getting to a place where I could forgive him. Forgiveness doesn't get the person who's done you wrong off the hook. It does not acquit them for their wrong-doing. Forgiveness means that you release the wrongs done to you so you're no longer prisoner to them."

"Fred Fischer is dead," said Hugh mechanically.

"Not in your heart and mind, though. How much do I want to bet you can still hear your pa yelling at you? Or see him standing in the doorway of the barn? Does he show up in your dreams? I bet you make speeches to him in your head!"

The look of surprise on his face said it all. It was as though he were saying, *How can you see so clearly inside me?*

Ellie continued. "I once heard somebody say, or maybe I read it somewhere, that unforgiveness is the poison you drink while waiting for someone else to die. I want to stop drinking that poison and making myself sick. I also want you to be well, Hugh."

Hugh wasn't at all comfortable with the direction of this conversation. In fact, he felt downright angry. On the one hand, he wanted to send her away for tearing off the scabs on his youthful wounds. On the other hand, she was addressing his core issues like no one in his life ever had. If relief was possible, shouldn't he want to hear about it, in the same way that a starving man craves food?

"Every person on this planet is broken, not just you and me," Ellie said. "But the problem is that we can't fix ourselves. Neither can anyone else, including doctors, psychologists, and preachers. Thank God that there's one person who can take away our pain and broken-ness and heal us from within. His name is Jesus Christ. Here's the deal, though: you have to come to Him and admit that you need help."

"What are you talking about?" Hugh demanded. "Is this about religion now? If it is, then I had a taste of it when I lived with the Turners. I've been to church. Besides not getting anything out of it, it was as boring as watching paint dry. So no thanks."

Hugh turned away and started tearing off boards again.

Ellie would not be dismissed so easily. "I believe in God the Father, Jesus His Son, and the Holy Spirit. I also believe that every word in the Bible is true. But I don't consider myself to be religious. The way I see it, religion is about following a set of procedures established by some church in order to please God. Religion tells us that God will be angry with us if we don't perform those particular formulas. But I believe that God is part and parcel of our everyday reality... like nature and the relationships we have with other people. It's just that we're broken and He's the only one who can fix us. That's because He made us..."

She could see that he wasn't interested, but she pressed forward anyway. No turning back now.

"You know," Ellie said, gesturing toward the truck in the driveway, "if something were to go wrong with your truck, who would you take it to? The dealership where you got it, or someone else entirely? Only the manufacturer is going to expertly diagnose the problem and fix it. I believe that God created humans, and therefore He's the right doctor to heal us when we're broken and sick. The fact is that He's already fixed these problems, and the solution is available to us upon request. All we have to do is show up at His clinic."

Hugh didn't argue. He kept at his work as if he was ignoring her spiel, but in fact was still listening...

Ellie wasn't quite finished. "You have every right to reject Jesus as the healer of your heart and soul. But I'm not going to let you discard Him without knowing what it is you're discarding. Wouldn't you be a fool if you found a wallet but threw it away without first checking if there was money inside? I would suggest that you read from the Bible sometime, or let me show you what it says. You could come to church with me, if nothing else. And after a reasonable amount of time, if you still think it's all a bunch of hogwash, I won't say anything more about it."

Hugh felt his dander gradually subside. But somehow his male pride wouldn't allow him to blithely agree to Ellie's speech. The truth was that her confidence in identifying the source of his pain impressed him, as well as her conviction that turning one's pain over to Jesus would bring relief. But he didn't understand how any of that worked even though she made it sound logical.

"I'll think about it," was all he said.

About an hour later, he had finished hammering apart the last of the old and decrepit granaries. Hugh felt the joy of having accomplished this mission.

Nine

THE FOLLOWING MORNING, Ellie got up extra early to keep her appointment with the Lord Jesus. She found that she looked forward to these times. They were having a noticeable effect on how she dealt with the rest of her day. She was less uptight, more cheerful, rarely preoccupied with herself, and usually patient and interested in the lives of others. Although her "big sin," as she thought of it, still had the power to discourage and depress her, she experienced flashes of joy. She was grateful that Hugh was letting her play a part in the renewal of his family farm. The work kept her from brooding.

She showed up at Hugh's place at about nine o'clock and found that he had removed all of the boards over the first-storey farmhouse windows. To remove the ones from the second storey, he would have to back up his truck and set up a ladder from within the truck's box. Ellie helped by steadying the ladder.

To her amazement and relief, the job got done without calamity.

Afterward she showed Hugh the latest drawings she'd made of the farmyard. They laid out two very different options that took into account the permanent features of the farm that couldn't be altered. As before, he was highly impressed with the clarity of her proposals and how beautifully she had depicted them.

Working together, they reorganized the piles of salvageable lumber near the site where Hugh planned to build his summer cabin, a.k.a. "The Ritz."

By the time they finished up for the evening, Hugh told Ellie that he planned to be in Swan River the following day to take care of several items of business. Ellie planned to use that time to work on the third phase of her Fischer Farms proposal.

~

The next morning, Hugh took care to wash himself from head to toe, shave his face, don clean clothes, and style his hair carefully. If the day turned out as he hoped it might, he wanted to look his best.

By eight-thirty, he was on the road singing along with Kenny Rogers on the radio. Hugh could hold a tune pretty well.

His first item of business was to make arrangements for electric power to be restored to the farm. The second was to have his well water tested. The third was to buy nails, screws, and any other pertinent hardware he'd need to construct the summer cabin.

But he had another mission in mind, something that had preoccupied him ever since the somewhat heated discussion with Ellie two days earlier. She had pointed out the value of knowing one's family history and Hugh had to admit that he knew precious little about his roots. Logically, of course, he knew he must have had grandparents, but he had no recollection of ever meeting them.

In fact, he only had a single hazy memory of meeting any relative outside his immediate family, and that was his mother's older sister. Hugh figured he must have been about five years old when they'd had a Christmas dinner at an aunty and uncle's house in Swan River. He especially remembered being gifted with a toy pickup truck. It had been red and instantly became the most precious possession of his young life.

He had wracked his memories trying to come up with their names. For the life of him, he couldn't remember what his uncle had been called, but he thought his aunty might have gone by the name Gertie.

After making his purchases, Hugh slowly drove up and down the streets of the oldest neighbourhoods in town. He felt, merely by impression, that the house had been located north of downtown. His vague recollections couldn't supply the house colour or its shape or style. He remembered only white—the colour of winter and Christmas.

Suddenly Hugh slammed on the brakes. There was a woman kneeling in front of her flowerbed, wearing a wide-brimmed straw hat. Wearing garden gloves, she wielded a small hand spade.

Hugh had no idea who this woman might be, but he hoped she might be able to furnish some possibilities if he provided her with his scant clues.

"Hello, ma'am," he said after parking the truck on the side of the street.

The woman looked his way and waited for him to introduce himself.

"I'm looking for someone… an aunt I haven't seen since I was five years old. I think her name was Gertie, but I cannot recall a last name. I'm not at all sure I have the right neighbourhood. But it seems to me we turned north off the main road to go to her house for a Christmas dinner many years ago. I know that's not much to go on, but is there any chance you know someone named Gertie, or maybe Gertrude, from Swan River? I figure she'd be in her late fifties, approximately."

The woman stood up and seemed to be concentrating. "The only Gertrude I know is Trudy Johnson, a fellow member of the Horticultural Society here in town," she said. "I guess she's old enough to be your aunt."

"I assume she's married, because I had an uncle at the time. Although I don't remember his name at all. I think they had a son, too, but he was older than me. Does this fit with your friend Trudy?"

"It may, but why don't we go over and find out? She lives not far from here on Sixth Avenue."

Still carrying her hand spade, the woman led Hugh on a walk less than three blocks away to a small, tidy bungalow painted light yellow with green trim. The lawn was perfectly manicured. A few flowering shrubs graced the foundation on each side of the front door.

The woman gingerly climbed the three steps and called through the screen door, "Yoohoo! Trudy, are you there? It's Leslie."

There was a pause. Then they heard the sound of slippered feet padding toward the front door from inside.

The salon-blond-haired woman who came to the door was of medium build and clad in blue gingham, her seersucker pedal pushers matching her sleeveless shirt. She smiled in recognition of her friend and didn't seem to notice Hugh standing a short distance away.

"What brings you here all dressed in garden gear? Oh gosh, now I'm a poet." She laughed.

"This young man." Leslie nodded in Hugh's direction. "He claims to be looking for an aunt he hasn't seen since he was five years old. He thought her name was Gertrude, and since you're the only Gertrude I know, I thought we would start with you."

"That's his only clue? I very much doubt..." Trudy had stepped out of the house and onto the landing so she could have a look at Leslie's "young man."

Just then, Hugh stepped forward. As soon as he saw her face, he knew he'd hit paydirt. The resemblance to his mother was unmistakable.

"Aunt Gertie," he said huskily. "It's me..."

"Hugh," finished Gertie, becoming misty-eyed.

"Well, I see you've found the proverbial needle in the haystack, improbable as it was," said Leslie, somewhat astonished. "I'll leave you two to getting to know each other again while I tend to my gardens. Glad I could be of help."

And off she trundled back to her own place.

"Come inside, son-of-Alice." Gertie moved sideways so Hugh could enter. Leading him into the kitchen she said, "There's so much to talk about that I don't know where to begin."

She indicated a chair for him to sit on. Then she took a pair of mugs from the cupboard, intending to fix them both some coffee. The radio played in the background, temporarily filling the void that the shocking, unexpected reunion had produced.

Hugh couldn't take his eyes off his aunt. While he had hoped against hope that he would find her, he honestly hadn't expected to be successful. The chances of her living in the same house after twenty-five years had seemed like a long shot at best.

He needed a minute to collect himself. By all appearances, Gertie did too.

"You've been gone so long," she said. "Nobody seemed to know where you'd got to. I thought you must have fallen off the face of the earth. I had reason to want to get in touch with you some time ago and I had no idea where to begin. Your sisters seem to have disappeared as well. The last time I saw them was when we buried your folks three years ago. You weren't with them. Maybe you were lost to them too."

It was more question than statement.

Hugh shifted his weight uneasily. "Quite frankly, it's because they're gone that I considered coming home. I've only kept in touch with Margo." Well, that wasn't quite true. "Actually, it's the other way around. She's kept in touch with me."

"What's brought you back now, Hugh?"

"I'm thinking of beginning a new chapter at the farm."

Gertie's mouth dropped open in great surprise. "Are you serious, Hugh? There can't be anything there that's liveable. Why, it was a ruin even while Alice and Fred lived there."

"You're right. I got here a week and a half ago and I've already started on the demolition. I have a few ideas on how to go about rebuilding it... but that's not why I came looking for you. As far as I know, besides my sisters, you are the only living relative I have. I know almost nothing about my family history. I'm hoping you can fill me in."

For a moment, no one spoke. Gertie set a plate of store-bought cookies on the table, then poured the freshly percolated coffee into the mugs and set one in front of Hugh.

Sitting across from him, she took a sip. "Fair enough. You deserve to know the truth, however painful and ugly it might be. What is it you want to know?"

"Everything. Start at the beginning. I don't even know how my parents met. I remember asking Ma about it once. She looked at me strangely and said, 'It doesn't matter. I made a foolish mistake and now I have to live with it.' Then she walked off, as if her lips were sealed."

Gertie looked away and sighed. "In a way, her story begins with me..."

It turned out that Gertrude and Alice were the daughters of Gerald and Mavis Hunt. There would have been a brother between them, but he'd died unexplainably not many weeks after he was born. It was recorded simply as "crib death." The family made their home in Brandon, where their father had worked as an accountant. They had been a very average family, neither wealthy nor poor, always having enough.

The girls had developed very different personalities. Gertie described herself as the sensible and responsible one, while Alice, five years her junior, was always hankering after adventure, wanting to participate in this, that, and the other thing if only for the fun of it. She frequently complained that their parents were fuddy-duddy dull and never did anything exciting or even interesting.

At the proper age of twenty-two, Gertie had married Edwin Johnson, who had a good job as loans manager with a bank in Swan River. The money they received as wedding gifts provided the downpayment for their house-of-dreams.

"As you can see, we're still living here after all these years," Gertie commented. "The place has seen some renovations and upgrades over time, but we never outgrew it. Edwin and I only ever had one child... David, if you remember." She took another sip of coffee. "But back to family matters..."

Hugh smiled patiently.

In the third year after Gertie and Ed moved to Swan River, Alice came up for a visit and to practice being an aunty to Gertie's little boy. She also planned to attend a wedding social and dance for one of her friends. Young Freddie Fischer had been in attendance, along with a few other unattached guys. Someone had introduced Alice to Freddie, and thereafter they spent quite a lot of the evening together shaking up a storm on the dance floor.

Alice stayed an extra week to go out with Freddie every day, often not returning until extremely late, causing Gertie and Ed considerable consternation. But Alice was smitten.

At the end of the week, she announced that she and Freddie were in love and planned to marry in the near future. No amount of cautionary talk could penetrate Alice's resolve. She believed she was well enough acquainted with Freddie to be sure he was a good catch. He was handsome, exciting, lots of fun, and made her feel good.

Alice's parents were also dismayed. They tasked Ed and Gertie with looking into the nature and character of the Fischers, and Freddie in particular. It was Ed who uncovered the fact that he lived in the district of Minitonas, having recently inherited his father's farm. Beyond that, he had a reputation for being fast with the ladies, hanging out a lot at the hotel bar, and being quick to brawl. Not the kind of suiter the Hunts wanted for their daughter.

When confronted with these facts, Alice would not be dissuaded. She was different from all of Freddie's former girlfriends, she insisted; she was the right kind of girl for Freddie and if he was deficient in character, she would be the correcting influence once they were married.

Gertie sighed sadly, then paused a moment before continuing.

"They say love is blind, and for good reason," she said. "People in love seem to be incapable of seeing beyond their feelings to the obvious facts that everyone else can. I have no idea what Fred's thoughts were, but Alice seemed to be under a kind of spell. Others could see that this was trouble striking a match with naivety, a recipe for disaster and heartbreak… but she couldn't or wouldn't see it."

The wedding between Alice and Fred had taken place in September, around eight weeks after the couple's introduction. Freddie never did come to Brandon to meet Alice's parents beforehand. It was with considerable trepidation that Gerald Hunt walked his lovely daughter Alice down the nave of the United Church in Brandon and placed her hand on the palm of the dubious Freddie Fischer.

Not everything went south immediately, recalled Gertie, and yet it didn't take long for Freddie to show his true colours. What Alice had originally seen as exciting was gradually revealed as rough and controlling. Any attempt at reasonable discussion was met with intimidation. It was his way or his way.

In those first few months Alice went from having a happy disposition to one marked with stress and anxiety. When Gertie had asked about it, her younger sister brushed it off by saying that their marriage adjustments were taking longer than expected.

"At one point, Alice wanted to come into Swan River to attend another dance, but Freddie wasn't interested," recollected Gertie. "She came anyway and attended with me and Ed. But she stayed late and drank a lot and couldn't drive home. So she slept overnight at our place. When she did go home the next day, she was met with hostility and a barrage of every evil name Freddie could think of, from sleaze to whore. Alice swore up and down that she hadn't been unfaithful, but he wouldn't believe a word of it. She never went anywhere alone after that."

Gertie let out a long sigh and pushed her coffee mug aside.

"A couple of months later, she announced that she was pregnant. Freddie said it wasn't his child and no amount of insistence could convince him otherwise."

"Is that why he never called me by my given name?" asked Hugh. "Only *bastard*."

"Are you serious?" she exclaimed. "He never once addressed you by your name?"

"It was *bastard* or *boy*. Nothing else."

"Oh, Hugh, I'm so sorry it was like that for you. I'm surprised he never saw his likeness in you, because you do rather obviously resemble him."

Gertie got up and refilled their coffee mugs. Afterward they sat in silence for a couple of minutes.

"There isn't much more to tell," she said. "Except this one thing, which is very hard for me. It shows how hard-hearted I was at the time."

She went on to describe the Christmas dinner she and Ed had hosted when Hugh was about five years old. Margo had been around three, and his younger sister Diane just a baby. The sisters' parents had come up from Brandon to be with their children... and especially to see their grandchildren.

While the men sipped rum-spiked eggnog in the living room and Mavis kept busy peeling potatoes in the kitchen, Alice had manoeuvred Gertie into the basement to frantically ask for help in getting her and her children away from Freddie. She wanted to leave him — permanently. But Gertie would have none of it. She reminded Alice of all the warnings she'd been given; she'd made her bed and now she had to sleep in it.

Somehow they'd all gotten through the rest of that Christmas dinner, behaving as if everything in the world was simply marvellous.

In the spring, Gertie and Ed had driven out to the farm to see Alice and the family, Gertie having felt anxious to restore the frosty relationship. But before they could get out of their car, Freddie had gone out to tell them they weren't welcome. He wouldn't let any outsiders on the farm anymore — and if they tried to come any closer, he'd get his shotgun. The smell of alcohol had been rather strong on his breath, but it was enough to shock Gertie and Ed into leaving.

As they drove away, Gertie remembered looking back and seeing Alice standing in the doorway of the farmhouse, watching the car go with a stressed, smileless look on her face, arms akimbo. Gertie felt terrible for not taking Alice's trouble seriously enough. It seems things hadn't just gone from bad to worse, but from worse to dangerous.

Upon returning home, Gertie and Ed talked about what they should do. In the end, they decided to just stay away. They thought the best way to help Alice was not to antagonize Fred.

There were no further extended family get-togethers after that.

"I still don't know if that was the right decision," said Gertie, tears streaming down her cheeks. "I've relived that conversation at Christmas dinner a thousand times. If I could do it all over again, I would have worked out a plan to get Alice and you kids out of there. She could have gone home to Brandon and devised a fresh start. She made a big mistake, sure, but we all make mistakes. That doesn't necessarily mean we have to be saddled with the consequences forever. We should be able to make amends. Don't you think so, Hugh?"

Hugh nodded. The story had the effect of making him feel depressed all over again. The heavy weight he'd carried for most of his young life once again settled over him.

A part of him wanted to get up and leave, to go outside for some fresh air, but there was more he needed to know.

"What do you know about the Fischer side of the family?" he asked, changing the subject.

"Not very much. Apparently, Freddie's father was a heavy drinker as well and died young of liver disease. We heard he had a sister who eloped with some guy to Ontario. After the senior Fischer died, the mother went east to visit her daughter and didn't, or wouldn't, come back. That's how Fred came into his inheritance of the farm. That's all I know, though I have no way of verifying it."

Hugh furrowed his brows. "So I have relatives somewhere in Ontario?"

"Possibly, if the tale is true. There may yet be seniors around here who knew them back in the day. Would you like me to make inquiries?"

"I'm not sure. Maybe. Let me think about it."

He'd answered honestly. He had mixed feelings at best when it came to anything associated with his pa.

"You know, it's almost lunchtime and your Uncle Ed will be coming home expecting lunch to be ready," Gertie said, suddenly sounding cheerful again. "Why don't you relax in the living room while I fix something to eat?"

The noon meal was comprised of ham, cheese, and lettuce sandwiches with pickles on the side. Uncle Ed was, of course, greatly surprised to meet Hugh again after so many years, but he expressed joy at seeing him anew. He offered his full support for what Hugh hoped to do regarding the farm. And since he was a banker, he offered financial counsel in the endeavour.

After lunch, once Ed had returned to work, Gertie talked about their son, and Hugh's cousin, David. After high school, he had enrolled in law school and graduated at the top of his class. He now practiced law in one of the large firms in Toronto. They were very proud of him, of course, although sadly they almost never saw him anymore. Apparently there had been nothing for him in Swan River.

It was obvious to Hugh that his aunt ached with loneliness and disappointment over how this had turned out. But she didn't dwell on it.   •

"Hugh, can you share anything of your life after you ran away?"

This gave Hugh pause. There was only so much he was willing to disclose, and Gertie was still something of a stranger. Still, since she had been forthright with him, he felt she was entitled to some information.

"In October, about two weeks before my sixteenth birthday, I had a last-straw experience with my pa." Hugh flashed a stern look meant to dissuade Gertie from enquiring further; she received it and said nothing. "I made up my mind that on my birthday I would run away to the city and lose myself there so Pa would never find me. Every day for the next two weeks, I took a few extra clothes with me to school to hide in my locker.

"On the morning of my birthday, when I left on the school bus, I was careful to act like it was just another day. I never said goodbye to anyone, not even my sisters. All I did was write a note to Margo, briefly explaining my plan. I sealed it the envelope and gave it to one of the girls in my class to pass on to her. Then I placed all my clothes in my backpack, left all my schoolwork behind, and lit out."

Gertie relaxed back in her armchair, her eyes fastened on her nephew.

Hugh continued his story with a faraway look in his eyes, telling of how he had walked to the highway and held out his thumb to the vehicles passing by. Eventually the driver of a large delivery truck had stopped and asked where he was headed.

"Winnipeg," Hugh had told him.

"Hop in."

On their way to the city, the driver had introduced himself as Brian Turner—and Hugh introduced himself as Tom... Tom Sawyer. As soon as he'd said it, he realized it was an obvious lie, but he hadn't wanted to risk giving his real name in case the guy planned to turn him over to the police or something.

Even though Brian must have known it was a false name, he let it pass and began to converse nonchalantly. Soon he succeeded in getting Hugh to relax and earn enough of his trust to understand why the young man was running away from home.

Upon reaching Winnipeg, Brian asked where "Tom" wanted to be dropped off.

"Anywhere," Hugh had said. "Maybe the youth hostel?"

Brian had sighed. "I wish you'd come home with me. We can figure out the best course of action from there."

After introducing the boy to his wife Marcie and son Kevin, the Turners decided to hold a family meeting. They promised not to turn Hugh over to the police or abandon him to the streets. But if he would come clean about his name and circumstances, they committed themselves to helping him make a new beginning.

That had been music to Hugh's ears.

Mrs. Turner became tearful when Hugh told his story, especially upon learning that it was his sixteenth birthday.

In exchange for a roof over his head, Hugh agreed to abide by the family's rules and complete his high school education. That night, for the first time in his life, he slept in a real bed—one that was long enough to support his feet and wide enough in which to turn over. He understood instinctively that, by some stroke of luck, he'd been given a gift of kindness.

As they all grew to know each other, the Turners encouraged Hugh to participate in school sports and taught him the basics about preparing simple meals, doing laundry, cleaning up after himself and maintaining a vehicle. Not long after, he got a weekend job pumping gas. Except for a little pocket money, he turned over most of his wages to Mrs. Turner to help cover the cost of his keep. She in turn saw that Hugh was properly clothed in and out of season.

"If it wasn't for the Turners, I don't know where I'd be today," concluded Hugh. "Maybe skid row."

Gertie looked incredulous. "You sure did get a lucky break, nephew. And I'm glad you did. Your mother must have been frantic, though."

"Well, that's another thing. Mrs. Turner made me write to Margo, care of the high school, and tell her that I had arrived in Winnipeg safely. I gave her the Turners' address and phone number, so she could stay in touch. Soon after, she wrote to assure me that she told no one where I was except Ma and Diane. Ma was sad that she hadn't gotten to say goodbye, but also relieved that I was holed up in a safe place. Apparently, Pa never asked about me and kept more to himself after I was gone. He didn't bother the girls much anymore, nor Ma either."

"Maybe Fred was scared that the Fischer that got away would bring down repercussions on him," Gertie mused.

Hugh chuckled at the pun. "Very funny, aunty. Truth is, I couldn't care less."

It was close to four in the afternoon when Hugh decided to get going, despite the invitation to stay for dinner—or even to spend the night in the guest room. Gertie backed off, seeing that Hugh had made up his mind.

"In that case, I have one more thing to tell you," she said. Hugh raised his eyebrows at this. "This morning, I told you that I had tried to get a hold of someone in your family but had no idea where to look. Every one of you kids seemed to have vanished into thin air."

Gertie paused for a moment, as if making up her mind about something. Then, with a determined look about her, she pressed on.

"I have an important announcement to make, but it's best I make it to all three of you at the same time." She got up, went to the kitchen, and returned with a calendar in her hand. "Ed and I will host a dinner with you and your sisters in about a month, if you can get hold of them and invite them on my behalf. Let's do it Saturday, July 19. If that doesn't work for anyone, then make it for the week after... or the week after that. We'll work around any date that works for all three of you. And trust me, you'll be glad you did. I promise it'll be worth your while."

"I can get in touch with Margo," said Hugh. "She'll know how to reach Diane, I think. Can you give me more of a hint than that?"

"No." Her voice was firm. "Just let me know about the date as soon as possible so I can make arrangements on my end."

Hugh raised his brows a second time, but Gertie shook her head resolutely.

He left shortly after, promising to stop by often for visits. On a piece of paper, she wrote down her address and phone number so they wouldn't lose touch again.

On the drive home, he wondered what could be so important to her that it would necessitate a family reunion. It seemed impossible to guess.

Ten

HUGH TOOK HIS time returning to the farm. The unexpected discovery of his aunt and all the disclosures they'd shared had tired him out. In fact, he felt exhausted. Although he would have liked to have enjoyed his aunt's homemade dinner and slept in a real bed again, instead of the sleeping bag on a cot, he had reached the end of his rope and hadn't been able to take any more socializing.

Instead of heading straight home, he turned off the highway and drove along the backroads. He needed time to process everything he'd learned, so he went slowly, observed how the crops were coming along, and noted the various homesteads in the area.

By the time he finally rolled into his own yard, it was after six.

Following an uninteresting supper consisting of a can of spaghetti and storebought cookies, Hugh felt restless. He didn't want to linger in any further reflection concerning his past. He wanted to bury it. Again.

Having to look at the dilapidated house was making him grumpier by the day, so he decided that it had to go, asap. That resolve led to the next decision: the next time Ellie showed up, they would take out all the furnishings, and anything else she deemed salvageable, and store it in the barn.

He just needed to clean out the barn.

Hugh got on it with gusto. After opening the big doors on both ends, he jumped into the old farm truck and turned the key. The engine whined and sputtered, trying to turn over, but couldn't seem to get it done.

Hugh got out, raised the hood, and tinkered with a few wires and sparkplugs. This time it fired up after only a couple of coughs.

He let it run for a few minutes, then drove it slowly out of the barn and parked it near the machine shed. The barn now seemed quite spacious. With the light of day still strong, Hugh went from stall to stall, cleaning out the messes and sorting through the odds and ends that had been tossed there. Ellie would be proud to see that he hadn't automatically thrown everything out. He set aside spades, shovels, axes, rope, chains, bale hooks, and anything else that looked functional. He placed a few glass jugs and bottles, as well as some crockery, to the side for Ellie to look through.

The project took until dark to accomplish, but the work helped Hugh get over his edginess. It also made him hungry again.

Since he wasn't sleepy enough to turn in, Hugh lit on fire the pile of trash he had taken out of the barn and used its heat to roast a couple of wieners. Afterward he fell asleep easily—but not like the proverbial baby; the night was fraught with dreams of his mother.

Ellie woke to the boisterous sounds of birds as early as 4:00 a.m. The birdsong coming through the open window of her bedroom sounded happy, the cheerful melodies carrying so loudly that they reminded her of praise. And praise was a great way to start the day.

Although awake, Ellie wasn't ready to stand up, so she spent the next hour in bed thinking of Hugh and how she might be a good and wise sister to him, all the while remaining ready and able to share about Jesus.

When she was ready to resume her soul work, she rose, dressed in grubby clothing, and ate a hearty breakfast. In her assignment journal she wrote the title of the next page: *10 Top Priorities.*

The scripture she reviewed came from 1 Thessalonians. She found the book especially interesting in that she hadn't given any thought to the idea of Jesus's literal return. She appreciated the reminder that faith in Jesus had a goal beyond one's trouble-stricken life on earth. Living in a sin-free environment with Him was definitely something to look forward to.

In her other journal, Ellie added some thoughts to her previous discussions with the Lord.

A little after eight o'clock, she was ready to go back to the Fischer farm and hopefully assist Hugh with getting The Ritz erected. If he wasn't around, she could start moving things out of the derelict house. She put a few boxes and totes in the car, just in case she needed them.

When she drove into the yard, she found Hugh standing in front of the antiquated farm truck, the hood propped up as he examined the motor underneath. He smiled as he saw her emerge from her vehicle.

"Good morning," she said. "You look extra happy. What's new?"

"Come with me. I've got something to show you. Something that should make you proud."

He led her to the barn, slid the big doors open, and stepped inside with Ellie right behind him. At first she didn't know what to look for, and then she realized the stalls were empty and swept clean, except for one which held a tidy arrangement of crocks, jugs, and variously shaped bottles. Another stall held the original cast-iron cookstove Hugh had grown up with.

Delighted, she crouched down to examine the items. "My my, Hugh-go... I do believe you're catching on! Well done."

"What did you just call me? My name is Hugh. Only Hugh. Not Hugo."

"Ah. Well, here's what," said Ellie, standing up again. "One-syllable names seem unfinished to me, like they need a little something extra to complete them. Take the name Ann, for example. You seldom meet someone who just gets called Ann. It's often stretched out to Annie, or

Annabelle, or Anita... or something. Your name seems too short. My tongue wants to stretch it out a little... how about Hugh-ston?"

She winked at him.

"You're full of it. That argument goes both ways. People named Ronald get called Ron. Theodore becomes Ted. Maximillian boils down to Max."

"You know a Maximillian? That's impressive."

Hugh shook his head. "If you're going to make fun of my name, you're gonna get it right back, Ell-louise."

She let out a laugh. "You're on! Let the games begin."

"Later. I have some things to tell you," said Hugh. "I'm on the waiting list to get a new meter back on the hydro pole, but it might take a couple of days. And I don't want to start on the cabin until I can use my power tools. In the meantime, we can empty the house. That's why I cleared out the barn, to make room for all that stuff. The sooner I can knock that house down and burn it, the happier I'll be."

Ellie sighed. Sure, the house was fully decrepit and had served its purpose. It was just that she knew its demise would not contribute one whit to resolving Hugh's bitterness.

But he would have to learn that for himself.

"Alrighty, let's get at it." Ellie went back to the car to retrieve her work gloves and one of the boxes she'd brought along.

Hugh backed up his half-ton so they could begin loading the larger items. The small refrigerator and stove came out first, followed by the Hoosier cabinet. The houseware items it had contained were put in one of Ellie's cardboard boxes. They loaded as many items as they could fit from the back room, then drove to the barn and unloaded it all. There, Ellie sorted the items to go into different stalls—those to keep, those to be sold or given away, and those to be repaired.

The wooden table and set of partially broken chairs were set aside as well as the old sofa and chair. She wanted to take these home at once and begin the work of repairing and refinishing them.

After the house was emptied, Hugh helped take Ellie's projects to her place, depositing the table and chairs in the workshop and storing the sofa in the Quonset. Ellie grabbed some large garbage bags and stuffed the clothing and linens into them.

They stopped for a wiener roast lunch. During this break, Hugh told Ellie about his visit with his aunt.

"No way!" she said, wide-eyed. "Finding her must have been nothing short of a miracle."

"Yeah. I was thinking I had the favour of the gods, or else a golden horseshoe stuck up my arse."

"That would be the one true God of the universe, not *gods*," said Ellie. "And I do believe He's on your case because He loves you and wants you to want to be a member of His family."

His face darkened. "Oh really? It would have been nice if He'd shown up when we were kids living in this hellhole."

"Yes, really. Just so you know, there *is* another god, small g, who's after your body and soul as well. That would be the god of evil and he goes by several names. Satan. The beast. Lucifer. The devil. It would appear he had a firm grip on your father, and he was going after you too. But God was watching over you the whole time. Think about your aunt, who blessed you as a little boy with a special toy that represented hope. Or think of your mom, who cared for you as best she could in difficult circumstances. Think about how you got your education, or about how you got out of Dodge when your life was in jeopardy. Think about the Turners, good people who took you in when you needed help the most. You didn't have to spend even one night on the cold streets of Winnipeg. How's that for starters?"

Hugh said nothing. There was Ellie, piecing together the puzzle of his life in a whole different way than he ever had. Again.

"From where I stand, it's easy to follow the hand of God in your life," Ellie said. "But apparently you, Hugh-misphere, are blind in one eye and can't see out the other one. But I digress. What did your newly found aunt have to say?"

Calling him Hugh-misphere broke the tension. Hugh smiled and resumed telling her the story of finding his aunt. He even related the tale of how his parents had met and gotten hitched.

When he told how his mother had been seeking excitement and adventure, Ellie began to squirm uncomfortably.

Hugh noticed. "What's the matter now?"

"I'm thinking that maybe your mother and I have similar personalities. It was my craving for fun and adventure, without being smart about it, that caused me to go off the rails myself. I paid for it—not in the same way your poor mom did, though."

Ellie got very quiet then, and for a few moments nothing more was said between them. Both appeared to sink deeper into their own thoughts.

"I suppose it satisfied my curiosity to hear about my family history," Hugh eventually spoke. "But I left Aunt Gertie's place depressed all over again, a get-out-or-be-crushed feeling that came over me after hearing about my parent's miserable lives. I was part of it. So were my sisters. And we had no choice in the matter." There was bitterness in his tone. "You said I would feel better if I knew my family history, Ellie, but I don't. Not even a little. I wish I hadn't dug it all up."

"I didn't say it would make you feel *better*," said Ellie rather sharply. "I said that knowing the truth would give you *understanding* as to how things had come to be. Where there's a fruit, there's a root. There's a huge difference."

"Right. You did say that. I admit that it does help... a bit. About my ma, at least."

"Did your aunt know much about your dad's side of the family?" asked Ellie.

"A mere skeleton of the full story. She couldn't distinguish between fact and hearsay, but she offered to seek out people who knew Pa's family first-hand. I do have a smidgeon of curiosity... but whenever I think about it for longer than, say, a minute, I get so riled up that I want to hit something."

"Hmmmm. Why do you think that is?"

"That's easy. Pa was a selfish, unpredictable, angry, wife-beating sot! I'd still like to pay him back for what he put us through."

"Did he have the same tendency as you to fly off the handle?"

Hugh opened his mouth, then clamped it shut. Enough said. Time to change the subject. Time to go back to work.

With the house now empty, Hugh carefully pulled out the electrical wiring. It wasn't difficult, since the wires were stapled to the wall and along baseboards. He intended to reuse these wires, as well as the outlets, switches, and lightbulb receptacles.

Meanwhile, Ellie began the task of removing the interior doors and unscrewing their corresponding hinges and strikers. These, too, could be salvaged. She wanted the windows removed for the same reason, though it would have to be done another time; she was getting tired and wanted to call it a day.

Around mid-afternoon, they heard the sounds of a vehicle turning into the driveway. Hugh poked his head out beyond the porch to see who it was, hoping it was the people from the hydro company.

It wasn't. Gertie Johnson pulled in and was slowly getting out of her turquoise car.

Eleven

"IT'S MY AUNT," announced Hugh, surprised. "I wonder why she's here."

He dropped his tools and went outside to meet her, clapping his hands together to clear them of dust and debris.

"Hello, Aunt Gertie!" he called. "What brings you to my neck of the woods?"

Gertie gazed around the farmyard, turning in a complete circle, before finally acknowledging her nephew.

"Oh, Hugh, I do hope you don't mind me showing up unannounced. After our discussion yesterday, I couldn't get settled." Gertie sighed heavily. "The memories and feelings just wouldn't go away. Ed and I talked things over like we hadn't in years."

Hugh nodded. He didn't know what else to do or say.

Ellie watched from inside the house, uncertain whether she should join the scene outside. It might be too personal to get involved with.

"I just had to come," continued Gertie. "It seemed like I'd get no peace until I saw for myself how things were. Is it all right if I look around, Hugh? I won't get in your way."

Hugh exhaled a long breath and raked his fingers through his hair. "I… I don't know what you want to see… or how it will help you," he stammered. "If you want to look through the house, you came at the right time because I hope to knock it down and burn it as soon as I can."

"Yes, please. I'd like to do that."

Hugh led her into the empty house. Their footsteps sounded hollow, echoing off the walls with every step.

Ellie stood at the entrance to the living room with a door leaning against her and a screwdriver in hand. She smiled at Gertie.

Gertie, in turn, was startled to see her.

"This is Ellie, my neighbour from up the road," Hugh said by way of introduction. "She comes by to help with some of my projects." He gestured to his aunt. "Meet Gertie Johnson, my mother's sister."

Ellie extended a gloved hand. "Pleased to meet you, Mrs. Johnson."

"Hullo. I'm sorry, I didn't realize Hugh had company," said Gertie, a bit flustered. "I… I won't get in your way. And I won't stay long. I just needed to see the place where my sister lived."

"Of course," said Ellie, stepping aside.

She parked the door she had removed with the others in the kitchen and then cast a look toward Hugh, as though asking for direction on whether to stay or go. Hugh shrugged.

"You can go upstairs," Hugh said to his aunt. "But the steps aren't in very good shape."

Gertie nodded and proceeded to ascend, although she paused midway as the creaks and groans grew somewhat frightening. After a moment she bravely carried on. Soon she could be heard wandering around in the little rooms above.

It wasn't long before she ran back down, moving as quickly as she could. Ellie and Hugh could see that she was on the verge of tears.

"Were you very cold in the winter, Hugh?" Gertie had a tremor in her voice. "It seems like such a drafty house."

"We managed," said Hugh.

"You must remember, the house has been vacant for three years or more," put in Ellie. "Houses deteriorate very quickly when they aren't lived in."

Gertie nodded. "Yes, I suppose you're right. There's some comfort in that." She turned to Hugh. "I'd like to help you get things turned around here. I missed my cue the first time, but I'm determined not to miss it again. What can I do to help?"

"Ah, I really don't have anything suitable right now, aunty, unless you're a mechanic." Hugh looked around the room, not sure how to answer. "I've got a few pieces of farm equipment that need to be checked out to see if they're in running condition. Maybe down the road..."

"Come with me, Mrs. Johnson," said Ellie. "I can think of a couple of things that need doing. Your help would be most appreciated."

Hugh sent Ellie a confused look, but Gertie looked relieved and followed Ellie out of the house toward the barn. Not knowing what else to do, Hugh trailed behind.

As they walked, Ellie explained the plan to build a summer cabin and recycle as much as they could. But of course everything they'd taken out of the house would need a thorough cleaning before it could be pressed back into service.

"It would really be helpful to have the fridge and stove thoroughly cleaned before they're put to use again in Hugh's cabin. Would that interest you, Mrs. Johnson?" asked Ellie politely.

"I would love to do that for him!" assured Gertie enthusiastically. "I'm no stranger to scrub brush or scouring pads."

"Wonderful. What about sewing? Do you use a sewing machine?"

"Well... yes. I don't sew a lot, but I think I can still sew a straight line. What needs stitching?"

At this point, Hugh got bored with all the women talk. He excused himself and returned to the house to finish removing the electrical wiring.

Ellie was just as glad because she hoped her next idea would serve as a surprise gift one day.

"Come with me," said Ellie, leading Gertie into one of the stalls. "These bags are full of the clothing and linens that got left behind. They all need laundering. Beyond that, I suggest we sort them into colour groups and cut them up to make quilts. One for your nephew and each of your nieces. They could be Christmas or birthday presents. What do you think?"

Gertie nodded thoughtfully. "I have to confess, I haven't made quilts before. All them little pieces… it looks hard and complicated."

Ellie shook her head. "It's not really. But what if, after this is all washed, I sort out the colours and cut them up into kits? Then you can sew them at your leisure."

Gertie lit up like a lightbulb. "If you'll do the hard part, I'll be glad as a bowl of Mexican jumping beans to do the easy part… as long as the pattern isn't too complicated. I've seen quilts that look like you'd need a textbook to put them together."

"I promise to keep it simple and straightforward," said Ellie, chuckling. "I'm also thinking of staging a yard sale one of these weekends. Neither Hugh nor his sisters want what's left since their parents' demise. Would you be interested in putting on a yard sale with me?"

"What does Hugh have to say about it?"

"If it was up to him, he'd burn everything here along with the rest of the dilapidated buildings. He's given me the antiques to me as a 'wage' for all the manual help. I'm interested in a few pieces, but not all. There's enough remaining to justify a yard sale."

"You know, that's a good idea. It'll give me an opportunity to go through my things too. Give me a call when you've got a calendar in front of you."

Together the ladies carried the bags stuffed with clothing and linens to Gertie's car. Then they exchanged phone numbers.

Before getting in her car to return to Swan River, Gertie went back into the house to say goodbye to Hugh. She found him organizing the wires into neat coils.

"I'm heading back to Swan now," she said. "I'll be back in a few days to clean your appliances."

Gertie looked around to see if Ellie was within earshot. Satisfied that they were alone, she added conspiratorially, "I don't know where you found that girl, but she's a keeper!"

As she left, she waved goodbye to Ellie.

"It was nice to meet you, Mrs. Johnson," Ellie shouted.

Gertie laughed. "Just call me Gertie!" she called through the open window.

Twelve

ELLIE SLEPT LONGER than usual on Thursday morning because she and Hugh had agreed the evening before that she wouldn't return until he had functioning electricity. He wanted to use the time to work on the old farm truck.

After a leisurely breakfast, Ellie began her soul work in her pyjamas. There was a particular question she felt the Lord wanting to discuss: *What would be a fulfilling life for you?* She pondered it for quite a while before writing a response to this thought-provoking topic.

Around noon, she felt she'd been lazy long enough. She dressed in some shabby clothes and went into the machine shop to plan out how to repair and refinish the wooden table and chairs. She wished Rob was around so she could get some advice, but he'd been busy looking after the crops.

Of the five chairs, only one was whole—the captain's chair with armrests. However, its legs were wobbly and needed to be reglued. The bottoms of the other chairs were intact but the backs had missing spindles. If she took them apart, Ellie reasoned, she could rebuild two whole chairs but would be a spindle short for a third. Perhaps she could find a replacement...

Using a mallet, she was successful at taking apart the chairs and arranging the pieces in sets. Afterward she began with the sanding—a dirty, tedious job.

It was mid-afternoon when she heard Rob return to the yard in a tractor. Moments later, he entered the shop.

"Hey, girl! Seems like a long time since we've seen you," he said, smiling. "What are you up to?"

Then his gaze fell on the pieces of furniture arranged all over the floor.

"Where did you get those?" he asked.

"From the old Fischer house. I'm hoping you can help. I want to make the tabletop smaller and bevel the edges with a router, but I have limited experience with power tools, so..."

Rob came over to get a closer look. He ran his hand over the surface, noting the partially split seam. "Yeah. It wouldn't take much to cut this down."

He walked to the back wall where a radial arm saw was covered with a tarp. As he readied the machine, Ellie explained that she wanted the tabletop cut square, using only the best parts. Rob assessed which portion to use, bypassing the split seam, and made his pencil markings. With Ellie holding one end, it was soon sliced into a single piece measuring thirty-nine inches per side. Rob then used the router to round the edges.

Ellie beamed at the excellent work.

"I came in here thirsty, and I'm still thirsty," said Rob. "Do you have anything interesting to drink in the house?"

"Will soda do?"

Rob nodded and they walked back to the house together. While Ellie poured two glasses and looked for a snack to go with it, Rob glanced at the mess of drawings still cluttering the kitchen table.

"What's this all about?" he asked.

"I'm working on a housing proposal for Hugh Fischer. I offered to help him with some ideas."

Rob raised his eyebrows. "Why?"

"Because he lacks imagination, and I have some to spare. Plus, I need some kind of activity to keep myself amused."

"I've seen your car there sometimes and wondered what was going on."

"If you're thinking we're getting into a *relationship*, you're wrong," she replied evenly. "Neither of us is interested in the dating game, although he seems to be a nice enough guy. He's not for me."

She set the glass of soda in front of him as her brother took a chair at the table. She sat as well, placing the cookie jar in the centre.

"It would be good to stop by and befriend him yourself," she added. "Hugh says he's come back to start over, but I'm not sure he has a right understanding of what farming involves these days. He has limited experience, and everything he does know came from his father fifteen years ago. I doubt very many people around here admired Fred Fischer's farming practices."

Rob raised his eyebrows a second time. "True. Do you think he's a chip off the old block?"

"Not really. He's actually very conscientious about *not* being like his dad."

Ellie sighed deeply, then began to share a few carefully curated details from Hugh's story, sticking to generalities so as not to betray his trust in her. She talked about her goal of rescuing the antiques from his desire to burn the entire property to the ground.

When Ellie finished her story, Rob was looking past her with a faraway look in his eyes. They sipped their sodas in silence, neither saying anything for a couple of moments.

At last Rob spoke. "You are so very like our mother, Ellie. It's both beautiful and painful to watch."

"What do you mean?"

"It's painful because seeing her in you causes me to miss her terribly. On the other hand, didn't you notice over the years that it was almost always Mom who had the ideas and the vision for what to do around this place? About what to do and how things should get done?"

"It seemed to me that Dad and Mom discussed things."

"Sure, but Dad did nothing without conferring with Mom. He wasn't stupid. I'm not saying that. But she had the *imagination*, as you call it. The creative vision and the wisdom. He had the brawn and skills to make it happen."

"I see what you're saying," said Ellie. "But if I'm like Mom, who are our siblings like?"

"Gus is a lot like Dad. And Harold? I'd say he has a bit of both of them."

Ellie put down her glass, amazed at her brother's insight. "When did you get to be so observant?"

"When did you?"

"You're suggesting you're like Mom too," she said.

"What do you think?"

Ellie thought about it for a moment. "Well, given how you've taken this farm, adding to and improving it, keeping current with farm science… yeah, I'd have to agree you're much more like Mom than Dad. But then Sarah…?"

"She loves me and supports me in whatever I mean to do. I bounce my ideas off her and she checks them for flaws. Sarah is the perfect wife for me."

"Aww. I love hearing you say that. I love her too and find her easy to talk to." Ellie's eyes filled with tears. "I wonder if I will ever have what you have, Rob."

"Just be patient, sis. There's someone out there that's just right for you. But from what you've told me, Hugh's character is along the same lines as Dad. Which means he's probably falling for you right now, despite what he says. He may be getting to be a little too dependent on you."

Rob made a sweeping gesture at the papers on the table.

"He's not a believer," Ellie said. "I will never yoke myself with an unbeliever!"

"Okay. Smart girl. But his beliefs could change, and we hope they will, don't we? But if not and you have to step back from his life, do it carefully. Like weaning an infant from the bottle. A man's heart will break every bit as easily as a woman's."

"Are you saying this out of experience?"

"It's a serious mistake for women to assume that men don't have deep feelings just because they aren't inclined to show them as often."

"I'll be careful, I promise," said Ellie. "I wouldn't want to add more hurt to the likes of Hugh Fischer. His biggest need is not for a good woman in his life, but for Jesus to come in and take away the hate and bitterness that's eating him alive. I've spoken to him about that, but he doesn't hear me."

She paused for a moment.

"The thing is, I think he sees himself as a victim, as a good guy who's been hard done by. To be sure, he's been wronged, in more ways than I yet understand. But it's like he feels he has no need for a Saviour. The problem is other people, like his dad. He thinks he's justified in feeling bitter. The idea of forgiving his father, for his own peace of heart, sounds ludicrous to him. He says that his pa doesn't deserve forgiveness."

Rob shrugged. "Hmmm. I think I may take your advice and look in on him. At the very least, it's the neighbourly thing to do."

"I'm glad to hear it," said Ellie happily. "We Baumans weren't savvy enough to see what was going on with their family. I think this time we should help out."

"I'll do what I reasonably can, Ellie."

She went on to mention some of the areas where she felt Hugh could use her brother's knowhow: draining the dirt cellar of water, digging a pit to burn trash safely, checking the structure of the barn, assessing the old farm equipment—

"Whoa there," Rob interrupted. "Just let me meet the guy first!"

"Okay, but you need to know that he's highly motivated to get rid of all the old buildings as soon as he can. Not just because they're long past serviceability but because they're linked with his idea that he can't move forward until they're gone."

"I see. I suppose I can understand the concept of beginning anew as with a blank sheet of paper."

"Yeah. Well, his blank sheet of paper involves more than out-with-the-old-and-in-with-the-new buildings. For him, starting over is also about trying to make up his mind whether to take up farming, like you, or offer services in mechanics."

"At least he's narrowed down his options to just two. That's better than having too many choices or none at all."

Ellie's face clouded over.

"What's the matter now?" asked Rob, downing the last of his soda.

"I... I just wish I knew what starting over looked like for me," she said sadly. "I know I don't want to go back to Winnipeg, but I'm not sure I should stay in these parts either. It's great to be home for now, but I also feel like I may have outgrown this town... like a shirt that's one size too small."

"I don't think I need to tell you that this is exactly the sort of question you leave with the Lord and then pay attention as you wait for the answer. At the right time it will present itself and you'll know it. Just be patient. It's not like you need to know by Friday." He rose, walked over to the kitchen sink and set his glass inside.

Ellie nodded. That was the right answer, but it didn't make her feel better.

"By the way, I have something else to ask of you," Rob said before taking his leave. "Since I'm caught up with my work in the field, I'd like to take Sarah for a weekend away. Just the two of us. Will you keep company with my kids while we're gone?"

"Of course. When?"

"I haven't put it to Sarah yet. We'll get back to you."

Thirteen

IT WAS SHORTLY after eight in the morning when Hugh sped up the driveway of Bauman Farms. His face shone with excitement when Ellie, still in her pyjamas and chenille robe, met him at the back door and let him in.

"Your power must have been restored" were her first words.

"It was! And that's what I came to tell you, in case you still want to build the cabin with me."

"Of course I do. I have to make sure you do it right," she teased.

"Can I use your phone to make a call to Margo? I want to catch her before she goes to work."

"Yeah, sure." Ellie pointed to the old-fashioned radial dial phone mounted on the kitchen wall. Then she slipped away to her room to change into daywear.

Hugh made no attempt to keep his conversation private, thus Ellie overheard him invite Margo to dinner at Aunt Gertie's for July 19. She was to contact Diane and make the same invitation to her.

"No, I don't know what she wants us for," he said. There was a pause. "She said it would be very much worth our while." Another pause. "Then call her yourself. The number is…"

And that was that. Hugh hung up.

When Ellie came out of her room, Hugh turned to her.

"Want to ride back with me?" he asked.

"Actually, I'd like to follow on my bike. I have a couple of things to do first."

For Ellie, her soul work had to be prioritized. This new habit was becoming increasingly important to her, especially since she could gauge its results. The practice was changing her, in a good way, by keeping her buoyed when depression might otherwise have taken over.

The journaling was slowing down, however. She didn't sense so many pointed questions coming up for personal reflection lately. The journals stayed nearby, though, in case she needed the therapy of writing something out.

Her daily scripture reading hadn't wavered. She keenly understood the importance of knowing her Bible, and to know it as well as she knew any room of her house.

This morning, she decided to read a couple of psalms and afterward discuss matters with Jesus that were important to her. She prayed again for Hugh, especially that he would lay down his bitterness and receive Christ into his heart. It was the missing link to gaining the kind of peace he starved for. He just didn't know it yet.

When she was done, Ellie packed a picnic lunch of sandwiches, bananas, cookies, a jar of lemonade with a sprig of mint and ice cubes, and a thermos of coffee.

Nearly an hour after Hugh had called on her, she pedalled her bike onto the Fischer farmyard.

"Sorry for the delay, Hugh-manoid, but I had to do my soul work," she said while parking her bike. She set the lunch box near his tent. "And I took the time to make us something to eat later."

"Right. Soul work. That's what I'm doing now. This is *my* soul work." Hugh indicated his tools. "Humanoid, eh? What's in the lunchbox you packed for later, El-derberry?"

Ellie smiled at the joke, appreciating that their friendship had grown close enough that they could poke a little fun at each other.

The old wooden granaries had been small and short, meaning that the resulting boards would have to be doubled up, spliced, and screwed together to create the appropriate lengths for the size of cabin they were building.

Even so, by mid-morning the floor joists were well constructed and the plywood, which had formerly covered the windows of the old house, had been screwed down neatly to become the floor.

To celebrate, they took a coffee break.

Afterward Ellie talked Hugh into taking out a couple of windows from the second floor of the farmhouse to reuse in the cabin. This was no easy feat, but after some struggle they managed to accomplish it without breaking the panes.

Next they turned their attention to constructing the walls. As before, the studs needed to be doubled, spliced, and screwed together to lend strength and the necessary height.

Hugh and Ellie spoke very little while working. Their focus was on getting the job done without dillydallying.

Ellie found that all the time she'd spent as a young woman watching and aiding her dad and older brothers had paid off. She had a pretty good understanding of how to construct a simple building and therefore could anticipate each step of the process and prepare for it. As soon as one doubled-up stud was finished, Ellie had another one ready for Hugh to assemble. It was good teamwork.

The back wall, which would have no windows or doors, went up quickly. The side walls each had to accommodate a window, which meant the process didn't go as fast. Their hope was to get the skeleton of the structure erected by the end of the day. If there was enough daylight, and they had the energy, they would start on the siding—but that would be a bonus.

No sooner had they begun preparing studs for the side walls than a vehicle approached from the south, a blue and white pickup which slowed down and then turned into the driveway.

"Oh wow!" exclaimed Ellie. "It's my brother, Rob."

"Now what would he want?" asked Hugh, suddenly uneasy.

"Let's find out. Come on."

Rob had stopped his vehicle in the middle of the yard. When he emerged from the truck, he had a wide grin stretched across his tanned face. He was topped with a cowboy hat instead of the usual baseball cap he wore during field work.

"Hello there." Rob extended his hand to Hugh. "I thought it was high time I came to welcome my new neighbour. I'm Rob Bauman, Ellie's elder brother."

Hugh and Rob shook hands firmly.

"Good to meet you sir. I'm Hugh Fischer."

"Ellie says you're planning to make a lot of changes around here and that you want to take up farming."

Hugh smiled. "She told you right."

"Good for you. What are you working on now?" asked Rob, looking over to the building site.

Hugh led him closer and explained his desire for a better shelter over the course of the summer. When Rob showed sincere interest, Hugh went on to explain their plan to salvage as much as they could from the farm's other structures—and to keep expenses as low as possible.

"I had planned to work on something else in my shop, but it can wait," Rob said. "Let me help for a bit."

Hugh showed Rob his supply of salvaged wood and the drawings Ellie had made of the finished product.

"Ellie drew this up, did she?" Rob turned his attention to his sister, winking. "Is this the best you can do?"

Ellie playfully stuck out her tongue at him.

For the next couple of hours, Rob was the one helping Hugh construct the studs while Ellie stood in the background, waiting to fetch things as needed. Both men were experienced in carpentry, so the work progressed even more quickly.

While Ellie and Hugh had worked without much talking, Rob used the time to ask neighbourly questions of Hugh.

"What kind of farming would you like to get into?" he wondered.

This got Hugh talking, and he seemed to grow more and more comfortable with each sentence. Rob was generous with his knowledge, suggestions, and support for Hugh's ambitions. Soon they were talking about farm equipment and Rob offered to help him assess the machinery he'd inherited, old though they may be.

And then another wall was ready to be erected.

It was long past noon now and Ellie started laying out her picnic lunch, but Rob interrupted her preparations.

"Ellie, I need you to go back to the shop and get the power drill," he said. "This work will go much quicker if we don't have to share tools."

She immediately started walking toward the driveway.

"Oh!" Rob added. "And can you call Sarah? Let her know I won't get home until supper."

"All right. But don't say anything interesting while I'm gone. I don't want to miss it."

She hurried away toward Rob's truck.

After she left, Rob turned to Hugh. "Ellie says the root cellar beneath the house is filled with water. Let me have a look. I may be able to help with that too."

"I don't want to trouble you."

But Rob waved him off.

Hugh led him into the house and showed him the cellar. As before, the water had filled the cavity to within a foot of the main floor. It stank of stale, rotten things.

They then walked around the house to see where the water had gotten in and found the breach on the east side. Most likely some kind of rodent had dug a den and broke through into the cellar. Probably a racoon or a skunk. With rain and melting snow, that hole had gradually filled with water that had nowhere else to go but down.

"Even if you demolish and burn the building, you should get rid of the water first," said Rob. "The house will burn better. Besides, there may be things you want to salvage."

Hugh highly doubted this, but he didn't argue. He was beginning to wonder if the Baumans might be hoarders. They sure did seem to want to hang on to a lot of old things.

Ellie returned with Rob's electric drill and a small container of bits. Only now, though, did Rob realize he also needed the gas-powered water pump located on a shelf in the Quonset, along with a couple of hoses. So Ellie turned right around and went back.

Soon the two men were busy erecting the third wall. Once done, Rob set up the pump and started pulling the water up and out toward the roadside ditch. It became Ellie's job to monitor the pump while the men continued construction of the cabin.

After a while, Ellie decided to check on the progress of the cellar. She took a flashlight from Rob's truck, donned some gloves, and went inside. Standing at the top of the stairs, she could see that more than half of the water had been pumped out. Already she could see some of what had originally been stored down in the cellar, including some jars of home-canned food and a few crocks. That was it so far.

In the meantime, the fourth and last wall went up, including the main doorway. The men then got ready to start on the rafters. Ellie couldn't hear their discussion, but she watched as Rob slid into the role of elder brother. The two men were joking with each other and debating. Rob seemed happy to have a reason to swing a hammer and make the wood submit to his will.

As for Hugh, she hadn't yet seen him so relaxed and talkative—and he was no slouch when it came to work. He obviously knew what he was doing.

Ellie wondered if it was normal for two men who barely knew each other to get on so well as they worked in concert. She knew it was the way of farmers in the valley to help one another. It was how people around here had survived since the 20s and 30s, back when people had come from far and wide to build homesteads.

From her vantage point, it sure looked like Rob and Hugh were enjoying each other's company. The sight warmed her heart. Just as women needed other women for comradery and understanding, so it was for men.

As far as she knew, aside from his aunt, Hugh hadn't reached out to reconnect with any former friends, if he had any. She remembered that he had once remarked that he was better off not socializing with people. But Ellie didn't believe that for a minute. Whoever had said no man was an island was absolutely right!

By suppertime, which happened at exactly 5:45 p.m. according to Rob's wristwatch, the structure was complete. It was now ready to be closed in.

Rob collected his personal tools and laid them in his truck, with Hugh's assistance.

"Appreciate you coming by and for your help in throwing up this building," Hugh said.

"You're welcome, neighbour. I enjoyed the work and the break from my own list of things to do."

"You've given me a lot of pertinent information to think on."

"Anytime you want to talk farming, I'll be happy to chew the fat."

With that, Rob drove back in the direction of Minitonas.

"I've got my own chores to catch up on too," said Ellie, collecting her things. "See ya tomorrow."

Hugh took a break long enough to feed himself some pork and beans with bread. On a full stomach, he began to apply siding to his cabin. He was somewhat tired, but not enough to justify going to sleep just yet. He usually found that if he worked until he was drop-dead tired, he didn't lie awake thinking about "ghosts" lurking in the night, watching him. He told himself these fears came from the lack of a yard light and promised to install one soon. In the meantime, he needed to curb his overactive imagination.

Thus, Hugh cut and hammered away until ten o'clock, getting two outside walls covered in siding before calling it quits. Then he fell on his cot and slept like the dead.

Hugh woke later than usual the following morning and quickly realized that every muscle in his tall, lean body was sore. But the summer sun was already causing the inside of his tent to crackle with stifling heat. If he didn't get outside, he'd choke on the hot, dry air.

Walking around and stretching helped loosen his aching muscles. And after a leisurely breakfast of brewed coffee, fried eggs, and canned ham, he felt ready to swing his hammer again.

Ellie showed up mid-morning. The forecast was for a hotter than average day, so she'd worn a sleeveless shirt and a baseball cap so she wouldn't have to squint too much.

Hugh was well into installing siding along the third wall when she joined in. It was tedious work requiring lots of measuring and cutting, but with Ellie's help the day progressed a lot faster than it would have otherwise.

Shortly after they started siding the fourth wall, they heard a vehicle approaching from the south. Ellie looked to see who it was, wondering if Rob was going to join the work bee once again.

But no, it was a faded navy-blue truck from the 60s. The vehicle slowed down as it approached the end of the driveway. Hugh peered hard, trying to figure out who these visitors were. Then he recognized the person sitting in the passenger seat.

"Aw, shit!" he spat.

Fourteen

HUGH ANGRILY DROPPED his hammer and almost ran out to meet the truck before anyone could step out. But he wasn't quick enough. The short, elderly passenger emerged and Hugh confirmed that it was the same old dude who had approached him outside the grocery store the first time he had gone into Minitonas. That had been a week and a half earlier, but he wore the same soiled clothing as before and the smell of him was every bit as rank.

Hugh backed up a step at the odour. "Why did you come, old man?" he growled.

"Ya remembers me, don't ya? I'm Tipper, one of yer pa's buddies." The old codger flashed a leering smile, revealing missing teeth.

"I don't care. You and your cronies aren't welcome here. You can get right back into the truck and skedaddle," said Hugh, nodding toward the driver.

Tipper's countenance changed immediately. "I came to get what's mine."

"And what would that be?"

"A whole bunch of money, or a whole bunch of liquor. One or t'other."

"Really? You're crazy... or just stupid. Or both!" fired Hugh. "I don't know you. I've seen you once at the grocery store for a couple of minutes. We've never had dealings with each other, so there's no way I can owe you anything. Get lost!"

On that note, the driver of the truck stepped out. He was considerably taller than Tipper and his long black hair was tied back in a ponytail at the base of his neck. His head was topped with a worn black cowboy hat. He cut an intimidating figure as he slowly walked around the front of the truck. His attitude conveyed that he should not be trifled with.

Ellie, who had been watching nervously from the rear of the cabin, became frightened. It looked like something awful was about to happen and she didn't like those two men appearing to gang up against one.

Without further thought, she picked up the crowbar that had been lying on the grass nearby and ran to join Hugh. What she planned to do with the crowbar, she didn't know. It just made her feel better to have something that could serve as a weapon.

The two visitors looked upon her with surprise.

"Get out of here, Ellie," Hugh said. "This is not your argument."

"I know, but whatever these guys want, I'm gonna make sure it's two against two." She turned to Tipper. "What exactly do you want anyway?"

"I want my money back," he replied cooly. "Or my liquor."

"Did you make this deal with Hugh?"

"No! With his old man, Freddie Fischer."

"Then take it up with him," Hugh said through curled lips. "It's got nothing to do with me!"

The taller of the men took another step toward Hugh, who in response took a step backward.

"Who's this guy?" Hugh asked Tipper. "Your personal bouncer?"

"This is Chiclets. He knew your pa right well hisself. And he wouldn't take no guff from him either. Ya know why we call him Chiclets?"

Hugh and Ellie waited for the answer.

"Because when people try to cross him, he hits them in the choppers and then their broken teeth lie on the floor — like bloody Chiclets." Tipper smirked.

That's when Ellie noticed the brass knuckles on Chiclets's right hand.

"There is absolutely no reason to get into a physical fight here," she said indignantly. "But you, Tipper, do have to be clear about why you think Hugh can help you with a deal you made with his father."

"Because the firewater will be here somewhere. And so will the money."

"I've been here thirteen days so far and I've done a *lot* of clean-up," began Hugh. "In the house. In the barn. In all the wooden grana-ries that used to be here. And I haven't found a drop of liquor or a single coin. Honest to God!"

Ellie nodded. "I second that, and I've been here a lot helping out."

Suddenly, Hugh had a hunch. A suspicion. "Have you been here looking around for yourselves? Lately?" he asked the men.

Chiclets didn't so much as twitch, but Tipper's eyes shifted uneasily.

"If I catch either one of you, or anyone else, trespassing on my property, I'll have you bloody well arrested," threatened Hugh in the most menacing voice he could muster.

Neither showed any fear whatsoever.

Tipper leaned forward and said in a low, chilling tone, "This here place has lots of secrets. Nasty secrets. Any one of them could land ya in big trouble. So I wouldn't be too quick to call in the cops."

"Where do you live, Tipper?" asked Ellie, still annoyed.

"Why do you want to know?"

"Because if we did find what you're looking for, how would we get it to you? Oh, and exactly how much money did you give Fred-die?"

"Ahhhh." Tipper seemed to be debating what to tell her. "I got me a place southeast of Minitonas. Go a half-mile south of town and then go east a ways. Ya can't miss it. It looks a lot like this dump. And… if ya never find the liquor, he owes me two hundred and fifty bucks."

"And how much booze did that buy?" asked Ellie.

"The whole frick'n batch!" said Chiclets darkly. They were the only words he'd said throughout the encounter.

Tipper nodded in agreement.

"Right then," said Ellie stiffly. "I'd say this meeting is over. How about we all go back to our work now?"

Tipper and Chiclets looked at each other, nodded slightly, and got back into their truck.

"Don't come back here," warned Hugh with a hard glare.

During the confrontation, Ellie had remained cool as a cucumber. Calm, clear thinking, and fully articulate. But after the unwelcome visitors were no longer in sight, she realized she was trembling all over.

Hugh noticed. "Are you all right?"

"I'm not sure." Ellie's voice shook.

"Come here." He opened his arms to embrace her. "Just calm down. We're going to be fine. Shhhhhhh."

The fact was, he needed just about as much reassurance as Ellie did.

"What do you think he meant by this place being full of secrets?" asked Ellie a moment later, stepping out of Hugh's arms.

"So far, I only know about one," said Hugh. "Have you got sturdy shoes on? Good. I'll show you."

He led her on a zigzagging course through the bush on the northwest end of farmyard, evading the many heaps of refuse and rusting farm implements. It was a graveyard in its own right and gave Ellie the creeps.

After they passed through the trashy area, not only was the path easier but Ellie found it beautiful. She felt a pang of jealousy that there were no meadows or natural stands of trees and shrubs like this on the Bauman farm. All the Bauman trees were planted in strict formation, tidily trimmed shelterbelts.

They came to a stop in front of the same natural pond Hugh had visited some twelve days earlier.

"Is this the secret? It's… it's beautiful!" In awe, Ellie walked to the water's edge, coming up to a great flat rock.

"I would say it's one of the nicest features of this property," said Hugh with a note of pride. "And I don't think it has anything to do with Tipper's secrets." He raised his arm and pointed to the left. "I think that does, though."

Ellie followed his finger and noticed a tiny shack partially hidden by a copse of quaking aspens.

"Do I want to know what's in there?"

"Nothing that will bite you."

To reach the shack, they walked through another meadow overgrown with tall grass, shrubs, and wildflowers. They approached the door and Hugh reached for the block of wood that kept it closed, giving it a simple turn. The door creaked open.

"That's a… a…"

"A still," finished Hugh. "You make whiskey with it."

"Oh my gosh," said Ellie breathlessly. "Now it makes sense. Tipper is out an entire batch of booze. Your pa was in the moonshine business! That's off-the-charts crazy…"

"I don't know yet what I'm going to do about it. Come on. Let's go back by the pond."

"Wait," she said. "Let's look around a bit. Maybe his money is in here too."

"Go ahead, but I doubt it. I think Pa would have been clever about hiding it. If that moonshine money is on the farm, I bet it's somewhere completely unpredictable. He wouldn't keep it in a mattress or cookie jar or coffee tin the way normal people do. He'd be more likely to hide it in the trash somehow, or maybe the furnace. You know what I mean?"

"Let's look anyway. Just to rule it out."

"Be my guest," said Hugh, stepping aside.

He waited outside while Ellie crawled over the main tank and gingerly stepped around everything else cluttering up the space. She shook her head after she had concluded her search.

Empty-handed, they made their way back toward the pond.

"I'm positive Tipper has been scoping out the place and still hasn't found anything," Hugh said. "These guys might be the reason I sometimes get the feeling that I'm being watched."

Ellie shivered. Other than some of the stupid things a few of her friends had done when she was much younger, this was as close as she'd ever gotten to a criminal enterprise. She felt a little afraid.

"I think the secret of the still might be a problem," he added. "I would need a permit to have one, and of course I don't. That's what Tipper is threatening me with."

"Why don't you just get rid of it?"

"Great," he said wryly. "What a brilliant idea."

"Seriously. Why can't you just dig a deep hole and bury it? Do it in the field somewhere. Then grow wheat or barley on top of it."

"I'd rather get it off the property altogether."

"What if you gave it to Tipper? Then he could deal with the logistics."

Hugh thought about this for a moment. "Assuming he knows where it is, he's had three years to take it if he wanted it."

Ellie pondered that in silence as they began making their way back toward the construction site. It was time for them to get back to work.

Although they resumed installation of the siding along the final wall of the cabin, the unexpected visit from Tipper and Chiclet had deflated their enthusiasm.

Nonetheless, the time soon came for them to tackle the roof. Hugh looked at the much smaller pile of wood left over and made a decision.

"I'm not going to close it in using this lumber," he said. "There might not be enough and I'm tired of cutting and fitting so many pieces. I'm just going to cover the roof with plywood."

"Shouldn't we stick to using salvage? What about the boards from the fence behind the barn?"

Hugh shook his head. "This is a good sound structure, and it should have a decent roof—not to mention that it will only take a few minutes to put on a few sheets of plywood. Using all these little pieces of wood would take all day. I'm not so strapped that I can't buy some plywood."

A few minutes later, they hopped into Hugh's truck and headed for Swan River. Besides plywood, they also needed to pick up shingles. For a greatly reduced price, they could buy leftover packages of different colours. Hugh didn't care about the colours; he just cared about keeping the rain out.

Ellie, on the other hand, wanted to at least arrange the motley assortment of coloured shingles into an attractive rickrack pattern. Hugh just rolled his eyes, groaned, and slapped his forehead.

The last thing he shopped for were two panes of glass cut to exact measurements. He intended to replace the top two wooden panels on the door with windows.

Thus supplied, they headed back to the farm.

At the end of the day, the carpentry work was complete. The roof was also in place, as were the shingles, arranged in horizontal zigzag stripes…

Hugh had made one amendment to Ellie's drawings, having extended the roof's front peak so he could install a porchlight beneath the eaves. Ellie liked this added feature. It lent the cabin some character.

The only tasks left to take on was adding trim to each corner of the cabin, and installing the door with replacement glass panes.

Afterward they stood back and admired their handiwork. Despite the cabin's colour being the same drab grey as all the other decrepit buildings in the yard, it was a handsome structure.

Hugh felt a great deal of pride over what he had achieved in the first two weeks since his arrival. A *lot* had been cleaned up, whether trashed or reorganized. And this little one-room cabin represented a new beginning, one he thought he could be proud of.

It was true that new worries were beginning to surface, but he felt he could deal with them. Good people such as the Baumans and his aunt and uncle were supporting him.

Which also reminded him that he wouldn't be able to enjoy any of his accomplishments so far if it hadn't been for Ellie. He watched as she walked around the cabin, collecting the odd bits and pieces of wood that were left scattered over the ground. She heaped them together near the spot where Hugh often built a campfire.

When she looked up, she noticed Hugh staring at her.

"What?" she asked.

"The cabin is great, Ellie. But I'm not blind to the fact that hardly any of what's gotten done in the last ten days would have happened if it wasn't for you. I want you to know that I appreciate you very much. I don't know how to adequately thank you, or make it up to you..."

"Stop, Hugh-loughby," she said, smiling. "You're welcome. Helping one another is the right, neighbourly thing to do. Anyway, I need to get home. I'm tired and hungry—and of course, tomorrow is Sunday. Will you be coming to church with me?"

Hugh struggled to answer. He knew that Ellie earnestly wanted him to check it out with her, but he also knew he earnestly wanted to get the electric power wired into the cabin.

"I'll see," he said, waffling. "I want to get started on the electrical. You understand, don't you?"

Ellie sighed, then nodded. "Sure..."

Fifteen

THE FIRST THING Ellie took care of was feeding herself from a few leftovers in the fridge. Afterward she felt refreshed enough to head into the shop to continue the work of refinishing the table and chairs. She completed the sanding and then glued the backs of the chairs together. She also applied primer to all the pieces so they would be ready for painting.

Rob had told her that she could help herself to any of the partially used cans of paint stowed on the shelves, and that included the spray paint. There wasn't enough of any one colour, so she planned for the table to be white, the captain's chair black, and each of the regular chairs red, yellow, and blue respectively; she had found some doweling which fit close enough to replace the missing spindle and thus complete a third chair. She determined to return the fourth, backless chair to Hugh's barn to be used as a stool.

The table had to be painted using a brush, which took quite a bit of time. But the chairs could be done with spray paint. Ellie dared to leave those pieces on cardboard overnight, trusting that an unexpected rain wouldn't come along and ruin them.

She showered and then called Gertie Johnson, who was most delighted to hear from her. All Ellie wanted to do was tell her about the cabin and that Hugh would be moving in as soon as the wiring was done. Monday at the latest.

But Gertie wanted to chat.

"I've been thinking about how Hugh wants nothing to do with anything associated with his former life on the farm," the older woman said. "Well, I went through my drawers and cupboards and set aside dishes, cutlery, and even a few pots and pans I thought he could use. Do you think that's a good idea?"

"Do I?" Ellie replied. "Not only is it a good idea, I think it's awfully thoughtful as well."

"Oh good. I've also been thinking about giving him the single bed in our guest room. It bothers me that he sleeps on a cot. That can't possibly be good for his back. And it'll mean I can set up a double bed for when we have guests. I've even got a highboy dresser I wouldn't mind giving away so he could keep clothing organized. Would he like that, do you think?"

"I have no doubt. He'd be thrilled to sleep on a real bed again. And the dresser is a great bonus. You really are very generous, Gertie."

There was more. "I hesitate to ask, but I really do wish I had something of Alice to remember her by."

"I understand. I'd probably feel the same if it were me."

Gertie sounded relieved. "Thank you. Would it be possible for me to buy that tall dresser with the tiltable mirror? I realize she probably didn't purchase the piece herself, but she likely kept her clothing in it. That's close enough for me."

"You know what? If the dresser has that kind of meaning for you, you can just have it. It's a sweet old piece, but I have no sentimental attachment."

"Thank you, dear," Gertie replied gratefully. "That is so kind and unselfish of you."

There was more still.

"Now, I've laundered everything that was in the plastic bags you sent home with me," the woman continued. "What is next to be done with them? You mentioned quilts."

"Right, I did," Ellie said. "But they aren't a priority yet. However, if you've got the time, you can take apart the cotton-like items and flatten them for cutting. Anything that's silky or stretchy won't be suitable and can either be given away or cut up for rags."

"I understand. Well, it's been a delight talking with you. Thank you, and I look forward to seeing you on Monday."

A conversation that probably only needed to last five minutes had lasted a full twenty-seven, but Ellie didn't allow herself to be annoyed. The woman was thoughtful and generous. She was also lonely and seemed to be looking for something purposeful to do. Like so many of the older generation, she had been left to feel passé, not knowing what meaningful pursuits she could do with her time after having spent her life putting her family before herself.

That line of thinking had definitely become passé.

Gertie was only being motherly to the one person who could receive what she best had to offer—and that was all it took for Ellie to suddenly, and overwhelmingly, miss her own mother. Unhindered tears filled her eyes.

"I miss you, Mom," said Ellie to herself. "It's been a really crazy day, and I wish I could get your take on some things…"

For the next few minutes, she grieved without restraint.

Sometime later, Ellie went down to the basement to do a load of laundry. The basement was strictly a functional space, used to store miscellaneous and seasonal housewares and utilities such as the furnace, hot water tank, and laundry machines. There was also a cold room for potatoes and home-canned fruits and vegetables, and of course the deep freezer chest.

Once the laundry was underway, Ellie took a look around to see what her mother had considered valuable enough to keep. She noticed jigsaw puzzles, tabletop games, the kind of extra-large pots and bowls used during canning season, a couple of suitcases, and then, leaning upright in the corner, rolled-up linoleum tied up with string. Ellie recognized it as the flooring that had been in her parents' bedroom before they'd replaced it with carpet. Apparently Elizabeth Bauman had thought there might another use for it someday.

Good thinking, thought Ellie. *I know exactly where its next use will be.*

She ran outside and back to the machine shop to spray another light coat of paint on each chair. Standing back to admire her work, she decided that they were coming along nicely. She also gave the tabletop another coat of white enamel. It would need several to survive the inevitable wear and tear.

Back in the house, Ellie changed into pyjamas and prepared herself to read from the Bible, pray, and write in her journals. She had just got herself settled in her favourite armchair when she heard the sound of a vehicle coming up the driveway.

A glance through the window confirmed that it was Hugh. What did he want now?

~

After Ellie had left, Hugh finished putting away his tools and then warmed up a tin of chili for his supper. He was getting mighty sick of store-bought canned food but consoled himself that it wouldn't be long until he could keep fresh food in the fridge and eat healthier, not to mention tastier.

He soon returned to the cabin and began to plot just where the lightbulb receptacles would be placed, as well as the outlets, marking the spots with a felt pen. He would have liked to have done more, but he had to admit he was tired. Gosh, he could smell himself. When was the last time he had bathed?

All right then. He would go to Ellie's place, have a shower, and agree to go to church with her in the morning. He only had to go once. If he didn't like it, he could say so and she would leave him alone on that score. She had promised that.

He brought all things electrical into the cabin so they would be on hand when he next worked on it. Then he threw his duffle bag in his truck and drove the quarter-mile to Ellie's place.

~

"Come in!" yelled Ellie from the living room when she heard Hugh knocking. She had just gotten comfy and didn't feel like getting up. "I'm in the front room. Although I'm surprised to see you. I thought you'd be sick of me by now."

"Nope, not quite," kidded Hugh. "Do you mind if I have a shower? I stink, even to myself."

"Not at all. Wash some clothes if you need to. I'm caught up with my stuff."

Upon that invitation, Hugh loaded the washer and took his shower. A little later, he joined Ellie in the living room in sweatpants and a T-shirt.

"That's a whole lot better," he said, sitting on the sofa. "I feel human again. Would it be rude if I stretched out on the couch?"

"No, silly. Make yourself at home. Are you hungry? I'm sure I can find something to snack on."

Ellie automatically got up and went to the kitchen. She returned with a bowl of potato chips and an oval platter bearing some fruit. She set them on the coffee table and then went back for a pitcher of juice and a couple of glasses.

"You are the most hospitable person I've ever met," said Hugh.

"It's in my upbringing. If anyone stops by, you automatically get out the coffee or teapot, and lay the table with whatever you have on hand." She smiled, but then her face took on a more serious expression. "I've been thinking about Tipper's claim, that your farm is riddled with potentially harmful secrets. Before you knock down the house, I think we should go through it with a fine-toothed comb. There might be important items concealed under loose floorboards, or behind heat registers, or in the attic. Or even in the cellar! Now that the water's out, we can explore what's down there."

"You are also the nosiest person I've ever met," said Hugh. "We? It's not your concern, Ellie. But you're probably right. I should do a thorough search. Not before I'm settled in the cabin, though. When one project is done, I can start another."

"It's not about being nosy for me. I'm quite bugged about Tipper and Chiclet's threat. After all you've been through, I'd hate to see more bad incidents added to your woes. That's all."

"Thank you for caring," said Hugh quietly. Then he noticed her books piled on the sidetable. "Read something to me."

"Seriously? Can I read from the Bible?"

"Sure."

"Then I'm going to read to you from Genesis… about how we all became broken people living in a broken world."

Hugh turned on his side and leaned on his elbow toward her.

Ellie opened her Bible to Genesis 1 and began to read. An elementary school teacher would have remarked that she read with "expression"; she read aloud in such a way that Hugh could see the story in his mind's eye, like a movie. The tale got especially interesting when the talking serpent enticed Eve to eat the forbidden fruit. Kaboom! It was a game-changer of epic proportions.

Ellie stopped at the end of Genesis 3 and looked up at Hugh expectantly.

"That's a great story," said Hugh. "It's the first time I've heard the original. Do you really believe it? I mean… a talking serpent?"

"I very much do believe it," she replied. "It makes a heck of a lot more sense than the illogical theory of evolution that science teachers want us to swallow. That requires more faith, or gullibility, than I can spare for such nonsense. As for the talking serpent, the text doesn't suggest that *all* snakes spoke. It's more like the devil, also known as Satan, either entered into the snake or manifested himself as one. Do you actually get what happened there at the beginning of time?" Suddenly, an idea occurred to her. "Here. Let me show you another way."

Ellie rose and went into the kitchen, returning with a blank sheet of paper and a fine-point felt pen. She knelt at the coffee table and began to draw. She started with Adam and Eve as stick people on the left, representing the Earth, and on the right she made some markings to represent the celestial city of heaven, where God dwelt.

"In the beginning, when everything was still 'very good,' there was no barrier between heaven and Earth to prevent Adam and Eve from having access to God, or to prevent God from regularly and freely fellowshipping with His creation. When Eve got tricked into eating the forbidden fruit, her sin of disobedience immediately caused a chasm between God and the people, who had been created in His image. Their uninterrupted access to Him was cut off, like a snipped electrical cord."

Ellie marked two lines representing a chasm between her drawings of Earth and heaven.

"What God then said to the serpent was tantamount to declaring His intention to repair the damage. But He didn't do it immediately. For four thousand years, give or take, God let humans multiply and experience the misery and hardship of life when lived apart from Him. Then, at just the right time, He sent His solution—His only Son—to Earth to experience humanity for Himself. We know Him as Jesus, the Christ. Because He lived as a human for over thirty years without getting tricked into sin like Adam and Eve, His sinlessness qualified Him to die on behalf of all people, for every sin ever committed throughout history. That's what we celebrate at Easter… it has nothing whatsoever to do with bunnies or eggs.

"It had to be this way because the penalty for sin was death. *Is* death. The sacrifice of Jesus's perfect life, dying on my behalf and yours, satisfied God so well that we now once again enjoy easy access to God, similar to what Adam and Eve originally had. I say *similar*, because it's only possible by crossing a narrow bridge—the bridge of the cross upon which Jesus died in our place. Do you get it? He substituted Himself for you… and me…"

Ellie drew the shape of a cross. It extended across the paper, bridging the Earth to heaven, over the chasm.

"That's what we have to do if we… you… I… want to enjoy a relationship with God and all the benefits, like peace instead of troubled minds, that comes with it. It's also what we have to do to experience eternal life, living with Jesus forever, even after we die on this earth. We have to come to God through Jesus, claiming His sacrifice on the cross on our behalf. There is no other way. Believe me, people try other tactics, but they don't work. They can never work. And that is the abbreviated version of the Gospel, meaning the good news, regarding Jesus Christ!"

She concluded it with a smile, after which silence reigned for a couple of minutes. It was a thoughtful, friendly silence during which Hugh picked up Ellie's drawing and studied it while lying on his back on the couch.

"I've never heard this before," he said at last. "Not even at the church the Turners took me to in Winnipeg, or from the Turners themselves."

"Well, now you have," said Ellie softly. "What are you gonna do about it?"

"I'm gonna think about it." Hugh sat back up. "It's getting late. I should collect my things and go."

"Stay. Sleep in my brothers' room like you did before. It will make it easier to get ready for church in the morning."

"You're serious?"

Ellie nodded.

"Then I will. I've forgotten what it's like to sleep in a real bed."

Before breakfast the next morning, while Hugh still slept, Ellie painted another layer on each of the chairs and the table.

At 10:30 a.m., she and Hugh left for the First Baptist Church in Minitonas, taking Ellie's car. Hugh complained that he had to fold up his limbs like a grasshopper to sit in the passenger seat.

Once at church, Hugh was amazed that so many people would take the time to greet him and introduce themselves. Many seemed not to recognize his surname, which was a relief. There were a couple of young women and one guy, though, who recalled him as a class-mate from their public-school days. All were married now and had started families of their own. They were surprised to see him at church, also as Ellie's friend, but they welcomed him warmly nonetheless.

The service started with music which sounded a lot different than anything Hugh had heard at the Turners' church. The music there had been classical and formal, like something from a previous era. These Baptists in Minitonas sang in a more down-to-earth style.

As it turned out, they had special guests that morning. Instead of the usual choir, a gospel quartet from another province was singing energetically, as a kind of advertisement for a concert the church would host that evening. Hugh had to grudgingly admit that he enjoyed their music. They reminded him of a few country music artists he liked.

When the time came for the sermon, the pastor spoke about one of Jesus's parables from the Gospel of Luke: the story of the rich fool. What struck Hugh was that the pastor presented his message in plain English, relating it to the practical issues of life... anyone's life. The conclusion, of course, made an elaborate point on the importance of cultivating a rich relationship with God over and above all one's other relationships and priorities.

Hugh thought of Ellie's drawing the evening before and how much the pastor's words complemented what she had said.

All in all, Hugh's first experience at FBC was a good one, and he was truly surprised. It was hardly like the earlier church he had experi-enced in Winnipeg. He might let Ellie talk him into coming again. And he was pretty sure he wouldn't mind coming out that evening to hear the toe-tapping gospel quartet.

After the service was over, Rob's wife Sarah sought them out and invited them to come to their house for lunch. There was a stuffed chicken roasting in the oven and more than enough to share. Hugh agreed, since this meal promised to be ever so much superior to anything out of a tin can. Then again, Ellie held the keys to the vehicle in which they'd come to town. He was rather at her mercy.

At Rob and Sarah's house, Hugh met their three children. The oldest was Trevor, who was fifteen, blond, tall for his age, and slim albeit athletically built, which corresponded to his love for sports. Next was Charlotte, thirteen, who was also blond and had long hair that reached the middle of her back. She enjoyed crafting and baking with her mom in the kitchen.

Finally Hugh was introduced to the little girl, Beanie, who was petite for a seven-year-old. She'd been registered as Bernadette at birth, in honour of Sarah's beloved grandmother, but once she was referred to as Beanie, well, it stuck. In her own words, she liked to read and draw.

Hugh had never interacted with young children and wasn't sure how to go about holding a meaningful conversation with one. Thankfully, Rob rescued the moment by asking about the building of his cabin. Hugh was only too happy to provide an update.

Soon after, everyone was invited to the table. Hugh couldn't believe his eyes. The only occasions on which he'd seen tables spread with that much delicious-looking food was Christmas and Thanksgiving.

"Wow!" he blurted out. "What's the occasion?"

"Just Sunday fare," Sarah answered with a smile.

This family held hands while asking the blessing. Hugh held hands with Ellie on his right and Beanie on his left, instantly aware of how good it felt to touch someone and be touched.

The table talk included stories from school and expressions of anticipation for the summer holiday. Quite a lot of time was given to discussing the church picnic, which was coming up the next Saturday. It was to be held on the grounds of the Bible Camp at Wellman Lake located a half-hour away in Duck Mountain Provincial Park.

"Why is the park called Duck Mountain when it's really just a few average hills?" Charlotte asked.

"I know the area was home to more than the average number of ducks, at one time at least," answered Trevor. "We talked about it in social studies. And the difference in altitude is because the Swan Valley was carved out by a glacier. But you're right. Whoever named it a mountain must have been making a joke, because if these hills are mountains, what should we call the Rockies? Gargantains?"

Everyone around the table looked at each other with raised eyebrows.

"But they would still be mountains to mouses and bumble bees," said Beanie, adding her two cents.

"You mean mice, Bean, not mouses," said her brother. "And that doesn't count at all."

The table talk returned to the church picnic and the annual softball tournament. Four of the youth were tasked with forming softball teams for the planned tournament. Trevor was one of them and had enlisted eight people, including his dad. But he needed one more.

"Mr. Fischer, would you please join my ball team?" asked Trevor politely.

"Are you sure you're allowed to ask me? I don't belong to your church."

"That's okay. Even if it is a church picnic, it's really a kind of community thing and anybody who wants to come is welcome."

Rob nodded in agreement.

"I played a little ball in high school, but not since," confessed Hugh. "I'm pretty rusty, and I don't have a glove anymore."

"Aww, that's okay. Most everybody will be rusty. Especially my dad." Trevor chuckled and ducked—but not quick enough. Rob's light punch got him in the shoulder. "I'm sure I can find you a glove. Aunt Ellie, will you be my spare in case somebody doesn't show up?"

"Spare!" exclaimed Ellie. It sounded like a yelp. "I bet I could still show you a thing or two about playing ball. And I'm sure my old glove is around somewhere."

"Oh yeah? I bet you couldn't hit the broad side of a barn…"

And on and on it went. Hugh could only smile and sit in amazement. He had never seen such playfulness amongst family members, not even in the Turner family. If this was what a healthy family looked like, he had most definitely missed out.

After dinner, the board games were brought out. Ellie searched Hugh's eyes to discern if he was okay with staying longer. He certainly seemed to be, since he agreed to play checkers with Trevor, then a round of Battleship after that. Time passed quickly without anyone realizing it, and soon it was five o'clock and Sarah was laying out a light supper.

"Are you coming to the concert tonight?" asked Trevor.

To Ellie's amazement, Hugh answered quickly. "Sure. They sound pretty good. They remind me of the Oakridge Boys."

The next thing she knew, they were all sitting in church, taking up an entire pew. Hugh was flanked on one side by Trevor and the other side by Charlotte while Beanie sat on his lap.

My, my, who'd have thunk, she thought.

It was a good concert that included oldies for the seniors and some newer songs the younger people appreciated. For Hugh, all the tunes were new, but he liked them. They had an encouraging effect on him, and not many things in his circle of experience did that for him.

After the concert, when Hugh and Ellie returned to Bauman Farms, Hugh jumped into his truck to go back to his own place.

He rolled down the window. "Ellie, was this a typical Sunday for you?"

"I guess so... all except the concert. That's a rare treat."

"Today might have been one of the single best days I've ever had. Thanks for including me in your family. Would you know what I meant if I said I learned a lot?"

"I think so. Glad you joined us today!"

"Good night, Ell-ementary."

"Good night, Hugh-betcha!"

Sixteen

EARLY MONDAY MORNING, before she did anything else, Ellie went to the shop to reassemble the table and apply a final coat of white paint. Pleased with how it turned out, she placed it outside so the sun would shine on it, ensuring that it would dry quickly.

She then sprayed a final coat of paint on each of the four chairs. To her, they looked adorable and anticipated that Hugh would feel the same way. They looked nothing like they had. The bright colours, she hoped, would inspire cheer.

Then she hauled the rolled-up linoleum up from the basement and placed it in the backseat of her car. Of course, half of it stuck out the open window, but that couldn't be helped.

She fixed herself a mug of coffee and grabbed a couple of oatmeal raisin cookies, reasoning that they were a variation of porridge. She sat in the living room to read a few more psalms while eating "breakfast." When the coffee was drained, she dressed in jeans and a faded tie-dyed T-shirt, ready to put in another day's work.

She found Hugh working on exactly the project she had expected: the wiring. A lot of it was already in place, as he'd been up since 6:00 a.m., refreshed and raring to go. He'd installed the panel box high up on the rear wall. A number of wires dangled near it, soon to be connected with circuit breakers. The lightbulb receptacles and most of the power outlets were in place.

But something was different, and it took a moment for Ellie to figure out what it was. Hugh was whistling!

"Good morning, Ell-egance!"

"Top of the morning to you too, Hugh-ligan. How come you're so cheerful?"

"Cuz the sun is shining," he said, smiling broadly. "The Ritz is almost ready to move into. I slept well. How's that for starters?"

"Great! I brought you something. Come see."

Ellie led him outside and showed him the linoleum. They took off the strings and carefully stretched it out.

"I appreciate your thoughtfulness, neighbour, but it's got... polka dots," finished Hugh lamely.

It was true. The pattern was made up of primary-coloured polka dots against a white background. Not exactly his style.

Ellie laughed. "It's a bit of salvage my mother kept in the basement. I'm donating it to your cause so you won't get slivers in your bare feet."

"Right. The salvage rule. I get your drift. Actually, it'll probably cheer up the room with everything else being so grey. Thank you."

They heard the sound of wheels on gravel and turned to see a van slow down on the road and carefully turn into the driveway. It took a few seconds for them to realize it was Gertie.

His aunt was all-smiles as she got out of the vehicle.

"I hear you're going to move into the cabin today," she said. "I've come to clean those appliances like I promised. And I brought you some things I thought you could use."

Hugh greeted her with a brief hug. "That's very kind of you."

He went back to the wiring while Ellie helped Gertie unload. She'd had the presence of mind to bring hot water in pails with lids, along with soap and cloths. Suddenly, Ellie couldn't wait to start scrubbing the fridge and stove right alongside of her.

No sooner had they gotten started than they heard another vehicle approaching. This time it was Rob and Sarah.

"Once the kids left for school, we looked at each other and said, 'Why don't we go and help our neighbour too?'" Sarah said. "So here we are."

Rob immediately got involved with the wiring while Sarah took on the project of washing down the Hoosier cabinet.

Because of the visiting that went on while they worked, it took until noon to clean the appliances, but it didn't matter. The camaraderie was most enjoyable, as it always was when women join forces for a common cause. The same could be said when men teamed up to hunt, fish, or raise a barn. Work that might otherwise amount to drudgery could be quite tolerable when one had good people to work alongside.

As for Hugh, he wasn't used to being the reason for people coming together, much less the recipient of such support. He felt humbled, and more than a little awkward. Not knowing what to do with all this attention, he went with the flow and let things unfold as they would.

Close to noon, Sarah offered to return home to make up some sandwiches. This caused Gertie to suddenly remember that she'd brought a picnic hamper. With the help of the other women, she rolled out an old blanket and set down an amazing spread of sandwiches, pickles, sliced cheeses, veggies, and potato chips. She hadn't known there would be so many people, but in her enthusiasm she'd already prepared enough for a small army.

They enjoyed a wonderful, upbeat picnic in the late June sunshine. Rob told funny stories about Ellie, depicting her as a kid who wanted to be involved in all the same things as her brothers. As everyone laughed, Ellie's face went crimson in remembrance.

For dessert, Gertie pulled out some paper plates and plastic forks with which to serve an apple pie she'd baked the day before. The men groaned, for they were already full, but they gladly consumed a slice anyway.

After the veritable feast, the men completed the wiring and tested their workmanship: the lights worked, as did the outlets.

Installing the polka-dot linoleum came next. Rob and Hugh efficiently trimmed and set the flooring in place with glue and secured the edges with a staple gun. Even before the furniture was brought in, Ellie thought it was an appealing space.

The exciting moment had finally arrived: moving in. Rob and Hugh started by carrying over the avocado-green fridge and plugging it in. What a relief it was when they first heard its familiar hum! Next came the harvest-gold stove. After installation, their tests showed that the oven and all the burners were in good working order. Lastly, the men carried in the Hoosier cabinet and set it between the fridge and stove.

If the cabin had appeared comfy before, it looked downright homey now.

At this point, Rob and Sarah began to say their goodbyes. It was mid-afternoon and they wanted to be home when their kids got back from school.

Hugh tried to express his deep appreciation, but the words stuck in his throat.

Rob clapped him on the back. "Not a problem, neighbour. Glad to help you get started. Call if ever you have need."

After they left, Ellie stepped closer to Hugh. "You're going to want fresh groceries, right? How about you go get them now so your aunt and I can set up a few surprises for you?"

"What surprises? You're not going to turn my cabin into something girlish, are you?" asked Hugh suspiciously.

"Wouldn't dream of it."

Gertie winked. "Of course not."

"We'll need about forty-five minutes," said Ellie. "So don't hurry back."

For a moment, Hugh debated with himself whether to go. At last he jumped into his truck and drove off toward Minitonas.

Moving quickly, Ellie and Gertie unloaded from the van all the parts for the single bed she had brought over from her guest room. They quickly assembled the bed and clothed it with a set of blue sheets and a lightweight comforter, with a blue bedspread on top. A box full of extra linens were stowed under the bed.

"There," Gertie pronounced with confidence. "Blue is a traditional boys colour, right? He can't complain this is too feminine for a bachelor."

Ellie smiled. "It looks great!"

They carried in the highboy dresser and set it across from the bed on the opposite side of the cabin. Next up, they retrieved the table and chairs. Once these were unloaded and set in place, the furnishings were arranged.

The cabin now looked more than homey; it had graduated all the way to cozy. The different colours of chairs and the blue bedspread matched the bright polka-dotted floor. Although the colour of the fridge and stove were off shade, the final effect was still pleasing.

Since Hugh still hadn't returned, the women began to unpack the housewares Gertie had donated. They arranged them in the cabinet and in the cutlery drawer underneath the tabletop.

Gertie was still interested in taking home the antique bureau used by her sister Alice. Ellie helped load that piece of furniture into the van.

More time had passed and still there was no sign of Hugh. Gertie was becoming antsy, as she wanted to leave for home. Ed would be expecting supper on time. But she didn't want to miss out on seeing Hugh's reaction.

To pass the time, Gertie pinned up a calendar on a stud between the refrigerator and the bed. Ellie found Hugh's boombox in the barn, plugged it in, and set it on top of the highboy. They bustled around a while longer, adding miscellaneous but useful items. Gertie placed a final box beside the dresser, filled with items Hugh would have to sort through.

At last they heard an approaching vehicle. They went outside to find Hugh pulling up.

"You're fifteen minutes late," chided Gertie, but not angrily.

"I thought I would give you extra time in case you needed it."

"Never mind." She beamed with excitement, as giddy as a child on their birthday. "Just go and look inside—now."

Ellie watched from a short distance away. This was a special moment between Hugh and his aunt. She wasn't about to steal Gertie's thunder.

Hugh approached the cabin and swung open the door. He stood there, stunned.

"Do you like it?" asked Gertie. It sounded like a plea.

"It's… it's… nothing less than fantastic." Hugh stepped inside, with Gertie following. "You brought me all this?"

"I brought you the bed and dresser, and all the dishes, pots and pans… everything you'll find in the cupboard and drawers."

Hugh choked up. "Aunty, I don't know what to say."

"'Thank you' and a big hug is all. I'm going to have to run. Your Uncle Ed will wonder what's become of me."

He did thank his aunt, and he did give her a warm, appreciative hug. The elder woman's eyes glistened.

After she drove off, Hugh turned his attention to Ellie. "Are the table and chairs from you then?"

Ellie shrugged. "Do you recognize them?"

"No. Should I?"

"That's the same set you ate off of in your old house. I had the table cut to a smaller size and took apart the chairs, rebuilding them and then giving them fresh paint. Salvaged paint, I might add. They've got a whole new look!" She smiled. "Do you like them?"

Hugh nodded but couldn't seem to speak. He kept blinking to stave away the tears that threatened to roll down his cheeks. His heart was deeply touched.

"Ellie—"

"You're welcome. Let's put away your groceries."

Between them, they brought in three large brown paper bags full of provisions. They also brought in the duffle bag of Hugh's clothing to place in drawers. Using some leftover hardware from the old house,

Hugh hung hooks for the shirts. On another stud, he installed a double hook to hold his jacket. He stowed his plastic bin of odds and ends at the foot of his bed.

The cabinet had to be moved over a bit to set up a stool with his drinking water drum on top. Once the lidded wastebasket was in place, another gift from Gertie, it seemed all his practical needs were looked after.

Ellie took out the drawings she'd made for the future farmyard and laid them on the table. "Have you decided which yard plan you're going to carry out?" she asked.

He showed her the one he like best.

With a little gasp, Ellie remembered something. She ran out to her car, then returned a minute later with the picture frame she had bought a few days earlier. She picked up the drawing Hugh had selected and secured it in the frame.

"There," she said. "Now you have a picture on the wall to help you stay motivated in your quest to rejuvenate this place."

Hugh produced a nail and hung the frame near his bed.

"But I want the other one up somewhere too," he said.

She frowned, not understanding what he meant. He opened his bin of odds and ends and pulled out the drawing she'd made during their talk on Saturday—the one she'd used to illustrate how the world had been broken until Jesus bridged the chasm.

With great surprise, Ellie watched him tack the picture on the wall between the studs near the head of the bed. In that position, he would be able to see it every time he lay down on the bed.

"That's it then," she said. "You're moved in. Congratulations! I'm sure you'll be ever so much more comfortable here than you were in your canvas tent."

"Even without running water, I feel like I'm living in luxury. It's aptly named The Ritz, after all. Maybe I should make up a piece of board with that name and nail it above the door."

"That would be fun," said Ellie as she took a few steps toward the door.

"Stay, won't you?" he said. "I'd like to share my first supper here with you."

"I think I should go. Got other things to catch up on."

Hugh reached out and placed his hand on her arm, "Please stay," he said with pleading eyes; they were as large and irresistible as a puppy's.

Ellie stayed.

Seventeen

WITH HUGH'S FIRST building project completed, Ellie was able to take the following day off. She rose later than usual, feeling no pressure to be anywhere. She took lots of time going through her morning routine, and that included her soul work. Yet it didn't feel as sweet as other days. The fact was that she was restless. It was one of those days when you want something but don't know what. She thought of all the things on her to-do list, but none of it appealed to her. She wished she could talk to someone, someone wise, about life, purpose, and fulfillment.

Ellie realized that was it. She wanted a conversation of depth with someone of her kind—a fellow woman. A member of the sisterhood.

The girls she had once hung out with as a girl were either no longer in the area or were now married with children, and she hadn't kept up with them. She couldn't think of any older women at FBC with whom she felt close enough to bare her thoughts. There was Sarah, of course, but she wasn't the right fit today.

Then it came to her. Aunt Ruth! Her mother's younger sister, Ruth, was easy to talk to and had a warm, generous heart. As a bonus, she didn't live too far away. She and her husband Herb still lived on their farm in the district of Bowsman.

The thought of having a long conversation with Aunt Ruth energized Ellie. She dressed quickly in a skirt with a pretty top, taking the time to apply makeup and style her blond tresses into a simple updo. It made her feel feminine and boosted her spirits.

Ellie grabbed her handbag and drove away, aiming her car in a northerly direction.

Driving through the fields of the Swan Valley never failed to inspire her. The farmers were prudent and kept their fields clean and healthy. The breadbasket of middle Manitoba was looking good. Hopefully it would stay that way until the harvest was complete and the grain could be safely stored in bins.

Twenty minutes later, Ellie arrived at her aunt and uncle's place, pleased with herself for having remembered how to get there. As she parked, her aunt Ruth, every bit as silvery-haired and plump as when Ellie had last seen her, came out of the house to see who her visitor was. She squealed with delight when she recognized Ellie.

"Aren't I the lucky one to have my favourite sister's only daughter come to see me," she cried, smiling from ear to ear.

Ellie's mother had been Ruth's only sister, so it was a joke to claim that she'd been her favourite.

"What brings you to my corner of the world?" Ruth asked.

Ellie reached out to embrace her aunt. "I had time on my hands— and after thinking about it, I decided I wanted to spend it with you."

"Well, isn't that nice! Come inside. Have you had anything to eat? Let me fix you something."

"I've had breakfast, aunty. But no one in the whole valley beats your cookery. Whatever you have will be delicious."

In the kitchen, Ellie noticed a pan on the counter half-filled with moist chocolate cake, slathered with thick, creamy icing. Ruth cut generous pieces for herself and Ellie. The kettle on the stove boiled water for their tea.

At last Ruth finished fussing about and sat down. "Tell me about yourself, my girl. How is it with you?"

"Oh, not too bad, I guess," answered Ellie. But her eyes betrayed a sad heart.

"You miss your mother, don't you?"

Ellie nodded.

"Of course you do. I do too. She was my best friend. I have no one to talk with like I did with her."

The kind, sympathetic words encouraged Ellie to let a couple of tears escape, though she promptly wiped them away. "I'm fine, aunty, I really am. Mostly. It's just that I feel *lost.* I don't know any other way to put it. I don't know what I should do with myself…"

"You don't like being a nurse anymore?" asked Ruth, surprised.

"I don't mind being a nurse. It's more about *where* I should be a nurse. I took a sabbatical from the hospital in Winnipeg. But honestly, I'm not too interested in going back to the city. I don't know what to look forward to."

"What about the hospital in Swan River?"

"I haven't checked for any positions yet. I'm not sure coming home to stay is a good fit. Like I told my brother, it feels like an item of clothing that's at least a size too small, as if I've outgrown the place."

"I see." Ruth sounded thoughtful. There was a short pause before she spoke again. "Is it just about the job, Ellie?"

"I don't think so. Truthfully, I thought my life would look different at this point."

"What do you mean, Ellie dear? Tell me about it."

"I thought I'd be living in a big house, be married to a wonderful man, and have at least a couple of snotty-nosed kids hanging onto my legs by now. At FBC last Sunday, I noticed that women at least five years younger than me were married with kids. What's the matter with me?"

"Did you not meet any fine men while you were in Winnipeg?"

"Not many. Although I must admit, I thought my last boyfriend was the cat's meow. He was handsome and fun and training to be a doctor. We broke up a few weeks ago, round about the time Mom passed away. It was a bad breakup."

"Oh dear. No wonder you feel sad and lost. I think you should be easier on yourself. Great sorrows require a lot of time to heal, more time than we might think," said Ruth. "But you know, the Lord sees you and knows all about your troubles. Tell Him about it and leave it with Him. He knows what's best. When we trust Him, He answers our prayers at just the right time and in just the right way."

It was the standard response, the one any Christian might give to a struggling brother or sister. It wasn't new or clever, only the simple truth. The sage counsel was meant to encourage.

"I wonder if I'll ever marry," said Ellie. "I think the people at FBC must already think of me as a spinster."

"Nonsense! Your mother was at least thirty before she tied the knot. You're much too young to think your ship has sailed." Ruth hesitated a moment. "Having said that, I want to tell you something. May I?"

"I'm listening, aunty."

"Marriage *is* a good thing. To have a mate, have children, build a life together... these are good things. On the other hand, you must understand that being single is *not* a bad thing. In fact, I'll go so far as to say that it is better to be single than to be badly married. When people make mistakes about their choice in a mate, their lives are a misery. What I'm saying, Ellie, is this: don't let your age pressure you into marrying unwisely. Marry only when all the right qualities have come together, even if that turns out to be when you're forty-nine. Which I'm sure it won't."

"I know you're right, aunty. I just needed to hear it."

"Good. Now, the other thing I wanted to say is that married women often make the mistake of thinking their husband is supposed to meet all their needs, or some foolishness like that."

Ellie raised her eyebrows. "What do you mean?"

"Look. A husband ought to love his wife with tenderness and affection, give her children, provide her with a home and her material needs and all that... Likewise, a wife should love her husband, care for him in practical ways, and create a home that's loving and calm without adding to the stress put on him by this harsh world. But fulfillment and satisfaction in life? Well, that's another thing. That's something only Jesus can do for us when we put our faith in Him. So many young people look to their spouses for wholeness. They can't give that! It's not in their power. Then you hear about people divorcing because 'He doesn't fulfill me...' or 'She doesn't satisfy me...' Oy vey! I don't believe God ever intended that. That's not what is meant by two-becoming-one."

"I think I understand," Ellie said, nodding. "It makes good sense. I'll try to remember the difference between being loved by a husband, which is desirable, and being fulfilled by a husband, which is impossible, and not mix them up." She looked directly into her aunt's eyes. "But I do have Jesus in my heart. Still, some days my longing for more is almost greater than I can stand. That's when I don't feel like Jesus is enough. Do you know what I mean?"

"Sweetheart, if I understood everything and knew all the answers, I'd be a wise woman indeed! I understand your longing, Ellie. It comes to me in waves sometimes too. But you know what I think it means?"

Ellie shook her head.

"I think it means our spirits within are longing to be reunited with our Saviour and Creator," said Ruth. "The psalmist wrote, *'As a hart longs for flowing streams, so longs my soul for thee, O God.'*[4] What a wonderful day it will be when we go to be with Jesus, just as He has promised to those who trust in Him."

"I agree, aunty. But my friends and I have prayed. 'Jesus, can You wait until I experience love and marriage first, and the birth of a child? Then You can come.'"

Ruth laughed heartily. "Yes, all young people seem to want that. It's normal. As long as the Lord tarries, we should carry on and pursue these things. The Bible doesn't put a time limit on 'be fruitful and multiply.' But there's an implication here that bothers me—that the heavenly realm isn't as good, exciting, or delightful as what we have on the earth. That's very unfortunate. I believe most Christians greatly underestimate the wonder of heaven and of being together with Jesus. If someone gets there without being married first, I'm sure they won't think they will have missed out on anything this poor old broken world had to offer. At least, that's what I believe."

---

[4] Psalm 42:1, RSV.

"Point taken." Ellie drained the last mouthful of tea and looked up at the clock on the wall. She saw that it was nearly noon. "Will Uncle Herb be coming home for lunch?"

"He may, or he may not. It's no matter. There's lots of food on hand if it comes to that. He went into Swan River to meet with a bunch of the old farmers who like to talk farming and politics over a bottomless cup of coffee. It's a weekly habit."

Ruth rose and began to clean the table.

"But you know what?" she said. "I can't sit around yakking it up all day neither. There's a community supper party being planned for the town of Bowsman. It's a kind of celebration for the end of school and a launch of the summer holidays. They asked me to make six apple pies and I have to do it this afternoon. I'm not saying you have to go. But if you stay, we'll have to talk while I make pies."

"I'd love to help you with that," said Ellie. "It will be fun."

Aunt Ruth found an apron for Ellie, and soon Ruth was combining lard and flour for the pastry while Ellie peeled and sliced apples. They carried on talking, with Ruth bringing Ellie up to date on the activities of her cousins. Ellie talked about befriending her new neighbour, who had once been her previous neighbour, and his ambitions to reform the family farm.

Ruth talked about the changes in her health and energy, ascribing them to aging. Growing old was not for the faint of heart!

"Oh, the world sure is changing in an awful hurry," Ruth lamented. "And not many of these changes look to be for the better! In fact, I'm sure if the nation continues on its present course, it'll soon be going to hell in a handbasket."

"Are you tracking the feminist movement?" asked Ellie, curious about what her aunt might think of the current societal trends.

"Do you mean all the noise about women's rights, equality with men, abortion rights, and that sort of thing?" Ruth spoke sharply.

Ellie guessed she was in for an earful. "It would include all those things, yes."

Ruth sighed. She sprinkled another round of flour on the counter, placed a lump of pastry dough in the centre, sprinkled a bit more flour on the lump, and then applied her rolling pin, spreading the dough into a thin circular shape. All the while, she spoke earnestly.

"I don't think it's a topic with easy conclusions. If I were to respond to all those men out there..." Ruth made a right-armed sweeping motion. "...who feel they are superior to women by virtue of being male, if they are unfair—or worse, abusive—or if it's about men who lord themselves over women like taskmasters showing little or no respect, then these feminists have my sympathy and support. That's not right by any standard."

Ellie listened intently. She could feel a *but* coming.

"But it seems to me that today's women want to usurp men and their role. Their clamour doesn't sound like a call for the men in our society to smarten up. Neither does it seem like a call to live in harmony together. It sounds more like they want to emasculate the men and be in power over them. Or am I missing something? What do you think?"

Ellie thought for a moment before answering. "What you say does describe the more radical women I've heard," she said. "I think the average woman, myself being one of them, just wants to live in a mutually loving and fair relationship, with roles not so severely divided as they have been in times past."

"Yes, well... the world is changing and we have to adapt with it, at least to some extent. Although God's principles function perfectly, as they should in any culture and any era. These should never be watered down or compromised." Ruth kept working the dough in front of her. "On the other hand, it seems to me your generation has opened Pandora's box. I don't see anything good coming out of a generation that categorically rejects traditional biblical morality. Couples want merely to live together without commitment, and then separate and recouple. Sex isn't sacred anymore. It's done like the animals do—shamelessly, with many partners. I don't know what this world is coming to, Ellie. I fear for the nation. I really do. History shows that nations are only as strong as their family units. Our family units are falling apart left, right, and centre!"

Ellie nodded, then changed the subject. "Dr. Morgentaler is in the news again."

"Oh, well there's another thing that gets my goat." Ruth sounded more intense than ever. "How can a doctor who takes an oath to preserve human life take the life of an unborn child without compunction? It's shocking to me. I understand that sometimes a woman, perhaps single girls especially, aren't able to raise their children. But then why not allow another couple who can't have children to adopt them for their own? It saves the baby's life and brings happiness to others. Abortion seems very selfish to me. Not to mention, it's tantamount to murder."

"You're preaching to the choir, Aunty Ruth." Yet Ellie wanted to take the discussion a step further. "When I was living in Winnipeg, I knew a girl who had an abortion. What would you say to her, after the fact?"

"Oh, that's a shame." Ruth's voice softened in a split second. "The poor girl... is she a believer?"

"I would say she knew about Jesus when she was young but went astray after she left home."

"Oh dear, that seems to happen to so many of our young people today..."

"True. But what about my friend?"

Ruth didn't answer immediately. "I think it would depend on the girl," said Ruth slowly. "If she was *repentant*, my heart would go out to her. I would do all I could to reassure her that the blood of Jesus covered that sin on the cross too. I would tell her that Jesus still loves and forgives her. She could, in God's grace, move on. But if the girl was *not* repentant, if she justified herself and was proud and haughty, I would be very disappointed. Even heartbroken. I'm pretty sure I would have a hard time talking to her. Maybe I couldn't. I don't know. I haven't been tested in a situation like this."

"I hear you, Aunt Ruth," said Ellie softly. "Actually, I think yours is a good answer."

146

All together they made eight apple pies—six for the community supper, one for Ruth and Herb, and the eighth one for Ellie to take home as a reward for all her labour.

It was after four o'clock when Ellie announced she should get going. She wanted to stop for a few groceries before the stores closed.

"I can't tell you how good it is that you stopped by," said Ruth warmly as they walked out into the yard. "It was good to talk our hearts out, wasn't it? It did me some good to express my thoughts. Kind of sorts them out in the telling. You're welcome any time, Ellie."

Ellie got in her car, waved goodbye, and drove away.

On her way to Minitonas, Ellie thought back over some of the highlights of her visit. Then she got to thinking about the still-warm apple pie on the passenger seat—and with it came the thought that she should share it with someone. She felt she was being prompted to do this.

"Who would You like me to share this pie with?" she prayed aloud, waiting on the Lord for insight.

"Give half of it to Hugh Fischer."

"Why him? There must be someone else."

"Give it to Hugh. It will bless him more than you know."

"I'm afraid he'll think I'm getting interested in him as a sweetheart."

"I'm asking you to show him My love as a neighbour, not as a girl-friend."

"I'm afraid of sending mixed messages."

"I will look after his heart. Just be obedient."

"Fine, Lord. But I hope he can tell the difference!"

～

An hour later, Ellie had completed her errands and was on the road toward home. When she slowed down to turn into Hugh's driveway, she saw that he was in the process of cutting the grass using a rotary mower hitched behind the tractor. Most of it was already done.

A lot of clean-up had occurred in the last two weeks, she reflected as she pulled up. The yard looked considerably tidier than it had when Hugh had first arrived.

Ellie parked by the cabin and stepped out.

Hugh drove the tractor and mower in her direction, then stopped and shut it down. He hopped off the tractor to meet her.

"Looks like you've been busy," said Ellie.

"Actually, I did get a lot done. I put away the camping gear and tinkered with the farm truck. I think its roadworthy now. Then I came across the mower and decided to get the grass cut. Makes the yard look bigger somehow. I even moved the outhouse behind the machine shed. Allows for more privacy."

"Looks nice! Anyway, I brought you something." She held out the apple pie. "I've just come from spending an awesome day with my aunt Ruth. We made pies together and she sent this one home with me. And it may sound weird to you, but as I was driving home I got a very strong impression that Jesus wanted me to give you half of this pie."

"You're right, that is weird." He cocked an eyebrow, looking sceptical. "Besides hearing supernatural voices, how do you know you're supposed to give it to me?"

"Because I really wanted the whole thing for myself. I also tried to think of someone other than you with whom to share it. Couldn't come up with a single name."

"And why would God... uhhh, Jesus... want me to have some of this apple pie?"

She shrugged her shoulders. "Because He wants you to know that He notices you and loves you and wants you to be blessed, even in a little matter like pie."

"I'm sure I've never told you, but apple pie is my most favourite dessert," said Hugh, somewhat awed by the apparent coincidence.

"You're right, I didn't know. But Jesus did. You have Him to thank more than me. So let's take it inside and divvy it up."

Eighteen

ON WEDNESDAY, ELLIE dressed again in work clothes. After dividing up the pie the previous evening, Hugh had pressed her to hurry up and comb through the farmhouse like she had suggested. He planned to burn it.

The truth was, she *was* keen to look through the old place. Knowing what little history she did, it seemed to her that a closer inspection could yield more insight into how the Fischers had lived. She wasn't sure why she was so interested when Hugh wasn't. It wasn't her history to care about.

Nonetheless, Ellie was truly fascinated by the mystery surrounding his parents' sad, irregular lives, and even the lives of his grandparents before them, though he had apparently never met them.

She understood, at least to some extent, Hugh's disinterest. The house represented a great deal of pain and shame. By suppressing all that former misery, he could keep his emotions in check. Buried, in fact. Yet she believed the day would come when he would regret not having some mementos associated with his forbearers, at least his mother. That's why she felt such a strong responsibility to do for him what he could not yet do for himself.

Besides, it really would be fun to explore the old house—or snoop around, as Hugh would have said.

For this job, Ellie chose to bring close-fitting garden gloves and a flashlight with a strong beam, just in case she came across any dark spaces beneath floorboards or behind walls. And if she needed any other tools, she felt confident she'd find them in Hugh's collection.

Thus outfitted, Ellie climbed onto her bike and rode to Hugh's place.

She found him sitting outside the cabin on his only lawn chair, nursing a mug of black coffee. The door was wide open and the radio blared a weather forecast on his favourite country music station.

Ellie parked her bike along the side of the cabin with a bit of a bang.

"Hey, hey! Watch it, lady. Don't scratch my new house," teased Hugh.

"Phffff." Ellie grunted and rolled her eyes. "Are we working together or am I the only detective on this assignment?"

"I thought you should have this bit of fun all to yourself. I've got my eye on tearing down that old chicken coop over there."

Ellie followed his gaze to a small, partially fallen structure south of the house.

"Be sure to check for liquid gold or a treasure chest while you're at it," said Ellie. It was an oblique reference to the assertions Tipper had made several days earlier.

"Yes'm, boss-lady!" returned Hugh, shaking his head in mild annoyance.

Ellie snorted a second time.

Taking only a crowbar along with her flashlight, she walked into the house and began her search in the lean-to off the kitchen. The pitcher pump to the cistern remained, as Hugh still drew water from it. There was nothing suspicious to explore, but it was the first time she had noticed the separation of the lean-to from the house. A crack along the ceiling exposed the outdoors.

Next she explored the kitchen, which also yielded nothing.

She chose to leave the cellar for last. Although the water had been drained, it was still very damp and reeked of must.

The sitting area, or living room, was where Ellie went next. Hugh had, at her request, systematically removed the windows, which now allowed birds to fly in and out. A family of barn swallows was building a nest in one of the corners in the living room.

That's a mistake, birdies, warned Ellie. *You're fixing to go down with this ship...*

The flies, too, were ubiquitous. But she could find nothing suspicious.

Upstairs, she combed the girls room hoping that either Margo or Diane had stuffed notes from their school days into various crevices. There was no evidence of this.

The extra small spaces which had served as a sewing room and Hugh's bedroom respectively yielded no surprises, nor did the large closet, to the disappointment of Ellie's romantic notions.

She had high hopes for the bedroom used by Hugh's parents, but nada; it didn't have so much as a loose floorboard.

"Well, I'm disappointed in you, Alice Fischer," spoke Ellie aloud. "I thought you might have squirreled away coins or small bills to one day make a great escape. Obviously not. Not even a secret diary."

A bird flew overhead, causing Ellie to look up. There, in the middle of the hallway, was the access hatch to the attic. She would need a ladder to get to it, however.

Ellie bounded down the creaking stairs and strode over to Hugh, who was heaping the rotten boards of the chicken coop into a somewhat compact heap. The chicken wire fencing that had once upon a time contained the hens had been dismantled, tidily rolled up, and set aside.

"Find anything interesting?" asked Hugh without stopping his work.

"Not yet. I need a long enough ladder to get into the attic. Do you have one?"

Hugh thought for a moment, then nodded. "Yeah, there are a couple in the barn."

He went there with Ellie following and soon found what she asked for. Hugh went into the house with her carrying a ten-foot wooden ladder, climbed the sitars, and set up the ladder through the attic hatch.

"You or me?" asked Ellie.

"This is your party, not mine. I'll hold the ladder steady while you look."

Ellie climbed up and shone her flashlight in a full circle. Suddenly, she let out a gasp.

"Eureka! I see something. But it's beyond my reach." She backed down the ladder. "There's a suitcase up there, or maybe a metal box. See if you can get it."

Hugh went up as soon as Ellie stepped aside. His eyes had to adjust to the darkness before he saw the item Ellie had seen. Taking another step up, he was able to reach out and nudge the box-like object closer. He then gingerly withdrew it from the attic and passed it to Ellie so he could descend the ladder safely.

It was about the size of a suitcase, and all metal, like a small traveling trunk. It was rusting in places but overall remained a sturdy container. The ends bore leather handles while the opening side had two latches on either end of the central lock. Without a key, of course, they would have to pick the lock to see what was inside.

Ellie was giddy with excitement over this discovery while Hugh remained as nonchalant as ever.

They carried the ladder and the metal suitcase out of the house and laid them on the grass.

"Do you know how to pick locks?" asked Ellie.

"Not really, but I can try." Hugh tried a number of small metal objects, angling them into the old-fashioned lock to release it.

After several minutes, he finally succeeded. Ellie held her breath while Hugh lifted the lid.

Inside they discovered a man's suit. No; it was a uniform... a soldier's uniform made of coarse wool in army green. The edges of the collar, jacket, and sleeves were finished in red piping. At least ten silver-coated buttons from throat to hem fastened the front panels together. They also found a helmet with a spike standing up from its centre.

Hugh lifted the jacket. Underneath lay the matching pants and a white undershirt. Below it were leather straps designed to carry miscellaneous items on one's back, as well as pouches in front of the chest.

The next layer was a pair of polished black boots, high enough to reach one's knee, and beneath the boots lay a long object wrapped in cloth. Hugh removed the wrappings to reveal the blade of a bayonet. It gleamed in the sunshine and caused chills to run up and down Ellie's spine. Hugh felt the edge with his thumb and found it still razor sharp.

At the bottom of the box lay a few papers. Hugh lifted these carefully, as the sheets were old and yellowed. The writing was clear, but not in English. Ellie recognized it as cursive German.

"That must be the owner's name, up there." She pointed to a line near the top of the paper. "Helmut Rudolf Fischer. And look at the date: 1916. Oh my gosh, Hugh, this is a German uniform from World War I. That war began in 1914 and didn't end until 1918. Maybe this Helmut guy was conscripted in 1916."

Another paper carried a date of February 11, 1898. His birthdate, perhaps?

A photo fell out from between the sheets in Hugh's hands. It showed a soldier in full uniform, by all accounts the same one Hugh had unpacked from the metal suitcase. The man stood tall and proud with his bayonet in hand.

"I'm guessing we're looking at your granddad as a young man," said Ellie unnecessarily.

Hugh nodded. "What's wrong with this picture?"

"Well, he was a soldier fighting with the German army..." She caught the significance. "Which means he was on the side of the enemy, not the Allies."

Ellie and Hugh looked at each other, their faces inches apart.

"That would constitute a secret, wouldn't it," Hugh said. It was a statement, not a question.

"At least socially. I can't imagine this information would go well with our predominately conservative neighbourhood," said Ellie. "It's hard to imagine that Canada's Department of Immigration would admit an enemy when he came to Canada... unless he used a false name. Do you see any immigration papers in there?"

Hugh leafed through the thin stack. No immigration papers were included.

"If he used a false name, that would be two secrets... of the kind that would make you want to look over your shoulder every day of your life," said Hugh, thinking hard. "I've just made up my mind to take up Aunt Gertie's offer. I'm going to ask her to inquire about anyone who knew my pa and his family. I didn't think I was interested in the history of the Fischers. Now I am."

Ellie furrowed her eyebrows. "But surely this isn't one of Tipper's secrets, do you think?"

"I greatly doubt it." Hugh repacked the uniform in the same order he'd found it. The one difference was that he placed the aged paperwork on top where it could be readily accessed. "I'd be surprised if he even knew my grandad. But you never know. I think Tipper only has a thirst for alcohol, and the past glory of belonging to a country gang of no-gooders. That's the way I read him."

Ellie nodded. It seemed like an accurate assessment.

After the small trunk was repacked, Hugh carried it into the cabin and stowed it under his bed. When he came back out, he said to Ellie, "Say it. I know you want to."

"Whatever do you mean?" asked Ellie with feigned innocence.

"You want to rub it in. The fact that this rather amazing discovery would have been totally destroyed, all that interesting information lost forever, if you hadn't insisted on searching the house. So go ahead and say it. 'I told you so...'"

"I don't have to. You just did." Ellie smirked. "And I'm not quite done yet. There's still the cellar to explore. I'd really like you to be part of that, because it's so wet and slippery down there. It's also nearly pitch-black. Creeps me out."

"Is Ell-dorado admitting she's afraid of the dark?" teased Hugh.

"I'm admitting that Ell-dorado is afraid of *that* dark space, and Hugh-berdasher should make like a knight in shining armour and assist the poor maiden!"

"You crack me up."

Hugh laughed as he followed Ellie back into the farmhouse. They paused before the doorless entrance to the cellar. It *was* pitch-black and creepy. Hugh had no desire to descend the steep, water-soaked wooden steps to look around at things he didn't give a hoot about, but his manliness had somehow been cleverly challenged. Thus, he felt he must rise to the occasion.

"I'll need your flashlight," he said, taking the device from Ellie. He shone it around the dark from the top of the stairs. The light didn't reveal anything untoward or frightening, only a couple of shallow puddles on the muddy dirt floor.

Reassured, Hugh descended the steps backwards, and Ellie followed close behind in the same manner. Upon reaching the final step, Hugh's feet went right through the wood as if it were sponge. The unexpected falter caused him to lurch, which then caused Ellie to slip. Unable to keep his footing steady, he plummeted with a yell onto the oozy mud floor. Ellie landed on top of him, adding a shriek of her own.

"Well, that's just great," grumbled Hugh darkly. "There can't be anything down here worth this much trouble."

Ellie tried to get up with some dignity. "I'm fine, thanks for asking."

The flashlight was lying on its side on the still-wet floor, shedding no light at all on their situation. To turn over so she could establish her feet beneath her, Ellie dug her elbow into Hugh's gut.

"Oww!" he yelped, pushing her off him into a miry puddle.

"Sorry, sorry."

She grasped the flashlight and shone it over Hugh, who still sat on the mud floor. Although his expression was all glare, Ellie began to giggle.

"I'm sure this is *not* funny."

"Oh, but it is," said Ellie, continuing to laugh. "You should look at yourself, Hugh-beas corpus."

Hugh tried to hold on to his frustration but couldn't. Ellie's giggles were contagious, and pretty soon the corners of his mouth were twitching.

He began to chuckle. "You're quite the sight yourself."

Ellie managed to get to her feet by holding on to the stringer of the sodden treads. She held out a hand to help Hugh get up as well. Him being heavier, they almost fell again, but he managed to right himself, all muddied notwithstanding.

The cellar ceiling was so low that neither of them could stand upright. They maintained a hunched posture as they scanned the three irregular walls. The fourth wall represented one of the walls of the cistern.

"Stop," said Ellie. "Shine your light back there again."

He aimed the beam of light between the treads to the region just behind them. "Well, I'll be…"

Hugh swore under his breath.

"Bingo," echoed Ellie softly.

Altogether, Hugh handed forty-nine unlabelled bottles of moonshine whiskey up the stairs where Ellie received them and placed them in four cardboard boxes of a dozen each. The last one stood alone on the floor.

Then they traded places while Ellie retrieved the articles she wanted for salvage and Hugh set them aside for her to relocate later. She sent up assorted small crocks, empty glass jars as well as some with home-canned food, and a couple of old-fashioned kerosene lamps. She also found some collectable tins still in good shape having been stowed on the topmost shelf.

As usual, Hugh complained endlessly about her penchant for hoarding junk, but Ellie had become used to his drivel on the subject and ignored him completely.

Before leaving the cellar forever, Ellie used the flashlight to scrutinize every hole and crevice to make sure no valuables were unknowingly left behind. If there was a treasure to be found, she meant to find it—no stone unturned, no corner unexamined, no container unopened. For Hugh's sake, of course.

Outside, Hugh loaded the forty-eight bottles of firewater into the cab of his truck. Meanwhile Ellie transferred her salvaged items and stowed them in the barn along with the other housewares they had taken out of the house.

She watched Hugh pick up the one lone remaining bottle of moonshine, contemplating it. Suddenly he gripped the cork tightly and twisted it until it popped out. As if daring himself, he swallowed a mouthful. Immediately he began to cough and sputter, tears streaming down his face. He danced around like a flopping fish out of water and thought he might be dying. Wide-eyed, Ellie thought he could be dying too, but didn't know how to help.

Eventually he seemed to recover from the shock, at least well enough to speak again.

"That stuff... is pure evil... in a bottle," he said, alternating choking and panting.

"You'll throw it out then?"

"Heck no!" snapped Hugh. "I'm gonna make a label for it with a picture of a skull and crossbones and the words *rubbing alcohol*. If I ever get hurt and need to clean a wound, I'll use this for disinfectant. No germ would survive once doused with this hooch!"

Nineteen

AFTER ELLIE HAD taken the latest salvage from the house to the barn, and after Hugh had burned the pile of rotten wood that had once been the chicken coop, she made an offhand remark.

"You should deliver the whiskey as well as the still to Tipper and let him deal with its disposal. After all, he was in cahoots with your dad."

Hugh thought about it for a moment and decided that it was a good idea. He got into his pickup and drove along the space between the bush and the wheat field until he judged he was near the location of the old shack. Ellie came along and helped him transfer the large copper pots and related apparatus to the back of his truck.

However, as they slowly drove back to the main yard, Ellie began to have misgivings. "I'm not so sure anymore that this is a good idea…"

"Really? Why not?"

"I just feel you… we… would be contributing to someone's alcoholism. I feel like we're somehow being irresponsible by supplying Tipper with the means that could kill him, or at least keep him really sick…" She trailed off in thought. "I wonder what his real name is…"

"Don't know. Don't care." Hugh suddenly sounded annoyed. "And no, I don't feel one ounce of responsibility for him being an alcoholic. Turning over the moonshine, which he clearly insists is his due, doesn't make me an accessory to his addiction."

"I'm not so sure…"

"Look. All I'm doing is completing a transaction this Tipper guy made with Pa years ago. I wasn't involved in any part of that shady business. The only reason I'm involved now is that he threatened me!"

"I'm not sure I see it that way. Even participating in this small way could be immoral…"

"Being the delivery boy doesn't make me responsible for his addiction and ill health," he insisted crossly. "The post office delivers millions of parcels every year, some of which must contain illegal substances. Does that make the post office culpable?"

"I'll wager that if they were aware they were handling bomb parts, for example, they would at least turn them over to the police."

"I don't know how they go about screening packages," he said. "But they're in the business of getting things from here to there, not concerning themselves with policing people or governing their customers' morality. It's as simple as that. And as far as I know, it's not illegal to have homemade whiskey. It's only illegal to sell it. And the reason it's illegal to sell it is because the government is greedy about the taxes they would lose from their own liquor sales. So there."

Ellie still had doubts, but she didn't say anything more.

Even so, Hugh could tell he hadn't convinced her. "Ellie, you're killin' me. I thought you were on my side. Why can't I get Tipper and his cronies out of my hair? This is what we have to do. If I destroy the moonshine instead of turning it over to him, he'll still be an alcoholic… and he'll still pester me for Pa's cash. My 'good morals,' as you put it, will have achieved nothing."

Ellie sighed. "I suppose you're right."

Relieved, Hugh moved on. He wanted help with his plan to deliver the hooch to Tipper the following day. If she came along, there would at least be a witness. That way, Tipper couldn't later claim that he hadn't gotten his order.

Ellie nodded and consented to come along, surprising Hugh given their recent war of words, but he didn't push it. Maybe he'd finally gotten something through her thick skull…

That evening, Ellie recorded the amazing developments of the day in one of her journals. She also used her black pen to write out a question to the Lord: *What do You think about me and Hugh turning over a stash of high-proof alcohol over to the likes of Tipper?* She prayed for insight and stilled her heart to listen.

After a while, she began to write out the thoughts that came to her. The Bible discussed situations in which no amount of urging, exhorting, challenging, threatening, or prodding could convince a person to stop sinning. In such cases, God had *"given them over to corrupted minds, so that they do the things that they should not do."*[5] This meant that they were allowed to experience the full consequences of their stubborn desires.

It helped Ellie to see that very likely Hugh was right. Tipper was committed to his own destruction via alcohol, and that commitment in no way reflected on Hugh or herself.

That wasn't the only insight Ellie received. The seed of another idea came to mind, and it began to grow the longer she thought about it.

"Yes, Lord," she said aloud. "I'll get right on that tomorrow morning."

By mid-morning the next day, Ellie was waiting impatiently for Hugh to pick her up. She had gotten a few things ready to bring along. The first was a folder with three new ideas for Hugh to consider for the farm. She would also pass along the magazine she'd bought with all the house plans. Additionally, she had prepared a substantial lunch packed in a brown paper bag.

And of course she also had her handbag.

---

[5] Romans 1:28, GNB.

At last Ellie saw Hugh coming up the driveway. She stepped outside and walked out to meet him.

Hugh seemed surprised to see her climb aboard with so much paraphernalia, but he chose not to say anything about it just then.

"Do you remember the directions to get to Tipper's place?" he asked instead.

"Yes, I think so. We're supposed to go through Minitonas to the south side, then take the first road east. Look for a yard that looks similar to yours. Assuming he's home, though, I think he may be shocked to see us."

"Could be. I just want to get this business over with." It had an air of finality.

They drove along in amicable silence while listening to country tunes on the radio, and before long they had passed through town and took the first road heading east. They immediately found themselves in farm country with very few residences to be seen.

They soon approached a stand of trees on the left which looked to have a bit of driveway winding through it. Hugh steered his truck in that direction, and a few yards in Ellie pointed to a sign, pinned to a tree: *KEEP OUT.*

"I bet this is the place," she said.

Suddenly they came into a clearing which revealed a very old square bungalow. Its roof was pointed in the centre and sloped down on all four sides. It was all-weather grey, similar to the old Fischer house, yet there were a few patches, such as right under the eaves, that suggested it was once painted pink. The remnants of a garage, leaning precariously, faced south; it didn't have a door, leaving the contents—a horde of broken, rusted junk—exposed to the elements. There was no evidence of a vehicle, not even a relic from times past.

The centre of the yard was covered in gravel, but weeds and grass were taking over. No attempt had been made to keep the green growth mowed.

Across the clearing from the house were a couple of tumble-down granaries of the same sort Hugh had recently torn down at his own place. Surrounding the small yard was a thick belt of mature trees that provided complete privacy.

Hugh drove up to the time-worn residence and pressed out a short toot of the truck's horn. Right away, the front door opened. Tipper stood there, unsmiling and glaring as he sought to know who had violated his privacy.

Even when Hugh stepped out of his truck, Tipper continued to glower in silence.

"It's your lucky day, old man," said Hugh. "I found what you wanted and brought it over, special delivery."

He began to slide the boxes of unlabelled whiskey out of the truck. He set the first box on the ground near the door to Tipper's house; the bottles tinkled a little in the process.

As Hugh then turned to get another, Tipper looked closely at the bottles and finally realized what they were.

"Weeell, looky here," he said, exchanging his nasty expression for a grin. "I told ya it was there somewhere, didn't I?"

He pulled one of the bottles out of the box to examine it more closely.

Hugh set down the second box beside the first. Ellie brought a third box, and Hugh then dropped the last twelve bottles in place.

He rested his hands on his hips. "I brought you something else too. One of your 'secrets,' I think. I don't want anything to do with it."

Tipper looked at him, puzzled.

"I found the still, hidden way back in the bush at our place. I'm giving it to you. If you don't want to use it yourself, I'm sure you'll know somebody you can sell it to."

With that, Hugh turned on his heel and walked to the back of his truck. Together, he and Ellie lifted the green-tarnished copper contraption out and carried it onto the grass. Next to it they deposited boxes of hoses and a mix of sundry parts.

"Okay, that's everything," Hugh said, keeping his eye on Ellie as she strolled nearby, trying to see what she could learn about Tipper apart from his interest in alcoholic beverages. "Now, I want to hear you say that your deal with my pa is complete, and that I don't owe you anything. Then we'll shake hands on it."

"Weeell now, I dunno," Tipper replied, stalling. "How do I know it's what I paid for? Mebbe it's just water in them bottles."

"Open one and taste it. If that doesn't burn your insides out, nothing will."

Tipper pulled at the cork of the bottle in his hand until it popped out. He knocked back a mouthful. Whereas Hugh had flopped around from the shock to his system, Tipper stood like a statue. His mouth hung open as if he couldn't get his breath.

Then he shuddered all over. "Oh yesss, that's the good stuff," he gasped.

"Tipper, I see you have a bit of a garden here," said Ellie.

Tipper looked at her quizzically. "Yah, I got me some taters and other roots. Why?"

"Nothing. I'm just a little surprised you're interested in gardening. Have you always lived here? I mean, is this your childhood home?"

Both Hugh and Tipper looked at her with furrowed brows.

Ellie ignored their puzzled looks and asked something else. "What's your real name? The one your mother gave you?"

"By golly, that was a helluva long time ago…"

"I brought you something." Ellie returned to the passenger side of Hugh's truck and pulled out her paper sack. She carried it over to where Tipper stood. "When you were out at Hugh's farm a few days ago, I got the impression you might be hungry for real food. Woman-cooked food. So I brought you some."

Tipper took the bag from her cautiously, then peeked inside. The topmost item was a sandwich, surrounded with wax paper. And there was more where that came from. His eyes opened wide at the sight of the generous filling of sliced meat, tomato, lettuce, and cheese between slices of rye bread.

His mouth quivered with desire to eat, but he looked up at Ellie first with a question in his eyes.

"Go ahead. It's all yours," said Ellie encouragingly.

"What is it ya want, lady?"

"I really do want you to have some good food to eat. You don't look very healthy to me. I'm a nurse. I notice these things. Besides that, I'm hoping you can answer some questions about the past, you being quite a bit older and all." She looked around for something they could use for seating. She couldn't spot anything suitable. "Do you have any chairs?"

Tipper handed her the sandwich along with the brown bag, recorked the whiskey bottle, and set it back in the box. He disappeared into his ramshackle house.

"Ellie, what the heck are you up to now?" asked Hugh in a loud whisper.

"I'm hoping he can give us some answers," she whispered back. "He's pretty old. He might know things about your grandad, amongst other things."

"I have no idea why you care." Hugh shook his head. "I'm pretty sure I don't want to be part of this."

As though in protest, he went back to his truck and leaned against it, arms folded across his chest.

Tipper emerged with two well-worn wooden chairs and set them down in the tall grass. Ellie adjusted hers so she sat across from him and returned his sandwich. Tipper gulped it down hungrily.

"So what should I call you, not-Tipper? Mr. Smith? Mr. Jones?" asked Ellie, reaching into the sack to give him another sandwich.

"Da bloomin' guv'ment makes out my measly pension to Leonard Wallen." Tipper chuckled at his own cleverness. "Back when I was a lad, my ma called me Lenny."

"Awww. I bet you miss that."

Tipper shrugged, unwrapped the second sandwich, and chowed it down.

"Do you have family?"

"I had an older brother. He did the farmin'. He's gone now. Quite a while ago."

"What did you do for a living then?"

"All kinds o' things. Whatever job I could find. I helped the farmers puttin' in crops or harvestin' it off. Done a bit o' truck driving. Got onto a crew once for paintin' someone's big barn. Odd jobs here and there."

"If you've lived in this area all your life, you must know a lot of people."

Tipper, a.k.a. Leonard, shrugged. "Mebbe yes, mebbe no," he said, eyeing Ellie's brown paper sack once more. No doubt he was wondering what else it contained.

"Hugh told me the other day he had never met his grandpa. Did you know him, Mr. Wallen?"

"Who?"

Ellie reached into the paper sack and pulled out a muffin.

"Freddie's old man? Nah." He eagerly took the muffin. "I b'lieve he was outta the picture by the time I took up with Freddie."

"How did you and Freddie meet?"

"We was both regulars at the hotel bar."

"You know I was neighbours with him all my years of growing up and don't recall meeting him even once."

"Weeell, ya didn't miss much. He weren't the kind decent folks took to, and fer good reason. He weren't the kind a body could trust, ya know? The rest of us boys had to keep him in our sights all the time fer fear he'd rip us off." Tipper ended his answer with a chuckle.

"Well, someone tried to trust him. After all, he got married."

Tipper snickered. "That was another thing we never did figure, is why he done that. Sure didn't stop him from messin' around with other women any time he got a chance."

Ellie sighed. Was she never going to hear even one redeeming thing about Frederick Fischer? It wasn't possible for a human being to become so utterly incorrigible, was it?

She looked over to where Hugh stood leaning against his truck and saw the look of impatience in his face. Clearly he wanted to get going.

Turning back to Tipper, she said, "Just one more thing. You mentioned there were a lot of secrets at the Fischer farm. Could you tell me, please, how many secrets we're talking about? What kind of secrets?"

She reached into the brown bag, brought out a couple of home-made chocolate chip cookies, and handed them over.

He grasped them gladly and took a bite of one before answering. "I don't rightly know. The auld bugger was a bag of secrets. He prob'ly took most of them to his grave and that's just as well." He took another bite. "Ya found the still and the moonshine. Where was it, by the way?"

"Underground," answered Ellie ambiguously.

"Weeell, somewhere, sometime ya should find his moonshine cash. He didn't trust the banks with any o' that. Couldn't risk anybody asking questions, ya know. Always had to be cash." He polished off the first cookie. "I only knows about another secret, and it's a big one. But I can't talk about it 'cuz it would mean lotsa trouble. It's best that one stay hidden."

"Please tell us... I don't want Hugh to get into trouble for something he had nothing to do with."

"Nope! Anyways, I b'lieve Freddie took care of it good. Shouldn't be a problem for his boy."

Hugh waved to get Ellie's attention and then pointed to his watch.

Ellie nodded. "I have to go now. Thanks a lot for helping me understand things better, Mr. Wallen. Here, you keep the rest of this lunch."

She handed over the brown paper bag as they walked over to where Hugh stood next to his truck.

"Our business with each other is done now, right?" asked Hugh.

Tipper nodded and put out his grubby hand. Hugh grasped it.

After that, Ellie took Tipper's hand to shake it as well. She wanted him to understand that he was confirming the conclusion of their business with her too.

~

It only took a minute or two to drive back to Minitonas, where Hugh stopped at the post office to pick up mail. There was nothing of interest in the Bauman mailbox, but Hugh had received a reply regarding the well water sample he'd had sent off for testing. The news was relatively good; if the water was treated properly with chlorine, it would be suitable for human consumption. The envelope included pamphlets and instructions. He and Ellie high-fived each other.

"I need to go into Swan for a bit, but I don't mind taking you home first if you like," offered Hugh as he backed out of his parking space. "I want to stop in and talk to my aunt."

"I have nothing pressing to do and would be delighted to see Gertie again. That is, if it isn't interfering..."

"Nah. There's nothing I want to discuss with my aunt that you don't already know about."

"Then I'm in."

Nothing was said between them until they reached Highway 10 north of town and turned left.

"So... are you going to tell me what you and old man Tipper were talking about?" Hugh finally ventured. "I overheard a bit here and there, but not much. And why did you bring him all that food?"

"I judge he's around seventy and knows a lot about the people who used to live around here," she said. "Been around long enough to know the answers to many of questions that have arisen lately. And as for the food? Well, it met an obvious need. It was disarming too. My mom claimed many times that the way to a man's heart is through his stomach. She also said, of course, that you catch more flies with honey than with vinegar."

"And did you learn anything interesting?"

"I did..."

She proceeded to fill him in on all the details of their discussion. As she spoke, he kept his thoughts to himself.

"Thanks Ellie," he said finally. "You're a lot better with people than I am. I guess I'm more like vinegar than honey. I'm surprised you still hang out with me."

"Well, I should tell you that I think you handled Tipper—er, Mr. Wallen—pretty well. Man to man, you had to be very firm or he wouldn't have respected you and probably would have tried to take advantage. He might even have resorted to blackmail. Who knows? But you handled him with authority. You did good."

"It's not often I've been told that," said Hugh with genuine appreciation. "But tell me honestly: why are you so interested in my family's history? When most folks get a whiff of how disgusting and poor and different we were, they hightail it and run. You're not running. You're leaning in. I don't get it."

"I can think of a couple of reasons. One is, I'm genuinely curious about this mystery surrounding your grandparents. Whatever happened in that family led to the kind of man your pa became. What went into creating a hard, abusive man like Freddie Fischer? I believe that if we live with constant criticism, we learn to be critical. If we live with violence, we learn to be violent. If we live with love and kindness… well, you get the picture. My upbringing couldn't have been more different than yours. When you told me what it was like growing up in your family, you could have knocked me over with a feather. I was that shocked. I don't have any personal experience with that kind of abuse."

Hugh tapped the steering wheel wistfully. "When I was with your family for dinner last Sunday, that was the first time I saw with my own eyes what it's like for parents and kids to be so easy and funny and loving with each other. I felt like a kid looking through the window into another world, longing to be part of it."

"Hmm. I believe I can safely say that the Baumans have adopted you into the family," she said. "I have three older brothers. Having one more is fine with me. Even Rob's kids relate to you as an uncle of sorts. Obviously Beanie thinks you're wonderful, crawling onto your lap like she did. Little kids are a bit like dogs; they seem to innately sense who's good and safe and who isn't." She turned to him with a smile on her face. "Anyway, if you want to belong with a family, the Baumans will happily include you."

"Thanks. You guys have shown me lots of support and I sure didn't expect it."

They drove along quietly for the next several miles, each of them lost in their own thoughts.

"I don't see myself as being like my pa," said Hugh solemnly after a few minutes. "I'm doing everything I can to be as different from him as possible. I want the buck to stop with me."

"If only it worked that way," said Ellie ruefully. "Granted, you were miraculously dropped into the laps of the Turners once you ran away. That counts for a lot. But it doesn't cancel out the sixteen years of abuse Freddie poured into you. Like it or not, it's part of you. If you got married and after the honeymoon your wife did something to make you mad, I'd bet the whole farm that you would lash out at her the way your dad did to your mom. If you had little kids who didn't behave, you'd probably parent them the same way you were parented. We all have those default reactions, the ones we ourselves have learned through experience. Patterns are passed down from one generation to the next."

Hugh slumped, his hands gripping the steering wheel so hard that his knuckles turned white. "I feel like you've just handed me a death sentence."

"That is absolutely *not* my intention," said Ellie as seriously yet kindly as she knew how. "It's another angle to what we were talking about a week ago, another way of showing how every single member of the human race is born broken and needs Dr. God to put them back together. If anyone goes to Him and admits they're broken and sinful, which is kind of the same thing, He cleanses and restores them to wholeness through His Spirit. And only then do we bust free of our slavery—and yes, it *is* slavery—to those generational patterns."

He nodded along, thinking back to the picture she'd drawn. The one he had tacked to the wall next to his bed.

"I have been thinking about it," he assured her. "Every night before I fall into my bed, in fact. I've even prayed to your God. I said, 'God, if You're as real as Ellie says You are, then do something to prove it to me—personally. Do something that's tailored to me alone so I can't explain it any other way. Then I'll be convinced forever.'" He paused, looking out at the fields as they whirred past. "I'm still waiting."

After that, Ellie didn't know what to say.

"I wasn't going to tell you that," said Hugh after a while.

"Well, I'm glad you told me. And I'm awfully interested in what God's going to do in answer to your prayer. I expect you to tell me as soon as you get your proof."

That conversation had taken them all the way into Swan River, which had just appeared over the horizon. In moments, they were headed up Sixth Avenue North and parking in front of Gertie's house.

Twenty

ELLIE AND HUGH were hardly out of the truck when Gertie came flying out of the house.

"How nice of you to come and see us," she gushed as she flung her arms around Hugh's neck. She welcomed Ellie with a big smile but stopped short of hugging her. "We're still having lunch, but you can join us. Come right inside."

"Oops," said Ellie, somewhat embarrassed. "We had a busy morning and got to talking so earnestly that neither of us checked the time."

"She's right," Hugh said. "We can come back later."

"No way! What kind of aunt would I be if I didn't feed my nephew once in a while?" Gertie smiled, then added, "And his friend."

She ushered them to the kitchen table where Hugh's Uncle Ed was already seated and eating his noon meal.

"Well, I know who this handsome young man is. But who is the pretty young lady?" Ed rose and extended a large, plump hand toward her.

"This is my neighbour and friend, Ellie Bauman. Ellie, this is my uncle, Ed Johnson."

Everyone sat down.

"We're having a make-your-own-sandwich lunch," said Gertie. "Take some of that bread from the basket and fill it with whatever you like."

The table was laid out with multiple selections of sliced meats, cheeses, lettuce, and more.

"I've heard all about your summer cabin," said Ed. "How do you like living in it compared to the tent?"

"It's going great, Uncle Ed," answered Hugh. "I'm set up to sleep well, eat well, and cook well. I have all the comforts of home, except for running water, but I'm fine with carrying it the old-fashioned way. Of course, I'll have to come up with a winter-proof solution by fall. For now, it's terrific!"

Ed got busy fixing himself a second sandwich. "Glad to hear that. Someday we'll come by so I can see what you've got going there."

"There's not much to see yet," said Hugh. "I've been tearing down the old buildings. All the smallest ones are gone. I'm demolishing the old house now. By this time next week, it'll hopefully be reduced to a pile of ash."

"Seems right ambitious of you since you haven't been here that long," noted Ed.

"Yeah, well, I'm not going to lie—it's kind of therapeutic. It's not possible to replace the old buildings fast enough. I need new buildings to start a new life."

Gertie and Ellie exchanged glances.

"More power to you," said Ed, seeming to understand. "If you'll all excuse me, though, I need to get back to the office. Good to see you, Hugh. And you too, Ellie."

He nodded to the women, then set a hat on his balding head and walked out the back door.

After a moment, Gertie asked, "What brought you to Swan River this time?"

"A couple of things," Hugh said. "Taking you up on an offer was one of them."

"Which one would that be?

"Arranging a visit with any seniors who might have known my grandparents on the Fischer side."

"Aha! I knew your curiosity would sooner or later get the best of you," said Gertie with a smile. "After our big talk, my curiosity was raised too. I asked some of the older people I know and eventually learned that Leah and Dan Bredin knew them a little—and some friends of their in Minitonas knew them much better. When are you available, Hugh? I'll call Leah and make a date."

Hugh looked at Ellie, who shrugged her shoulders. "Any time is good, aunty. I don't have any commitments on the calendar."

"Yes, you do. When you flip the page to July in a few days, you'll see you and your sisters booked for a six o'clock supper here and a big announcement. That's Saturday, July 19. You do *not* want to miss that, Hugh. And no disrespect to you, Ellie, but just keep in mind that this will be a family-only dinner."

Ellie nodded heartily. "Absolutely!"

"Right then. I'll call the Bredins and see when they're available."

The women collaborated on the task of putting away the leftovers from lunch. Hugh and Ellie then waited in the living room while Gertie phoned the Bredins.

After a brief conversation, she hung up and waited a few moments. Less than ten minutes later, the phone rang again.

"All right then," Gertie announced, coming into the living room. "It's too short notice to get together today, but tomorrow evening is good for both couples. So I propose you come for supper and they can join us for dessert at seven o'clock. What do you say?"

"Sounds great," Hugh said. "But I'd like to bring Ellie too, if I may."

"Are you sure? The information could be sensitive..."

"She knows as much about me and the family as you do, aunty. I told her the whole sad story myself."

Gertie looked surprised for a moment, but then she just smiled. "I'm thinking you two spend so much time together that you're beginning to look alike!"

"Wait. No, aunty. It's not like that..." Hugh began to blush.

"Never mind. Just kidding!"

Ellie changed the subject promptly. "The reason I came along today was to look at the fabrics you washed, ironed, and took apart to be cut up and sewn into quilts. I didn't come to infringe on family matters."

"That's right. I forgot about that. They're downstairs. We can look at them now, if you'd like."

Hugh stood up. "If you ladies are going to talk about sewing, I'm going uptown to arrange to have a telephone installed at my place."

"Good idea!" chorused Gertie and Ellie at the same time.

The women inspected and discussed the organized piles of fabric.

"Now that we've separated the colours and prints that go together, I suppose you want me to start cutting them up," said Gertie hesitantly. "Let me remind you I have no previous experience in constructing quilts, even though I'm quite aware they're a popular craft at present."

"Like I said, I don't mind cutting up these groups into kits. There's a cutting wheel and mat in my mother's sewing cupboard. If you don't mind doing the sewing and quilting, I'll gladly look after this step."

"Phew! I appreciate that."

The fabrics were folded and placed into a large box, which was a bit heavy. When Hugh returned, he carried it easily and loaded it onto his truck.

"I'd like to contribute to tomorrow night's supper. I could bring a salad or perhaps a dessert. What would you prefer?" asked Ellie graciously.

"Oh that won't be necessary," Gertie protested, "I have everything we'll need."

"Honestly, I'd like to contribute."

"Well, if you really want to… how about a salad?"

"Perfect! Anything in particular?"

"Whatever's your favourite will be fine, dear,"

Hugh then asked, "What can I bring.?"

Aunt Gertie patted his arm. "You need only to bring your handsome self. I'll take care of the rest."

Hugh let it go, but on the drive home he said to Ellie, "I don't feel right about coming to dinner empty-handed. What do you suggest I bring?"

"A gift to the hostess is usually a bouquet of flowers, or a box of chocolates. Sometimes a bottle of wine is done as well," answered Ellie candidly. "Any of those would thrill her, I think. She's pretty taken with you."

After he dropped Ellie off at her house and carried the big box of cloths inside, he returned home. He turned off the ignition, then noticed the folder lying on the passenger seat beside him. Ellie had brought it with her that morning, but they hadn't taken the time to discuss the matter.

He took the folder into the cabin and leafed through the plans and drawings while sitting at the table. Ellie had written a letter of explanation regarding the three new drawings, so he had all the necessary information to understand them. Browsing the proposal gave him a break from all the hard physical labour he'd engaged in recently.

With country music playing in the background, he also looked carefully through the magazine, paying attention to the plans with the smallest square footage homes. In the end, he decided that none were better than what Ellie had come up with herself.

Ellie had sketched out three plans. He dismissed the smallest one pretty quickly. It was a tiny house that would have been no larger than a camper trailer.

The midsized plan would be adequate for one person, or perhaps a childless couple, and built on a slab or crawlspace foundation. It was attractive but simple, something he felt he could build for himself.

The largest one, on the other hand, was only slightly bigger than her midsized proposal, although it had more deluxe features, like a finished loft, attached garage, and full basement.

Yes, the midsized plan most appealed to him.

Feeling sure of his decision, he felt tired enough to go to bed early and fell asleep promptly.

Yet he didn't stay asleep. Somewhere in the third watch of the night, he awoke. Instead of falling right back to sleep, he gave in to deep and complicated thoughts. His mind dwelled on the small trunk under his bed, the one with the German military uniform. He also considered the secrets Tipper claimed were contained on his property. He thought about how much money he would need to spend on a house to adequately prepare for the winter. He wondered if he was really cut out to be a farmer, what with his lack of field experience.

All these worries and doubts gnawed at him and kept him awake until the sun shone brightly through the window. By then, sheer exhaustion caused him to drift off in spite of himself. He didn't wake again until nearly ten o'clock.

The first thing Ellie did when she got home was sit in the armchair where she did her soul work. She didn't read or write; she just sat and pondered while staring off into space. Honestly, she felt nettled by Gertie's remark that she and Hugh spent so much time together that they were beginning to look alike.

"Is that true, Lord?" she asked aloud.

After reviewing the events of the past two weeks, she was able to let the comment slide like water off a duck. Gertie Johnson really had no idea how much time they spent together or how they spent it. Their focus was almost entirely on work, and their few social interactions were carried out in friendship, nothing more.

Her thoughts turned to the fabrics in the box. She got up and sorted them into groups, setting aside a stack made up of all-blue prints, another that contained strong-coloured florals, and a third for assorted light pastels.

Before cutting the material, she brought out her graph paper and sketched three lap quilts, so called because they wouldn't be large enough to cover an adult-sized bed. One was to depict a log cabin with the blocks arranged in furrows; she thought the blue stack would be best for that. The second quilt would be fashioned from a combination of squares and triangles that looked like stars when assembled; for this pattern, the dark florals would show off well. For the pastels, she planned a nine-patch block with solid light squares between them.

The borders for all three quilts would be similar, with a white strip to surround the blocks like a frame, then another strip of assorted plaids, and a final white strip to encase it all. On paper, the quilts looked very attractive.

The evening was nigh and Ellie pushed herself to do what she did not feel like doing. The nine-patch pattern was the easiest to cut quickly and so she went for it, keenly aware of the dark cloud of depression once again poised just above her head. To help offset this mood, she played some gospel recordings. It helped, but only enough to keep her on task.

As she completed her cutting, she could no longer stop tears from spilling over onto her cheeks. She'd had enough.

Ellie lay down her cutting wheel, turned off the lights and stereo, and went to bed. Not for the first time, she cried herself to sleep, yet again grieving her losses. Mercifully, sleep covered her senses the entire night with no bad dreams or unnecessary awakenings.

$\sim$

She felt better when she awoke no longer crying. But the sadness remained, and it didn't help that the sun wasn't shining. The morning dawned grey, with the smell of rain in the air.

She followed through on her routine, making herself a mug of hot coffee and settling in the big armchair wrapped in a plush blanket. She was still reading through the Psalms, and this morning she focused entirely on one: Psalm 119. She read it over quietly. Every line reflected what she felt and what she wanted the Lord to do for her. Even though it was long, she read it a second time, this time aloud as a prayer from the depths of her heart.

In the larger journal, she wrote out the question she sensed the Lord asking: *What are you feeling? Why do you think you're feeling this way?* Then she poured out her heart, flooding the page with her grief.

Afterward she assigned herself a task in the little journal: *Write down words of worship to the Lord.* Her list was extensive:

- Holy, holy, holy.
- Lover of my soul.
- Friend and confidant.
- Worthy to be praised.
- Always good.
- All-powerful.
- Provider of all my needs.
- Healer of all my sorrows.
- Master of everything.
- Above all things.
- All-knowing.
- Nothing is too hard for Him.

It was a good exercise and it accomplished its purpose of lifting her spirits and helping her to trust the Lord despite feeling low.

When she returned to the kitchen, she saw that she had cut more cloth than she remembered. It didn't take much more time to complete the process of assembling two kits for Gertie.

Next she looked for and found shoeboxes her mother had saved, and placed the kits inside them, complete with the graph paper drawings and a few notes that demonstrated how the quilts were meant to be constructed.

Realizing that she was running out of time, she put away the blue fabrics to be tackled another day.

By the afternoon, the light rain had progressed into a steady downpour. The house became rather dark and cheerless. Putting on some worship music, Ellie switched on the ceiling lights to dispel the grey mood.

She decided to bring a Caesar salad to Gertie's dinner, since she had all the ingredients on hand. She made the dressing extra-garlicy and set it aside to be poured over the lettuce when she arrived.

There was now a mere hour to get ready before Hugh came by to pick her up. She got through her ablutions in good time and emerged wearing a denim skirt and multicoloured knit pullover. She fixed her hair in a tidy French roll, leaving a few tendrils to curl around her face. She kept the makeup light and subtle.

Right on time, Hugh pulled up to her house.

~

Upon arrival at Gertie and Ed's place, Hugh presented his aunt with a bouquet of pink carnations and baby's breath. She came close to crying, unable to remember the last time anyone had brought her flowers. At this, Uncle Ed looked a bit sheepish.

Ellie presented her with the two lap quilt kits. Gertie was amazed with the quickness of her efforts and looked forward to working on them in the days and weeks ahead.

The Caesar salad Ellie had brought turned out to go well with Gertie's supper of roast beef and mashed potatoes, drawing compliments for its piquant flavour.

The ladies had barely managed to tidy up the kitchen after the meal when the doorbell rang. Their guests had arrived.

The Bredins introduced their friends from Minitonas, Henry and Beatrice Klein. The introductions continued all around as each person got comfortable.

It was Henry who addressed Hugh first. "You must be Freddie Fischer's son. The resemblance is remarkable."

"So I've been told," said Hugh, hoping the resemblance ended there but stopped short of saying so.

"I'm so happy you all could come by this evening," Gertie said to the Bredins and Kleins. "We're hoping you can fill in some local history for us. My nephew Hugh has returned to our neck of the woods after living in Winnipeg the past fourteen years. He mentioned that he'd never met his Fischer grandparents, nor had he been told much about them. That's where the four of you come in."

There was a short pause during which the guests seemed to think hard without actually saying anything.

"As I recall, he and his wife got here as homesteaders before us," Henry began. He turned to his wife. "Wasn't it so, Bea?"

Beatrice nodded. "Someone introduced us to them because we spoke fluent German back in those days and they knew very little English. They were happy to have someone to talk with."

"What did they look like?" asked Ellie. "What were their names? Did they bring children?"

"Oh no," answered Beatrice, shedding any remaining reticence. "They were just a young couple, still in their twenties. They were real Germans, from Germany, come to make their fortune in a new country, like so many others at that time."

Henry inclined his head, apparently in agreement.

"They must have had quite a bit of money, because they were able to put up a much finer house than the rest of us." Beatrice was losing herself in the memory. "We started out in a two-room cabin built from trees we felled on our own land. That was typical of most homesteaders—that is, until we got our feet under us. They may have used the trees they had on their land too, but they must have had it sawn into lumber. Is that how you remember it. Henry?"

180

Beatrice looked at her husband directly, who nodded yet again.

"Mr. Fischer's name was Rudy, which I suppose was short for Rudolf," Leah remarked. "He was a little taller than average, as I recall, and always walked very straight and proper. Some people were put off by it. He often came across as arrogant."

Dan sighed. "That was probably because he had a pronounced limp. I believe it was due to some injuries he sustained in the Great War. You know, the war that was supposed to end all wars?"

"Did he ever talk about it? What regiment did he fight with?" asked Hugh with interest.

The four of them looked at each other as if uncertain.

"I don't know. I don't believe it ever came up," Henry replied. "None of the veterans who returned from that conflict wanted to talk about it. And you can't blame them. It was a terrible, terrible time."

Everyone one in the room collectively nodded.

"Mrs. Fischer's name was Huldah," said Leah, starting another track.

By this time, everyone was comfortable enough to share their memories, freely jumping in with their comments, which came one on top of the other.

About Mrs. Huldah Fischer, they recalled that she had been a tiny woman who'd worn her hair tight against her head with a braid that coiled into a bun at the nape of her neck. She'd had a small mouth, sharp nose, and eyes that seemed to be alert to everything. She had reminded people of a mouse, little but quick.

"I think she was unhappy from the moment she arrived to the day she left for good," said Leah thoughtfully.

"What makes you say that?" asked Gertie.

"She seemed to find homesteading so *hard*, as I recall," answered Leah.

That prompted a memory for Beatrice. "I think you're right, Leah. I remember an occasion when she was clearly homesick, which happened quite frequently, I might add. She said she had come from a large and wealthy German family that lived in a mansion of a house with servants. She was a city girl who, until emigrating to Canada, led an exciting social life. But she had no idea about how to perform the traditional women's role of looking after children, cooking, and maintaining a house. Neither did she like living in isolation. She missed the shops and theatres. And yet they'd come to Canada after getting married in search of the new promised land."

Leah jumped in. "I think the romantic adventure wore off really quick!"

"Oh yes," agreed Beatrice. "But she wasn't the only one. Those early days of homesteading were hard for everyone. Lots of roughing it. Lots of making do…"

"But you know, for all Huldah's inexperience, she rose to the occasion," credited Leah.

"She had to or they wouldn't have survived."

"She got to be a pretty good cook and became known for a few gourmet dishes, such as the heavy cake she drizzled with some alcoholic beverage or another." Leah smiled in remembrance. "And her famous rum-pot. Every summer, she collected a variety of fruits and diced them up to be steeped for weeks and months in sugar and rum. And not just a little; her cellar had a long row of rum-pot—rumtopf, Huldah called it—sousing in one-gallon crocks!"

Ellie and Hugh exchanged knowing glances; they had found a lot of crockery around the Fischer farm, and they'd taken many small ones out of the dirt cellar.

Changing the subject, Hugh asked, "What more can you tell me about my grandfather?"

"Oh, let's see… well, he became a decent farmer and had ambitions to add to his holdings, with a view to becoming a wealthy landowner," said Henry, nodding his head.

"That's about right," agreed Dan. "Though he fell short of his goal when he died young. Was purported to have been from a diseased liver."

"That's no surprise. The man drank like a fish," put in Henry wryly. "Although I doubt many people caught on. He held his liquor well."

Dan shrugged. "I believe he used alcohol to numb the chronic pain of his war-damaged leg and hip."

Hugh then asked, "Did Rudolf make his own whiskey?"

"Not that I know of," answered Henry frankly. "But wine, yes. Much of the fruit they grew went into making homemade wine. And, of course, the rum-pot…"

Ellie stepped in with a question of her own. "Did they go to church anywhere?"

The answer was a collective resounding "No!"

"Not that they weren't invited," said Beatrice. "Several invitations came their way from the neighbours. Minitonas offered numerous houses of God, as accorded one's preference. Rudolf seemed proud of the fact that he was an atheist. Huldah shared that sentiment."

"What about family?" Gertie asked.

Leah replied, "The Fischers had only two children. The eldest was a daughter, Renata. A couple years after she was born, they had a son. That would have been Frederick."

"That's right. I remember now. Renata was an easy first baby, but Frederick was colic. Huldah had a hard time with him," added Beatrice. Then a new revelation dawned on her. "You know, I wonder if it wasn't Freddie's own mother who inadvertently led him to develop a drinking problem."

Realizing what she had just said, she clamped her mouth shut and looked guiltily at Hugh.

"It's okay," he assured her. "I'm well acquainted with my father's shortcomings. Carry on."

Beatrice visibly relaxed. "It's just that she used the 'juice' from the rum-pot to quiet Frederick down, one teaspoon at a time. She did it to get him to sleep, especially when her frustrations with his colic reached their zenith. After that, she used it to soothe his gums when he teethed… and as a cough syrup whenever he came down with a cold or sore throat… or a headache… or a sleep aid…"

"You make it sound like Huldah was trying to turn Freddie in an alcoholic," Leah said, looking uncomfortable. "I'm sure she had no such intention. She was just trying to do her best with what she had."

Beatrice offered a shrug. "I'm sure you're right. But you know what they say—alcoholism starts with the first drink."

Leah grumbled a bit at this and Ellie squirmed, anxious to change the subject.

"Tell us more about Renata," Ellie broke in. "Hugh has never met his aunt."

Renata was described as a girl built with large bones, like her father, as opposed to her tiny, wiry mother. That said, she had resembled her mother more in facial features. At school, she could be argumentative with the teacher and bossy with the other children. She had been good friends with one of the Lindberg girls too, which is how she'd become acquainted with their older brother, Mervin. It wasn't common knowledge that Renata and Mervin had been an item. Their choice to run away together to elope and live in Toronto had created quite a kerfuffle. Rudolf had been deeply angered; Huldah, heartbroken.

They didn't chase after her, though. She was of age, after all.

When the discussion turned to Freddie as a lad, it was recalled that he had been a little imp from the get-go—and it had earned him lots of straps applied to his behind. Although none of that discipline seemed to cure him of his contrary ways. He had been inclined to be the class clown at school, not to mention a mischief-maker.

It was at school where he'd gotten the name Freddie, since he had been called Frederick at home. That was all right, as far as it went, but as a teenager he had fallen in with a bad crowd and his parents hadn't been able to steer him straight.

"There were lots of heated arguments between Frederick and Rudolf," Henry recalled.

"I remember that too," agreed Dan.

Henry nodded. "The boy grew into a tall, strapping young man who eventually prevailed against his aging, partially crippled sire if and when he took a notion to manhandle him."

"Freddie could be as charming and endearing as any kitten or as disrespectful and spiteful as the devil himself," said Leah.

"That's true." Henry sighed, then added, "He was gaining a reputation for those traits too."

"When did Rudolf Fischer pass away?" ventured Ellie.

"Gosh, I don't remember the year," Dan said. "It will say on his stone in the Minitonas cemetery, I'm sure."

Henry was quiet for a moment, straining to recall memories from long ago. "I do remember the funeral, though. Now that was a strange affair. They had claimed to be atheists, and Huldah stuck to that view even after her husband passed. There was no church service, but she did find someone to say a few words in memory of him. I think he was the guy who acted as justice of the peace when there was call for it. Then they lowered the casket. Neither Fred nor Huldah shed any tears. They were as stoic as I've ever seen. And that was that. It was over. I think the whole business lasted maybe fifteen minutes. Everybody went home."

"We offered to go home with Huldah, to sit with her for a few hours, but she dismissed us," said Beatrice. "She wasn't in need of company and preferred to be alone. We honoured that request. But next we heard, she had packed a big suitcase and told Freddie that she was going to Toronto to visit his sister. She never came back. That was a shocker, I'll tell you."

"I don't think that went well with Freddie," opined Henry. "She turned over the farm to him, but I believe he was angry that his mother had left him for good. Like he'd been abandoned by the one person he'd thought was in his corner. He hadn't seen it coming. None of us did. And after that we didn't see the Fischers again, including Freddie. He didn't keep up with his parents' friends..."

Henry trailed off, looking thoughtful. Something seemed to be coming back to him, perhaps something he hadn't thought about for many years.

"Rudolf once dropped a strange comment with regards to World War I, something about how the war hadn't ended well and there would most likely be another to end it properly. That's a strange saying, isn't it? There was another war too, twenty-five years later, and Freddie followed news of that conflict as religiously as the rest of us. But now that I think back, it's not clear that he was rooting for the Allies. You don't suppose Rudy was pulling for the Germans, now do you?"

Dan rose to his feet. "Rudolf did have an air of mystery around him, I'll give you that." He turned to Leah. "Are you ready to go? I don't want to miss my beauty sleep."

"Oh no..." Gertie got up as well, clearly embarrassed. "Wait, there's still dessert! I got so caught up in your stories that I completely forgot about it."

"We'll do it another night," said Leah. "It's getting late for us old-timers."

But Gertie wouldn't let them go until she had hurriedly divided her pan of chocolate cake in quarters—one each for the Kleins, the Bredins, and Hugh with instructions to share with Ellie.

Once Ellie and Hugh had climbed back into the truck and were preparing to leave, Ellie turned to him with a strange, pensive look on her face.

"That was an interesting evening," she mused.

"Yup. Yup, it was."

While undressing for bed, Hugh distinctly heard the sole bottle of moonshine, parked atop the Hoosier, speaking to him. Not out loud, of course, but he couldn't seem to ignore it.

"Take another mouthful," it urged. "It won't be as shocking to your system as last time. It gets easier as you get used to it. Come on, try some. It'll probably help you sleep better too. Just a mouthful. Like before..."

The temptation probably would have worked, save for one thing. It spoke to him in the voice of his pa. And he wasn't having any of that!

Clad only in his underwear, Hugh picked up the bottle with one hand, his flashlight in the other, and transported the talking hooch to the machine shed. He set it on a rough shelf next to an old rusty tin where the words *Rat Poison* could still be made out.

"There," he murmured. "You two can talk to each other all night if you want."

Twenty-One

A BRIGHT SUN dawned on the morning of FBC's community picnic. Hugh and Ellie drove as far as Rob and Sarah's place, then rode with the family in their station wagon. They all arrived at the Wellman Lake Bible campground around 9:00 a.m., with a steady stream of traffic both ahead and behind them. The summer heat was already causing a few to sweat. Children ran around joyfully with their Sunday school friends. Women carried dishes of food to the dining hall, as well as baked goods and handcrafted wares for the afternoon auction. Meanwhile, the men chatted in groups of three or four.

After a pancake breakfast, fried and served by a few of the menfolk, the time came for a series of races between the Sunday school children, beginning with the tots. It was as entertaining to watch the toddlers run helter-skelter to the finish line as it was to watch them perform in a Christmas program. Utterly adorable!

Next, the school-aged kids were paired up for the three-legged race, and again for the wheelbarrow race. After the races, the kids were divided into small groups for the annual scavenger hunt. Those lucky enough to win ribbons were told they could turn them in later for sweet treats.

The schedule called for the softball games to begin at 10:30 a.m. The teams were given designated numbers by the umpire. Trevor Bauman's team was referred to as Team 2, slated to play Team 1 in the first round of the tournament. But Team 1 was short a player, and they recruited Ellie. She was only too glad to participate, since she preferred participating to spectating.

Following a bat toss, Team 1 took the field first, with Ellie assigned the position of shortstop. Old Abram Keller had been recruited as umpire. His years of interest in baseball made him the perfect choice, but it was rather comical to see a confirmed senior take his stance behind the back catcher like a professional, twisting his cap backwards. He took his role very seriously!

Trevor was up to bat first. On the second pitch, he hit the ball along the ground and made it to first base.

The next batter was Hugh. He let the first pitch pass.

"Steee-rike!" yelled Abram.

Hugh got a piece of the next pitch, but it went foul. The third pitch, too, went wide. Ball one.

On the fourth pitch, Hugh made good contact and gave the ball a ride to an empty spot between right and centre field. It was enough to get him to first base and Trevor to second.

The next batter struck out. Nonetheless, Trevor and Hugh were able to advance to their next bases.

Batter number four was Rob, and immediately the fielders backed up. He didn't disappoint. On the second pitch, he hit the ball high and far. It landed somewhere on the beach of the lake, making it easy for Trevor and Hugh to run home. Rob held the honour of scoring the day's first homerun.

By the end of the first inning, Trevor's team had managed to rack up four runs.

Team 2 had chosen Hugh to be pitcher, since no one else seemed to want to play this important position. He threw the ball quite well. Three batters made it to base, but two others were tidily struck out.

Then Ellie was up to bat.

"All right, Hugh-billy," she called from the plate, loud and sassy. "Let's see what you got!"

A few of the spectators chuckled.

Hugh pitched, but Ellie let it pass.

"Steee-rike!" hollered Abram.

Hugh pitched again. It went wide.

"Ball one!"

On the third pitch, Ellie swung and connected—but it went foul to the right. The fourth pitch almost hit her; she backed away just in time.

"Hey, watch it, will ya?" she yelled.

"Ball two, inside!" declared Abram.

The next pitch was quite a lot higher than the strike zone.

"Ball three, high!" Abram then added, "Full count: three balls, two strikes."

Ellie gripped the bat and focused. She really wanted to hit this last pitch out of the park, like Rob had.

The ball came in nice and straight. Ellie wound up, took the swing... and missed! Her mouth dropped open in an expression of utter shock.

She was a good sport about it, though, and quickly broke into laughter.

"Ellie-Mae-Clampett has struck out!" Hugh called, just as loud and sassy as she had been to him.

The moment of levity subtly changed the tenor of the whole game. From that point forward, the match became a contest of prowess, especially between the men and boys. The banter caused players and spectators to relax.

At the end of the game, Team 2 came out ahead by a score of 10–7.

Tables were set up for lunch and the picnickers enjoyed their hotdogs and hamburgers in the open air. It was wonderful, at least for those who didn't mind swatting at the horde of horseflies.

Hugh made up his burger and sat down at a table with Trevor and Rob. Right behind him, a few of the other men sauntered over.

"Hey, you throw a mean ball, buddy," said one of them. He then extended his hand. "Irvin here. And you are?"

"Hugh Fischer." He returned the handshake.

"Yeah, you're pretty good," agreed another man, who introduced himself as Pete.

"Thanks. I'm surprised I can still throw and catch a ball, since I haven't done so since high school."

"I'm thinkin' you're new here," put in a third man, who went by the name Murray. "What do you do for a living?"

"I'm trained in motor vehicle mechanics."

"Uh-huh. What does that include? Like ordinary cars and trucks, or are you one of them heavy-duty mechanics for those semis and highway tractors pulling big logs and such like?" This came from Irvin.

"I don't have a specialty, per se. So far, my knowledge and experience cover general mechanics," clarified Hugh. "I'm not the one you want to call to fix a highway tractor, at least not yet."

"What about old-time vehicles?" asked Pete. "I got a vintage coupe sitting idle in a shed that used to belong to my grandpa. It would be fun to get it running again."

"Me too! I got an old half-ton rusting in the bush out back on our farm," Murray said. "I don't think it's too far gone to get back on the road again."

"What about mowers?"

"What about appliances?"

"I could probably could handle them, provided I could get parts," replied Hugh between bites of his burger.

There was a collective "Ahh" and nods of comprehension. That was the rub—getting parts for vintage.

"It's less of a problem if you have the means to *make* the parts," Rob remarked.

Hugh looked toward him. "I've never tried my hand at that, so I don't know..."

"What about autobody?" asked Irvin. "Can you repair and refinish dents and other damage?"

"Well, so far I've only done that kind of work on my own vehicles." He was thinking of the little subcompact he had driven around Winnipeg for a while.

"Let me know if and when you set up shop," said Pete. "I'll likely have work for you."

Irvin and Murray murmured the same sentiment.

One by one, the men all left to get more food. Hugh was about to get up as well when someone new came over and sat across from him. He was a nice-looking fellow under his strawberry-blond crew-cut. Although he was a full-grown man, he retained a certain baby-face.

"Hi, I'm Rory Lang," said the man, extending his hand.

Hugh shook it. "Hugh Fischer here."

"I think I remember seeing you back in junior or senior high. Are you here to take up farming, or...?"

"I have a farm, just not sure what I'm going to do with it yet." Hugh felt slightly uneasy with the young man's question and his reference to their former school days.

"I've seen you at church a couple of times with Ellie Bauman."

"Yeah. We're friends." Where was this going?

"Well... like, are you two dating or something?"

"We're neighbours. We get together and help each other out."

"Then she's fair game."

Hugh looked somewhat flustered. "Ummm, you'll have to ask Ellie about that."

"Good. I will."

Without another word, Rory rose and left.

I walked into that one, he thought. Yet the short conversation had perturbed him. While it was true that he and Ellie weren't dating—that they had agreed to relate to each other as brother and sister—it didn't sit well that other men might enter the picture. For all the time they spent together, he did sort of think of her as "his girl."

He was about to get up again when a young brunette wearing short shorts and a tanktop sat across from him and set down a plastic glass filled with orange juice.

"I saw you didn't have a drink, so I brought you one," she said, smiling. "I'm Rhonda. And you are...?"

"Hugh Fischer," answered Hugh with a much smaller smile.

"Nice to meet you. You're new around here, aren't you?"

"You could say so. It will be three weeks as of Monday."

"How 'bout you tell me about yourself?"

To Hugh, she reminded him of a chirping bird. "Well, I don't know what to tell you."

"Where do you work? What do you do?" prompted the chirping bird.

"Actually, I'm still sorting that out." He went on to briefly tell her about the farm, but he wasn't in the mood for this. The girl was beginning to get on his nerves.

"That's so cool," Rhonda said. "I see you're not wearing a wedding ring. Does it follow that you're single?"

At that moment, little Beanie Bauman approached their table and climbed onto Hugh's lap.

"Not quite single," answered Hugh. "Beanie is my girlfriend, aren't you?"

He gave the girl a little squeeze. Beanie clapped her hand to her mouth in an attempt to shyly hide her ear-to-ear grin.

"Awww, that's so sweet," cooed Rhonda.

It was Sarah who saved the day by coming by to collect Beanie for the next kids event. It provided the perfect excuse for him to take his leave of Rhonda.

The second ball game got underway as the kids went on a treasure hunt. Hugh opted to watch the softball game. From the top of the bleachers, he could see clear across the yard to where Ellie sat at a picnic table across from Rory Lange. She was smiling and nodding by turns.

The sight rankled him, and there wasn't a thing he could do about it. He tried to concentrate on the game.

~

Having concluded her conversation with Rory, Ellie joined another table of women she had known since childhood. Together they nattered on about recipes, children, gardening, and the hot weather.

A few minutes later, the hugely pregnant Darcey Unger showed up and sat next to Ellie. Ellie gladly moved over to accommodate her. She liked Darcey and always had. Darcey was a couple of years older, had married in her early twenties, and was now about to have her third child. She and her family lived in Minitonas, just up the street from Rob and Sarah.

Darcey was one of those what-you-see-is-what-you-get kind of women. She was self-assured and unafraid to say what she thought. Truth was, there were times when she really ought to have kept her mouth shut. Mind you, what she lacked in sensitivity she gained in perception. More often than not, she made the right call when she shot from the hip.

Darcey was tall and big-boned, standing nearly six feet, but no one could say she was fat or ungainly. In fact, she was quite athletic. She exuded strength and confidence in a way that some found intimidating. She was not to be taken lightly.

"So what's the news with the FBC hens today?" said Darcey in her characteristic big voice.

"You likely know more than any of us," remarked one of the hens with a short laugh.

"When's your baby due?" asked another.

"Already overdue. By a week," Darcey panted. She wore a bandana around her head and used it to wipe the sweat off her brow. "This baby can't come out soon enough. If I stick out any farther, I'll be tripping over myself."

"Haven't you taken a risk coming out today if you could pop any minute?"

"That's *why* I came! To dare the little one into getting this show on the road."

And then, as if on cue, it happened—Darcey's water broke. She felt the warm liquid run down the insides of both thighs and immediately stood up. Another woman might have been embarrassed by such an occurrence. Not Darcey.

"Thar she blows!" She looked down at the wet mark she'd left on the bench. "Oh crap! Sorry… pardon my French," she said hastily.

Clearly the elder FBC women didn't like hearing her use such bad language, but Ellie thought it was funny.

Within a few minutes, Darcey's parents came around to look after her two kids while her husband Tony stepped out of the softball game to drive her to the hospital in Swan River. Rory, who was sitting in the bleachers, was invited to replace Tony in the game. He seemed very pleased to have been asked.

In their wake, excitement rippled through the crowd. Some were even gossiping that Darcey had resorted to having the baby somewhere on the campgrounds!

A little bored with the women's chatter, Ellie decided to watch the ball game. The third and final game in the tournament was underway. Team 2 was taking on Team 3, with Trevor, Rob, and Hugh all fielding the same positions as before.

After climbing the steps to the top of the bleachers to get the best view, she noticed Rory sitting on the bench amongst the batters.

This might prove interesting, she thought.

~

The game was more than half over and going well for Trevor's team. They were leading six to four with three innings left to go. Hugh hefted the ball and looked from the pitcher's mound to the plate, where Rory had stepped up. His rival was swinging the bat back and forth, preparing to hit it out of the park.

He had decided that he didn't like the guy. To be fair, he didn't want to hurt him either, but he hoped to scare him a little. For sure he wanted to strike him out.

Hugh looked toward the batter with steely eyes, then wound up and threw the first pitch. Although this was softball, the ball flew across the plate—fast.

Rory backed away and let it pass.

"Steee-rike!" boomed Abram.

Rory stepped up to the plate again, swinging the bat to indicate he was ready.

Hugh let another one fly—and Rory swung. And missed. Hugh exhaled in relief.

Zing! The next pitch came right across the plate, but on the line between a strike and a ball. Rory jumped back.

They both turned toward Abram, who hesitated for a second before declaring his verdict: "Steee-rike three! Batter's out."

Embarrassed, Rory glumly retreated to the batter's bench. Hugh hoped that besides foiling Rory's ambitions at bat, he had somehow discouraged his interest in Ellie too.

The game ended shortly thereafter, with Trevor's team losing in the final stretch by a score of eight to seven. But nobody cared much. It was all about having a good time.

Within moments of the game ending, everything turned at the sound of whoops and hollers drifting up from the beach. One of the groups of treasure hunters had dug up something of interest—a metal box secured with a padlock—and one of the picnic's organizers promised the kids it would be opened after supper.

The last activity planned before supper was the auction. The money it raised would go toward the cost of running the camp. A table was set out for would-be buyers to look at the merchandise before bidding.

Hugh noted a lemon meringue pie which interested him; lemon pie came right after apple pie on his list of favourite desserts. Amongst the crafts he saw a watercolour painting set inside a white frame. There was something familiar about that image.

Then he got it. It was a painting of the pond on his own property. Ellie must have done it.

Sure enough, on close inspection he saw the tiny initials ERB printed along a blade of grass. She had captured its charm perfectly.

He would bid on that and let the lemon pie go if he had to.

The auction progressed quickly, with none other than Abram Keller in the role of auctioneer. When the watercolour came up for sale, Abram opened the bidding at five dollars. Hugh put up his hand. Abram raised it to ten.

For a while, it didn't seem like anyone else would join the tendering. Suddenly, a woman put up her hand.

"Now fifteen dollars, jibbity-jibbity-jibbity," said Abram.

Hugh raised his hand.

"Now twenty dollars, jibbity-jibbity-jibbity…"

The woman slowly raised her hand a second time.

"I got twenty dollars. Who will give me twenty-five?"

Again, Hugh raised his hand.

"I got twenty-five. Who will make it thirty? Jibbity-jibbity-jibbity…"

This time, the woman shook her head.

"*Sold* for twenty-five dollars to the young man in the blue cap…" And with that, Abram moved on to the next item.

Hugh was pleased with his purchase. The more he looked at the depiction of his pond, the more he liked it.

Ellie watched the transaction from the far side of the crowd. It pleased her that her picture had gone to someone who would appreciate it. She remembered very well that this pond had probably been the only feature on Hugh's property to bring him any measure of joy.

For supper, the women arranged a potluck of lasagnes and salads. Dessert consisted of large pieces of puffed wheat cake and rice crispy squares together with the watermelon from lunch.

The children were getting tired by this time in the day, perhaps having gotten too much sun, and their noises were distinctly less cheerful. Nonetheless, many people were still eating when the pastor, Leland Wirt, called the children to gather around at the front of the dining hall.

"Are you ready to see the treasure?" he asked the children.

They clapped and hopped up and down. "Yes!"

Pastor Leland produced a key and opened the padlock. Carefully and slowly, he lifted the lid as the children strained to see what was inside.

He lifted out… a book.

"Do you know what this is?" he asked.

"A Bible," answered a confident boy.

"That's right. Did you know that the Bible speaks often of treasures?" The pastor smiled at the mix of nods and shaking of heads. "Let me read you a few verses. Then you'll know for sure. First, Matthew 6:19–21: *'Lay not up for yourselves treasures upon earth, where moth and rust doth corrupt, and where thieves break through and steal: but lay up for yourselves treasures in heaven, where neither moth nor rust doth corrupt, and where thieves do not break through nor steal: for where your treasure is, there will your heart be also.'*[6]

"Now children, what is your treasure? Is it candy? Is it your toys? Is it something else? Jesus is telling us that whatever the most important thing is to us, it's going to show up as the thing we chase after in this life. If it's not Jesus and the things of heaven, it will all prove to be worthless in the end.

"Here's another one, from Colossians 2:2–3: *'…to the acknowledgment of the mystery of God, and of the Father and of Christ; in whom are hid all the treasures of wisdom and knowledge.'*[7] Here we are told that in Jesus we have everything we need—everything that can give us joy and happiness, and everything that can help us get through our troubles and trials. We're also told that when we want to know what is true and right, we can ask Jesus, because He knows perfectly what is good and what is bad. And He and helps us to know it too.

"Now the next one, this time in Matthew 13:44: *'Again, the kingdom of heaven is like unto treasure hid in a field; the which when a man hath found, he hideth, and for joy thereof goeth and selleth all*

[6] KJV.
[7] KJV.

that he hath, and buyeth that field.'[8] Jesus is telling us that the kingdom of God isn't so easy to see. It's not obvious to the naked eye in the same way that trees and flowers are. But when you do find it, the smart person lets go of everything else to have the treasure that is Jesus and everything He represents.

"Lastly, listen to 2 Corinthians 4:7: *'But we have this treasure in earthen vessels, that the excellency of the power may be of God, and not of us.'*[9] The treasure the apostle Paul is talking about here is Jesus, and the earthen vessels are you and me. Everyone who invites Jesus to be their saviour receives the spirit of Jesus, who comes to live in each of us, and then God's power can be shown through our hands and feet and heart and mind.

"This is just a small sampling of what the Bible has to say about the treasures of this world and the treasures we have in heaven if we belong to the Lord Jesus. It also speaks of the treasure we have in Jesus Himself, as well as His holy Word. Now, who would like to look in this treasure chest here to see if there's anything else inside?"

All the kids' hands went up and the pastor invited one little girl to take a look. She put her hand into the box and pulled out some packages of paper.

Pastor Leland took these from her. "These are tracts which can help to show someone who doesn't know the love of Jesus how to become His child. I want every one of you to take at least one tract to share with someone else who might not have Jesus in their heart."

He paused for a moment, his eyes moving across his entire audience.

"Now for the last item on the schedule for today," he continued. "This morning, as you all were passing through the pancake breakfast line, you were asked to put your name on a list. The purpose of that list was to enter you into a draw for this brand-new Good News Bible, in modern English. Would our Sunday school superintendent please draw one of those names?"

---

[8] KJV.
[9] KJV.

The superintendent came up and swished his hand around in the ice cream pail full of little papers of names. At last he pulled one out, seeming a bit puzzled with what he read. He then handed the strip to Pastor Leland.

"The winner is… Hugh Fischer!"

Everyone in the dining hall clapped their hands. Hugh was mightily surprised that his name had been called, but he calmly went up to Pastor Leland and accepted the book. He got lots of stares, since most people had no idea who he was.

"May you read it and be blessed," said Pastor Leland as he placed the Bible in Hugh's hands.

The pastor then closed with a word of prayer. The people were dismissed to stay or go as they wished. The church's community picnic was officially over for another year.

On the ride home, Beanie sat between Ellie and Hugh. She pressed a tract into Hugh's hand.

"I took two so you could have one," she said.

"That was thoughtful of you, Bean, thank you," said Hugh, tousling her hair. He tucked it into his new Bible.

When they got to the house, Hugh and Ellie were about to get in his truck and drive home when Sarah stopped them.

"Ellie, I have a favour to ask," she said.

Ellie turned to her. "Anything, Sarah. Just ask."

"I've noticed how good you are with the kids. Would you mind terribly much taking them for a few days this week so Rob and I can go away on a little vacation for ourselves?"

"Absolutely. I'd be happy to."

The children, standing nearby, had overheard. They ran off into the house, cheering in anticipation of being able to spend some more time with their Aunt Ellie.

A few minutes later, she and Hugh were riding through the country in silence.

"Did you have a good time?" Ellie finally asked.

"Yeah, I did. I met a few more men who encouraged me to set up a mechanics shop. They have machines and vehicles that need repairs. Got some new ideas to chew on. You?"

"It was all right. What do you think of your new Bible?'

Hugh shrugged.

"Could winning it be the answer to your prayer?" she said. "You know, the one for God to do something personal for you so you can be sure He's real?"

"Anyone could have won this, Ellie. It's not unique." He paused, and his voice took on an air of nonchalance. "So who was that blond guy you were having so much fun talking with?"

"What blond guy? I wasn't talking... oh. Do you mean Rory Lang? I wasn't 'having so much fun,' as you put it. I went to school with him. We were in the same class."

She looked out the window, the fields blurring as they raced past.

"He did ask me out, though," she admitted. "I put him off by saying that I wasn't in an emotionally healthy place to be dating anyone. Rory isn't my type. Like, *really* not my type. I don't think I'll ever be in an emotionally healthy enough place to date him."

Ellie looked sidelong at Hugh. Was it just her or did he seem almost relieved?

"I saw Rhonda making eyes at you around lunchtime," she added.

"Rhonda? Oh, you mean the chick who wouldn't stop chirping like a bird. Yeah... she struck me as someone who might be twenty-one going on sixteen."

"No attraction there then?" asked Ellie cautiously.

"Not for a moment."

Ellie let out an inward sigh of relief. All was well. The world was still right-side-up.

Twenty-Two

ONE OF THE first announcements at church the next morning was that Tony and Darcey Unger had welcomed another girl, Abigail, into their family. A not-so-little sister, weighing eleven pounds and four ounces, for Carrie and Lorraine. The congregation clapped for the Unger family.

Pastor Wirt preached on the subject of another parable, the one famously centred on the prodigal son.

"This is my story," Ellie whispered, leaning close to Hugh, who had again consented to come to church with her. "I'm the prodigal who's come back home…"

Hugh nodded, though he wasn't at all sure what she meant by it.

Afterward in the foyer, the people greeted one another warmly. Seeing Ellie standing alone, Rory sidled up to her.

"Good morning, Ellie," he said in an intimate tone. "I want to thank you for sharing with me yesterday. Know that I'm praying for you, that God would heal your heart and emotions back to good health."

She smiled weakly. "Uh, sure. That's nice of you, Rory. Thanks."

Hugh soon finished a conversation with a new friend he had made at the picnic and rejoined Ellie. Without making eye contact or greeting Hugh, Rory departed for another area of the foyer.

On the drive home, Ellie reflected on how much she looked forward to spending a quiet afternoon by herself. After Hugh dropped her off, she ate a light lunch, then packed a tote bag with her Bible, a couple of journals, and a sketchpad. She biked down to the Roaring River for some rest and relaxation. She had a good afternoon reading, writing, listening to the calming sounds of nature, and wading in the shallow water.

~

For his part, Hugh rolled up a towel, picked up his new Bible, and negotiated the plethora of trashed items in the bush until he came to his favourite spot and best kept secret on the property: the pond. Believing he was beyond the eyes of any human, he stripped off his clothing and dove into the water. The top few inches felt warm, but the depths were still cold. He emerged, teeth chattering and shivering.

He lay stretched out on the towel atop of the big rock. The sun soon warmed him and made him drowsy. It wasn't long before he fell asleep.

Hugh had no idea how long he slept, but he woke suddenly with his heart palpitating wildly. An unknown fear had gripped his mind and the hair at the base of his neck stood on end. Why? There was that feeling again; he was being watched.

He lifted his head and peered into the stand of trees that surrounded the pond, looking left and then right. As far as he could see, there was nothing out of the ordinary, unless one counted the old shack.

"That has to come down too," he said quietly to himself.

Not only did it represent the illegal business his pa had run, but it reminded him of the cruelty he had suffered at his hand. It was ugly and spoiled the scenery of that beautiful spot.

He calmed himself by taking even breaths. Forcing casualness, he redressed, picked up his towel, looped it around his neck, and began to walk back to the cabin.

After approximately fifteen yards, though, he turned on his heel and returned to the rock. There lay his new Bible, still unopened. He wasn't in the mood for it now, but he picked it up and carried it back with the towel.

At the cabin, he grabbed a cola from the refrigerator and plunked himself in the black captain's chair by the table. It was the second time he had felt the unexplained terror while on his own farm. The first time, he had chalked it up to an overactive imagination. This time? What could explain it? A daymare? Both experiences had occurred near the pond, and he wondered if there was any significance to that.

A memory emerged in the form of a vision. Hugh figured he was about thirteen years old. It was summer, like now, and he'd gone to the pond for a dip to cool off. He had lain himself down on the same big rock to dry while his pa had suddenly appeared in the clearing, hopping mad.

"There you are, you dumb ass. You're supposed to come when I call you!"

He jumped to his feet. "I didn't hear you, Pa. Honest I didn't!"

"I hollered good and loud," yelled Freddie, producing a cane of willow stripped of its leaves.

"I'm coming, Pa. I didn't hear you, or I would have been there!"

Panic was rising in his chest. He pulled on his shorts and began to run back to the farmyard. But as he passed his pa, Freddie grabbed him and strapped his bare back, buttocks, and legs with the willow switch, leaving bright red welts.

Hugh enduring the beating silently, trembling with unuttered sobs.

His pa then threw down the switch and grabbed him at the nape of his neck, marching him back to the main yard and into the machine shed. His pa wanted help lifting a heavy piece of motor out of a machine, placing it on a surface where he could work on it. It was all Hugh could do to lift his end. In fact, his end dropped abruptly onto the bench. It was too heavy for him to maintain his hold.

Freddie swore over Hugh's lack of strength. "That's all I needed. Get outta here!"

Hugh fled to the only other spot that offered a bit of refuge, the loft of the old barn. There he sank into some hay and sat for a long time with his head between his legs, miserable.

The memory, not thought of for eighteen years, hurt Hugh all over again. And then it rekindled his bitter rage. How could he escape from his past? Was this subliminal memory the root of the daymare? What would it take to have peace of mind and heart? Freedom from painful memories? The only conclusion he could think of was to get rid of all the things associated with his pa. Hopefully that would make the "bad air" go away.

"It starts today," he said resolutely to the refrigerator.

He downed the last of his cola and dressed in grubby work clothes. Amongst his tools he fished out a hardhat and some work gloves.

Carrying an axe, a sledgehammer, and some rope, he ascended the stairs of the old farmhouse, which creaked more ominously every time he mounted them. He set the axe and rope aside and began to swing with all his might at the walls first. The plaster fell apart easily; the slats behind them couldn't hold together under Hugh's relentless blows. Wood shavings and dust sprinkled down from the resultant split in the ceiling.

Then he tackled the longer, load-bearing wall of his sisters' room.

"This is for every time you called them dirty names," shouted Hugh, adding curse words. Wham! "This is for every time you pinched their bums and their little titties…" Smash!

Pretty soon the wall lay in tatters and the ceiling sagged even more.

He walked toward the last of the interior walls upstairs, the one that separated the hallway from the room his parents had slept in.

Hugh stopped for a few moments to catch his breath. He was well aware that he was giving in to his anger wholesale, but he didn't care. In fact, he wanted to vent his rage on the symbols that had caused his family so much hurt. He had held it in many a year. Today he would spend at least some of it.

He intended to utterly destroy the wretched house of his upbringing with his own fury and hate. It was the closest he could come to exacting revenge.

When he started swinging again, his next blow was as powerful as his strength could muster. The wall busted in half, plaster raining everywhere.

"That's for all the times you made Ma cry." Bang! "That's for all the times you grabbed her by the throat." Crash! "That's for every time you made her beg for money to feed us, and even your own sorry ass!" Boom!

The last portion of the wall blew apart.

Sweat poured down Hugh's face in rivulets, dripping off his chin onto his ragged T-shirt. The inner walls were down now, although some partial studs still hung from the ceiling like swords.

The ceiling sagged precariously, but that wasn't good enough for Hugh; he wanted it down. Now.

After a couple of moments' rest, he set the sledgehammer down by the stairs and fished for the axe. Finding it, he swung it at the lowest point of the sagging ceiling. Dust and shavings rained down, but most of the ceiling still held.

"Fall, dammit," ordered Hugh, swinging again.

More dust and woodchips fell, but the only difference was that the hole in the ceiling was a little bigger than before.

In a rush, he slashed again and again and again until he heard the groan of the ceiling joists grudgingly give way. His arms were tired and sore, begging him to stop, but his ire was in control and told him he couldn't quit. Enough was broken down for Hugh to see what looked to be old-fashioned trusses supporting the roof. Amazingly, they continued to hold.

Swearing again, he lunged at them with the axe but could barely make contact. Busting them would require another strategy.

When the upper level was nothing but a hollow bowl, the floor littered with a foot of debris, Hugh took his axe, sledgehammer, and rope down the creaking stairs and set them by the entrance. He intended to finish the job tomorrow, one way or another.

Outside, he removed his shirt to shake off the dust and wood shavings. Then he took off his pants. He had a gas-powered pump rigged to draw water from the well for his household use, and he started it now to rinse himself of all the sweat and filth. The water was icy cold, which made him gasp. Throughout the process his breathing calmed down, but his rage persisted.

In the cabin, he looked for something quick to eat. He was in no mood to cook. He settled on a tin of chili, which he ate cold directly out of the tin. It tasted terrible, but that wasn't a strong enough motivation to heat it up.

He suddenly stopped moving to listen. It sounded like a voice calling from far away...

Then realized what it was—that bottle of moonshine, calling out its temptation all the way from the machine shed.

"Just one swallow is all you need. You know you want it!"

But it once again came in the voice of his pa. Instead of luring him, it spurred him to flee.

Hugh jumped in his truck, started the engine, and sped up the driveway. He turned north, spinning his wheels on the gravel and sending a spray of stones behind him.

Just past the Bauman turnoff, he saw Ellie riding her bike on the road, headed for home. She noticed his approach and pulled off to her right. Hugh raced past and saw through the rearview mirror that she was staring after him. He didn't know if she recognized him or not, but he didn't care.

He fixed his eye on the road in front of him, not even watching for oncoming traffic, and very suddenly came within inches of T-boning a crossing car. That scared him. Hugh figured the other driver had probably wet their drawers.

The close call caused him to slow down and drive more responsibly.

He didn't know where he wanted to go, but returning home was out of the question. Since he was driving north, though, he decided he may as well poke around nearby Bowsman. As he entered the town, he was surprised to see how small it was.

After that, he swung back south on the main road and made his way toward Swan River. At the Highway 10 intersection, he debated with himself as to where to go next, and then turned west and drove as far as Benito. There wasn't too much to see there either, so he headed back east, through Swan and on past Minitonas until he roared by whatever was left of Renwer.

At last he came to Cowan. There he bought some gas, a chocolate bar, and a soda. It was getting dark, so the reasonable side of his brain persuaded him to return home.

Within a mile of his turn-off, Hugh balked again. He didn't want to go home, didn't want to confront that bottle of hooch that seemed to possess the power of speech. He sure didn't want to go up against the ghost of his pa, despite not believing in such things. The memories on the farm were just too sad and terrible.

Thus he turned off the road onto a field entrance, killed the engine, and laid down on the seat. It wasn't too comfortable, but he'd slept in worse conditions. Mercifully, sleep came quickly.

~

At four-thirty in the morning on Monday, the glare of sunlight woke Hugh. It took him a minute to realize where he was—and why he was there. His arms, shoulders, and even legs ached.

Feeling stiff, he slowly raised himself up, started his truck, and drove the mile back to his place. Once in his cabin, he flopped down on his bed and promptly fell asleep again.

~

The sound of knocking at his door roused him, but he didn't fully register the noise until the knock came a second time. He looked at the clock: 9:02 a.m.

With bleary eyes, he sluggishly rose and stretched his arms. He groaned from all the aches and pains that wracked his stiff body.

When he opened the door, he was standing in front of a representative from the telephone company.

"Is this the Fischer residence?" the man asked cheerily.

Hugh nodded.

"I've come to install your phone."

"Right! I'd forgotten about that." He forced himself toward greater alertness. "What do you need?"

"Just tell me where you want the telephone installed on the premises and choose the colour and style. The rest is up to me."

Hugh very quickly chose a desktop, push-button, classic white telephone. He then focused on preparing a large breakfast to fortify himself for all the work he intended to get done that day.

About an hour later, the telephone representative drove away, leaving a shiny new phone on his small table and a telephone book covering Swan River and the surrounding area.

For his first call, he dialled Ellie.

"It's Hugh," he said after she picked up.

"Hey, you must be calling from your new phone!"

"Yeah. But I called to tell you to stay away from here until I tell you otherwise."

There was a short pause. "I don't understand. What's up?"

"I'm tearing down the house. I started it yesterday afternoon. I don't want anyone coming around. Not even you." His voice was brusque. "It wouldn't be safe. Besides, it's something I have to do myself."

"It could be dangerous. What if you get hurt?"

"I have no intention of getting hurt. This is something you can't help me with, Ellie. I don't even want you to come around to watch.

Promise me you'll stay away until I call you when it's all over... after it's burnt..."

There was silence on the other end.

"Ellie?"

"I'm still here."

"Promise me."

"How about you promise me that you'll call after the demolition is done? Call before you burn it. That way, I won't worry that you're stuck under a pile of wreckage and can't get out."

"If I remember..."

He hung up.

~

Ellie had just about completed her soul work that morning when Hugh's call came. She wasn't surprised to hear that he was tearing down the house. That had been the plan ever since she'd introduced herself to him. His tone, however, troubled her. It betrayed a calculated and dangerous level of anger, something she hadn't heard him express before.

She returned to her armchair. "Lord, what's this about? What's going on?"

She waited for insight to come—and in due course, it did. She began to understand that, for Hugh, the house was like a punching bag that he needed to hit to vent his frustrations. He was asking for privacy to vent his hate and bitterness without the restraints others might expect of a civilized person. He wanted the time and space to go a little crazy without judgement.

"Okay, Lord. I think I can understand that..."

She followed that with prayers for his safety. She also acknowledged that the enemy of human souls had had his way on that farm for a good many years. She prayed that he wouldn't hinder or exacerbate Hugh's time of catharsis. She also prayed that this exercise would somehow serve as a stepping stone in the journey that would culminate in his coming to faith in Christ.

Normally Ellie would have been crazy curious to see what Hugh was up to, but having received this crucial understanding she was able to set aside the subject of Hugh Fischer and focus on matters in her own court. At least for now.

She gave Gertie a call and together they agreed to hold a yard sale on the weekend of July 12, a week before her special dinner date with Hugh and his sisters. They agreed that the sale would be big enough to warrant placing an ad in the local papers, in addition to putting up posters on community billboards.

That done, Ellie decided to cut the last set of blue print fabrics into strips for the construction of a small log cabin quilt. After the cutting was done, she took the kit to her mother's sewing area in the basement. She could have passed it along to Gertie, but it seemed like a good idea to keep it around so she would have something to do when there was nothing else to occupy her.

After that she caught up on household chores—and quite often, Hugh came to mind, forcing her curiosity to well up again.

He said I couldn't come to his place, she thought to herself, *but he didn't say I couldn't watch from mine...*

She went to the garage to look for a telescope or binoculars, and eventually she found a pair. Ellie trotted to the end of her driveway and hid in the row of spruce trees that grew there. Looking toward the Fischer farm, she spotted Hugh sitting on his tractor. The front was rigged with chains that were taut from pulling something. From the look of his mouth, he seemed to be bellowing—chanting.

"Fall! Fall! Fall!"

The expression on his face would have frightened little children.

Suddenly, Hugh turned his head and seemed to look directly at her. At least that's how it appeared.

Ellie guiltily put down her binoculars. She was sure he couldn't have seen her; she was too well hidden. But she realized that she shouldn't be spying when he'd asked her not to.

~

Hugh was having a frustrating time of it. Before knocking down the load-bearing wall on the main floor, he had gone upstairs to pull up some flooring and poke holes in the ceiling in strategic places so he could, hopefully, pull it down with chains.

Then he swiped at the old staircase with his axe, which came away fairly easily. The wall went down with no trouble, as had the walls upstairs the day before.

Surprisingly, the ceiling would not yield. The house should have caved in after the inner walls had been knocked out.

That's when he got out the chains and hooked them around the floor joists, as well as around the bar in front of the tractor. By applying steady pressure, he tried to collapse the house. It just didn't want to give.

Hugh was beginning to think the old building was a living thing that doggedly resisted his every effort to destroy it. But no way would he let the house triumph. By hook or by crook, it was going to fade into oblivion—even if it was the last thing he did.

He rocked the tractor forward and backward several times in quick succession, and finally he heard the sound of wood snapping, squealing off its nails, capitulating to Hugh's merciless demands.

Despite their much-weakened state, the four outside walls continued to stand.

Exasperated, Hugh took up his axe again and chopped holes on each corner. He passed a chain around in a loop back to the tractor, secured it, and then backed up rather quickly. The corner gave way and fell inward.

Unbelievably, Hugh had to do the same for each corner until the antiquated house finally fell in on itself, fully ruined. Even then, the roof sat atop the heap, intact, further infuriating Hugh. He jumped up on to the wreckage with his sledgehammer and beat the roof until he could no longer lift the hammer.

He wanted to set fire to the ruin at once, but some spot in his brain that still functioned rationally told him to wait until he recovered his strength. If the fire should extend beyond the heap of decaying wood, he would need to rely on his wits and speed to curb it.

Somehow this thought led him to remember the other structure that needed to be demolished and burnt—the shack that had hidden the copper still. He tossed chains and axe into the cab of the tractor and drove along the edge of the bush until he had sidled up next to the structure. It took some fiddling with chains, but he managed to drag the shack back to the main yard whole.

By evening, the shack was decimated.

Wisdom and common sense once again told him to wait until morning before turning it into a conflagration. He did, but he spent the evening seated in his lawn chair staring at the shattered heap of wood that had once been his unhappy home, his long-standing rancour still intense and smouldering.

$\sim$

He awoke on Tuesday morning to find himself lying on the floor of his cabin. It took a minute to remember that he'd lain there, not wanting to soil his bed with his sweaty, dirty body. Head to toe, every one of his muscles ached from overexertion. And his back was worse than ever. Yet he ignored all the pain to see the job through.

Today was burn day.

To ensure a safe blaze, Hugh doused the grass surrounding the ruins of the farmhouse with water from the well. He even sprayed the trees and caraganas that lined the property no more than twenty feet from the east side of the old house. After that, he sprinkled a bit of gasoline on the wood. For safety reasons, again, he thought to get it started small and allow it to gradually burn up.

Nope. He greatly underestimated the speed with which the dry old timbers would catch fire. In all of a minute, the small fire raced through the boards and engulfed the entire pile, shooting flames high into the air. It burned exceedingly hot too. He couldn't stand anywhere near the blaze.

Thinking fast, he moved his truck well away from the fire, but he felt suddenly concerned for his newly built cabin. He sprayed its roof and siding with water.

Although Hugh chalked it up to his imagination, he believed he heard shrieks and screams rising out of the flames, fading into the sky above. It was the closest he could come to exacting vengeance, and he felt the satisfaction of having had the last word.

The fire burned as an inferno for about fifteen troubling minutes before dying. Hugh couldn't believe how fast it ended. He thought he'd be nursing the fire for the rest of the day. It was all over by noon— sooner, actually.

But Hugh was adamant that everything be burned down to powdery ash, so he kept the larger pieces burning through the use of a rake and shovel. He went back to angrily yelling accusations to his deceased father, calling him every dirty word he could think of.

Much of the ash tidily contained itself in the former dirt cellar, the only evidence that any building had once stood there. It suited Hugh well enough; the yard suddenly seemed so much more spacious.

He became aware of how filthy he was and longed for a shower. He would have one at Ellie's place, he told himself, and tell her it was okay to come by if she wanted.

~

"I've come to have a shower," said Hugh hoarsely after Ellie responded to the knock on her door.

Ellie nodded and stepped aside.

While he showered, she got the kettle boiling to make him a cup of tea with lemon and honey. It should soothe his sore throat.

Fifteen minutes later, he came into the kitchen looking more like his normal self, except that his face was very red, like sunburn, after having lingered near the fire so long.

Ellie indicated for him to take a seat at the kitchen table and placed the mug of honey-lemon tea in front of him.

"Thanks," croaked Hugh gratefully. "You can come back to my place when you want. It's over. Lots of things are over. At least I hope so."

"Did it work?" asked Ellie with a trace of doubt.

"What? I don't know what you mean."

"Do you feel better? Were you able to work off your anger? You know, get it out of your system?"

"Yeah, I think so," he rasped. "I feel calm. For years I've felt like I was burning up inside from all the repressed hatred for him—Pa, I mean. When I left, I tried to bury my memories. Buried my feelings too. I realize now that it didn't work. It's been smouldering underneath all along. Underneath my determination to finish high school, my training as a mechanic, even while I was busy working at that garage in Winnipeg. Since I've come back, my past has gotten in my face again. So I dumped all my resentment into that house and tore it down, purging myself of anything that remained as it burned, burned, burned... Now I feel quiet. Empty. Like the hate is gone. I sure hope it is. Being basically mad all the time is exhausting."

Ellie nodded. "I hope you know that, on the one hand, it's great. On the other hand, you're in a vulnerable place. Just sayin'. You want to be careful who gets to you now. I highly recommend inviting Jesus to come in and occupy your empty place so it's filled with someone good. Otherwise—"

"I'm still thinking about it, Ellie." He arched his back and squirmed under the ache of his muscles.

"I'm trained to give patients a massage when they need it. Would you like me to give you one?"

"Sure, that would be great."

Ellie left momentarily and returned with a bottle of lotion. In the meantime, Hugh removed his T-shirt. She couldn't help noticing how well-defined his muscles were.

Squirting some lotion on each shoulder near Hugh's neck, Ellie gently, and then more firmly, kneaded the muscles.

Hugh moaned with great appreciation.

~

Not long after that, Hugh went back to his own place to rest up. Meanwhile, Ellie readied herself to go into Minitonas to restock on groceries. She wanted to get it done before her nieces and nephews arrived to stay with her the next day.

Coming out of the grocery store, she saw a soiled, stooped figure standing near the entrance.

"Can ya spare me a dollar, ma'am?" he implored.

"Tipper!" she cried in recognition.

Tipper blinked and dropped his eyes, seemingly embarrassed.

"Don't go anywhere. I'll be right back." Ellie quickly deposited her sacks of groceries in the trunk of her car. "Are you hungry? Is that why you're asking for money?"

Tipper nodded, averting his eyes.

"Wait right here."

Ellie disappeared into the grocery store and took a few minutes to carefully choose a few items that would make for healthy eating and keep well. She paid for them and left the store.

She placed the large brown paper sack in the man's arms. "Here you go."

"Thank ya, ma'am," said Tipper, hurrying away.

Mrs. Bradley, an elderly woman from the town, approached, having watched the entire exchange from across the street. She stopped Ellie before she could get into her car.

"I saw what you just did, young lady," the woman said. "And I have to tell you, I don't appreciate it."

Ellie was taken aback.

"We want the town of Minitonas to be free of the riffraff standing around on our streets and begging from good, decent people," Mrs. Bradley continued. "They should get a job like everyone else and provide for themselves like all respectable folk. If you give them money, they will only spend it on more liquor. Because they are all drunks, you know. They won't spend it on the food for which they trick you into parting with your money. What you did just encourages them. If that keeps up, pretty soon our streets won't be safe for women and children to walk on."

She shook her index finger in Ellie's face.

"Well, well, Mrs. Bradley. And good day to you too, by the way." More than a little shocked, Ellie didn't quite know what to say. Then she quickly collected her thoughts. "You know, I understand what you're trying to say, and I might even agree with you on some points, but it's much harder to ignore the so-called riffraff if you know them. If the poor are anonymous, we can talk about them however we want. But that old man you saw me give groceries to? He's known around here as Tipper, and I know him. Maybe you should know a few things about him too. For example, his real name is Leonard Wallen. When he was a boy, his momma called him Lenny. He's not an anonymous face to me, and now he's not an anonymous face to you either. Yes, I know he's an alcoholic and I wish he would stop drinking, but I also know that he's genuinely hungry for food. Real food. Good food. He needs help, and that's what I gave him. I don't, and won't, apologize for that."

Mrs. Bradley reared back, looking stung. "Well, you needn't be so sharp! You sound like Darcey Unger talking like that!"

The woman hurriedly walked away on up the street.

"I'll take that as a compliment," said Ellie after her, miffed.

Twenty-Three

ROB AND SARAH dropped their kids off at the farm around nine in the morning on Thursday. After they'd gotten settled, Ellie asked what they wanted to do first. Charlotte wanted to bake. Beanie wanted to play a board game. Trevor rolled his eyes, not wanting to do either of those things—although when pressed, he suggested they go outside and play soccer; he and Charlotte against Aunt Ellie and the Bean would make for fair teams, he thought.

Luckily, their dad had been thoughtful enough to bring the kids' bikes. Ellie suggested they bike down to the Roaring River and jump rocks the way she had when she'd been their age. This had been a favourite pastime when she was a kid, and her mother had sometimes joined in. She treasured that wholesome memory.

The suggestion was accepted by all three.

With Ellie in the lead, they pedalled their way in a caravan of two-wheelers down to the bridge where they could access the river. The water was low, as it usually was in summer.

When they'd all climbed down the bank and stood at the water's edge, Ellie said, "The game is to jump from rock to rock down the river as far as we can go until we reach a deeper spot where there are no more rocks to jump on. Then we turn around and go back to where we started."

Off they went.

"Oh, and you have to do it without getting wet, so plan your steps before you jump," added Ellie.

Trevor, being older, athletically nimble, and having the longest legs, proceeded very well. He had good balance. Beanie needed the most help being the little peanut she was.

"When was the last time you kids played in a river like this?" asked Ellie, assessing the next rock to jump to.

Trevor and Charlotte answered at the same time. "Never."

"We just go to Wellman Lake. It's only a half hour away," added Trevor.

"It's great that you get to go to the lake," said Ellie after she had made her next move. "But you're missing out on some fun that's almost as close as your own backyard."

"This *is* fun," agreed Trevor. "But the river's no good for swimming on a hot day."

A pensive look came across Ellie's face. "Actually, I know about a little swimming hole nearby... but it's on private land."

"Where?" asked Trevor and Charlotte in unison.

"In the woodland at Hugh's place," she said. "We'd have to ask to use it. It wouldn't be right to go onto someone's property without permission."

"When we passed by today, we saw the big house is all gone," Charlotte observed. "Is that teeny little house sort of in the middle of the yard where he lives now?"

"It is. It's lots more comfortable for him than his tent used to be."

"But it's so *boring*. It looks like a junky old cabin. Why doesn't he paint it or something?"

"I'm sure it's because he has more important things to do," answered Ellie, though she privately agreed.

"Then why don't we do it?" suggested Charlotte.

"That would take a long time. Besides, one of the principles for building that cabin was that he could only use salvage. So the paint would have to be leftover, and I don't know where we'd get enough. And I don't know if Mr. Hugh would agree to it."

"What's salvage?" asked Beanie.

"Leftover stuff," her brother replied. He'd been following the conversation with mild interest.

"How about just the trim?" Charlotte pressed. "Even if we just painted the door and around the windows, that would cheer it up quite a bit, don't you think?"

It was getting close to noon. Time to get back to the Bauman farm.

Trevor led the bicyclers while Ellie rode tail. But when they got to the driveway, Charlotte didn't follow the others in; instead she sped straight in the direction of Hugh's place.

Ellie watched her go, finding this rather annoying. However, she didn't pursue her niece. She figured out what Charlotte was after.

When Charlotte got to the Fischers' driveway, she saw Hugh bent over the motor of his antique farm truck. He looked up upon hearing the bike's wheels crunch on the gravel.

When he recognized his visitor, he smiled broadly. "Hey girl, what brings you to my place?"

"I want to ask you something," said Charlotte, a little breathless. She brought her bike to a standstill beside him and got off.

"Shoot."

"Well, I was wondering…" Charlotte felt suddenly shy. "Could we paint the trim on your little house to cheer it up? It looks so sad being made of nothing but old grey boards."

Hugh narrowed his eyes in suspicion. "Did your Aunt Ellie put you up to this?"

"Oh no. It was my idea," admitted Charlotte proudly.

"Is it? What colours did you have in mind? I won't agree to girly colours like pink or baby blue."

"I don't know yet. Aunt Ellie said the rule was to use salvage, and we haven't yet checked out what we have for leftover paints."

"Well… I guess I'll say yes to you, Miss Charlotte. Because you're right! There's nothing cheerful about my cabin or anything else on this yard. We should do something about it." He paused, making direct eye contact. "When did you have in mind?"

"Probably after lunch. If we can get the paint business sorted out."

"Okay then. See you later, alligator."

"In a while, crocodile!"

They did a high five and then Charlotte biked happily back to Bauman Farms.

~

After a lunch of grilled cheese sandwiches, Ellie and the children descended on the machine shop where the many pails of leftover paint were stowed. They started by setting aside a few of them to be taken to the dump; they had dried up after many years of neglect. However, they did come up with a quarter-can of beige, and a quarter-can of pale yellow. When mixed with nearly half a gallon of leftover white, it came out the colour of cream. Ellie figured that should be enough to paint all the trim—and look good in the process.

They also discussed the possibility of painting the door and came up with some red and blue. Trevor wanted to mix it, and Ellie reluctantly gave in. The result was a deep purple.

"At least it isn't pink," said Charlotte.

Armed with assorted brushes and their pails of mixed paint, including primer, they set off for Hugh's place. Charlotte excitedly showed Hugh their palette.

"I'm fine with it if your aunt is," he said, giving Ellie a little wink.

Ellie smiled, appreciating that he would trust her judgment in the matter.

Trevor balked, however. "Isn't painting kind of a girl's job? If I'm gonna do something, it should be men's work."

Ellie rolled her eyes, but Hugh had more patience for him.

"Come with me, Trev," Hugh said. "I'm about to construct a cover for the well behind the barn. And then I want to install the pitcher pump on top of it. You can help with that. I promise you, that's not women's work."

Relieved, Trevor left the girls and followed him.

With everyone happily employed, the afternoon flew by. Charlotte primed and painted the vertical trim on each of the four corners of the cabin and the wide trim around the windows and door. Ellie painted the narrower frame around the windowpanes, as well as both sides of the door in purple. Being taller than Charlotte, she also painted the narrow facia board around the roof with the cream colour.

Beanie lasted about half an hour before she started whining about being tired and not wanting to paint anymore. She left to watch the work being done at the well.

Charlotte finished Beanie's job, which had been to paint the skirting boards around the bottom of the cabin.

Despite some misgivings, Ellie thought the final product looked very handsome. And yes, it made for a much more attractive structure.

"It kind of makes you want to add flowerboxes under the windows," Ellie remarked when Hugh came back to inspect the work; he and Trevor had finished installing the old pitcher pump. "You know, to complete the charm the cabin radiates now."

"Not a chance. I don't do flowerboxes. But you did a nice job, ladies. It looks really good."

He offered the Baumans a wiener roast supper, a chance they jumped at.

Afterward the kids begged to go up into the loft of the barn to find out how far they could see from high up.

While they were gone, Hugh told Ellie that he was thinking of moving every piece of equipment out of the old machine shed. That would allow him to use it as a mechanics shop until he was able to build himself a new facility.

"Are you still interested in all of the old junk we took out of the house?" Hugh asked.

"Are you still giving it to me? What if I want to sell some of it?"

"It's yours to keep, sell, give away, or trash."

"Just checking," she said. "I suppose you want it all out of your barn now."

"I do."

"The kids and I can do it tomorrow if you don't mind me using your truck to transfer everything over."

"I guess there's no other way to make it disappear."

~

By 10:00 p.m., the kids were all showered, pyjamaed, and ready for their first sleepover. Trevor was supposed to sleep in the guest room, the space where his dad and uncles had slept when they were kids. Both of the girls wanted to sleep with Ellie.

But as soon as the lights went out, the pillow talk began. Beanie wanted to play games like "Would You Rather…" and "What Kind of Animal…" and "What Is Your Favourite…" and "Twenty Questions." Ellie obliged her, and the result was a lot of giggling.

Not wanting to be left out, Trevor came walking back in, his blanket trailing behind him. They made quite a heap of humanity all bunched together in Ellie's bed.

In time, Beanie fell asleep first. Trevor was next, followed by Charlotte.

Ellie, snuggled between her two nieces, then lay awake for a long time thinking about how blessed she was to have family to love on, and to be loved on by. Alternately, she also found herself pining for a child of her own.

~

"All right, you lazy bones! Time to get up. We got work to do!"

Ellie shook the kids one after the other. Each turned away from her and buried their heads deeper under the covers. This caused her to rethink her strategy. When she began to tickle them, they all woke up giggling.

Ellie treated them to blueberry pancakes with crispy bacon strips. Then they piled into her car and aimed for Hugh's place.

Hugh had already been up for a couple of hours and had managed to load a number of pieces into the back of his truck singlehandedly. He was almost set to take over the first load when the Baumans showed up.

"Where's all this supposed to go?" asked Hugh, referring to the items in the back of his truck.

"It will have to go in the Quonset."

"Come with me, Trev." Hugh winked at the boy. "Let's build some muscles into those skinny arms of yours."

Many hands make light work and it wasn't long before the barn was void of its furnishings, housewares, windows, doors, and miscellany.

"Did you really just *give* Aunt Ellie all this stuff?" asked Charlotte upon the third load.

"Yep, I did. I wanted to trash everything and she wouldn't let me. So I said she could have it to do with whatever she wanted. And I meant it."

"I don't get it."

"You don't have to. But every load that gets taken away makes me feel happy."

The large wooden steamer trunk was the last thing to be taken over. Ellie put Trevor and Charlotte in charge of taking the old school desk out of her room, in favour of the trunk. The desk, of course, would be stored in the basement until a new use for it could be found. The trunk was a handsome piece made of hardwood, perhaps cherry, and bolstered with simple but effective wooden and metallic reinforcements. Its lock was likely fashioned of brass, as were the corners and rivets, though they were almost black now from years of neglect.

Given how much of what had been in the Fischer house was so shabby, the trunk was in surprisingly good shape.

And it was heavy to lift. Ellie insisted that the kids handle it with care until such time that it could be opened and its contents understood.

When it was finally set in place in her bedroom, Ellie realized that she loved it. The trunk added character, and she enjoyed the mystery of its yet unknown contents. Fuel for the imagination, she called it.

~

At breakfast on Saturday morning, Ellie made an announcement. Since the kids had worked so hard over the last couple of days, and since the weatherman promised a hot summer day, she declared they would go to Wellman Lake.

This was met with joy and excitement. Immediately the insulated picnic hamper was brought out and got filled with assorted picnic food and treats. They filled two gallon-sized thermoses with ice water and lemonade.

For swimming suits, towels, sand, and float toys, they would have to stop at the Bauman home in Minitonas.

Soon they were ready to go.

"Can we bring Mr. Fischerman too?" piped up Beanie.

"Do you mean Hugh?" asked Ellie. Beanie nodded. "Then his last name is Fischer, honey. Not Fischerman."

"Well, can he come?"

Ellie looked to Trevor and Charlotte. They looked at each other and then back at Ellie with a shrug.

"Sure," they said. "That's fine."

"Okay. We'll stop in at his place on our way out and see what he says. Get in the car, everybody!"

All three of the children's eyes went wide with surprise as they turned into Hugh's driveway. After emptying the barn, it turned out that Hugh had focused on emptying the machine shed. The yard was littered with old-fashioned farm equipment. The antiquated farm truck was back to being sheltered in the barn.

They caught Hugh in the act of removing the last item, a plough. He was pulling it out of the shed with the tractor.

Ellie rolled down the window of her car as Hugh descended from the tractor and walked toward them.

"The Bean wants to ask you something," she said.

With his arms resting on the roof of the car, Hugh looked through the window, past Ellie, to Beanie sitting in the passenger seat.

"Will you come to the beach with us?" asked Beanie, hopeful.

"You're having a beach day, are you?" Hugh stroked his chin in deliberation.

"All work and no play makes Jack a dull boy," quipped Trevor.

"Please come," pleaded Charlotte. "It will be fun."

Ellie gestured to all the farm implements, which Hugh had left scattered all over the yard. "This will all be here when you get back."

Hugh sighed. "It will, won't it..."

He stood up, removed his cap, and scratched his head. After a moment, he seemed to have made up his mind.

"All right. You talked me into it. Give me a minute to change."

A few minutes later, he emerged from The Ritz clad in cut-off denim shorts and a tank top with a towel hanging from his neck. He also carried swim trunks.

Beanie joined her sibling in the back seat to make room for him.

They still had to make a stop at the kids' home in Minitonas before they could carry on, but finally they were on their way, happy and full of anticipation for the summer adventure ahead.

"Let's sing camp songs," said Charlotte after their stop in Mini-tonas.

She immediately launched into a series of tunes, beginning with "There was an old woman who swallowed a fly..." followed by "There's a hole in the bottom of the sea..." and "There's a hole in the bucket, dear Lisa, dear Lisa..." They ended with another favourite, "Down by the bay…" The kids really hammed it up over making up funny lyrics. Several times, Hugh laughed out loud.

"You've never heard these silly songs before?" asked Ellie in surprise.

"Nope. Pretty sure I missed out on having a childhood, at least a normal one," he replied. "Hey, thanks for inviting me today. It's nice to be wanted. I'm not used to that."

"It was Beanie's idea." Ellie spoke in a low voice so the kids behind her would be less likely to hear.

"You didn't want me?"

"I didn't say that. I just mean that the kids think you're the cat's pyjamas. Last night, Charlotte told me that she was going to marry you when she grew up. I told her I thought she had said she was going to marry her daddy. Well, it turns out her mommy told her that daddy was already taken, so she'd have to find someone else. Seems like now she's picked you."

Hugh chuckled to himself. "I've discovered this week that kids can be pretty cool."

"Yeah, they can…"

When they arrived, the public beach at Wellman Lake was already peppered with families who'd had the same idea as Ellie. The Baumans, plus Hugh, rolled out their big blanket in the middle of the beach and set up their umbrella at one corner. Beneath it, they parked the picnic cooler plus the water and lemonade. They established a single rule: eat whenever you're hungry, as there would be no set lunchtime.

Then off they went, running into the water and splashing it up.

Ellie joined the kids in getting wet, although after a while they wanted to build a sandcastle. They implored Hugh to build with them, and then improved on that idea by making it a castle-building contest, with Hugh and Beanie competing against Trevor and Charlotte.

Ellie opted to sun herself on their beach blanket and observe the merriment. She loved the sight of her little crew getting along so happily. She couldn't help but notice how intently Hugh kept his eyes on them, as if he was learning by example how to be a kid himself.

Since the dark days at the beginning of the week, it did seem that he was able to finally relax. He was less edgy, more subdued.

A shadow fell across Ellie's face. "How come you're not in the water?" asked a woman in a strong voice.

"Darcey!" she exclaimed. "You're the last person I expected to see here today."

She moved over on the blanket so Darcey could join her.

"Why? I came home with Abby on Tuesday," Darcey said. "I was ready for an outing. Tony and the girls suggested a day at the beach, and I wasn't going to argue. Of course, I won't be going into the water. I might be crazy, but I'm not stupid."

Ellie looked up and down the beach. "Where's the rest of your family?"

"They're on the dock. Tony's trying to get them to jump into his arms. See?"

Sure enough, there they were.

"Can I see Miss Abigail?" Ellie asked, noticing the baby bucket carrier next to Darcey. It was covered with netting.

Darcey lifted the netting to reveal her newborn, capped with peach fuzz blond hair and swaddled with a light flannel receiving blanket.

"Wow, she's so new," Ellie remarked. "And yet so big, in a way. She came half grown up!"

"Well, that's what happens when you have a Clydesdale for a momma!"

"You look great, though. It's hard to tell you've just had a baby. Your tummy is pretty flat and it's been only a week.

"That's because I maintained an exercise regimen throughout my pregnancy. I can't help being big, but I don't want to be both big *and* ugly." Now it was Darcey's turn to look up and down the beach. "Who are you here with, Rob's kids?"

Ellie nodded and pointed them out.

"Who's that with them?"

"My neighbour, Hugh Fischer."

Darcey flashed Ellie a pointed look. "He looks good..."

"We're friends. Not sweethearts. We help each other out."

"So, no boyfriend?"

"Not at the moment. Only a boyfriend wannabe."

"Let me guess," said Darcey, grinning. "Rory Lang."

Ellie blushed, feeling slightly embarrassed. "How come that was so easy for you?"

"Because the guy is so obviously desperate. He follows unmarried girls around like a puppy. My guess is he's pushing thirty and already worried he'll wind up a bachelor for the rest of his days. He can't seem to get a girl to go for him, no matter what he does. It doesn't help that he has the face of a child and still lives with his parents, though I've heard he's taken over their farming operation."

"I thought of him as a nerd in high school, and it seems to me his nerdy ways haven't changed," Ellie said. "He cornered me last Saturday at the picnic. I didn't mind talking with him, but the thought of him touching me…"

"…might make you want to gag?"

"That seems a trifle unkind to say, but…"

"But… bang on, right? I used to date. I know how it is. I remember the days when it seemed that the boys I liked didn't like me, and the boys I didn't care a twig about were the ones trying to knock down my door. So glad those days are over."

"Yeah. That pretty much sums it up."

"Say, I need to use the restroom." Darcey began to get up from the blanket. "Can I leave Abby with you for a few minutes? I'll be right back."

"Of course."

Within a minute of Darcey's departure, the baby began to fuss. Ellie tried to put the pacifier in Abby's mouth, but every one of her efforts was rejected.

At last the baby began to cry in earnest. The sound of the newborn crying reached the ears of Charlotte and Beanie. They looked up to see their aunt lifting the baby out of the bucket carrier.

When they ran over to see, Trevor and Hugh weren't far behind.

"Awwww, she's so cute," cooed Charlotte.

"I wanna see," insisted Beanie. "Let me see too!"

Ellie adjusted the baby's position so Beanie could have a close look. Trevor and Hugh stood back, gazing down at the wee child from above while Ellie stroked her soft, delicate skin. It reminded her of a horse's muzzle.

"Aunty, what's the matter? Why are you crying?" asked Beanie, alarmed.

Ellie started, not having realized that tears were quietly spilling out of her eyes.

"I'm just thinking about a baby that died," replied Ellie, faltering.

She blinked and a couple more tears ran down her cheeks. Beanie wiped them off with sandy hands, creating a smudge on Ellie's face.

"What baby are you talking about?" asked Charlotte.

"It was in the hospital," answered Ellie carefully. "I'm a nurse, remember?"

All three kids accepted this. It was, after all, a totally reasonable explanation.

Hugh, on the other hand, stared intently at Ellie, who seemed to intentionally refuse to return his gaze. He heard what she had said, but he very much wondered what it was that she wasn't saying.

Twenty-Four

ROB AND SARAH had enjoyed the break from their family and regular routines, but now Rob was anxious to drive around the fields and monitor his crops. He was also ready to check on his harvesting equipment to ensure it was in good running order, even though the harvest was still several weeks away.

While rushing up Road 150W and passing by the Fischer farm, he jammed on the brakes to make an abrupt turn onto Hugh's driveway. Rob had noticed the younger man walking amidst an array of old farm equipment. It seemed a good time to chew the rag before continuing on with his day's business.

He pulled up in front of Hugh's cabin and cut the motor.

As soon as Hugh recognized his visitor, he turned on his heel and strode toward Rob.

"Hey! You must be able to read minds," Hugh said. "I was just thinking about you and wishing I had your opinion on a few things."

"I thought so. 'Fraid my opinion has a price, though." The corners of his mouth tipped upward.

Hugh did a quick double take. "All right… what's your price?"

"A cup of good coffee." Rob's face broke out in a grin. "Oh, and make sure it's coffee, not tar. I swear some people make coffee so strong the spoon could stand up by itself."

Hugh visibly relaxed. "I'm sure I still have some left in my coffee pot. Sugar? Cream?"

Rob shook his head.

Hugh disappeared into his cabin. While he was gone, Rob took a long look around the yard, taking in the many changes that had occurred since the last time he had dropped by, which hadn't been so very long ago.

Soon Hugh emerged with two steaming mugs of black coffee.

"It sure makes a difference with the old house being gone," said Rob, taking one of the mugs.

"In more ways than you know. What's your opinion on all these pieces of equipment? Are they worth anything? Are they even useful? I don't know what to do about them."

Rob didn't answer immediately. He took the time to walk around each machine, kicking the tires, looking at the motors, wiggling the gear sticks, occasionally passing a hand along a surface. He even peered closely at the spots of rust.

At last he circled back to where they had started in front of Hugh's cabin.

"There was a time when every one of these implements was just right for farmwork," Rob began. "Farms have grown considerably since your grandfather and mine homesteaded in the Swan Valley. Heck, even since I was a youngster, and I'm not that old. How much land do you own?"

"A half-section."

"That's quite a lot of land for these poor old beasts to keep up with. You already know they're not only old… they're worn out. You can run them if they'll go, but you're likely to spend as much time fixing them as you are to get any use of them in the field. They'll be lots slower and less efficient than the equipment available today. If this was my decision, I'd get rid of almost all of it. You can try to sell them, but I doubt you'll get much, if anything. Hobby farmers might be interested. They only work a few acres, usually forty to eighty is typical. There may be museums interested in some of the models, though they'd expect donations. You can also haul the items to the scrap metal yard. You won't get a lot, but it'll cover your gas and tidy up the farm."

Hugh nodded along as the man spoke. "None of that surprises me. I've been thinking along similar lines. But you said *almost*. What would you keep?"

"Well, as long as you live in the country, be it a full-scale farm or an acreage, a tractor is useful. Though if it was me, I'd give up this tractor as well. If I could only have one tractor, I'd have one with a front-end loader and the rear features of a live PTO and three-point hitch. That would take care of anything I had to do around the farmyard, summer or winter."

Hugh nodded with complete understanding.

"Can I ask you a question?" asked Rob.

"Go for it!"

"How badly do you want to farm? What I mean is, is it a passion for you? Can you hardly wait to get at it?"

"I honestly don't know," admitted Hugh. "To tell the truth, one of the reasons I cleared out the shed was to see if it was stable enough to use as a mechanics garage. I told you I'm trained in mechanics, didn't I?"

"You talked about it at the FBC picnic. If that's where your interests lean, you should give it serious thought." Rob looked around the property with an appraising eye. "See, it's different for me. I eat, drink, and sleep farming. I did it with my dad all through my youth. My brothers had to help too, but to them it was a chore. I loved it. After all these years, it's still fun to climb onto a tractor and put in a crop. It's still exciting to drive a combine and watch the rows of grain feed through the reel. I love to see the beautiful seeds in the bin. It's still a thrill to catch the blue blossoms of flax waving in the breeze like water, or the stunningly pure yellow of a canola crop. There's nothing more satisfying than looking at a golden field of ripe wheat. Barley looks good too, but you'll never get used to the itch! Nothing smells as good as fresh hay stacked under cover, unless it's my wife's home-made bread. That's hard to beat…"

Hugh smiled. "I think you should be a poet."

"Who says I'm not?" Rob smiled in return. "So what are you going to do for a house this winter?"

"I think I'd like to build one of the plans Ellie laid out for me. But I'm spinning my wheels trying to figure out whether I should put my energy into building the house or starting the business."

"Winter comes quickly, and it's not usually kind," Rob reminded him. "Show me what you're looking at."

Hugh retreated into the cabin and returned with the folder. He flipped through the pages until he came to the plan that most appealed to him. He handed it to Rob.

Rob studied it intently for a moment. "Looks like it has all you'd need. Simple structure. Wouldn't be hard to throw together."

"That's what I thought. I'll need a permit, of course. But do you think the floorplan will be accepted if I turned it in to the municipal office? Or do I have to get it officially drafted first? Like you said, it's simple and straightforward."

"I know everybody who sits on council. I don't mind putting in a word for you if it comes to that."

"Thanks. I appreciate that."

"You know…" Rob passed his hand across his chin, looking thoughtful. "I have an idea for how we could scratch each other's backs."

"I'm listening."

"When the fields are ripe, I usually need to hire someone to help, because time is of the essence and I have quite a lot of land to harvest. How about I help you put up this small house asap, and you help me take off my crops in August and September? The experience should help you figure out whether farming is something you truly want to do."

"I don't even need to think about it," Hugh replied. "That's a win-win proposition. Let's do it!"

He held out his hand, and Rob shook it firmly.

~

Ellie had four days, max, to get the antiques and housewares ready for the upcoming yard sale set for Saturday, July 12. She began with emptying the jars of home-canned food, sorely wishing her mother had opted to install an automatic dishwasher. To save time and energy carrying items back and forth, she set up a large plastic basin with hot soapy water in the Quonset and washed the housewares there.

Going through all the boxes, she was sad to note that there wasn't anything of particularly high quality to set aside. She wasn't sad for herself, but for Alice, Hugh's mother, who seemed not to have had any nice possessions.

There were many crocks and Ellie set aside for herself a collection of one in every size from a half-gallon to the lidded ten-gallon container. It was easy to imagine the larger crocks had been used to make wine, as well as sauerkraut. Several glass bottles also needed to be cleaned; she recognized some that had contained horse liniment and wondered if these had been used to treat horses, or perhaps poor old Rudolf Fischer himself with his lame hip and leg.

While she was repacking the housewares into boxes, Rob pulled up in front of the Quonset. Ellie was happy to see him.

"You're exactly the person I wanted to talk to," she said as he stepped out of his truck and closed the door behind him.

Rob took in the large assortment of items littering the floor around the Quonset's entrance.

A feeling of foreboding seemed to rise up within him. "I'm afraid to ask, but why?"

"Most of this is destined for a yard sale in Swan River this weekend. I need your help getting it there."

"All of this stuff?" asked Rob incredulously.

"Most of it, except the sofa set and tall lamp table. Those I'm keeping for myself. That and the set of crocks over there." Ellie pointed to the collection next to the sofa. "But I'll also need to bring an old cast-iron woodstove and rather large stack of weathered boards that are still over at Hugh's place..." She finished weakly, casting her eyes to the ground.

"You've got to be kidding! All this stuff would fill my grain truck with no room left over. Why Swan River? Why not here? Our place isn't far from the main highway."

"Mrs. Johnson, Hugh's aunt, asked to have it at her place. We put ads in the local papers. I can't change it now."

"Does Mrs. Johnson know that this much paraphernalia is coming to her yard? I assume it's just a small city lot."

"I'm not sure she's on to the whole scope of this." Ellie waved her arm over the collection. "But she is very keen to help out. I'm sorry to trouble you with my projects, but I don't know who else to ask."

Rob exhaled loudly and made a 360-degree turn. He took off his cap, scratched the top of his head, and exhaled again. He was clearly displeased.

"I'm feeling like I don't really have a choice here." His cap returned to his head, his hands back on his hips. "But boy, kid, you owe me bigtime!"

Ellie sighed with relief and wrapped her arms around her brother in deep appreciation. "Thank you, this means a lot to me. I'll pay you for the gas!"

"I'm not worried about the gas. What if this stuff doesn't sell like you imagine it will and it all has to be brought back? I think then I'll be some upset. You'd better be right about this yard sale business. Oh, and you'd better arrange for some extra help. I can't do this all by myself..."

On Tuesday morning, Hugh marched into the municipal office in Minitonas and made a presentation in which he requested a building permit. The clerk, a thickly built woman who carried herself like the office chieftain, advised him that while the drawings were lovely, he would need to provide blueprints. Hugh surmised that it would be useless to argue with her.

His next stop was to the home of Rob Bauman, who could be found enjoying a leisurely breakfast with his family.

"Mrs. McDonald is very particular about doing things strictly by the book," said Rob dryly after Hugh explained his predicament. "Most of the time, that's a good quality. And then there's plain old common sense. I know every one of the counsellors and they're pretty reasonable. I'll see if they can move on this right away. Go back to Ellie and ask her to prepare a more detailed, blueprint-like drawing that shows window sizes, electrical outlets, etcetera. That should help gain council's approval without annoying Mrs. McDonald."

Hugh drove directly to the Bauman farm and parked in front of the open Quonset. Ellie was in the middle of washing out the cupboard his mother had once used as a pantry for kitchen staples. It gave him an odd feeling to see her put something like loving care into an old piece of furniture that nobody in his youth had seemed to give two hoots about.

"I need you to do something for me as soon as possible, please," he said respectfully before presenting to her the drawing she'd made. "Rob is going to make a case for the local counsellors to grant me a building permit, but we need it to look more like a blueprint. Could you expand on this floorplan by marking out more details and specifications?"

"Right now?"

"Right now."

Ellie sighed but dropped her cloth into the bucket and made her way toward the house, Hugh at her side. She went directly to her room and retrieved the flat box that held her papers and related supplies.

Close to three hours and a pot of coffee later, with Hugh watching the whole time and contributing suggestions, she completed the floorplan as well as four upright profiles to represent each of the four exterior walls, showing window and door placements.

"That's the best I can do," said Ellie. "I have no training in drafting. I'm merely a copycat."

"It looks great. The building is very basic," he remarked. "Thanks very much."

Without another thought, he picked up the freshly drawn papers and kissed her on the cheek.

He froze in horror, realizing what he had just done. "I'm sorry. I hope I haven't offended you."

"No. You didn't offend me." She grinned broadly. "But get outta here. I still have lots of work to do before Friday."

Her efforts were more than good enough, it turned out. By Thursday, he had his building permit in hand.

Twenty-Five

ELLIE AND ROB planned to begin loading his big grain truck at 1:00 p.m. on Friday. Since she felt she was still in her brother's debt, she wanted to be sure she wasn't personally late to help with the loading. Thus, she made a point of getting up early to concentrate on her soul work. She was still in the Psalms, a major theme of which was offering praise to God for His goodness and faithfulness. As Ellie reflected on that, she began to understand that praise was an effective antidote for any number of troubling things. Praising God brought one back to centre when chaos swirled all around.

With that insight, she spent most of her prayer time praising God and acknowledging His greatness, kindness, and goodness to her. She also invited Him to be present in the matter of the yard sale. However it turned out, she prayed that she would reflect the wise and loving spirit of Jesus within her with every interaction the day would bring.

The morning would be dedicated to setting up and staging the various artefacts she meant to bring, so she dressed in grubby jeans and an old plaid shirt. Her first task was to assign prices to each item. This turned out to be a long, thoughtful process and she often wondered if her expectations were too high.

I can always reduce the price if I'm overly optimistic, she thought.

Rob was late by half an hour, but when he arrived she saw that Hugh and Trevor were with him.

"I've made the executive decision that certain things, like the weathered boards and woodstove, will be offered for sale right off the truck," Rob explained. "There's no sense in handling them more than we absolutely have to."

That made good sense to Ellie.

For that reason, the windows and doors were loaded next, as they would stay on the truck throughout the sale as well.

After that, the items were added randomly. With three adults and one strapping teenager, the loading didn't take nearly so long as Ellie had feared. By 2:30 p.m., they were on their way to Swan River, Ellie leading the way in her car, which was also packed with boxes.

Gertie had borrowed some long folding tables from her church and set them up, wiped and ready. As Ellie unloaded the boxes from her car, Gertie unpacked them and arranged the antiques to their best effect, adding them to the items she hoped to sell from her own house. The driveway was short, so the furnishings had to be arranged close together along each side. The crocks were lined up along the front walk.

When everything was in place, Ed produced a pair of sawhorses to let passers-by know that the sale wouldn't open until 9:00 a.m. on Saturday.

Before they returned home, Ellie noticed Hugh wandering through the furnishings with a puzzled look on his face.

"Are you experiencing giver's remorse?" she asked. "Do you want some of these things back?"

"Nope. But somehow they don't look like the same items I used to see around the house. You've done something to them."

"All I did was give them a thorough cleaning or polishing. I also effected a few repairs where needed. And I didn't want the cupboards and dresser to smell musty." Ellie smiled. "Poke your nose in the pantry cupboard."

Hugh opened the door and sniffed. "Cinnamon?"

She nodded. "I hope the lovely scent helps entice someone to take it home. Sniff the dresser drawers."

"Some kind of perfume, I think."

"Right again, Hugh-liport!"

"You've gone to a lot of trouble, Ell-icopter. I sincerely hope this turns out well for you."

~

To help with the final preparations, Ellie arrived at Gertie's house shortly after eight o'clock the next morning.

Gertie took Ellie aside. "I'll make the first sale of the day by giving you this." She handed her an envelope that contained $150 in cash. "It's for the dresser I took from you. I don't feel right just taking it."

"It was mine to give, and I'm glad to have done so. Especially since it has meaning for you."

"No. You keep the cash. I want to contribute to my nephew's new beginning." Gertie patted Ellie's arm and walked away.

That made no sense at all, thought Ellie to herself, shaking her head. *I don't think she understands the arrangement I have with Hugh about these things.*

Nonetheless, she placed the envelope in the moneybox. She removed the tailgate from Rob's big truck to show the items available for sale in the box.

A few minutes later, Sarah arrived with her daughters. Together they set up their card table from home, using it to create a lemonade and cookies stand.

By quarter of nine, people were lining up behind Ed's rope.

When Ed made his appearance, Ellie had to stifle a laugh. He had dressed for the occasion by donning a white golf shirt over bold plaid Bermuda shorts that exposed his comically thin legs. Atop his head he wore a fishing hat with a few lures pinned to it. A piece of wide masking tape was affixed to his shirt with the words *ASK ME* written in black felt pen.

In keeping with his appearance, he seemed to be in a rare clownish mood. About a minute before nine, Ed stood in front of the ropes, chatting with the women at the front of the line.

At ten seconds to nine, Ed yelled out a countdown and the small crowd joined in. "Ten... nine... eight... seven... six... five... four... three... two... one... Bombs away!"

He ripped down the ropes and immediately the yard was filled with a throng of people, primarily women. It sounded like the buzzing of bees. Ellie closed her eyes for a minute to focus on the comments she heard.

"Love this cabinet! It's so shabby chic and smells like cinnamon!"

"That tube radio cabinet is just like the one my grandparents had..."

"Look! It's a real treadle sewing machine. Do you know how to use it?"

"I slept in a bed like this when I was a kid. They don't make 'em like that anymore..."

"This old washing machine would be perfect for our cabin..."

"I love it, but where would I put it?"

Pretty soon people were lining up to make purchases. Some buyers asked Ellie if she would consider taking a lower price. Her answer was always that if the item was still available after three o'clock, she would consider a discount then.

"Never mind," they invariably replied before paying the asking price.

Ed handled the contents of the big truck like an auctioneer. A pair of women were discussing the bundle of weathered boards, which was priced at $375 for the whole lot or five dollars per board. Apparently, the women were craft designers and had in mind to recycle them by creating quaint birdhouses, picture frames, and other country décor items.

Before they could decide, a married couple came up behind them with Ed in tow and declared, "We'll take the whole stack for $375."

The ladies were immediately indignant and countered, "We'll take the whole lot for $400!"

The couple looked at each other, and then at Ed. "$425."

Which caused the crafters to exchange glances and announce, in one voice, "$450!"

As for the married couple, it seemed the husband was ready to bow out, but the wife insisted they offer more.

"These boards will make a fantastic feature wall in the family room," she said. Thereupon she turned to Ed and announced: "The entire bundle for $500!"

Ed turned to the crafting ladies, who shook their heads in defeat.

He led the couple to the sales table and relayed the sum to Gertie, who at first looked surprised and then smiled like a Cheshire cat.

A similar sequence of events occurred with regards to the cast-iron woodstove. Ellie had taken great pains to clean and polish it so it gleamed like new. She had put a sticker on it asking for $500.

One woman had fallen in love with it and said to Ed, "I really want this stove, but I ought to talk with my husband first. Can you hold it for me?"

Ed intended to say yes, but that's when a gentleman who had overheard the conversation stepped in. "I'm also interested. Since it's so very well cleaned and polished, I'll give you $600."

Ed turned to the woman.

"I'll raise that to $650," she said while looking at the other bidder with steely eyes.

The gentleman glared right back. "I'll give you $725 for it."

The woman hung her head. "I can't raise that without speaking to my husband. I guess it's yours. Drat!"

"Sold to the gentleman with the moustache for $725," declared Ed and led him to the sales table.

Mid-morning, an antique dealer came along from somewhere out of town with a large van and took all the doors and windows, as well as the two cast-iron radiators and many of the crocks. He picked through the housewares, bottles, and jars too and would have liked to include the old tin tub but could spare no room for it.

As soon as the tub was set back down on the driveway, another woman claimed it immediately. "We'll use it at our cabin at the lake to rinse our sandy feet."

A group of women who had been present at the opening of the sale returned later in the day with cash and half-ton trucks to carry away the dresser with the oval mirror, the crude pantry cupboard that smelled of cinnamon, the dear old secretary, the treadle sewing machine, and the small sideboard. Other cabin owners carried away the bedframes.

The last piece of furniture to go was the washstand. It was the least attractive of all the antique pieces, having sustained many water marks. When Ellie lowered the price, it went with the next visitor.

By four o'clock, no one was coming around anymore so the sale was declared closed.

Sadly, Gertie's table sold very little. She made a sum total of $22.25. Privately, Ellie understood why. Gertie had set out things that were outdated but not truly antique. They were the sorts of things one saw at every yard sale because the items had become passé.

The lemonade and cookie stand, on the other hand, had done a booming business, most likely due to the fact that Beanie had plaintively implored everyone who passed by, "Would you please buy my cookies?" And they usually did. Charlotte scored a few sales as well, following up her sister's pleas with a more cheery, "How about a glass of lemonade to go with that?" Sarah had turned this into a teaching opportunity on business fundamentals. The deal was that the young entrepreneurs had to repay their mother for the ingredients that had gone into making the cookies and lemonade; after that, the profits were all theirs.

The girls were thrilled to have earned somewhere between fifteen and twenty dollars each for all their efforts.

The big winner, of course, was Ellie. At the end of the day, all that remained were a few glass bottles, canning jars, and sundry housewares. All the big items were gone and anything truly antique from the small items, such as the crocks, kerosene lamps, and tins, had sold in a heartbeat. When Gertie and Sarah added up Ellie's sales, it came to a whopping $3,185!

Ellie gasped. "That's unbelievable!"

Sarah beamed, happy for Ellie's success. "Good for you!"

Gertie's smile was weak and seemed pained. Ellie noticed.

"Would you like your money back?" asked Ellie softly.

"Oh no," she said, after hesitating. "It's just that I feel it should go to Hugh directly so he can buy something new and useful when he has his own house. Obviously you don't need it."

Ellie recognized this as an oblique reference to the large sum of money she herself had made that day on what Gertie considered to have been Hugh's things, not her own.

"But Mrs. Johnson," piped up Charlotte. "I heard Hugh say—"

"Never mind, Charlotte," interrupted Ellie. She turned to Gertie. "I will be sure to pass along your envelope to Hugh."

"Thank you," said Gertie, thus mollified.

There wasn't a lot to clean up, but everyone pitched in to repack everything that was now destined for the secondhand store. Gertie insisted she do it, so after repacking the boxes they were loaded into the trunk and back seat of her car.

Ellie graciously proposed to take everyone out for supper, including Rob, Hugh, and Trevor. It was her treat and expression of thanks for everyone's help. The gesture was happily accepted since they'd all had a tiring day and no one felt like cooking.

When Hugh and Rob learned of the results of Ellie's sale, they were astonished. Neither would have believed the junk would sell so well.

Ellie tried to give Rob some gas money, but he waved her off; it was enough recompense that he didn't have to haul the stuff home again.

As promised, Ellie gave Hugh the envelope of cash she'd gotten from Gertie for the dresser. Hugh didn't understand and was entirely confused.

"I'll explain later," whispered Ellie.

~

"So explain to me why I have this envelop full of cash," Hugh said when he and Ellie were alone later that evening.

"Your aunt wanted the dresser that your mother used when she lived on your farm, as a remembrance of her. I gave her the dresser free of charge, but she didn't feel right about not paying for it. She believes the money really belongs to you, not me, so she wanted me to make sure you got it."

Hugh sighed audibly. "All right, you did as she asked. But I'm giving it back to you because I'm a man of my word. I really did give you those things with no strings attached. Aunt Gertie can't change that."

"Hmmm. I don't think I can get away with it. This money has been designated for something nice and useful for when you've built your house. I'm sure she'll want to see exactly what it was spent on."

"Fine. Keep it and buy me something nice and useful. And it's okay if you happen to forget all about it." Hugh let out another long, deep sigh. "I expect eventually she will too."

Twenty-Six

THE WEEK FLEW by for Hugh. He and Rob determined that they should get some men in the concrete business to build a cistern. It seemed the soonest this could get done was the following week.

Hugh lined up all the farm equipment in a tight row along the south end of the farmyard, in the location where he'd taken down the granaries. He then erected a plywood sign nearby where it could be seen from the road. With a paintbrush and black paint, he crudely spelled out the message: *For sale, apply within or call...* The phone number was included in large letters. Ellie's great success had him hoping for some interest in the outdated farm equipment.

With these chores out of the way, Rob helped break down the old cistern, filling it in and then packing and levelling the ground. The site was now ready for a new shop to be built upon it, whenever Hugh decided he could afford the project. In the meantime, he would use the old machine shed as a workshop, such as it was.

As the sun set that Friday and Hugh retired for the night, he thought about how far he'd come in just five and a half weeks. He had reconnected with his roots, prepared to live an isolated life as a recluse, only for his nearest neighbour to worm her way into his life with irresistible kindness. In fact, all of the Baumans, from Rob down to teeny-weeny Beanie, had embraced him, making him feel not only

welcome but encouraged in word and deed. Their unexpected friendship had assured him that he mattered.

More than that, they made him feel *wanted*. He wondered, for the
umpteenth time, why they cared. In former days, the Baumans and
Fischers had had almost nothing to do with each other. Hugh realized
that was surely the way his father had wanted it. He had forced their
entire family to keep their distance from the neighbours.

"They're proud people who think they're better than us," his pa
had said during one of his tirades. "I saw old John driving a new
pick-up—didn't even notice me, the old fool. All them Baumans think
they're so high and mighty…"

He now understood that his father had been the arrogant one,
jealous of the fruits of the Baumans' hard-earned labour.

Hugh's own experience had revealed a family who wanted him
to succeed as least as much as they had, and they were more than
willing to help him get on his way.

The only other people who had given a rip about him had been
Brian and Marcie Turner. He realized that he could now add his long-
lost aunt and uncle to that short list. He wondered whether he would
ever get used to that.

An image of Ellie flashed through his mind. He had never known
another girl like her. Mind you, it was a truth that he didn't know many
women, even if he included his mother and two sisters. Still, he had
found her highly attractive the day she'd welcomed him into the
community with bran-apple muffins. As he'd gotten to work with her,
she had fast become, in his eyes, the most beautiful and level-headed
woman he had ever met. She seemed to understand him, which was
a rare and precious thing.

He had often ribbed her for having a penchant for hoarding, yet
her savvy instincts had proven correct. She had turned all his castoffs
into a handsome sum of money. For that, he was a little jealous; it
would most certainly have been helpful if put toward his building projects, but only a little. She had more than earned it with all the creative

efforts she had poured into every aspect of the farm's renewal so far. She had his undying respect and admiration.

Hugh realized with great clarity that Ellie had something he was short on: vision for the future. He flew by the seat of his pants, running from idea to idea without a coherent long-term goal. A girl like Ellie would make a great life partner.

But that was the rub; Ellie had made it clear that she would only relate to him as a sister, and she had maintained that stance. Even the small amount of affection she had shown him was limited to the same tender expressions she bestowed on her brother and his family.

Would she be willing to change the rules of their relationship? For his part, he was ready to take it to the next level.

Ah, but that was the other rub. Ellie knew almost everything there was to know about himself and his family history. To put it crassly, she knew full well what a bunch of losers they had been. For Hugh, it meant he was out of her league. For all his changing feelings toward her, he did indeed feel unworthy as a suitor.

On the other hand, he had to admit that she never made him feel as though he was beneath her. Even so, if she would only show him the least bit of encouragement, he would open the doors of his heart and love her with abandon.

As it was, he had to keep his feelings in check or he would get lost in the misery of unrequited love. It was better to nurse an insufficient friendship than no relationship at all, Hugh figured as he turned over in his bed. He no longer resisted sleep.

~

Ellie's week had gone through its own ups and downs. Now that the sale was over, she no longer had a reason to frequent the Fischer farm. It seemed like her current life was spent in alternating states of feast and famine. Either she was run-off-her-feet busy or had next to nothing to do.

Presently, she had time on her hands.

One remaining project was the log cabin quilt. She went into her mother's sewing area to see if she could get herself excited about that activity. Ellie cut and then arranged the strips with dark prints on one side and light on the other, but she wasn't quite pleased with the result.

It needs a dash of bright colour in the centre, she thought.

She went to her mother's fabric cupboard to look for something suitable. The stash of fabrics was quite diverse, which came as no surprise. Liz Bauman had sewn everything from baby clothes to Sunday suits for her three sons, and probably even her husband.

A piece of bright yellow cloth caught Ellie's eye. When she pulled it out of the stack, she recognized it as something she had worn as a young girl. It had been a Sunday dress with a fitted top and full gathered skirt. She remembered how she had liked to twirl in it so that the skirt flared up in a circle around her waist. Nostalgia for those simpler days washed over her.

She snapped herself back to the present. This piece would be quite perfect for the quilt motif she had in mind. The cloth was canary yellow but covered in small bouquets of blue forget-me-nots, ideal for the predominantly blue-themed quilt top.

It was an interesting way to pass the time—at least, until she had completed six blocks. Then she tired of sewing and found herself looking for something else to occupy herself.

Midweek, Ellie wandered into the Quonset to look again at the sofa set and lamp table she had kept for herself. The accent table would look lots better refinished, she decided. To do that, she would need to get some stripper, stain, and varnish.

On that note, she fetched her purse and started up the car, sure that she needn't go any further than the community store in Minitonas.

As she passed the Fischer driveway, she noticed Rob on one of his tractors packing and levelling the ground where the old house used to stand. It pleased her that her brother was becoming good friends with Hugh and doing his part as a caring neighbour to help him get off to a good start.

Her first errand, however, was to clean out her mailbox at the post office. She swung open the door and nearly crashed into Rory Lang, who was on his way out of the building.

"Ellie!" he said, obviously happy to see her. "You have no idea how often I think of you. The Lord must have arranged for you to be here at the same time as me. How about we go over to the café and have a cup of coffee?"

"Ummm. Well, I haven't got my mail yet," answered Ellie, hedging.

"Oh! Sure. I'll wait."

In the minute it took Ellie to empty the mailbox, she decided that she would accept his invitation to hear what he had to say, if for no other reason than that she was a bit bored.

They sat across from each other in one of the booths at the café.

"I'll have coffee and a piece of your rhubarb pie," Rory said when the waitress came by to take his order. "Have whatever you would like, Ellie. It's on me."

"I'll just have a cup of tea with a wedge of lemon, thanks," said Ellie.

The woman nodded and hurried away.

Ellie looked around the café, memories from childhood coming back to her. "I remember when this place used to be called Lindy's Lunch. I was just a kid, but... this town seems to shrink a little more with every passing year. It worries me that Minitonas as we know it may one day disappear like Renwer. That little place barely has a cluster of houses left."

Rory nodded, but he didn't seem eager to philosophize about the noticeable decline of so many rural towns across the prairies.

"I wanted to ask how you were doing," he said instead.

"I'm fine. What do you mean?"

"A few weeks ago, you said you were still grieving the loss of your mother, amongst other things."

"Right. Well, some days are harder than others, but in general I'm on the road to healing. Thanks for asking."

Their orders arrived. Ellie squeezed the juice out of the lemon wedge into her little teapot. Rory stirred both sugar and cream in his coffee.

"That's good to hear." He looked directly into her eyes. "I want you to know that I pray for you every day, Ellie. I care about you."

This was a mistake...

Aloud, she said, "It's nice to be cared for, but I might need to correct you on a few things. Why don't you tell me what you mean..."

When he replied, he was surprisingly straightforward. "Well, I've prayed about it and I believe the Lord wants us to be together. I think we'd make a good team, you and me."

It was one of those dreaded moments when one has to set straight an errant suitor. It could be such a difficult thing, one involving the delicacy of the heart, a supersensitive emotional organ.

On the other hand, the sooner the mismatch could be dealt with, the better for all concerned.

"With all due respect, I don't believe that," said Ellie. "The Lord hasn't communicated it to me. I don't have any feelings for you... that way."

"I'm sure if we spent time together, got to know each other better, it would happen." Traces of desperation were coming through in his tone. "We just need to give it a chance."

"Rory, I honestly don't want to hurt your feelings. I'm sure there's a girl out there who's just right for you. It's just not me." She spoke firmly. "I have to go now. Thanks for the tea."

She got up and left the café, looking back only once as she closed the door. Rory looked like he might cry.

Ellie hurriedly picked up some stripper, dark oak stain, and a varnish to get cracking on her new project. She intended to go straight home, but at the last second she turned right on Third Street and drove toward Darcey's place. She hoped her friend wouldn't mind the spontaneous visit.

"Well, well, well," said Darcey upon answering the doorbell. "To what do I owe the pleasure of your company?"

"Just the need for a little girl talk."

"That would suit me too," Darcey confessed. "Would you like a cuppa something?"

"No thanks, I've just had tea. How's it going with the new baby?"

"Great. She sleeps through most of the night now. That's almost all she has to do to make her momma happy."

Darcey led Ellie into the living room and invited her to sit.

It was the first time Ellie had been in Darcey's home, and she was most surprised by what she saw. Given Darcey's bold personality, she would have guessed her friend would have had a clean-enough-to-be-healthy, dirty-enough-to-be-happy philosophy of housekeeping. Rather, the place looked squeaky clean!

"How do you do it?" Ellie asked, awe in her voice. "Your house looks like I could eat off the floor! And you have three little kids. My place doesn't look like this, and there's no one there except me."

Darcey shrugged. "I like things to be in order. Helps me think straight. Keeps me from getting grumpy. I just don't let things fall behind."

"I hadn't realized you were such a disciplined person."

"So what's on your mind, sista?" As usual, Darcey was taking the direct approach.

"Well, I just needed to tell someone... that it's over between Rory and me."

Darcey stared hard at Ellie. The corners of her mouth twitched ever so slightly, and then her shoulders and belly began to shake. Finally she burst out laughing so hard that tears filled her eyes. Ellie giggled right along.

"Gosh, I needed that," Darcey said, trying to hold herself together. "A good belly laugh, I mean. But sorry, you must be feeling terrible."

"Actually, I do feel bad... for him."

"Why? Is he crying somewhere?"

"Maybe. He tried to tell me that the Lord told him we—me and him—belong together. I told him that couldn't be true because the Lord hadn't communicated the same with me." All over again, Ellie felt irritated. "It bugs me to no end when people invoke the name of the Lord to force their personal agendas on others. Like, who can argue with that? 'The Lord' trumps any feeling or opinion. Well, you know what I mean. It's a terrible attempt at manipulation."

"Yes, I do. I hear you, and I'm with you," said Darcey. "So Rory is out. Shocking! What about the other guy?"

"What other guy?"

"That tall, handsome dude you bring to church? You two look good together."

"His name is Hugh Fischer. He's our new neighbour. Lives almost directly across the road from our farm." Ellie shifted her weight and put her feet up on a nearby footstool. "He's a great guy. Smart. Great work ethic. Generous. Good sense of humour."

"I hear a 'but' coming…"

"But he's an unbeliever—a non-Christian. I don't dare give my heart away *again* to someone who isn't on the same page as me in terms of faith. I've been there, done that, bought the T-shirt. It ends in disaster. So not worth it."

"Sounds like you've been burned bad," said Darcey gently.

"You don't know the half of it. And no, I don't want to talk about it." She put the emphasis on *don't*.

"I can respect that. But tell me more about Hugh. He comes to church. Do you suppose he's close to making a decision for Christ?"

"I don't know," said Ellie, disheartened. "Every time I ask him, he says he's still thinking about it. I'm beginning to wonder if he's a slow learner or something."

"I rather doubt it. I bet he takes everything you say, and everything he hears at church, very seriously. I bet he turns it over and over in his mind. When he's ready to make a decision, it will be the real deal. Authentic. He'll passionately sing the chorus of 'I Have Decided to Follow Jesus' as his personal testimony."

Darcey sang the last refrain to solidify her point.

"I hope you're right, Darcey, I really do. If you are, I confess that he would be of real interest to me."

"I saw the poster for a yard sale you staged in Swan River. How did that go?" asked Darcey, changing the subject.

"It went very well. I sold almost everything! And that reminds me, do you know of anyone in these parts who does upholstery? I have an antique sofa set I'd like to get redone."

Darcey smiled confidently. "Yes, I do. Talk to my neighbour Cynthia across the street. She's a brilliant seamstress and furniture upholsterer. The stuff she turns out is better than anything you can buy. I'm serious. Tell her what you have in mind and she'll outdo it!"

"With a reference like that, I'm sure I will!"

The cries of a newborn reached their ears in the living room.

"Someone's hungry," Darcey said, getting up. "Again."

"I'll take that as my cue to head on home. I have another project lined up anyway." She leaned in to give her friend a hug. "Thanks for listening, Darcey. You're a good friend."

It took Ellie the rest of the week to strip, clean, sand, stain, and revarnish the taller-than-average antique sidetable. She didn't enjoy the messy process, but the results, due to her fussy, careful work, were awesome. As far as she was concerned, she had a showpiece.

Another project crossed off her list.

Twenty-Seven

HUGH WOKE UP on Saturday morning understanding that it would be an important day, but he couldn't immediately remember why. He had to study the calendar to realize it was July 19, the very important supper date at Aunt Gertie's that would include his sisters.

He had seen Margo for a brief visit five weeks ago on his drive up from Winnipeg. They had very occasionally gotten together over the course of the last fourteen years. He more or less knew what to expect from seeing her again.

Diane was a different matter. She would have been eleven when he left, and aside from a couple of short, vague letters she had sent via Margo in the first few months after he'd run away, they had lost touch. Their relationship had been a casualty of his decision to flee.

The only thing he knew about Diane was that she had married someone from Saskatchewan and now had a couple of kids.

He felt bad for not making more of an effort to include Diane in his life. Mind you, he reasoned, that argument went both ways. If Diane had been interested in maintaining a relationship with her brother, she could have sought him out.

The realization that all three siblings would be reunited that evening triggered a confused feeling of excitement and apprehension. He rose, deciding to clean the cabin until it was spic and span.

Chances were pretty good that Margo would stop by to see what he had done with the farm.

His instincts told him this would be a special occasion, even if he didn't yet understand why, so he also decided to show up for Gertie's supper in the finest clothing he owned, looking his best from top to bottom. With that in mind, he polished his cowboy boots until they shone. He also needed a haircut and a thorough cleaning—and that meant going over to the Bauman farm to use their bathroom and laundry facilities; he was running out of clean clothes.

Ellie happened to be outside mowing the lawn when he pulled up, and she cheerfully let him into the house. He opted to take a bath, hoping a soak in the tub would help settle the growing sense of butterflies in his stomach.

When he had completed his ablutions, he returned to the kitchen to find Ellie standing against the counter, her arms folded across her chest.

"Are you excited about your family dinner this evening?" she asked.

"I can't decide if I'm excited or anxious. I'm not sure what to expect. How would you prepare for a night like tonight?"

"Well, first I would assume that your aunt has planned the evening to be a wonderful surprise. So don't worry. From the little I know about Gertie, she's all about wanting to bless you as generously as possible. Also, I would take another bouquet of flowers, or maybe a box of chocolates."

Hugh nodded. "I already thought of that. I'll pick something up when I go for a haircut."

"What about your sisters?" asked Ellie, raising her eyebrows.

"What about them?"

"Didn't you tell me you hadn't seen Diane since you left Minitonas fourteen years ago? And that you and Margo don't get together much?"

Hugh hung his head sheepishly. "I may have. It's true, after all."

"Well, if it was me, and I was the one to have neglected my siblings for so many years for it-doesn't-matter-what reason, one way to break the ice would be to bring a gift. It could also be flowers or sweets. Maybe a piece of jewellery or a collectible."

"It hadn't occurred to me. Now that you've pointed it out, it sounds like a really good idea." Hugh smiled, grateful for the suggestion. "But I'm no good at this sort of thing. Would you mind coming to town and helping me choose something nice?"

"I suppose I could. It's liable to add up, though. I don't mind giving you some yard sale money to cover it."

"That's real thoughtful of you, but I think I can manage." He stopped and looked at her more closely. More meaningfully. "You're a great friend, Ellie. Like... a best friend."

At quarter of five, Hugh was ready to make the drive to Swan River. He had safely stowed three beautiful and distinct bouquets of flower arrangements in the cab of his truck so they wouldn't fall over. He dressed in black denim pants and a dark shirt with a bit of blue showing around the collar. His hair was coiffed and his fingernails freshly clipped. He couldn't remember the last time he'd dressed up for anything special!

The butterflies returned to his stomach, but he ignored them as he climbed into his recently washed and wiped down truck.

"Aunt Gertie, here I come," he murmured.

As it turned out, Hugh was the first to arrive. He couldn't carry all the vases at once so he approached the door with the one he meant to give his aunt.

Gertie threw the door open wide upon his arrival. It seemed she had been watching for her guests' arrival.

"These are for you," said Hugh, placing the rose filled vase in her hands.

"Oh my! My favourite colour too. You are the best nephew an aunt could have," she gushed. "Thank you so much. Please come in."

"You're welcome. I'll be right back. I've brought flowers for my sisters too."

Hugh turned on his heel and retrieved two more vases from the floor of his truck. Gertie held the door open for him so he could come inside unhindered.

"What beautiful flowers! Your sisters will be thrilled by your thoughtfulness. I certainly am."

She indicated that he could set them down on the coffee table while she placed her gift of roses on one of the sidetables. Hugh didn't correct her assumption, since none of this would have happened if Ellie hadn't suggested it.

Ten minutes later, Diane pulled up and parked along the curb. Hugh watched from the living room window as she tentatively surveyed the house. She was a taller, filled-out version of the dark-haired, blue-eyed, fair-skinned little sister he remembered. She wore crisp white pants and a pale blue blouse that matched her luminous eyes. If he had to choose, he would say that she resembled the Fischer side of the family more than the Hunts.

"You're at the right place!" declared Gertie, who ran out to greet her with a hug.

Diane smiled in return, though she retained a look of apprehension as she followed her aunt into the house.

Gertie took Hugh's arm and pulled him toward his sister. "Let me be the one to introduce you to your very own brother…"

Diane gasped. "Hugh! You look different than I remember. You're so tall! My gosh, you look like Pa. I mean… you're very handsome. I mean—"

"Everyone seems to think I look like Pa, but I'm *not* Pa," said Hugh, fighting a wave of powerful emotions he hadn't expected. "You don't have to be afraid of me."

He opened his arms and squeezed Diane hard. They held each other for several seconds before separating and holding each other at arms' length to look each other over in wonder.

Uncle Ed entered the room with a tray of stemware filled with red wine.

"Welcome here, pretty niece," he said, smiling sweetly. "And you too, nephew. You cut a fine figure, I must say."

He held out the tray and each took a glass of wine.

When Margo arrived, she strode confidently to the front door, looking very professional in a navy-blue pantsuit and colourful blouse that went perfectly with her tanned skin. Her brown hair had natural red highlights with salon-added blond streaks; it was styled in the latest shag fashion.

For the first time, Hugh noticed how much she resembled their mother.

"Sorry I'm late," said Margo upon entering the house. "I stopped in at the farm on my way in. Lots of changes there. I must have just missed you." She embraced Hugh, then noticed Diane. "Good to see you too, sweetie."

Margo stepped out of Hugh's arms to wrap hers around Diane.

"Glad to meet you again, aunt and uncle!" she added jauntily, turning to Gertie and Ed. "Thanks for hosting this reunion."

When the greetings were done, Hugh presented his sisters with their floral arrangements to their great surprise. They each got a little emotional when he placed the vases in their hands. This was followed by another round of hugs.

Gertie got a little sidetracked from preparing supper, not wanting to miss anything. But at last she put it all together and called the group to the table.

She had gone all out, setting the table with a lace cloth and laying out her finest bone china. The centrepiece was made from fresh flowers selected from her own gardens and inset with long tapered candles. The care she'd put into the arrangement conveyed to her guests how special they were to her.

The fine meal began with a spinach salad, followed by a main course of roasted rock Cornish hens with rice stuffing and garden-fresh beans. Before dessert, Gertie presented each at the table with a small dish of lemon sorbet; "to cleanse the palette," she said. After that she served strawberry shortcake with fresh berries and whipped cream. She made sure they were given a fine dining experience as prelude to the night's business.

Throughout the dinner conversation, no one made any reference to the difficult past they had endured. Neither did they make any allusion to their parents.

However, Margo wasn't shy about talking about her life. She had worked as a salesclerk in Dauphin after moving there with her new husband. She had stayed with the same shop ever since, and just four weeks ago she had been promoted to manager. It was easy to see how thrilled she was with this latest development. Everyone around the table expressed their sincere congratulations.

"Will you and your husband be starting a family?" Gertie asked.

"Not yet," answered Margo between bites. "Actually, I haven't made up my mind about whether I even want children. I think it would be hard to be a parent and maintain a career at the same time. I like going to work. I like being able to afford nice clothes. I like being independent. I'm afraid that having a child would end that. I'm not sure I want to make the sacrifice."

After a slight pause, Gertie invited Diane to talk about her life in Saskatchewan.

Diane became immediately shy. "I don't have anything exciting to tell like Margo," she said. "I'm just a stay-at-home-mom to two little kids."

"There's nothing wrong with that," Gertie returned stoutly. "There was a time when we said, 'the hand that rocks the cradle rules the world.' I want to believe there's still truth to that. Don't let anyone tell you you're *just* a mom. If you have children, it's an important job, and don't you forget it!"

Uncle Ed coughed into his closed fist, a reminder to his wife to stay clear of cultural politics. "Tell us, dear, how did you come to live in Saskatchewan?"

"Well, I met my husband while working as a waitress at a truck stop. He was a driver then, and a regular customer. We fell in love, got married, and moved to Yorkton, where he grew up. Before you know it, the babies started coming." Diane's voice was quiet. "I thought about going back to work, but after we did the math it didn't seem like it would be worth it. Just about my whole paycheque would have gone to the babysitter. What's the point of that? So I stayed home with my kids and I don't mind it at all. They're fun to play with. They make me happy."

"That's wonderful, dear," said Gertie. "Tell us about your children."

"I have a three-year-old daughter, Amanda, and a nearly one-year-old boy, Sean."

"I'm sure they're charming. Congratulations!" Uncle Ed turned to Hugh. "Would you like to bring us all up to speed on your latest endeavours?"

All eyes looked his way.

"I don't have much to tell yet. I've gone back to the farm and started tearing down the old buildings. They're mostly gone now, except the machine shed and the barn. I intend to rid the landscape of them too, though, as I get the time. I'm considering starting up a mechanics shop. We'll see how it goes."

Margo gave him a hard look. "I thought you wanted to farm."

"Pa's old equipment isn't up to the task," he answered with matching directness. "I'd need to save up a lot of money to purchase adequate machinery. In the meantime, we'll have to keep renting out the land."

Margo nodded. "No surprise there."

Hugh suddenly noticed that Gertie's gaze kept darting to the clock mounted on the wall behind the table.

"You'll need to finish your dessert soon," she said. "The main reason I invited you all to come should be here any minute."

On the dot of seven, the doorbell rang. Ed got up to answer the door while Gertie ushered her guests into the living room.

"Come in, sir," said Ed with stilted friendliness.

A moment later, he led a short balding man into the room. He wore a pinstriped suit and sat in the seat designated for him. The others were facing him in a circle.

He exuded self-importance as he set down his briefcase and made himself comfortable. When he was settled, he nodded to Ed and Gertie. Whatever he had come to say, it seemed he was ready to proceed.

"Right then," began Gertie. "I called you here to tell you that your last grandparent, Mavis Hunt, passed away as of January this year. I realize you didn't get to know your mother's parents. Be that as it may, after the will was read, it was learned that the estate was to be divided equally between the two daughters, myself and your mother."

She let that sink in for a few seconds, then gestured to the newcomer.

"This is Mr. Rodney Dearborn, esquire, who was appointed executor of the estate," she continued.

Mr. Dearborn acknowledged the introduction with a slight bow from his sitting position.

"I've received my portion of the inheritance," Gertie said. "He is here to send each of you home with your mother's inheritance, divided equally."

The room got quiet. So quiet that they could hear the tap dripping in the kitchen.

Margo broke the silence. "Just how much inheritance are we talking about, Aunt Gertie?"

"I can answer that," Mr. Dearborn interjected. "Each of you will receive a cheque for $71,300."

There was dead air for half a minute. To Hugh, it felt like an eternity.

"Is this for real or some kind of joke?" asked Margo sharply. "I think you just said we won the lottery! And that's impossible because I didn't buy a ticket."

"I assure you, Miss Margo, this is no joke," said Mr. Dearborn. "You and your siblings are indeed heirs to a tidy sum of money."

None of the Fischers could speak. They were utterly dumbfounded.

"I'm quite aware that each of you has experienced a difficult child-hood," said Gertie at last, meeting each of their gaze by turn. "I can only hope this will in some small way make up for a bit of it."

Having got the siblings' names and spellings beforehand, Mr. Dearborn passed out a series of envelopes, then closed his briefcase and departed, leaving the family to discuss the matter amongst them-selves.

"I have one more thing to share," said Gertie after he was gone. "One of your grandmother's hobbies was collecting Royal Doulton figurines. If you're not familiar with them, they're considered the highest quality in porcelain, bone china figurines, crafted in England. They're numbered as limited editions and aren't cheap. At any rate, your grandmother Hunt thought they were beautiful and treated herself to one each year. I've brought them all home and set them out in the back room. I invite each of you to choose one to take home as a reminder that, once, you really did have grandparents."

It was a lot to take in. Hugh, Margo, and Diane all looked at each other, and then at their aunt and uncle, looking somewhat like a trio of deer caught in headlights.

Margo elbowed Diane and said, "Come with me."

She took Diane outside and the two of them sat in her car, where they remained talking for a half-hour, if not a little longer.

"I wonder what that's about," said Gertie, sounding uneasy.

"I have no idea."

The longer it took for the girls to rejoin the party, the more uncom-fortable Hugh became. In the meantime, he expressed his gratitude for his aunt and uncle hosting the evening. The inheritance, he felt, was the surprise of a lifetime. It was going to take care of a number of his financial worries.

At last Margo and Diane returned, Margo carrying a cardboard filing case that resembled the bellows of an accordion.

When they were all reseated, Margo cleared her throat. "Diane and I have reached an agreement."

Hugh inhaled sharply. He couldn't imagine what was coming, but his insides were already twisting.

"We've been thinking about this for several weeks, so it's not an impulsive decision," Margo said. "The inheritance we have received today, totally unexpected as it was, has tipped the scales. We, Diane and I, would like to hand over the farm to our brother Hugh. We want it to belong to him alone."

Hugh sank back in his chair.

Margo turned to him. "Diane and I know what Pa did to you, how he treated you worse than dirt. If anything good can come of it, it should be that you get to keep the farm for yourself. There is one catch, although I don't think you'll mind too much."

Diane, seated next to Hugh, smiled sweetly and patted his arm.

"The farm account has about $10,000 in it," Margo said, all eyes trained on her. "According to the law, Mom was entitled to half. Hugh, if you'd be willing to give up Mom's half, about $5,000, and split it between Diane and me, you can have the rest, as well as all the land, and do whatever you want with it. It's yours."

"Are you serious?" asked their stunned brother.

"Dead serious."

Hugh turned to Diane.

"What she said," confirmed Diane. "I don't want the farm or anything to do with it. It should be all yours. You deserve it."

Hugh wept.

The party ended soon after, since everyone's hearts were too full to visit in any sort of light-hearted way. Addresses and phone numbers were exchanged and promises made to get together on a regular basis. Perhaps Thanksgiving. Possibly Christmas.

A cheque for $2,500 was made out to Margo and another one to Diane. Then the cardboard file, with all the farm-related paperwork and chequebook, was handed over to Hugh.

Gertie invited the girls to stay overnight, but each demurred, preferring to get home.

As for the porcelain figurines, Diane chose a Christmas sculpture depicting a rooftop Santa with an armful of toys.

"My kids will like it," she said.

Margo's choice featured a woman in a yellow and white gown wearing a hat and purse, carrying a parasol.

Privately, Hugh wasn't particularly interested in any of the figurines, but he understood why his aunt was making a gift of them. He settled on a princess-like figurine with long blond hair, prettily gowned in strapless blue with a matching wrap."

"Remind you of someone, does she?" asked Aunt Gertie coquettishly.

Hugh didn't answer.

Twenty-Eight

HUGH LEFT GERTIE'S house shortly after nine o'clock after an evening so full of bombshells that he could hardly process it. It seemed too good to be true. One thing he knew for sure: he wanted to talk to someone. He was bursting with... joy. Was that the right word? He needed to share it with someone. A best friend who would understand and be happy for him.

So far, he only had one of those.

~

Ellie was already in her pyjamas and housecoat when she saw the headlights of Hugh's truck come up the driveway. She wasn't too surprised that he'd want to tell her how the evening had unfolded, although she'd figured he would at least wait until the morning.

Since he couldn't seem to wait, she assumed the news must be either very, very good or very, very bad.

She met him at the back door and let him in.

Hugh did his best to put on a glum face as he pulled out a kitchen chair and sat at the table, making every effort to appear dejected.

Ellie put on the kettle and studied him. "I don't believe this act. You had a wonderful evening, didn't you?"

Hugh gave it up and smiled broadly. "I don't know where to begin."

"The beginning is always a good place to start." She handed him a mug of chamomile tea and took one for herself.

They moved to the living room and took their traditional places, she in the big armchair and he on the sofa with his feet on the coffee table.

"So tell me, was it awkward seeing your sisters again after so long?" asked Ellie.

"Not nearly so awkward as I feared."

He started by telling her about his sisters, including their reactions to the bouquets, then described every detail of the fancy dinner Gertie had prepared for them. When he had her in the palm of his hand, he dropped the big news about his inheritance.

Ellie's eyes went wide and her jaw dropped. "I knew it! I just *knew* Gertie had something wonderful in the works. I'm so happy for you, Hugh. That money is really going to help you get the farm going, won't it?"

"It sure will," Hugh said. "Wait, though. It gets even better."

But he had to pause. A lump formed in his throat and his eyes got misty; he literally couldn't speak for a minute.

"After we found out about the inheritance, Margo and Diane announced that they're going to give over the entire farm to me—as the sole owner, free and clear."

Hugh tried to sniff away the tears, but they came anyway. He wiped them away with the back of his hand and looked over at Ellie. Tears were streaming down her face too.

"That might be the most selfless act of love I've ever heard," she said. "You know what this means, don't you?"

"I'm not following you."

"Seriously, Hugh... what does your whole wonderful, beautiful, amazing evening add up to?"

"I have a family," he declared in awe. "I have a normal, loving family after all."

"Okay, that too. But what else? This shouldn't be hard for you, bro."

Hugh shook his head. "I don't know what you want me to say."

"Your prayer, idiot!" The words were sharp, but her tone was warm and tender. "Don't you get it? This proves that God is real. He's proved Himself to you in the unique way you wanted. If you don't get that, you really are as blind as a bat and have the brains of an amoeba."

His mouth dropped and he got a faraway look in his eyes. He didn't answer right away.

She sat up straight. "Hugh-mophilia Fischer-Price, if you tell me once more that you have to think about it, I'm going to get up and fetch my mother's rolling pin and beat your dim-witted head until I bang some sense together!"

"Well, you could try!" Hugh started to laugh out loud. "You're absolutely right, Ellie. God *did* answer my prayer. Okay, I cave. I believe! What do I do next?"

Now Ellie became dubious. "You're serious? You're not kidding with me?"

"I'm one hundred percent serious. I want what you have."

"Then get on your knees with me and pray something like this..." She got out of the chair and knelt on the living room floor. "It's okay if you change the words a little to make them your own."

Hugh joined her on the floor. They faced each other, separated by the coffee table, and closed their eyes. When they began to pray, Hugh echoed Ellie's words.

"Heavenly Father, I come before You, admitting that I'm a hurt, sinful, and broken man in need of Your cleansing and forgiveness. Wash me clean in the shed blood of Your Son, Jesus, who died in my place. Fill me with Your Holy Spirit and begin the work of making me a brand-new person in Christ. Thank You for the sacrifice of Jesus that makes this possible. Thank You for loving me and making me one of Your own. Raise me up to become a man after Your own heart. Help me to learn Your Word and live it all the rest of my life. In the name of Jesus Christ, I ask, amen."

When Hugh finished the prayer and opened his eyes, a warmth swept through him. It was accomplished.

Ellie smiled. Another child had wisely come home.

She stole a look in Hugh's direction and saw that his eyes were moist again, but there was something else. Something she'd never seen from him.

"What?" she asked.

"I've never felt this way before," he replied slowly. "I believe the right word to describe it would be 'peace.' I thought I felt it after I destroyed the old house and burnt it, but I know now, by comparison, that was just a kind of emptiness from releasing my bitter, stored-up rage. What I feel now is different. It's like something I've been looking for all my life... and I finally found it, just now. I'm sure this must be what people mean when they say they're at peace..."

It seemed very much to Ellie like the right thing to do would be to give the guy a hug. So she came around to Hugh's side of the coffee table and put her arms around his shoulders. She held him like that in comfortable nearness for a minute or so.

At last, he pulled away. He had a lopsided grin on his face.

"I believe I'll sleep well tonight," he said. "Maybe for the first time ever."

"That's par for the course. Why don't you do that in my brothers' bedroom tonight? You're already dressed for church."

"You're sure you don't mind?"

Ellie shook her head.

"Thanks. Then I will."

Moments later, he crawled into bed and slept like the proverbial baby.

Thus, at approximately 11:38 p.m. on July 19, 1980, all the angels above rejoiced that another son of Adam had been birthed into the kingdom of heaven. This time, the babe in Christ was a six-foot-one man weighing around a hundred eighty pounds. Everyone said he looked like his Father. Some said he bore His very image.

The joy of the Lord was still very much with Hugh when he got up the next morning.

"I feel like I want to tell someone," he said while sitting at the kitchen table sipping from a mug of coffee. "Like I want to get a megaphone and blast my good news up and down the streets of Minitonas."

Ellie listened in awe. She couldn't remember the last time she had been with a newborn believer and seen the excitement they exuded. It was catching, like the flu or the giggles. She wanted to do a happy dance around the kitchen as she prepared breakfast.

"Rob and Sarah will be excited for you," said Ellie. "So will Pastor Leland. And my friend Darcey too."

"Darcey, the big girl? Why?"

"I just know she's taken an interest in you. Tell her about this when we get to church."

Hugh spotted Rob as soon as he pulled into the parking lot and tooted his truck's horn. Rob heard the sound and turned. Just then, Sarah came into view by the building's front door. The couple stopped and waited for Hugh and Ellie to park and catch up.

As Hugh hurried forward, Ellie lagged behind, purposely wanting him to have his moment. It took a while for Rob and Sarah to finally understand what Hugh was babbling on about. Rob clapped him on the back while Sarah hugged his neck. The joy was spreading!

Sarah winked at Ellie and gave her the thumbs up.

Once they got inside, Pastor Leland expressed a more subdued joy. He took Hugh's phone number, as well as directions to get to the Fischer farm; he intended to pay his new parishioner a visit.

Hugh soon noticed Darcey making her way to the nursery and immediately launched into the full story. She responded like the Baumans had—overjoyed. Rather loudly, Darcey declared him to be her new brother!

Once again, Ellie was hanging back, but she caught the knowing look Darcey cast in her direction.

Hugh experienced the church service differently this time. He wasn't an outsider looking in, but rather part of the family. There was something very comforting in that. A kind of security that he hadn't previously known. Soaking in this new experience, it felt very like he had come home. It felt good.

~

"I can hardly wait to tell my sisters and Aunt Gertie," said Hugh to Ellie while they lounged in the shade of the trees fronting the Roaring River. Ellie had talked him into coming down here to jump rocks and wade in the water.

"My advice is to do it in person, not on the phone," said Ellie. "She and Ed will need to see the change in your countenance. Otherwise they may not take you seriously. I think it was St. Francis of Assisi who said, 'Preach the Gospel at all times, and when necessary, use words.' He meant, of course, that our actions and who we are speak louder than anything we say."

Twenty-Nine

IT WAS ANOTHER frantic week for Rob and Hugh as they got started on building the new farmhouse. Rob brought over his tractor with the front-end loader and dug a deep hole to prepare for installing the cistern and septic tank; it would be large enough to accommodate a larger family home in the future, should such a day come. Rob had expected it to be a fairly easy task, except he encountered an extra-large stone while excavating that proved stubborn. Removing it required a number of chains and Rob's most powerful tractor. Eventually it was rolled out of the way and positioned near the entrance of the driveway—at Ellie's recommendation.

"You could paint *Fischer Farms* on it," she suggested.

Bright and early on Wednesday morning, a crew came and set up the forms for the cistern and septic tank. They worked quickly and the next day the cement truck came and went several times.

While that was going on, Rob and Hugh constructed the wooden beams to support the house.

On Saturday, the two men began work on the floor joists. Sometime before noon, Hugh looked up and noticed in the distance that someone was approaching on a bike.

His gaze caught the attention of Rob, who looked up and watched the biker pedal up the driveway.

"It's Trevor," said Rob, surprised and curious all at once.

"Dad!" Trevor shouted when he was still several meters away. "Dad, you should come home now."

Rob became fully alarmed. "What's happened?"

"Mom is crying. She's started packing a suitcase," he said, panting. "I think Uncle Gerry got killed falling off a ladder when he was trying to replace some shingles on his barn... or something like that..."

Rob quickly explained to Hugh that Gerry was Sarah's elder brother. He farmed near Russell, Manitoba. They were a close family, which meant Sarah would be taking the news hard.

"That's it for me today," said Rob, already packing up his tools. When they were gathered, he started picking through his billfold. He withdrew a pair of tickets. "Here, I won't be using these now. I had planned to take my bride on a date to the grandstand show at the rodeo and fair in Swan River this evening. Guess that's out of the picture now. You and a friend can enjoy the show instead."

A minute later, they had Trevor's bike placed in the back of Rob's pickup and were driving away.

The abruptness of these recent developments rattled Hugh. He finished securing the floor joist he had been working on and then began to collect his tools in order to return them to the machine shed. With his mind preoccupied by the crisis, he didn't notice the piece of rusted tin, slightly bent, that lay on the bench right next to the spot where he set down his hammer and carpenter's apron. As he withdrew his left hand, he sliced it on the tin, tearing open his palm all the way to the end of his little finger.

"Aaaacchhh!"

He winced in pain as he watched blood pour from the wound. With his good hand, he reached up for the bottle of moonshine he'd stored here, the one with the skull-and-crossbones mark taped to it.

Hugh headed for his cabin and used the washbasin to catch the runoff as he poured whiskey over the cut to disinfect it. He cried out again from the excruciating pain.

When he thought he could stand it, he poured a little more liquid and bit his lip until the sting subsided. At last he wrapped it in a great wad of paper towel.

Ellie can fix this, he thought.

He recorked the bottle with his right hand and set it on top of the Hoosier cabinet. Then he jumped into the truck and sped to the neighbouring farm. Already the blood had seeped through the thick wad of paper towelling.

"You hurt yourself really good," said Ellie when he showed it to her. She examined the gash after removing the wadding. "By rights, you should go to the hospital and have it stitched up."

"I'd rather we just bandaged it tight," said Hugh through taut lips.

She was getting ready to disinfect the wound with hydrogen peroxide when Hugh told her that he had already doused it with the moonshine.

"I'm sure it's clean, and it probably killed half of the good flesh along with the germs," he said grimly.

Just to be sure, Ellie swabbed the bloody cut with the hydrogen peroxide and began the meticulous procedure of bandaging the wound so the fleshy parts were brought as closely together as possible.

"There. That should do." She applied the last piece of medical tape. "You'll want to keep your hand elevated to keep it from throbbing too much. How about a sling? I could make one for you."

"Well, all right. But make sure it looks good to go out in public, because you and I have an outing today."

He pulled the tickets from his pocket and handed them to her. Ellie read them:

GRANDSTAND SHOW
July 28, 1980, 7 p.m.
Swan River, Manitoba

"When did you get these?" she asked. "I'd forgotten about this event. I think it's annual."

"Rob gave..." He trailed off, realizing that Ellie likely hadn't heard the news. Softening his voice, he explained what they'd heard from Trevor about the accident concerning Sarah's brother.

Ellie's face clouded. "That's too bad about Gerry," she said soberly. "Sarah's family is tight. This will be a hard blow..."

Hugh was respectfully silent for a whole minute before saying anything. "How about I pick you up at three? We can take in the fair displays and booths. Maybe eat a greasy burger for supper before the show starts. Go on some rides before coming back home."

"Sounds good," said Ellie.

He was about to leave for home to change his clothes when Ellie produced a vivid strip of cloth and offered it to Hugh to use as a sling. They laughed about the colourful pattern, but he agreed that it was crazy enough to be just right for its new purpose.

~

Wandering around the fair exhibitions turned into a nostalgic exercise for Ellie.

"My mom used to bring stuff to the fair. Mostly in the baking and preserves categories, but also entering some items she sewed. She often came away with several ribbons and prizes."

"Sounds like that's where you get your creative bent from."

"When I was a kid, I participated in the 4-H Club. That was when we Baumans still kept a few animals on the farm," she continued. "Twice, maybe three times, I entered a calf at the 4-H Show. One year I was lucky enough to win the blue ribbon."

"Cool. At what point did your family stop keeping farm critters?" wondered Hugh aloud.

"When my dad wanted to retire from farming. He sold it to the only son who was interested in carrying on the family tradition: Robert, the eldest. The difference was that Rob was interested only in grain farming, so the livestock and poultry either got sold outright or gradually discontinued…"

Walking through the sales booths was a lot of fun. Many of the venders sold western wear and accessories such as large belt buckles, rope neckties, cowboy hats, and bandanas in any colour you liked. They also came across a booth selling barnwood crafts including quaint birdhouses, little benches, and plaques with humorous sayings on them.

"See!" Ellie exclaimed. "What did I tell you? This is what some people do to recycle old, weathered boards and make a bit of coin from it."

Hugh had to reluctantly admit that she'd been right. This stuff wasn't "junk" after all. At least not to craftsmen and people who decorated their homes in country accessories.

They chose a supper of barbequed ribs with a cob of corn and coleslaw on the side. For rodeo fast food, it was delicious.

Afterward they took their seats for the grandstand show a little early, but in the meantime they amused themselves with people-watching and guessing the ages and professions of strangers. It was just something to pass the time.

They received a program when they presented their tickets at the gate to the grandstands. The show would begin with barrel races followed by calf-roping. Bull-riding came next and finally the chuckwagon races.

Yet when the show started, they realized they had no familiarity with the contestants for any of the various races, so they could only hedge their bets based on guesses. This was especially true when the chuckwagon races began.

"I think the red wagon team will win." Ellie eyed the caramel-coloured steeds with blond manes. "They've got the prettiest horses."

"I don't think you get how this works. It's not a beauty contest. It's about speed." He pointed across the stands. "I feel that team over there, the one that's all in black, has the best odds."

Neither of their choices won, but they enjoyed the country music band that played afterward.

When the program was over, the sky was dark but the grounds were alight with the flashing, gyrating lights of the midway.

"How about a ride on the Ferris wheel?" suggested Hugh. "It's always cool to look out over the world from up high."

"Sure. But don't expect me to go on that!" She was pointing to a thrill ride called the Drop of Doom. It slowly took riders up three stories and suddenly dropped them.

"Awww, come on," he goaded. "I never took you for a sissy."

"Not a sissy. Not a fool either!"

"Okay. I'll buy you a ride on the merry-go-round instead."

And he did. After the Ferris wheel, he produced tickets to ride the large carousel of horses. In a sentimental way, it proved to be just as fun as any other ride he'd been on.

"You are Hugh-larious this evening," said Ellie, grinning from ear to ear as she got down from her white fanciful horse.

Hugh chuckled, but he couldn't think of an appropriate comeback.

At about 11:00 p.m., they decided they'd had enough and began to zigzag their way out of the fairgrounds.

They were close to the exit when they heard the earnest cries of a child. Curious, they stepped into an alley between midway games—in this case, the ring toss and throwing darts to win a stuffed animal. Following the sounds, they encountered a large man spanking a young boy—his son, presumably.

Hugh sprang into action.

"What do you think you're doing?" he roared as he pulled the startled man away from the boy.

"What's your problem? Mind your own business!"

The child stopped crying at once and ran to the man's side. "Stop. Don't hit my dad," he said plaintively, his small chest heaving.

Hugh blinked, bewildered. Ellie was shocked too but still had the presence of mind to try and remove Hugh from the situation.

"Hugh! Look at me."

Hugh turned to her with a strange look on his face, one she had never seen before.

"Sorry to have bothered you," she said to the father. To Hugh she added in a firm voice, "We need to go—now. Come with me."

Taking his hand, she led him on a brisk walk to where they'd parked the truck. Hugh didn't speak, but his chest was heaving just like that of the boy.

"Keys?" Ellie prompted.

Hugh, somewhat trance-like, took the keys from his pocket and handed them to her. She unlocked the vehicle and got him settled in the passenger seat.

She got behind the steering wheel and started the truck. A glance at Hugh confirmed that not only was his chest heaving, but he was trembling all over—and blinking, a lot. She reached over and placed her hand on his arm, hoping to calm him.

Something big was about to happen, her instincts told her, but she had to get him to a safe place first. Home would be best.

"Hugh, you have to hold it together until we get home," she said as firmly as she could. "Then we'll talk about it. We'll deal with it, okay?"

She briefly removed her hand to manipulate the truck out of their parking spot. Once they were heading east on Highway 10, she reached over and placed her hand on his arm again. She drove as fast as she dared, hoping no cops were on speed patrol.

"You're doing great, Hugh. We'll soon be home. We'll be safe there. Very soon you can tell me everything. It's all going to be okay, I promise."

Hugh squirmed and allowed his head to fall back on the seat. He breathed heavily while staring straight ahead with vacant eyes. Ellie became increasingly uneasy…

Not sure of what else to try, she began to softly sing.

"Jesus loves me, this I know
for the Bible tell me so.
Little ones to him belong;

they are weak, but he is strong.
Yes, Jesus love me! Yes, Jesus loves me!
Yes, Jesus loves me! the Bible tells me so."[10]

She looked over at Hugh and in the moonlit cab of the truck saw his eyes glisten. She again squeezed his arm; he was still shaking like the proverbial leaf.

"Almost home, Hughie. Hang in there," she said encouragingly. Another song came to mind, so she sang again.

"What a friend we have in Jesus,
all our sins and griefs to bear!
What a privilege to carry
everything to God in prayer!
O what peace we often forfeit,
O what needless pain we bear,
all because we do not carry
everything to God in prayer!"[11]

After the last note, she said a silent prayer requesting Jesus's presence for whatever was about to happen. Her heart told her that Hugh was on the cusp of a meltdown, and it would be a doozy.

She turned into Hugh's driveway and cut the engine in front of the cabin. Immediately she scooted over to the centre of the seat and put an arm around his shoulders.

"Now tell me what this is about."

Hugh turned to look into her eyes. Even in the dim light of the cab, she could see the mountain of pain stored behind the pupils.

"Coach wanted me to join the basketball team," he began. "He said I was a good player. Liked the fact that I was tall. I told him I didn't think my pa would go for it. Coach said I wouldn't know for sure unless I asked. He offered to talk to my pa, but I didn't want him to

---

[10] Anna Bartlett Warner, "Jesus Loves Me, This I Know," 1859.
[11] Joseph Medlicott Scriven, "What a Friend We Have in Jesus," 1855.

see where we lived, or how. Besides, I knew my pa, and I thought that bringing Coach around would make things worse.

"That evening after supper, I told my pa that the coach wanted me to join the team. Games would be in the evenings and on weekends. Pa said no way, just like I expected. He wasn't interested in dragging my sorry ass all over hell's half-acre just to play stupid ball games, using up expensive gas for nothing. I knew better than to push it."

He paused there and Ellie began to feel anxious. Instinctively she understood there was something awful yet to tell.

"The next day, Coach asked if I had gotten the okay to join the team. I didn't say no. I just said that the problem was related to getting rides to and from games. He offered to take care of the travel details himself. So I agreed to it. This was the first time I defied my father like that. I knew it would mean trouble, but I had the idea that I should stand up to him. It wasn't like I wanted to do something *wrong*, for crying out loud.

"One day we had a game after school. We won. I scored a few baskets and felt really good about it. Coach gave me a ride home. Dropped me off at the end of the driveway like I asked."

Hugh paused again. He opened the door of the truck and stepped out onto the grass with Ellie right behind him, her heart beating wildly. She took his hand, wanting very much to communicate care and sympathy. He withdrew it, however, and slowly walked over to the hydro pole behind the cabin.

"Pa was waiting for me," he continued. "He asked me where I'd been. I told him I had played basketball with the team, but that it was okay because Coach would look after my rides so we didn't have to worry about gas or nothin'."

The scene played out like a movie behind Hugh's eyes, every detail as vivid as the day it had happened.

"I thought I told you no, boy," said Freddie in a quiet, menacing tone.

Hugh swallowed hard. He'd expected some trouble, but he hadn't expected this.

"Sorry, Pa. I'll quit tomorrow."

"Sorry!" shouted Freddie, so loud that it was possible the neighbours could hear. "Do you think 'sorry' is going to make up for crossing your pa?"

Quick as a blink, he had Hugh's wrist in a vice grip and marched him to the hydro pole...

Somehow—Hugh never did figure out how it was accomplished—his pa had gotten his arms tied and strung up so Hugh could neither defend himself nor run away.

Grabbing Hugh's shirt by the collar, Fred tore the shirt off Hugh's back in a single rip. Then Freddie removed his belt and snapped it twice, announcing his intention.

Hugh recalled the feeling of desperation and helplessness, mixed with fear. It came through in his retelling of the event.

Ellie had already begun to cry.

"This'll learn ya to cross your pa when I told you what," Fred snarled, lashing the leather end of his belt against Hugh's bare back.

"Sorry, Pa, sorry! I'll quit. I promise!"

But Freddie's ears seemed deaf. He strapped his son over and over without a break in the rhythm, until Hugh's back was as red as a sunburn.

Freddie stopped briefly to turn the belt around; now he was grasping the leather end. When he swung next, the buckle bit into Hugh's skin, drawing blood. In three strikes, Hugh's knees gave way and he slumped, hanging against the hydro pole by his wrists.

"I believed I was going to die that day..."

Ellie sobbed as with a broken heart.

"The last thing I remember before I passed out was my ma screaming, 'Stop, Fred, you'll kill him! You'll go to jail!'"

But the story was over, the shocking pain as fresh as the day it had happened. Hugh sank to the ground in front of the hydro pole and wept inconsolably. Ellie held him from the waist up and rocked him back and forth like a child. She could finally understand why Hugh had reached the end of his rope. There was nothing left; it was a rock bottom moment if ever there was one.

"It's okay to cry," she said, her own tears falling freely. "Just cry it out, Hughie."

Hugh wept from the depths of his heart for the boy who had been betrayed by the man who should have shown him a father's love and care. He wept for all the times he had been accused of wrongdoing just for being in the wrong place at the wrong time. He wept for having had to live in fear for most of his young life. He wept for the times his mother had dared not defend him because of the price of being beaten herself if she tried. He wept for the many injustices he, his sisters, and mother had endured—for not being properly fed, clothed, and cared for because those matters simply weren't a priority for Frederick R. Fischer.

He wept and wept and wept, his head and shoulders supported on Ellie's lap, the rest of him in the foetal position.

At long last, Hugh was still. Ellie determined that Hugh should rest in his bed. The last hour had been tremendously exhausting.

"You need to sleep now, Hugh," she said tenderly.

Hugh nodded and got up. Ellie walked him to his cabin, her arm around his waist.

Once inside, he fell onto his bed without even pulling back the covers or removing his cowboy boots.

Ellie watched as he fell asleep, instantly albeit not as peacefully as he might have wished. Occasionally a small cry or whimper escaped his lips.

In the dark, she sat on the edge of the bed and kept her hand on Hugh's arm, hoping that the compassionate touch of a fellow human would be of comfort in this dark night of the soul. Whispering, she prayed earnestly for his complete healing through his Saviour, Jesus Christ, and that come morning he would again know the joy of the Lord and peace that passes all understanding, as he had just one week earlier.

Eventually, though, she too needed to sleep. But given the weight of the evening, she dared not leave Hugh alone. She remembered that Gertie had left extra bedding in a box underneath the bed. In the dark, she felt around for it and to her relief found a light blanket. She partially wrapped it around herself, bunching up the remainder to use as a pillow. She sat in the captain's chair and placed the makeshift pillow on the table…

~

Ellie had no idea how long she dosed off, but she awoke suddenly with the hair on the base of her neck standing up. Her heart beat wildly. She was very much aware of an evil presence filling the cabin.

The first thing she thought of was that Freddie Fischer had returned to finish the job of killing Hugh. But that was impossible. Freddie had died a long time ago.

"Jesus," she whispered hoarsely, not wanting to wake Hugh. "We need help. There's an evil spirit here. Make it go away."

A strong impression spoke to her heart and mind: *"Send it away in My name, which is above every other name."* Ellie had never been in a situation like this before and had only a vague notion of how to face such a weird circumstance.

However, face it she must.

Speaking calmly yet forcefully, she addressed the evil spirit in the room.

"You have no business here. Both Hugh and I belong by choice to the King of Kings and Lord of Lords. You have to leave. By the shed blood of Jesus, God's only Son, who died in our place, I command you to leave this place, never, ever to return. Go right now!"

It didn't seem like anything changed. Had she left anything out?

"In the powerful name of Jesus, leave now!"

Hugh stirred. She heard a funny wobbling sound… and then, *crash!* She jumped up, terrified out of her wits.

Hugh instantly sat up, fully alert. The distinct odour of alcohol pervaded the cabin as Hugh reached over and turned on the light. Shards of the broken bottle of Freddie's moonshine whiskey lay on the stove and scattered across the floor. The clear fluid ran down the side of the stove and spread in all directions.

However, the evil entity had departed. The fearful presence had vanished.

It took quite a while to make things tidy again, as the bottle had literally exploded; it hadn't merely fallen off the top of the Hoosier.

While they worked to collect the glass and mop up the whiskey with paper towels, Ellie told him about what had happened.

Hugh listened in amazement. "I never told, but I felt that same frightening presence you just described. It's just that I wrote it off. Figured it was just a product of my overactive imagination. You know, a daymare..."

They both sincerely hoped this was the end of such unwelcome experiences.

"Come on, I'll take you home," said Hugh after the mess was cleaned up.

"Thank you. I'm so very tired. But will you stay with me? Sleep in the back bedroom like you have sometimes?"

"It's okay, Ell. I'll be fine alone at my own place."

"Well, after the heavy events of the last few hours, I'm not so sure *I* want to be alone. I'd appreciate another person in the house with me until the sun comes up."

"I understand. Of course I will."

Thirty

ROB AND THE family stayed in Russell for eight days, and during that time Hugh tried to keep working on the house. However, he found that he had little heart for it. He tired quickly and seemed to need a nap every day after lunch. When he told Ellie about this, she wasn't surprised. He was emotionally drained and needed more time to get back on track.

Nevertheless, he picked away at the project.

Pastor Leland, true to his word, paid Hugh a visit midweek. At first Hugh was a little shy, but the pastor set him at ease by showing sincere interest in his building project. He even asked Hugh to share how he had come to put his faith in Christ. Hugh gave him the condensed version, and in response the pastor encouraged him to read a little of the Bible every day and learn the Word. That would help him find comfort, wisdom, and instruction for life.

Before he left, he prayed for Hugh to be led by the Lord in all things. Hugh appreciated the prayer and the visit.

As for Ellie, she puttered around her house and kept herself occupied—sewing the log cabin quilt, baking, cleaning house, doing laundry, mowing grass, and reading and journalling while curled up in the big armchair. She also paid another visit to her beloved Aunt Ruth, who upon hearing about the events of the previous weekend showered her with kindness and wisdom, some of it in the form of sweet tea and freshly baked cinnamon buns. Ellie couldn't convey how much she appreciated being mothered.

By the time Rob and Sarah returned home with the kids, both Hugh and Ellie had recovered and their energy had returned to normal. They also realized that something had changed between them. Prior to Hugh's breakdown, they had been friends. Good friends. Now they had become much closer, although neither was quite sure how to proceed in this new normal. Consequently, they were rather shy with each other.

~

By August, the crops were beginning to turn to their ripened colours. Rob, especially, felt an urgency to get Hugh's house built before his attention had to be given over to the harvest. When the harvest arrived, everything else would have to wait until the grain was in the bins. This cardinal rule was not subject to negotiation.

Some time back, the building supply store had delivered a long list of material; piles of lumber, siding, and a pallet of shingles sat near the building site. Inside the old machine shed could be found the doors, windows, and drywall, amongst other necessities.

Within two weeks, Rob and Hugh had enough of the building constructed that it appeared finished from the outside, including the carport and five-foot covered porch across the front of the house. Hugh chose his colours for siding and shingles based on Ellie's drawings and illustrations. From the road, it looked like a classic white cottage with dark green shingles and trim.

Inside, a lot of work still needed to be done, such as the electrical and plumbing, before any attention could be turned to installing the insulation and drywall. Rob suggested these steps be handled by professionals. For one reason, to save time; swathing the crops had to begin come Monday.

While the men worked on the build, Ellie had other matters on her mind. She took a trip to Swan River to learn whether the hospital had any nursing positions available. She had come to the conclusion that she may as well find work nearby until something else turned up, if it ever did. It didn't seem to make sense to move someplace new, but she felt she was ready to re-enter the workforce. She filled out an application before leaving the hospital.

She didn't leave Swan River, though, without paying a short visit to Gertie. She'd brought along the blue-themed log cabin quilt. Gertie then brought out the other two quilts she had sewn, and the two women admired how well they had turned out. Gertie planned to give the quilts to Hugh and his sisters, so they would need to be done in time for Christmas. She intended to seek the help of the local quilting club.

Another notable piece of business for Ellie was making a call on Darcey's neighbour, Cynthia Clifford, the brilliant seamstress and furniture upholsterer. Ellie walked up to the house armed with a sketch of the sofa set she wanted to discuss.

When Cynthia met her at the door, they recognized each other from high school. Ellie noticed that she hadn't changed much; she was still the petite, natural redhead with whom Ellie had once shared classes.

Cynthia explained at length about her long-time interest in sewing. Her mother had been an excellent seamstress herself and had taught her all the tricks of the trade. Since starting her own home-based business, she was never without a project. It was a great way to supplement their household income.

"Darcey mentioned that you also do upholstery." Ellie remarked.

"Yes, I do!" answered Cynthia enthusiastically. "When we were getting ready to furnish our house, I realized that all the sofas and chairs I liked were far too expensive for our measly budget. So I decided to try my hand at making my own pieces. Well, I should say *we*. My husband Brent is pretty good at carpentry and he built the frames for me. We borrowed books from the library to get the springs right and I took it from there. Come, have a look…"

Cynthia led Ellie into her living room. There sat one of the most beautiful, one-of-a-kind sofas Ellie had ever laid her eyes upon. The design had an elegant simplicity to it, but the upholstery was both unique and stunning. Ellie was sufficiently wowed to know she had come to the right place.

"That's absolutely amazing," she said. "I do believe you are an artist, Cynthia."

"Thank you. I don't have any upholstery projects on the go right now, but I do have pictures if you want to see more."

Cynthia produced a photo album from a nearby shelf and gave it to Ellie. She flipped through the pages. Each sofa and chair looked great, but none were quite as stunning as Cynthia's personal piece.

"I think you're the right person to work with." She pulled out her sketch and handed it to Cynthia. "I rescued this set from certain extinction by fire. I believe it to be as old as the 1920s or 30s. Right now it's sitting in the Quonset at our farm. The upholstery is original, but it's worn and frayed. There's also a broken spring poking through one of the seats. What would you suggest?"

Cynthia studied the sketch for a moment. "The design is fairly heavy. It doesn't lend itself to anything floral or feminine…"

"I totally agree. I was wondering about leather—the kind of leather that's actual cowhide, not vinyl, and that you might find in a ranch house."

"I know exactly what you mean. But that would probably cost you a small fortune. The sofas of that type I've seen are priced around several thousands of dollars. What's your budget?"

"Oh well. It doesn't cost anything to dream." Ellie sighed. "My next idea was to combine a pair of coordinated fabrics in rich, deep colours. I like paisley, for instance. Maybe paisley and coordinating stripes?"

"That's a good idea too."

Cynthia cocked her head to one side, thinking hard. She walked to a shelf filled with interior design magazines. She flipped through one until she found what she was looking for. She showed it to Ellie.

"How about this?" she asked.

Ellie's mouth dropped. "It's perfect! Tartan! A classic Scottish plaid. It would suit the style of this sofa wonderfully."

"I totally agree. I know of a shop in Winnipeg that sells all things Scottish. Brent and I plan to go to Winnipeg next weekend. If you're serious about hiring me, I could order the yardage we'd need."

"Do you think it would exceed $3,000, including upholstery, repairs, and labour?"

"I think I could get it done for less than that."

Ellie nodded. "It's a deal. I'll write you a cheque for $1,500. Can Brent pick up the sofa? I only have my sedan."

"Yes, he can. Do you need it done very soon? I'm in the middle of a wedding dress that will take another week or two."

"No pressure, but sometime this fall would be great."

Ellie felt elated. She could already picture the finished sofa. Cynthia seemed equally excited by the challenge.

~

Not many days later, the harvest was in full swing, with Rob and Hugh operating the swather and combine interchangeably. It fell primarily to Sarah, Trevor, and Ellie to drive truck and haul the grain to the waiting bins at Bauman Farms. Sarah also prepared meals to be taken out to the fields and eaten together as a family. And when Sarah reached her limit, she asked Ellie to help.

The suppers were wonderful feasts—glorified picnics! The tailgate of Rob's half-ton served as a buffet for delicious casseroles, fried chicken, potato and other salads, corn-on-the-cob, and scrumptious desserts. Hugh was sure he had never before eaten so well in all his life.

The weather was consistently good, which meant they took few breaks, apart from getting a good night's rest.

At one point, Hugh took Ellie aside and pressed three twenty-dollar bills into her hand.

"I have no food left in my cabin for breakfast," he said. "Would you mind getting a few groceries for me?"

Ellie agreed. Before going to the grocery store, however, she stopped in to see for herself what his cupboards contained. She wasn't prepared for the shock of seeing his usually tidy cabin in such utter disarray. Stuffing his soiled clothing and linens in a black garbage bag, she put it in her car to be taken for laundering. After that, she swept the floor, washed the dishes, and emptied the garbage. Once the laundry was underway, she purchased food in Minitonas and replenished Hugh's pantry.

That evening, when he finally came home to sleep, Hugh was overjoyed to see the state of his cabin. On the table was a plate of bran muffins Ellie had baked. He also saw the sales receipt from the groceries, with a few cents of change lying on top. As far as he was concerned, she hadn't needed to leave the change, but the fact that she had only further demonstrated her integrity. His estimation of her rose still higher.

They hadn't spent much personal time together lately, though. He saw her at most of the field suppers, but that environment wasn't conducive to intimate conversation. He missed her input, including all the questions he had from reading his new Bible.

He still had to think about his new, incomplete house. Before resuming his duties in the field each morning, he made arrangements for the plumbing and electrical work.

About halfway through the harvest, it rained long enough to halt the process for three days. Rob came over and helped stuff the exterior walls with insulation, then cover them with vapour barrier and drywall.

While they were back on the field, another troupe of tradesmen came to tape and mud the drywall. Ellie then helped advance the project by painting all the interior walls with primer and white paint. It took almost four days, since she only had time between harvest-related jobs.

Whether he was assigned to operating the combine, the swather, or even driving the large grain truck, Hugh found the tasks conducive to deep thought. Most of it had to do with how he wanted to go about developing his property. He still liked the idea of starting a mechanics repair service and wondered if it could truly be a viable business. But he wasn't sure the valley could support another mechanics garage, especially an independent one.

Trading in his truck for a new model was another idea he often turned over in his mind. His current truck was four years old and he didn't want to drive the same one year after year until it had little or no value left. Driving a late-model truck was important to him. He entertained himself by thinking about the features each model offered. And he had the inheritance money to think about…

He also thought quite a bit about his newfound faith. It was still something of a wonder to him. He felt different from the inside-out. The anger that had once been his silent partner seemed to have left altogether. Never one for much patience, he noticed that he could happily wait for things to happen now without becoming annoyed. He also had a burning curiosity for the Bible. Whenever he was assigned to drive the grain truck, he brought it along to read while waiting for the grain box to be filled. The cover and pages were already beginning to curl.

Four weeks from the day they'd started, the harvest was in. It had been an intense yet joyful time with plenty of kind September weather. Despite a few breakdowns, the equipment had held up well, with Hugh being able to handle the minor repairs while Rob carried on without skipping a beat. They made a good team.

A few days later, after a thorough rest, Rob drove into Hugh's yard for a man-to-man visit over a cup of coffee. He also wanted to check on the construction of the new farmhouse.

"I'm curious, neighbour," said Rob. "What are your thoughts about farming now that you've had a taste of it?"

Hugh smiled. "I didn't hate it. But I also wouldn't wax all poetic like you. I think I didn't feel attached to the land because it wasn't mine, if that makes sense."

"I can appreciate that."

"It was fun driving the combine, though."

"Was that your favourite part?" asked Rob, taking another swallow of coffee.

"Second favourite. First favourite was the meals. Sarah is one great cook!"

"Yeah. She's great at everything. I'm one lucky guy."

Hugh could hear the love in his voice. What he didn't mention was the fact that he had also loved watching the Bauman family interact with each other. He'd learned from them. The kids wanted to tell their dad *everything* that happened at school—and he wanted to hear about it, no matter how mundane. The girls sometimes vied to sit on Rob's lap to the point of making it hard for him to eat his supper, but he took it in stride.

Occasionally, one of them might whine or start an argument. A word of authority would end the problem at once, and then the love would just carry on.

Hugh had never heard a father and son speak in such a good-natured and mutually respectful way as Rob and Trevor. Not even Brian and Kevin Turner had been so cordial with each other.

Sweetest of all were the tender ways in which Rob showed his love and appreciation to Sarah. They sometimes held hands while she brought him up-to-date on the latest news or asked for instruction on something around the house. More than once he'd seen Rob embrace her from behind while she set up the buffet on the tailgate of his pickup. They nearly always kissed goodbye at the end of a meal, and their goodbyes were always followed with "I love you!" Those verbal gestures were what Hugh admired most. They also made him feel sad. He couldn't come up with a single memory of someone having said to him, *"I love you..."*

Hugh came to the decision that Rob Bauman's family was not normal. Or if they were normal, they weren't average. As limited as his exposure was, he felt that what the Baumans had was precious and rare. Perhaps it was their faith in God and their commitment to living biblically.

Whatever it was, Hugh determined that if he should be so lucky as to have a wife and family of his own, he wanted to be the kind of husband and father he had witnessed in Rob.

Thirty-One

"SO WHAT ARE you going to do for a kitchen?" asked Ellie. They stood in the middle of Hugh's small house, discussing how to lay it out on a tight budget. And it still had to be aesthetically pleasing, of course.

"Until I know where I'm at with my finances, I'm just going to keep using the fridge, stove, and Hoosier cabinet." But one look at Ellie's face told Hugh that she didn't like this idea at all. "You don't agree."

"It doesn't matter what I think. It's your house. At the end of the day, it's not my circus—not my monkeys."

Despite this disclaimer, the disappointment she felt came through loud and clear. It didn't sit well with him. He had no way of changing the facts, though. Neither did he want to make any regrettable mistakes.

~

The main construction of the house was complete, and the electrical and plumbing was roughed in. Ready to begin the final phase of work, Hugh asked Ellie to come shop with him for light fixtures, flooring, bathroom commode, and other finishing touches.

Before they left, Hugh showed her the interior doors he had already purchased to be hung inside. By the look on her face, she clearly wasn't impressed.

"What's wrong with them?" asked Hugh, puzzled.

"You have a very tiny house. You should keep the design simple so it doesn't look cluttered. I painted the walls white so the rooms would feel spacious. If it was me, I'd stick to white doors, and keep the trim around the windows and baseboards white too. The house itself should remind one of a clean sheet of paper. Let the colours come from the furnishings and décor you bring inside."

After she'd explained this, it made sense to Hugh. So they loaded up the brown doors Hugh had purchased and planned to exchange them for white ones.

Shopping together wasn't easy. Hugh wanted to buy the cheapest items, but Ellie believed that price had to be weighed against quality.

"You get what you pay for," she reminded him. "And aesthetics matter. They can be the reason you look forward to coming home..."

She pointed out, for example, that the cheapest flooring wouldn't hold up to the wear-and-tear they would be subjected to in the home of a farmer or mechanic. That's why it made sense to spend more on a type of flooring that would go the distance.

Not everything had to be expensive, of course. They could save money on faucets and light fixtures, for example.

It took all afternoon, but Ellie's penchant for sniffing out a good buy paid off. Along the way, Hugh learned a few tips about the art of shopping.

Their last stop was to a secondhand store. Ellie called it "hunting for treasure."

"You never know when you might discover something wonderful," she remarked. "And for cheap!"

Unfortunately, it turned out that the shop displayed nothing of interest to her—except one item: a table lamp. The body was shaped like a Grecian pillar, made from navy ceramic, and had been set on a simple dark wood base. She knew the perfect spot for it.

"This is an example of save-versus-splurge," she explained as she made the five-dollar purchase.

A young woman approached the counter while Ellie and Hugh were checking out. She had a stash of baby clothing in one hand and a tiny babe wrapped up in her other arm. She set the clothing down but had trouble retrieving her wallet with the baby on her arm.

She turned her attention to Ellie. "Could you hold her for a second?"

"Of course!"

Ellie accepted the little one on her left arm. She looked down and saw that the baby was awake. The little girl was adorable, like the infant pictured on the labels of baby food, and smiled sweetly with tiny rosebud lips. Ellie responded with a smile of her own and stroked the downy cheek with her forefinger.

When the woman took her back, Ellie's eyes began to water. Two seconds later, tears were spilling onto her cheeks.

Hugh saw this and quickly ushered her out of the store. "Let's go," he said, leading her by the arm.

Once they were settled in his truck, he tore away and got onto Highway 10 as quickly as he could. Ellie continued to sniffle and wipe away tears with the back of her hands.

He reached across the seat and placed his right hand on her shoulder. "Please, tell me what this is about. Why do babies make you cry?"

Ellie didn't answer him. She looked straight ahead with pursed lips while the tears continued to slip down.

"Talk to me, Ellie," urged Hugh softly. "Whatever it is, I'm here for you and I'll help you work it out."

Ellie shook her head and turned away so that her back was to him and she faced the passenger window.

Hugh didn't push it.

They drove along the highway, down the hill that crossed the Roaring River bridge, and then back up the other side in silence, except for Ellie's stifled sobs.

Hugh tried again. "I told you about the worst thing that ever happened to me. It was hard for me to let that terrible secret out, but it was also liberating. It doesn't eat me alive anymore. You're the one who told me it would be like that. Just as He promised, Jesus has dissolved my pain. Let Him do it for you."

Ellie still didn't answer except to sob in earnest.

At last they turned north onto Road 150W. A minute later, they were near the Minitonas cemetery.

"Turn here!" said Ellie in a tearful voice.

"What?"

"Turn into the cemetery."

Hugh jammed on the brakes and turned into the second driveway. He stopped the truck and switched off the ignition.

Ellie opened the door, slid out, and ran amongst the plots without closing the door behind her. Hugh hurried after her.

Upon reaching the graves of her parents, Ellie fell to her knees. In a semi-prone position, she sobbed wretchedly. The scene pulled at Hugh's heart, but he didn't yet know how he could help beyond placing his hand on her back. He wanted her to know that he was near and that she had his unremitting support.

After a few minutes of this, Ellie quieted down, sat up, and composed herself.

"Momma, Daddy," she said softly, speaking toward the graves. "I have to tell you the rest of my story before it kills me. I think I left off telling you about my boyfriend, Paul Richter, the guy I met at the hospital in Winnipeg. Well, he was more than a boyfriend, Momma. We actually moved in together. Unmarried."

She paused and let that sink in for a couple of minutes.

Hugh became uneasy. He didn't have any idea what was coming, but he sure didn't like the idea that there might be another guy in the picture.

"We behaved like a married couple," she continued in a cracked voice. "I believed he loved me and I suppose I loved him too. We seemed to have so much fun doing things together. I thought life was great..."

Ellie paused again. Hugh could smell the "but" coming...

"I sometimes brought up the topic of getting married, but he didn't want to. He told me that true love didn't need a piece of paper. I knew it was wrong, but I went along with it." She took a deep breath. "Then, despite my precautions, I got pregnant."

More tears rolled down her face. Hugh squirmed but moved a bit closer to her and draped an arm around her shoulders. She didn't push him away.

"Paul blamed me for it. Said it was all my fault—like I could get pregnant all by myself." Her tone had the bite of acid. "I hoped being pregnant would solidify our relationship and provide a reason for us to get married and have a family. But I was wrong. I was very, very wrong."

Ellie stopped speaking. She seemed to be gathering strength for what she had to say next.

"He didn't want the baby. He said he wasn't ready to have a family, that he couldn't afford a child on his minimum income as an intern. He had a hundred other excuses. We fought a lot. He insisted that I have an abortion. He wanted for us to go back to the way things were before I got pregnant."

Now that she had said the A-word, talking about it became easier.

"Paul wore me down and I agreed to the abortion, which he arranged with some of his fellow interns. He was there at my side while the procedure took place. Just as the baby was taken away, so did all my feelings for Paul. As we were driving home, he tried to be so nice to me, so lovey-dovey. I couldn't stand him touching me. I couldn't get away from the thought that the baby had been murdered. That we had killed our baby... that I had killed my baby. I couldn't believe how much I hated him, and myself, at that moment. I was a wreck. I tried to carry on with my job as a nurse, but depression took hold of me and I could hardly function. That's why I put in for a sabbatical and came home. I'm trying to heal from this terrible thing I did. I've come back to Jesus and repented of everything." Her eyes were glued to her parents' headstones. "I know you're gone, but I still wanted to tell you myself. And this is the best I can do."

The tears were flowing again, but Hugh didn't let go. He squeezed her shoulders, reminding her that he was still there and wasn't going anywhere.

"I'm so sorry, Momma. Sorry for the whole mess I've made of everything. And I'm so sorry I killed your grandchild. How can you ever forgive me?"

And then Ellie lost it. She wept inconsolably with deep guttural cries.

Hugh turned slightly so he could embrace her with both arms and she fell on his chest, limp as a wet noodle.

Eventually, she was cried out and made the motions to stand.

Hugh got up as well. "Let's get you home."

When he pulled up to the Bauman farmhouse, Ellie jumped out and ran into the house even before the truck was shut down.

Hugh didn't follow immediately. He stayed in the cab and prayed for Ellie, particularly that she would know the Lord's comfort in this time of deep grief.

By the time he entered the house a few minutes later, Ellie had changed into pyjamas and put on her well-worn chenille housecoat.

"What can I fix you for supper?" asked Hugh upon stepping into the kitchen.

"Nothing. I'm not hungry." Her voice was subdued. "But feel free to raid the fridge. I need to lie down."

Hugh found some leftover fried chicken and potato salad to assuage the rumble in his stomach. After he ate, he looked in on Ellie, who was fast asleep.

Restlessness overtook him. He couldn't think about anything else but her. For Ellie's own sake, he felt very bad about her having had an abortion. He had never been personally close to this issue but could well imagine the devastation it might cause someone.

He asked himself if this disclosure made a difference in his feelings for her. The answer was a resounding no.

Something else niggled at him, however. He would have to wait until she was awake and strong enough to have a discussion.

To help pass the time, he softly played some records on the old stereo. The music provided a calm, sweet, safe atmosphere in which to rest for Ellie, and to relax and think for Hugh.

Around ten o'clock in the evening, Ellie came out of her bedroom, padded into the kitchen, and put on the kettle. Hugh got up from the sofa and followed her.

"You're still here," she said. "That's sweet of you. I'm fixing myself some chamomile. Would you like some?"

"Sure. But I should be the one making tea for you, not you for me."

"That's all right. I'm okay. I'm going to live." She smiled weakly, her face pink and puffy.

Hugh smiled back. "I'm very glad to hear that."

She prepared two mugs of tea, adding honey. Each took a mug and retired to the living room. Ellie automatically went over to the big armchair while Hugh went straight to his usual niche on the sofa.

They sipped their tea quietly.

"I'm thinking you want to ask me a question," Ellie murmured.

"One for sure, if you're up to it." Hugh sucked in his breath. "Do you still have feelings for this Paul guy? Are you hoping to get back together with him?"

Ellie's eyes went wide. "Heavens, no! Where did you get that idea? If I never see him again in this life, that will be fine with me. Why are you asking?"

"Just checking. It sounded like the two of you were very tight and I wondered if it was truly over," answered Hugh carefully.

"It's truly over. It's a relationship that never should have happened. The only reason it did is that I was blind as a bat, stupid as a rock, and foolish to boot! Not to mention rebellious to my parents—and Jesus too. What else would you like to know?"

"The only other thing I'm pondering is why you don't believe for yourself what you told me… what you asked me to believe."

Ellie raised her brows quizzically.

Hugh continued. "You told me, and Pastor Leland preaches it too, that Jesus died for all the sins of all the people for all time, so that

301

upon accepting His sacrifice we would be rid of our guilt and shame. I don't have to carry it around anymore like a ton of bricks. If that's true, why are you still carrying around your ton of bricks? Why aren't you set free? Were you kidding? Is the pastor kidding? Is the Bible kidding?"

There was a moment of loaded silence before Ellie responded. "No, Hugh, no one was kidding. It's true, and I need to do a better job of believing it. I'll only say that I've discovered that having an abortion isn't the same as having a tonsillectomy or an appendectomy, though there are many who would argue it's just that simple. I've thought about it for a million hours. I think the closest other surgery that may be comparable would be an amputation... losing a real physical part of yourself. I find that I can't get over it just like that." Ellie snapped her fingers. "It seems like I'm doing well, and then..."

"And then a newborn baby comes along."

"Right, and I'm undone! Back to square one." She let out a long sigh. "But I am doing better, really. My soul work—spending time in the Word, journaling, and praying every day—has helped a lot to overcome my caldron of many feelings. When I first came home, I was a basketcase."

"Not that I noticed," said Hugh. "You seemed to be in way better shape than I was. I was the basketcase being eaten alive with bitter hate and anger, thinking the only life left for me was the life of a recluse."

"The difference between us, dear friend, is that I knew where to go for help, and you didn't," she said softly. "Yet."

~

Hugh slept in his own bed that night. Although they had talked out the matter of Paul, he was still restless and unhappy. This thing between himself and Ellie needed to come to a head. Trying to relate as platonic friends was no longer working. Too much water had flowed under that bridge. Now that they had shared so many intimate moments and learned each other's secrets, it was time to pee or get off the pot, as Brian Turner had once told him.

But how should he approach the subject? It was tempting to talk to Rob about it, because he seemed to have the ability to talk about anything, and he would be sure to have some wisdom to share on the topic of love.

On second thought, Hugh rejected the idea. He needed to work this out for himself. He could certainly talk it over with the Lord Jesus, though, and in the hours that followed he poured out his heart to Him.

The next morning, however, he still felt agitated. He decided to keep praying until he was convinced of the answers he sought. One point of indecision revolved around whether to pursue Ellie and tell her how he felt or wait until she came to him. She was still recovering from a deeply emotional experience. It probably wasn't a good time to add another weighty matter.

He tried to keep himself preoccupied by hanging up the light fixtures in his new house: a ceiling fan with light in the front room, and a smaller yet similar model for the only bedroom. He then cut and nailed white trim around the windows. That kept him busy until mid-afternoon. By then, he had decided that if she didn't come to him by suppertime, he would go to her and tell her how he felt.

Hugh spent the rest of the afternoon cleaning the house.

For supper, he warmed up a tin of soup; his restless mood had produced a poor appetite, and he had even less motivation to cook a decent meal.

He was about to don his jean jacket and make the short trip to the neighbouring farm when he noticed someone walking along the road in his direction. A closer look revealed that it was Ellie.

His heart leapt in his chest and his legs felt a little wobbly. His moment had come.

"Please, Lord, don't let me blow this…"

Ellie's soul work did not go easily that morning. She couldn't concentrate on the scriptures and her attempts to journal quickly died. In her daily assignment journal, she decided to repeat an old topic: *Name ten things you are thankful for.* She wrote each item in the order it occurred to her:

- Hugh
- Jesus
- Hugh
- Hugh
- Rob and Sarah and family
- Hugh
- Hugh
- Hugh
- Hugh
- Hugh...

"I guess it's obvious we should be talking about Hugh today," said Ellie to the corner of the sofa where she usually pictured Jesus sitting. "Lord, I need help governing my feelings. Please guide me into truth. I don't want to waste my time getting mixed up with another man who isn't right for me..."

In the journal where she wrote down her questions to God, she asked, *What is Your will concerning me and Hugh?* In the past, insight had come to her fairly quickly, but this time she wasn't sure if she could trust it.

Ellie added an addendum to her entry: *Not my will, but Yours be done.*

She waited quite a long time for another idea to come to mind. When nothing else did, she gave it up and wrote, *I believe the Lord is showing me that we belong together... that we're meant to be together for life...*

In the journal where she answered questions that she felt God asking, she wrote, *What objections do you have in considering Hugh as your partner for life?* Weeks earlier, she would have said that he wasn't suitable because he wasn't a believer. That had changed. He had embraced the faith authentically and now exhibited a changed life. Apart from that, she found everything about him attractive.

After several minutes of reflection, she wrote her honest, single-word answer: *None.*

She closed her journals, showered, and took extra time to do her hair, apply a bit of makeup, and dress herself in something feminine. She half-expected Hugh to show up to check in on her after yesterday's outburst. On the other hand, she had sent him home insisting that she was fine.

Perhaps she should go to him to talk things out. Her heart could think of no reason not to, so she grabbed a sweater and headed for Hugh's place.

~

Hugh watched through the window to see if Ellie would walk on by or come up the driveway. When he saw her turn in, he rushed out the door to meet her.

"You're just the person I wanted to see," he said, all smiles as he closed the distance between them. "I was just getting ready to come to your place and check on how you were doing."

It was obvious to Ellie how glad he was to see her.

"Well, I've been wanting to see you too," she said. "You've been on my mind all day... in fact, I tried very hard to think about other things, but you kept interfering. Seemed like I wasn't going to have any peace until I gave you my undivided attention, so here I am. I think we need to talk..."

"I agree. And it sounds like your day was a lot like mine. I woke up with you on my mind and haven't been able to think about anyone or anything else."

They walked next to each other back toward The Ritz.

"There's things I need to say," he told her. "I'd like to go first, if it's all right with you. I may lose my nerve if I don't."

Her heart quickened. "Sure. Go ahead."

Hugh opened the door to his cabin and gestured for her to enter. Ladies first.

She went inside and sat in the red chair, while he sat adjacent to her in the blue chair. They looked at each other with expectancy, but suddenly Hugh found himself tongue-tied.

Ellie could see he was nervous and had an inkling about where this was going to go. If she was right, they were on the same page. The thought already thrilled her. Butterflies swarmed in her belly.

"Just relax, Hugh-labaloo!" She laughed lightly. "It's only me. What's on your mind?"

Hugh let out a laugh of his own. "I love how you come up with so many ways of taking my name in vain."

It worked, though. He already felt more relaxed, better able to just be himself.

"Ell, when you first started coming around in June, helping me get things going around here, we made a deal: to relate strictly as friends, like brother and sister..."

Ellie nodded. "I remember."

"Well, as time went on, that didn't work so well for me anymore. By the time of the FBC picnic, I was having feelings for you... feeling that were a lot more romantic than the way I'd feel about a sister. I just can't do it anymore. We've gone through a lot of seriously person- al stuff together. Day by day, you've become more important to me. The way you handled my meltdown after the rodeo and stayed with me all through the night... well, that's when I knew for certain that I loved you, that I didn't want to live without you by my side. And when I heard your secret story by your parents' grave yesterday, I knew something else for sure: I want to be the guy who gives you children. I want to be the guy who takes care of you all the rest of your days. I want to be the guy who helps you realize all your dreams. I want to be the guy you grow old with..."

Ellie's eyes began to glisten. She opened her mouth to say something.

"Wait! I'm not done." He put up a hand to stop her. "All last night and all day today, I've been praying to know whether I'm wrong, whether my feelings are inappropriate. 'God, please take these feelings away. Turn my heart in another direction.' But my feelings only got stronger, Ellie. All day long, my head and heart have been saying to me, 'We belong together. We're meant to be together for life.'"

"What? What did you just say?" Ellie asked, stunned.

"I said that I believe we belong together, that we're meant to be together for life. Why?"

"Because those are the *exact* words I wrote in my journal this morning when I asked God about His will for you and me," she said. "A few weeks ago, Rory Lang took me out for coffee at the café in Minitonas. He tried to tell me that the Lord told him that He wants us to be together... that we'd make a good team. I told him that it couldn't possibly be true because *I* had gotten no such word from the Lord. And here you are, quoting the exact words out of my journal, which you haven't seen. If that's not confirmation for me, I'm a complete idiot."

"Then you agree. We belong together, you and I."

"I do." But there was a note of hesitation in her voice. "That is, if you truly want me."

"Want you? Isn't that what I've been saying for the last five minutes?"

"It's just that since I've spilled my beans to you, I feel like I'm a kind of secondhand rose. You wouldn't be my first..."

"Good night, woman. There you go again. You don't believe your own Bible. There's this famous verse every Christian is supposed to know. Even I know it and I don't know much yet. *'If we confess our sins, he is faithful and just to forgive us our sins, and to cleanse us from all unrighteousness.*[12] If God has cleansed you, Ellie, and it's good enough for Him, then it's good enough for me too. You're *clean*, Ellie. You're not a secondhand rose! And yes, I want you. If you only knew how much."

He paused, this time feeling his own twinge of uncertainty.

"I could ask the same thing of you," he continued. "You know all about the troubling history of the Fischers, and that my family was a far cry from upstanding citizens. I don't come from good stock like you. Maybe you don't want me."

"Sometimes, Hugh Fischer, you can be such an ignoramus," returned Ellie, sounding relieved and exasperated at the same time. "This world rates people into upper and lower classes. It rates doctors and lawyers and prime ministers as being more valuable than waitresses and farmers and mechanics. But the cross of Jesus is a great leveller. Everyone is on the same plane at the foot of the cross. Everyone matters equally in the kingdom of heaven, regardless of the role they played on this side of eternity. You're good enough for me, Hugh. I love you and I want you."

Tears welled up in Hugh's eyes. "Do you mean it? No one has *ever* said the words 'I love you' to me before. I know, because I've been listening for them my whole life. If you don't mean it, don't say it. I couldn't bear that."

Ellie rose to her feet and stepped into Hugh's personal space. He stood, uncertain what to do next. She encircled her arms around his neck and looked softly into his deep brown eyes.

"I love you, Hugh," she said with all the ardency she could muster. "I *love* you. My beloved is mine and I am his…"

With tears trickling down his cheeks, he wrapped both of his arms around her and pulled her close to his chest. He kissed the top of her head, then her forehead… her nose… and finally his lips met hers. In that deliberate, lingering, breathtaking first kiss, he tried to express it all: that he loved her deeply ad infinitum.

---

[12] 1 John 1:9, KJV.

Thirty-Two

THE NEXT MORNING was Sunday and Hugh and Ellie entered the church foyer holding hands, beaming from ear to ear. Rob and Sarah had arrived ahead of them and were casually visiting with another couple. Sarah noticed Ellie first and elbowed Rob. He looked over and saw the two still holding hands and looking like they'd been shot with Cupid's arrow.

"I take it something has changed between you," said Rob, grinning as he walked over to them.

"Yeah, you could say that," answered Ellie shyly.

"Can't say that I'm all that surprised. Hugh here has been mooning over you for weeks now," Rob teased. "I suppose you think I didn't notice."

Hugh's face turned deep pink despite his tan. "I hope you don't mind that I love your sister…"

It was all he could think to say.

"No, I don't." Rob's reply was good-natured. "Just do it well. Women like that sort of thing."

After the service, Darcey noticed the pair. She marched up to them and broke the ice in her characteristic forward manner.

"Well, it's about time. Took you long enough. When's the big day?"

"We haven't decided," Ellie said. "We only agreed yesterday that we belong together."

She winked. "Congratulations! Honestly, I already know what your kids will look like."

Ellie laughed outright, but Hugh blushed.

Other folks who noticed the new development simply smiled as the couple spoke a word of greeting or passed by.

~

The third Sunday in September was a gorgeous day, neither too cool nor too hot. Ellie and Hugh shared a lunch at Hugh's cabin and then went for a stroll. They talked about weddings.

"I'm not interested in a long engagement," declared Hugh unequivocally. "What would the point be? We're not kids, after all."

"I hear you. But I only plan to marry once, and I'd like to have the wedding I've dreamt about since I was twelve: the big dress, fabulous wedding cake, gorgeous flowers, a big party of a couple hundred guests... the works!"

"Really? If it's that important to you then..."

"It is."

Hugh sighed with disappointment. Now that they had made the decision to be a couple, he preferred to get started on it as soon as possible. He had to try to understand the wedding production from her perspective.

"We should go into Swan River and look at wedding rings," he said, moving on to another topic, albeit a related one. "When are you available for that?"

"Not sure. I'll have to check the calendar. What do you have in mind? I'm not particularly interested in diamonds, in case you're wondering. I like the idea of matching bands. It's kind of the trend now anyway, if you're not aware."

"I wasn't aware, and to tell the truth I'm surprised. With all your hopes and dreams of a fancy wedding, I would have thought you'd want the biggest rock a finger could carry."

"Oh no. It's not in me to be ostentatious. In this case, I think less is more. Besides, it won't be as expensive, leaving dollars available for other things."

Hugh exhaled with relief. When it came to money matters, Ellie was sticking to her save-versus-splurge approach. On the one hand, he was more than willing to go along with tradition. On the other, he also appreciated that she was circumspect. Financially, they would get along.

"I don't know about you, but I've been considering wedding dates," said Ellie, turning her mind to another wedding issue.

"How about tomorrow? Or maybe next week? That should give you enough time to buy the big dress."

"Pfffff," grunted Ellie, shaking her head. She knew he was teasing, but she also recognized that it was a cover to communicate his honest desire. "I propose January 1. That would be a Thursday, but it'll be a day off for most guests. No need to show up for school or work. I also like the idea of starting the new year with a new life."

"I can probably wait that long." Hugh sighed as he squeezed her hand. "If I have to. But doesn't Pastor Leland have to agree? I assume he'll be officiating."

"Yes, and that's a good point. If he's not available, or if he's unwilling, we'll have to revisit the question."

They ducked under some low branches which brushed against their shoulders as they continued through the woodland on the edge of the Fischer property.

"Honey, it's only three months," Ellie reminded him. "And the time will fly by."

Hugh sighed again. "Truthfully, I don't know anything about throwing a wedding. The only one I've been to was for Kevin Turner, who got married a couple of years ago. That's the extent of my experience, and it's precious little. I wasn't asked to participate in any way other than being a guest."

"Well, lucky for you we Baumans are well-versed in the production of weddings. We'll gladly look after the gazillion details. If you would kindly show up at the church on time, that'll be enough for me."

"That's all, eh? Just show up on time?" Hugh looked at her disbelievingly but allowed himself a smile. "I think I can do better than that. In for a penny, in for a pound."

On Monday morning, Hugh went into Swan River to look up a jewellery store. While he was surprised Ellie didn't want a diamond engagement ring, it didn't sit well with him that her hand was altogether bare. He wanted the whole world to see that she was spoken for—that she was off the market.

Something she had said when they'd declared their love for each other had stuck with him. He'd heard of promise rings and wanted to learn more about them from the local jeweller. They discussed the matter until Hugh understood his options. Then he placed the order, asking for it to be filled expeditiously.

After leaving the jewellery shop but before returning home, he decided to seek out Ellie's friend, Darcey. He had a half-baked idea on his mind, but he'd need some help executing it. He got the sense that she would be the right person to talk to.

Darcey was surprised to see him at her door but admitted him gladly. They spoke for more than an hour, and when it was done they had settled on a delightful plan. It was subject to good weather, though, so they also worked out a few contingencies.

However it played out, it would have to be a surprise.

Since Hugh had returned to the valley, he hadn't been interested in visiting his parents' graves. Any curiosity he might have had was suppressed by deep anger and personal pain.

Today, however, for the very first time, he felt compelled to visit the site where they'd been laid to rest.

As Hugh approached the graveyard in his truck, he slowed down and came to a stop. He sat for a few moments behind the wheel, contemplating what to do next. The decision to come here had been truly spontaneous. He supposed the idea may have arisen from Ellie's graveside confession. Did he have some subconscious compulsion to settle up with his own parents?

Finally, he stepped out of the truck.

He walked through what looked like the oldest section of the cemetery and soon came across the faded and worn headstone of Rudolf Fischer. It was small and lay flat to the ground. The name was etched in plain lettering, as were the dates beneath it. He had passed away in 1945, four years before Hugh's birth.

Most of the headstones had touching albeit conventional phrases conveying the character of the deceased—"beloved husband" or "cherished wife" or "rest in peace" or "resting safe in the arms of Jesus…" Hugh felt sad that his grandfather had no such memorial added to his name.

He hadn't planned to spend any time thinking about the man's death. After all, he still felt intensely happy over his recent betrothal to, in his eyes, the most wonderful and beautiful woman the world had yet produced.

But somehow, the small, plain, neglected headstone of Rudolf Fischer, all but worn away, signified to Hugh that the life of his grandsire had not been worth remembering. His life hadn't mattered to anyone.

The thought hit him like a ton of bricks. To have lived, but not to have mattered, seemed the ultimate tragedy. The old Hugh might have plunged into existential sadness, but today his newfound faith came to his rescue.

I matter, thought Hugh. *I matter because God says I do. I matter so much that He sent His Son to die in my place so I could become His son, like Jesus. I matter to Ellie too. If I died tonight, she would mark my grave with the word "beloved" etched in stone so everyone who walked by would know that I was loved, that I was wanted, and that I mattered while I lived.*

Hugh moved along, searching for the graves of Alice and Frederick Fischer. He finally found them tucked in an obscure corner. He wondered if these had been the only plots available when Margo had made the arrangements. Or maybe there was a hidden message to be discerned from it.

Like the grave of Rudolf Fischer, these ones too were small, plain markers laid flat to the ground with nothing but names and dates. Had Margo decided on this lack of aesthetic because of the price point? Perhaps she honestly hadn't been able to come up with anything more positive. Hugh wouldn't have blamed her, although for his mother he might have added a simple *R.I.P.*

In the recent past, any thought of memorializing his father would have triggered intense rage. Yet here he was, cool as a cucumber. Instead of ire, he felt only great sorrow for what had been, and what might have been… if only…

Remembering how cathartic it had seemed for Ellie to speak to her parents, Hugh decided to try it for himself.

He stood at the base of Frederick R. Fischer's grave. "I understand now, Pa, that you were entangled with evil entities—powers of darkness that played a big part in enslaving you to alcohol, leading a lowbred life, and provoking you to treat your family very badly. It doesn't get you off the hook. You still did terrible things to us, and to me. Things that will always be inexcusable. But I forgive you. That's all I have to say."

Hugh turned his attention to his mother's grave. He squatted down onto his haunches as if to be nearer to her. For her, he removed his cap.

"Ma, I remember always being disappointed in you. It seemed like you were never strong for us, always afraid to defend your children. But I get it. You had very little to work with when bringing us up. It was all you could do to survive yourself. I forgive you too. I've come home, Ma. I'm going to make something good out of the farm. It's mine now. And I'm going to marry the girl next door. Yeah, Ellie Bauman and me. It's like a miracle. And another thing… I've discovered that God is real and I've given my life over to Him. I wish we had known about God before. It would have changed how we lived back then. I guess that's all I have to say. Good night."

His spur-of-the-moment business concluded, Hugh walked back to his truck. He felt better, lighter, like he'd lost a few pounds. More of the baggage he had been carrying around sloughed off. It felt good to be free of it.

On Monday, September 29, Hugh conferred again with Darcey. He had planned to take Ellie out for a surprise date, and the jeweller had ensured that the ring he'd special ordered would be ready for pickup right on time.

While at the store in town, he noticed generous price reductions on several end-of-season items. On impulse, he bought a riding mower. It would do a much better job than the rotary mower he had been pulling behind the tractor, and it could get into the tight places the larger mower couldn't.

More importantly, it would help him prepare for his upcoming surprise. The yard at Fischer Farms had never looked so spiffy.

And it truly would be a surprise. The only thing he'd told Ellie was to wear something special. She'd tried to worm a few more details out of him, plying him with question after question. But his lips remained sealed.

Finally he just shut her up with a long kiss.

The following evening, Hugh dressed in his black pants and shirt. Then, just before 6:30 p.m., he got in his pickup and drove next door. Ellie came out of the house in a loose-fitting dress with a pink floral print. It was cinched at the waist with a sash that created a blouson bodice, the top styled with a ruffled vee neckline. A short-sleeved white bolero jacket completed the outfit.

She wore her hair in soft, smooth waves around her shoulders. To Hugh, she had never looked more captivating. He greeted her with a kiss and offered her his arm as he led her to the truck for the short ride back to his place.

"Where are we going?" asked Ellie. "I don't know of any restaurant around here nice enough to justify dressing up like this..."

"You'll see," he replied cryptically as he turned into his driveway.

"Here? Seriously?"

Hugh stopped the truck, enjoying the shocked look on her face. "Don't move until I come around and open the door for you."

Like the perfect gentleman, Hugh helped her step out of the truck and placed her arm under his.

Ellie fully expected to be ushered into the cabin. She assumed he had cooked up a special supper for them.

It was therefore yet another surprise when he led her past the cabin altogether and strolled down a freshly mown grassy border alongside the bush.

"We're going to the pond, aren't we?" she guessed as they walked arm in arm.

"Yes."

Pretty soon, Ellie could hear strains of music coming from up ahead. It wasn't singing. Rather, the instrumentation blended with their natural surroundings. And the closer they got to the pond, the louder the music became.

Hugh made a sharp right turn, still following the freshly mown path, and they emerged into the clearing around the pond. There, on a Persian rug, stood a round dining table covered with a crisp white tablecloth that draped to the ground. The two dining chairs were also covered in white fitted cloth. On the table, in a sparkling crystal vase, was a stunning arrangement of a dozen red roses, white baby's breath, and fern. Beside it stood a glass hurricane jar with an aflame white candle. Two tall stemware glasses filled with a pink bubbly beverage completed the presentation.

Ellie's eyes went wide. It really was one of the most romantic displays she'd ever seen. The background of the pond and trees just beginning to show their fall colours was almost magical.

"You did all this?" asked Ellie, awed.

"It was my idea," he said. "But I admit to having had some help with the details."

He seated Ellie in one of the dining chairs and then sat across from her so he could look into her eyes.

"How about a toast?" He lifted his glass. "To us…"

Ellie tapped her glass against his and they each took a sip.

"Hugh-are-too-much, and I love you for it." She set down her glass. "I had no idea you were capable of such fantastic romance. I hope I'm going to keep discovering wonderful new things about you, even when we're old and grey."

"That goes both ways, babe."

Another person walked into the clearing carrying a tray. Ellie recognized Darcey immediately, dressed in black stockings, a black pencil skirt that ended just above her knees, and a dark blouse. Paired with a white Battenberg lace apron and lace cap, it was clear she was meant to resemble a traditional French maid. Being a big-boned woman, it might have looked comical if the costume were not so adorable.

"Bon soir, madame. Bon soir, monsieur." To Ellie's ears, her friend's French accent was almost impeccable. "Comment allez-vous ce soir?"

Darcey set down a salad plate first in front of Ellie and then Hugh.

"Darcey!" Ellie exclaimed. "I might have guessed you'd be in on this. I had no idea you spoke French. I'm so impressed."

"Well, that's all I learned from Coles Notes. It's back to English from now on." Darcey offered a broad smile. "Enjoy. I'll be back soon with your main course."

Ellie looked down at her salad: baby spinach sprinkled with blueberries, raspberries, and toasted almonds drizzled with a sweet dressing beautifully presented on a crystal plate. It tasted delicious too!

Neither Hugh nor Ellie said much—partly because they were eating, and partly because their hearts were beginning to feel full. Something special was happening and neither wanted to ruin it with unnecessary small talk.

A little while later, Darcey returned and erected a waiter's table. Like a well-trained server, she removed the salad plates and reset the table with new cutlery and cloth napkins. The stemware was refilled.

Then she brought out the main course: bone china plates featuring hot, roasted rock Cornish hens with wild rice stuffing and roasted vegetables alongside.

"Oh my," said Ellie. "Just like the meal Gertie made for you!"

He looked down sheepishly. "It was the fanciest thing I could think of."

"It's absolutely wonderful. You couldn't have done better."

Sometime later, Darcey removed the main course plates and asked Hugh if he was ready for dessert.

"Give us a few minutes first, please."

Darcey disappeared.

"Uh-oh," Ellie said. "I think I'm getting nervous."

Hugh reached into one of his pockets. After a moment of struggling, he withdrew a tiny ring box. He stood and came to Ellie's side of the table.

"I want to do this right. I know we've already agreed that we belong together, but that's not the same thing as making a proper proposal."

Hugh got down on one knee.

Ellie let out a small gasp. Her eyes began to fill with tears.

"I love you, Ella Rose Bauman, with all my heart and soul. Will you marry me?"

The tears had escaped and were running down her cheeks. Her heart was so full of joy and love that she had trouble getting her mouth to work.

She nodded first and finally croaked out, "Yes. Yes. A thousand times yes."

Hugh presented his promise ring. "I know you said no diamonds, but I wanted to see *something* on your hand to let the world know you're spoken for... that you're mine. It has the inscription of that wonderful thing you said to me a few days ago: *My beloved is mine and I am his*."

He slipped the ring on her finger and kissed her hand.

"Oh, Hugh, it's just perfect." She was overcome with emotion. "The quote is from the Song of Songs in the Bible... and I just love this ring. I'm going to keep wearing it even after we exchange wedding bands on our wedding day."

"Ahem."

She turned to Darcey, who pointedly indicated that it was time for their dessert: crème brûlée flecked with espresso bits and garnished with a chocolate-dipped strawberry.

The dish looked amazing, and its taste and texture turned out to be nothing short of divine.

Finally, Darcey also brought them cappuccinos to end the meal.

Ellie couldn't figure out how her friend had pulled it all off, considering there was no kitchen handy. Whatever her secret, she wasn't telling.

By now, the setting sun had cast a golden glow over the clearing. Hugh got up and lit two bamboo tiki torches, one on each side of the boulder that bordered the pond.

"May I have this dance?" he asked, bowing deeply.

"You so may."

Ellie stepped neatly into his arms and he led her to the large flat rock. He held her close while they shuffled to the romantic music playing on the portable stereo hidden, she assumed, some-where amongst the trees around the clearing. From time to time, he stopped and tipped her chin to place a sweet kiss on her lips. Then they'd dance some more.

Darcey made sure the music played nonstop. While they danced, she dismantled the dining room as inconspicuously as possible in the dim light. Not that she had to be overly careful; the two lovebirds only had eyes for each other. Which was as it should be.

When all was tidied up, Darcey quietly departed, leaving them to enjoy the rest of their blissful evening in privacy.

Eventually, though, the evening had to end. Hugh snuffed out the torches and they walked arm in arm back to the main yard, relying on a flashlight to light their way.

He drove her the short distance back to her house and walked her to the front door, like a proper traditional date. Before he could kiss her goodnight, though, she stopped him.

"You've given me an evening that rivals paradise, Hugh Fischer. I've never been so blessed in all my life. But I'm not so naïve as to believe there aren't going to be challenges ahead." She cast a glance toward the gentle incline of Duck Mountain Provincial Park in the distance. "The world has numerous mountains, and they're all made to climb. Tonight, though, was absolutely perfect. I'll never forget it. Nor how beautiful you've made me feel. Of all the things I've ever said to you, never forget this, because I mean it with everything in me: I love you."

To be continued in…
The Minitonas Diaries, Book Two:

And Then There's Life

About the Author

SANDRA VIVIAN KONECHNY is mother to two sons and two daughters, and grandmother to nine grandchildren. She and her husband Michael of close to fifty years live as retirees on an acreage northwest of Saskatoon, Saskatchewan. During the period when her nuclear family lived in Swan River, Manitoba, she accepted Jesus into her heart as Saviour and Lord. She was baptized two summers later at Wellman Lake in Duck Mountain Provincial Park off the shores of the Bible camp established there.

Her passion for story and dialogue began as a youngster playing with paper dolls. She would give the dolls a scenario to act out and lines for them to say. Apart from writing short stories, she has also done much in the area of crafting: sewing, quilting, cross-stitching, baking, and gardening. She enjoys word games and jigsaw puzzles. Some of her favourite blessings call her Grandma.

Rock Bottom is her first novel. She published one previous book in 2007, *When God Asks You...*, which examines thirteen questions in the Bible that God asked of various individuals.

She also has a children's book coming soon, titled *An Improbable Adventure at Grandma's House*. This tale was born out of playing a game with her grandchildren regarding a picture that hangs on the living room wall.